About the Author

Mark Bricknell was born on 16 September 1970 in Queenstown, South Africa, and has always aspired to be an author, dabbling with ideas, concepts and drafts for the past thirty years. He began his working career in the casino industry in 1993 to support himself while he concentrated on his writing, but his life and career caused a few detours along the way. Finally, having reached the pinnacle of his career as Gaming Manager in a world-renowned casino resort property, he used the Covid-19 lockdown period to 'dust off' his old notes and finish this work.

A Reason to Die

Mark Bricknell

A Reason to Die

Olympia Publishers
London

www.olympiapublishers.com
OLYMPIA PAPERBACK EDITION

A CIP catalogue record for this title is
available from the British Library.

ISBN: 978-1-80074-828-6

This is a work of fiction.
Names, characters, places and incidents originate from the writer's
imagination. Any resemblance to actual persons, living or dead, is
purely coincidental.

First Published in 2023

Olympia Publishers
Tallis House
2 Tallis Street
London
EC4Y 0AB

Printed in Great Britain

Chapter 1

Julia Swan lay motionless in her bed.

It was still early, and besides, the autumn mornings were becoming ostensibly cooler of late. She snuggled deeper into her duvet. It was warm and held her captive in its loving embrace.

She dozed a little, reluctant to get the day started.

Was that the buzzer?

She couldn't be sure, having drifted lazily between sleep and wakefulness for the past half hour.

Now listening attentively and fully roused from that state of flux where reality might just be imaginary, or vice versa.

She heard nothing. Complete silence.

Had she imagined it?

Had she dozed off again?

She finally succumbed to her curiosity and decided to leave the warmth and comfort of her bed.

She yawned, stretched and slipped her satin gown around her athletic and well-toned shoulders. She took a few minutes to smooth out the sheets, fluff the pillows and toss the duvet over the expanse of the bed.

The air was cool, but winter was still weeks away. No slippers required.

The apartment wasn't very expansive and within seconds she traversed the distance between her bedroom and the front door. She cautiously inspected the exterior passageway through the spy-hole in the door, but only the bright glare of the morning greeted her.

Julia retracted the dead-bolt, unlocked the door, and with the security chain still in place, gingerly opened the door a few centimetres.

There was, of course, an additional security gate between herself and the outside world, but then again, this was South Africa and nonchalance was not an option.

With around one-third of the eligible working population unemployed, the crime rate had spiked astronomically. Caution and street-smarts were consequently drummed into everyone from the moment they could walk. No-one could be too careful.

She flinched, as the glare from outside painfully assaulted her eyes. She had to squint until her eyes grew gradually accustomed to the onslaught of the bright light.

Nothing.

Nobody.

Maybe, the sound of the buzzer was just a part of her dream. A mere figment of her sleepy imagination.

She tentatively released the security chain and swung the door open to its limit.

On the door-mat, outside the security gate, lay an off-white envelope.

Now, who would ring the door-bell, drop a letter and run away?

Could it be that she had taken that long to surface from her dozing and to answer the door? She didn't think so. But then again, had she consciously heard the first or last of the buzzes? Or maybe, and more likely, had the deliverer been pressed for time and just rung once before dropping the letter? That actually sounded more feasible to Julia and since she had no letter slot in the door the deliverer had inevitably chosen the next best option and had just left the letter on the door-mat for her to find.

She would have slid the letter under the door if in the same predicament… but then again, each to their own.

Julia could have reached the letter through the security gate, but decided to check the passageway. Maybe the deliverer was still within eyeshot. Her range of vision through the security gate was largely limited, but she cautiously scanned from right to left before unlocking the gate and stepping out into the passageway.

Although the sky was bright and clear and later on it would be a beautifully warm autumnal day, the passageway, being open-plan, was at the mercy of the elements and a cool morning breeze whistled along its extent. Julia shivered slightly as her scant pyjamas and dressing gown offered no protection against the onslaught of the cool air.

The apartment block was a cream-coloured, brick building designed and built way back in the 1970s, but even to this day occupation was still in high demand owing to its excellent location on the beachfront.

Each apartment boasted a breath-taking view of the ocean and the small balconies offered a prime spot for sun-downers and socialising.

Fortunately, a lot of thought had gone into its design back in the day, including the peripheral land purchase, which prevented any construction between it and the ocean. This unmarred ocean view was a definite selling point and the wait list for an apartment was a mile long.

The resultant downside to each apartment having a one-hundred-and-eighty-degree sea-view, was that the open-plan passageways, which ran along the rear of the building to service the apartments on each level, were generally obscured from view by an overgrown thicket of unruly bushes and trees.

Julia, and frankly many of the tenants, both current and previous, had complained to the owner on many occasions about the security risk of these passageways, but to no avail.

The answer was always the same. The complex was enclosed by palisade fencing and fortified with electrified wire strands. The only point of entry or egress was guarded by a highly reputable twenty-four/seven security company with an impeccable track record and immutable credentials.

Since their onboarding, there had been no security incidents or breaches worth mentioning in the past twenty-three years.

And that was the end of that.

She scooped up the letter, turned it over a few times in her hands and retreated once more into her safely barricaded apartment.

She sipped on the freshly brewed cup of coffee and focused once more on the envelope, which now lay face-up on the coffee table.

Julia couldn't quite comprehend her trepidation, but it seemed so strange that someone had actually hand-delivered a physical letter in these digital days of internet and email.

Chapter 2

Julia studied the envelope more closely.

The only discernible marking was her name, typed neatly in bold, block letters in the centre of the envelope, staring back at her... **JULIA SWAN**...

Typed, printed and then hand-delivered... how strange was that?

There was also a very faint scent – perfume or deodorant – when she tentatively sniffed the envelope.

She didn't openly recognise the brand, but it could well be transfer left by the deliverer. The same scent had been slightly stronger in the passageway, even though the breeze had done its best to disperse it.

It became clearer the more she thought about it.

It could only have been a tenant who delivered the letter, and most likely someone she knew. Hopefully it wasn't a complaint letter. She searched for reasons for a complaint letter, but came up blank.

She was actually a very considerate and friendly neighbour. Nobody would have reason to complain to her or about her.

Who would write her a personalised letter?

She obviously didn't know all the residents, but her direct neighbours and those folks she encountered regularly on her way in and out of the building were always polite and talkative and often became acquaintances through commonalities.

More especially the older occupants, though, who were

generally quick to introduce themselves and share far more than was really necessary.

Julia doted on the elderly knowing full well that she would one day grow old and possibly be lonely and in need of attention or companionship too.

If it were a non-resident, the security guard at the main gate would have buzzed her and announced the visitor – no matter how familiar and without exception.

She instantly decided to phone down to the security control room and within a few rings the call was answered.

It was Phineas.

Phineas Nkambule was one of the longer serving security guards and Julia had got to know him quite well over the past few years.

He was a single father of three children, but lived alone in the nearby township. His wife had died a few years back after contracting and succumbing to the HIV virus. His daughter, aged eight, and his sons, aged fifteen and eleven, were in the care of his elderly mother.

Julia loved seeing the twinkle of admiration in his eyes when he spoke of his mother, always proclaiming how lucky he was to have her around to assist him.

There was, in any case, no space for his family in the tiny backyard single-room shack which he rented, so staying with his mother in the distant rural village of his birth, in their traditional home, was the only solution.

And even more aggravatingly, his twelve-hour work shifts really didn't allow for much family time anyway.

It wasn't an easy life for him and he could only pray that the cycle would end with him and that his children would somehow get a break and make a better success of their lives.

Knowing of his hardships, Julia would regularly slip him some extra cash on the side, hoping to make a slight difference in his life.

Julia placed the call on the intercom telephone, which connected each apartment to the guard-house.

"Hello, Ma' Julia?" Phineas answered the phone courteously, having seen her apartment number displayed on his console.

Julia could hear the smile in his voice even though she couldn't see him physically.

"Hi, Phineas," she responded, smiling in response to his friendliness.

It's true what they say… a smile is infectious.

"Phineas, how are you?" she asked, genuinely interested in his well-being.

"I'm fine, Ma' Julia, just the usual struggles. Oh, and also the tsotsi's broke into my room yesterday. I only have clothes and a bed, but they still stole my radio and battery."

In areas where electricity was not readily available, it was still common-practice to have an AM/FM radio powered by a hot-wired external nine-volt battery.

"Oh shame, Phineas, are you okay?" Julia asked, quite alarmed at the news.

Phineas replied quite indifferently, "I'm okay, Ma' Julia," as though this was a regular occurrence, which in reality it was.

There was generally nothing much between the haves and the have nots in the shanty towns and the have nots often just took from the haves when the opportunity arose. Fortunately, it was mostly opportunistic crime, as routines generally revolved around transport times and predictability was generally the enemy. The minibus taxis mostly departed for the city before the sun even raised its sleepy head and the shacks were left abandoned and at the mercy of these tsotsi's.

Julia, and possibly even Phineas, knew that she would make a plan to replace the radio as soon as she could.

Julia finally managed to change the topic to the reason for her call.

"Listen, Phineas, I found a letter outside my door this morning, maybe thirty minutes ago. Someone rang my door bell, but by the time I got to the door nobody was there... only the letter lying on the ground. Did anyone ask for me this morning, or ask to deliver a letter to me?"

"No, Ma' Julia, the morning is quiet. Nobody comes in. Only Mr Mathe went out for his run."

Julia marvelled for a second at how much his broken English had improved over the years. He wasn't in line to win any awards for grammar or pronunciation, but when she first met him, he was barely able to string a few words together.

There was a lot to be said about the effect of his regular interactions with all the English tenants.

"Thank you, Phineas," Julia muttered, "and there's no way anybody could get in besides past you?"

"No, Ma' Julia, I have been here from six o'clock and the fence is checked every day."

"Thanks, Phineas," Julia replied cordially, suppressing her consternation, "have a nice day."

Chapter 3

What's the harm, Julia finally decided after eyeing out the letter from her chair.

She finally picked it up again, rotated it, flipped it, and studied it.

Other than having that very faint scent of perfume or deodorant, it had no stamp which meant it was obviously destined for hand-delivery.

Absolutely nothing else seemed out of the ordinary.

No marks, besides her name.

No wires.

No powder.

By all accounts, it was a standard envelope, although slightly distended by the wadded letter it contained.

To her untrained eye, it certainly appeared safe enough to open, even though trepidation had been drummed into her and past experiences had nurtured, even demanded, a heightened sense of caution.

Should she call for back-up or was her paranoia just getting the better of her?

She inhaled deeply, subconsciously holding her breath, while slipping the tip of a paring knife beneath the fold and with a quick, cutting motion she slit the top of the envelope open.

Nothing happened… thankfully.

Although extremely anticlimactic, she exhaled abruptly out of relief that she was still in one piece, although remaining on high alert in case the letter was somehow still rigged to explode or shower her with fine white toxic powder.

She was familiar with all those stories and more so, it had been stringently impressed upon her from a young age to be intimately aware of any and all possibilities.

Who would really want to blow me up or poison me with ricin or anthrax?

Julia expelled a nervous giggle.

I'm just a lowly free-lance journalist.

But this wasn't quite true though and she knew it.

While she might be a nobody in her own capacity, she was the daughter of Alan Swan, the affluent and prominent self-made multi-millionaire.

Nobody reached that station in life without stepping on a few toes, whether intentionally or as a result of a business deal gone awry. And whilst always trying to be the good guy, casualties were often unavoidable.

He had, consequently, received a surfeit of threats over the years. Most of which were directed at himself, but more often than he would care to admit, they'd been levelled against his wife and daughter.

His strict instruction to both of them was to report any anomaly whatsoever to the home-base immediately, where his security team could initiate a full risk assessment and reaction plan. This had always seemed a bit excessive, but had on more than one occasion prevented a catastrophe.

Although readily aware of these dangers, Julia put them as far out of her mind as possible. Wouldn't she feel silly if the letter was nothing more than an invitation to some plush event, a love letter from some admirer or prospective suitor or just another overdue bill?

She wouldn't call in the troops for a simple letter.

Feeling slightly less apprehensive, Julia lifted the letter from the envelope and unfolded it.

Still no wires.

Still no noxious white powder.

Not even an elaborate font sprung out at her.

It was, in itself, rather innocuous.

There was no threat.

She looked it over intently. It was certainly no overdue bill. They were generally single-page statements containing nothing more than one-liners and figures.

This, on the other hand, was quite a substantial, multi-page letter.

Somebody had a lot to say.

It was a standard Calibri type font and whilst this was far more impressive than the mundane Arial type font, it was still fairly indifferent.

The paper was fairly standard as well. The typical A4 white printer paper was used. It was printed on one side only, hence the wad of pages folded and filling the envelope.

Waste of paper! Save the rainforests! Julia mused.

It was definitely addressed to her; with a cordial "Dear Julia" appearing in the top left quadrant of the first page. But from there on it was just paragraph after paragraph and page after page of typing. It reminded her of the old no-nonsense hand-written letters that her mother had sent her while she was away at university studying for her degree.

This would be a lengthy read.

She hadn't even washed her face or brushed her teeth yet.

She had originally planned to shower and wash her hair this morning, but she could not defer her burning curiosity.

It was non-negotiable, so she refreshed her coffee mug and snuggled back into her chair, prepared for the read... or so she thought.

Chapter 4

She gripped her second cup of coffee slightly tighter than intended when she read the opening sentence, until she realised that her knuckles had started to turn white, but she could not avert her eyes.

Dear Julia,

I know who you are, what you are and what you do! But please don't be alarmed, you are in no danger. I mean you no harm. In actual fact, I am writing this letter to you as I require your assistance.

I am about to embark on a mission of sorts and frankly, I require someone, more notably, you, to document and publicise my progress as well as the reasons for what could be construed, on the surface, as irrational and unsolicited actions.

The reason for approaching you should be obvious. But to offer some superfluous clarity and accolades; I have read all your articles, over the past year or so, with keen interest, and am extremely impressed with your command of the English language, the manner in which you captivate your readers and your association in general with the media – most notably The Daily Dispatch, *probably the oldest newspaper in East London, if not the entire Eastern Cape. Most importantly, though, your personal and regular stomping ground – the newspaper's online platform –* DispatchLIVE.

Local, national and possibly international coverage will be inevitable, but it will be you who sets the tone for this expected progression.

I am about to set in motion a series of events, which I quite simply blame on the government, both past and present.

South Africa's unemployment rate is spiralling out of control with no discernible, credible or effective short-, medium- or long-term plans to curb it. I believe the current estimate is around 30% of the employable workforce being unemployed. This is totally unacceptable, as the lack of employment has a direct correlation to the crime statistics in the country, especially in the number of housebreakings, thefts and vehicle hijackings. And while I cannot condone these actions, I certainly understand the reasons behind them. Right and wrong mean nothing to a hungry man, who must feed himself and his family. Now, combine a high unemployment rate, and thus a high crime rate, with an ill-equipped, under-qualified, out of shape and ineffective police force and you have a recipe for disaster – our disaster.

But I am getting ahead of myself – let me back up a bit and paint a proper picture for you.

South Africa has become inhospitable and uninhabitable. It is a small miracle that any of us are still alive. We travel in fear of being hijacked. Our female population live in constant fear of being abused, raped or even murdered. We lock ourselves away in our homes behind electrified fences and alarm systems. We subscribe to security companies, whose response times, we hope, will be effective in times of need, as we are damn sure that the police will not get to us in time. We cannot walk freely. We cannot let our children play freely. We cannot let our loved ones out of our sight. The scourge of crime in our neighbourhoods, towns and cities is growing exponentially each day. Forget about quality of life. We don't live any more, we merely survive.

It is estimated that there are about fifty murders each day.

And those are the reported cases. How many more have gone unreported? How many citizens have just gone missing? How many bodies have never been recovered?

Another significant and truly frightening statistic is that there is an average of around one hundred and eighty sexual assaults and rapes reported each day, which has been a concerning trend for many years now.

A study conducted by Jewkes in 2009 found that 25% of South African women are raped but only one in twenty-five actually reported the incident to the police. Imagine what the real figure is, bearing in mind that South Africa has a population of around sixty million people and approximately half of that population is female. To compound these horrendous figures, South Africa has the highest number of child and baby rape incidences in the world.

This is beyond comprehension and is absolutely despicable even on the most basic level of any society.

What is wrong with the men in our country? An abundance of sexual deviants.

This can only be described as a national crisis and the government is stumped as to how to resolve it! It's bad enough to be known as the "crime capital of the world" but it is with real concern and embarrassment that South Africa has now been referred to as "the rape capital of the world".

I am, by no means, a violent, irrational or irascible person by nature, but certain events, or more accurately, non-events, have driven me to the proverbial edge. So, to coin a phrase; "words are of little or no use any more – it's time for action".

There is, however, a solution, a light at the end of the proverbial tunnel. But it is extremely distant unless something is done right now. But unfortunately, those with the power to bring about this change somehow seem loathe to do anything about it. Why, you might ask? Well, that's the real question and the answer calls for all types of speculation, which I do not have the time or inclination to investigate. You may want to do your own research here.

We have a few state-of-the-art, automated, forensic science laboratories in South Africa. The Pretoria facility was constructed in 2005 at a cost of R75 million and at that time was the leading facility in the world for Genetic Sample Processing. The integrity of the system was unmatched, with minimum human intervention and results being automatically logged into databases and linked to case numbers. Human intervention would obviously be required to analyse the data, but the safety features meant that nothing could be altered or edited. In a word "Tamper-proof!" It was also designed specifically to process large quantities of DNA samples. Someone must have realised back in those days what a crime-ridden country South Africa would become. Typically, though, the GSP System is currently operating at less than half its capacity and that's probably at a stretch.

At the time, it was not the police who failed here, neither the technology nor, for that matter, the laboratory personnel. The authorities, higher up on the totem pole, were to blame.

As Chris Asplen was quoted in an article written at the time, "Nearly ten years after South Africa created one of the most advanced DNA laboratories in the world, the politicians have still failed to give the police force the legal authority to save literally thousands upon thousands of lives." He continued, "According to the United Nations, South Africa is ranked second in the world for murder and first for assaults and rapes per capita." You can almost sense his frustration, as he continues,

21

"The Parliamentary Portfolio Committee responsible for the legislation that would give police the ability to immediately begin taking rapists off the street has avoided acting on the law for years. The legislation sits in the committee while the worst sexual violence statistics in the world continue to pile up."

Now if this is not bad enough, South Africa also has one of the highest rates of recidivism in the world. Research has indicated that there is a high possibility of convicted offenders repeating crimes after their release. Call it poor rehabilitation or merely that these released convicts can't find jobs or have nothing better to do with their time. I don't have the answers here, but I do believe that a DNA database, containing at a minimum, the DNA of convicted felons, would certainly be a deterrent to these criminals reoffending.

It took the time and effort of Vanessa Lynch, who through her own tragic experiences, took a stand on the DNA issue in South Africa.

In association with like-minded individuals involved in the DNA Project, we finally had the DNA Act pass through parliament in 2013. This was only about twenty years after some of the first world countries had their DNA laws passed.

What took South Africa so long to realise the importance of this legislation and these processes?

Should we not have jumped on the bandwagon back then? Copy / Paste would have sufficed instead of trying to reinvent the wheel.

Remember, as each day passed, South Africa racked up another fifty murders and one hundred and eighty-three rapes. This should have sparked some sense of urgency, but no, nothing, nada – while we continue to bang the drum about sexual equality and women's rights, nothing is being done.

The debate about the right to privacy versus the right to safety and security; the interests of society versus the interests of the individual constantly rages on. Well, in my opinion, this should be a non-issue, as the intervention of any governing body to prevent people from harming or killing one another will inevitably result in some restriction of freedom or action. In essence, and I must plagiarise a quote I recently read, "Laws, by their very nature, restrict actions, but are in place to see that the greater good is achieved". When it comes to public safety and security, who cares about whose toes you stand on? The greater good is what matters. Get the laws in place. Give the authorities some legal support. Protect your public from the dangers that criminals impose upon society, and we will all live happily ever after.

Rights to privacy, what a joke? In this day and age, Big Brother is always watching. Internet connections and emails can and are being traced; cell phones have GPS functionalities; satellites and security cameras are the omniscient eyes in the sky. Privacy died in the dark ages, unless you live in a cave in Afghanistan and even there you might just be found, ask Osama Bin Laden.

As contradictory as it may seem, we willingly relinquish our DNA privacy rights to insurance companies when seeking life insurance or similar policy cover, but we dig in our heels and quote privacy laws when asked to do the right thing in combating or even preventing crime. It's an assault on common sense. Wake up people!

In a perfect world, everyone would voluntarily give up DNA samples. We should have massive databases, warehousing these unique genetic codes. Wouldn't that be the ultimate crime deterrent? Knowing that you will be apprehended because your DNA fingerprint is a key-stroke away? We would all be law-

abiding citizens. It's a no-brainer.

DNA is truly significant; it is not only examined to implicate a criminal; it is crucial in the elimination of potential suspects. And, ultimately, DNA is hardly ever used as evidence on its own, so routine investigative processes of collecting evidence are not suddenly gone and forgotten. It merely directs investigators to certain suspects.

Well, enough of the histrionics, I think I have made my point.

What will transpire from here on out is the following:

This might have the slight flavour of vigilantism but I see it more as correcting the unpunished wrongs of the past. These past-perpetrators need to atone for their past indiscretions, and with my assistance will tragically meet their maker.

I will, of course, ensure that some of my DNA accompanies these past-perpetrators on their final journeys, but don't expect me to make it too easy for the authorities. Oh, wait, if the 2014 audit report is anything to go by, there is still a backlog of around sixty-two thousand DNA tests to be completed to clear the slate. Now, based on this trend-line there will probably be well over a hundred thousand, or maybe even a hundred and fifty thousand tests outstanding in the next five years. Inept, totally inept!

Additionally, there are also reports of extreme lethargy or lack of resources in following up on DNA investigative leads and as at 31 March 2018 there were twenty-four thousand nine hundred and nineteen and eleven thousand nine hundred and ninety-one outcomes for known and unknown suspects respectively.

There just seems to be little or no inclination to locate, apprehend, arrest or even just question these individuals even though there is now solid evidence of their involvement in a crime.

I am really hoping that my actions will be a catalyst for change, but if the DNA processing turnaround time has not improved from between seven to thirteen months, I have serious doubts that my activities will have much of an impact. We can only hope!

It is possible that I will be apprehended one day, but common-sense dictates that this will only happen through a lapse in my concentration and judgement rather than through the application of the latest DNA and evidence analysis techniques. So, if everything goes according to plan, there will, in due course, be a few corpses over which the authorities will ponder. It is actually preposterous that in this day and age, I can be so confident that I will only be apprehended through my own carelessness and not through any advanced policing initiatives.

This now offers some clarity as to your inclusion in my plan.

Your task, as my journey unfolds, is not only to report on the current mundane murders, but to elucidate on the reasons for my actions. To give a little background to these events, you might say. To do a bit of research yourself and inform your readers of our little home-grown horror story and how simply it could have been prevented or resolved. Possibly even "glorify" my mission by explaining my pure intentions to your audience and maybe, just maybe, we'll get some results if there is a bit of public humiliation.

I apologise for this lengthy exposé, but your understanding and role is critical in the success of my undertaking.

I will remain in contact, but please do not waste your time in trying to track me down. You are in no immediate danger from me; so, let's keep it that way.

Best Regards,

Daniel Nathan Anderson

Chapter 5

Julia sat motionless. Her hand, which held the letter, trembled slightly.

What the hell, she thought.

Was this a joke?

Was someone playing the world's weirdest prank on her?

Where were the cameras?

This was far too surreal. It couldn't possibly be true.

If this was a prank, someone had gone to great lengths to make it look and sound very convincing.

But frankly, the effort required in researching these "facts" and then compiling this letter far outweighed the prank's comic value.

No way could this be a prank.

Julia shuddered. Goose-bumps prickled all over her body.

What to do? she wondered, still flabbergasted by what she had just read.

Her father's caution and instruction rang loudly in her ears.

This wasn't something she could keep to herself, irrelevant of whether it was fact or fiction. She had to tell someone.

Her father. Maybe the police, her editor or even her friends?

Well, it couldn't be the police right off the bat, could it? It probably wouldn't be taken very seriously or ultimately would just make its way straight into file thirteen amongst all the other unattended reports and cases. On the other hand, the letter could be interpreted as quite inflammatory and threatening and could quite possibly result in police action that would turn her world upside down.

She finally decided that they would have to wait to be brought into the loop.

Obviously, her editor would have to be brought into the loop, especially since she was expected to write articles on this nut-case's exploits.

This was certainly one of those occasions where you rued the fact that you were great at your job.

Daniel Nathan Anderson, she mused.

Why would he sign the letter? Surely it must be a pseudonym. No right minded person would sign such a seditious letter with his given name.

But, was he in his right mind?

Daniel Nathan Anderson.

She mulled it over in her mind for a few minutes.

No way, it can't be, she thought, as the penny suddenly dropped.

Daniel Nathan Anderson – DNA!

That surely wasn't a coincidence.

He must have planned for her to see the irony in his so-called initials all along.

She was a sucker for riddles and puzzles and the like. If he'd done his homework as he'd claimed to have, he would've known that she would decipher this in record time.

He obviously did know her… and far too well for her liking.

Or maybe… and this tilted her suspicion back to her friends again. They knew her well enough to include a little challenge like this in a fabricated letter to keep her intrigued.

Surely there'd be a phone-call soon with a bunch of giggling girls on the other end of the line, unable to contain themselves at the reaction they could visualise.

No, it couldn't be, she again decided. None of them would

put the time or effort into a prank as elaborate as this.

This must be the real deal.

If only she'd been a mediocre journalist. Someone else would have been chosen by 'DNA Dan' and the first time she'd have heard anything about this was on the evening news or whilst reading about it online or in the morning newspaper.

'DNA Dan', that's actually quite catchy, thought Julia.

She'd always been quick to coin a phrase or more appropriately in her occupation… a headline. Her love for wordplay again came to the fore and it titillated her the way she could always encapsulate a story with a few choice words.

Come on, pull yourself together, she reprimanded herself, *you need a plan.*

Her friends would never do this, but they would relish the adventure of being included in it and they would certainly be helpful and supportive in the long run… but not initially, Julia decided.

Her klatch would have to wait.

It would have to be her father, she decided. He'd been around the block more than a few times. He was a hardened businessman, whom she knew from her own involvement, had dealt with his fair share of whack-jobs in the past. He would definitely know what to do.

Besides, his instruction was crystal clear. She was to report any anomaly. Anything out of the ordinary. This letter surely slotted into that category.

While she treasured her independence, her father was correct. Some things were bigger than her. There were people out there who would employ any tactics to get at him, and his family was a relatively soft target.

Chapter 6

Alan Swan sat languidly on the sundeck of his mansion enjoying a late breakfast. It was a glorious morning and the warmth of the sun had over-powered the chill of the early morning. The view across the estate, from this vantage point, was absolutely magnificent.

He flipped through the pages of the morning newspapers, scanning for articles of interest. Even though he had the newspaper app on his iPad, he preferred the age old practice of flipping physical pages for local news. He only reverted to the electronic publications when pre-defined alerts prompted him to read articles of interest, which of course included all of Julia's work as well. In addition, national and international news were only available to him online, but these were routinely evening activities. His way to wind down with a whiskey after a hard day's work.

The challenging years and stress of his business life had taken their toll on him and even though he was only in his early fifties, he now sported a full head of distinguished grey hair. His olive-toned and unwrinkled complexion, however, ensured that he was still strikingly handsome in that Richard Gere, bespectacled, silver fox sort of way.

Alan had started his career in real estate sales in his early twenties and, after a few fortunate and lucrative deals, had decided to start investing in real estate himself. Flipping properties was a heady tonic for him and making a decent profit with each sale became utterly intoxicating.

Then, suddenly it wasn't; the buzz had dissipated.

His new drug of choice was procuring tracts of land in prime locations and investing heavily in the development of shopping malls, secure housing complexes and apartment flats.

The rental income was astounding and the best part was that his management team did all the hard yards, giving him time to speculate on further deals.

His portfolio currently included numerous beachfront properties and he wouldn't be happy until he owned the entire strip.

The refurbishment of the older properties he acquired complimented the more modern structures he erected, while elevating the beach front value and ambiance through the gentrification of the area.

His elusive white whale – his Moby Dick – was the apartment building in which Julia stayed. For years he had tediously negotiated the purchase thereof, but the owner was obstinate and would just not budge. Alan's offers were excessively higher than market value, but it seemed that no amount of money could influence a sale. The only restitution from his negotiations was that he would have the first option to buy when the time was right to sell.

It irked him though, that Julia still insisted on staying in that building and paying rent each month to boot, whereas she could stay for free in his ultra-modern apartment building only a few hundred metres further down the road.

She was just wired like that. No entitlement, no preferential rates and definitely no special treatment. She wanted to make it on her own.

Stubborn girl!

Each time Alan thought of this, he shook his head and smiled lovingly, knowing that her entire personality and demeanour echoed his own.

He already did and would do precisely the same thing all over again if he was placed in a similar position.

They were both stubborn like that!

He had the means and just wanted to dote on her and help make life a bit easier. Could an adoring father be blamed for that?

Why would she opt to live on a menial salary and struggle on a shoe-string budget when she could be part of his world?

Julia would make an excellent protégé, but she claimed to be following her dream by being a journalist and then, later in life, potentially write a few bestsellers.

It frustrated Alan, knowing the opportunities he could afford her. But he couldn't argue or disagree that at only twenty-four years of age, she was a brilliant columnist. The current drawback was that she was only a freelance reporter.

At this stage of her life, he would have thought that she should have secured a permanent position by now. But she seemed quite content with the arrangement of being paid for her submissions.

It just seemed a bit pedestrian to him in his frenetic world.

Once he had semi-jokingly offered to buy the newspaper or alternatively start a new newspaper for the East London area, which she could own and operate.

This offer was very quickly retracted when Julia totally flipped out.

Fortunately, the bond between them was and always had been phenomenal.

He would never jeopardise this. He only wanted the best for her, and ultimately to give her everything her heart desired.

One inevitability, which put his mind at ease, was that she would eventually inherit everything from him anyway.

She was, after all, their only child and she would never have to struggle in life.

Chapter 7

Moments later Alan's heart nearly skipped a beat.

Not in the critical, medical emergency way, but rather in the warm, loving and elated way.

Julia had suddenly appeared in the doorway and surprised him.

"Morning, Pops, great day out here."

"Morning, Jules," Alan responded through his warm toothy smile.

He relished her visits, whether planned or announced or neither.

She just brightened up his day.

He really missed having her around, even though he saw her quite frequently. That, combined with the fact that she lived only minutes away, made him count his blessings. It could have been way worse and he was actually very fortunate. Some children left home as soon as they could and moved away from their parents. Far away.

He was indeed lucky and he needed to remember that.

Julia needed her independence, he totally understood that, even though her childhood bedroom was off limits to everyone and was always freshly prepared for her return.

She casually strolled over to him and leaned in for a kiss followed by the requisite hug.

As usual, Alan hung on for longer than absolutely necessary, basking in his daughter's affection. His love for Julia was indescribable. Take the average affection between a father and his daughter and multiply that by a million.

"Got time for breakfast? The coffee's hot," he offered, finally releasing her from his loving embrace.

"Actually, today I do, Dad."

She pulled out a chair and absent-mindedly smoothed out the place setting in front of her.

"And there's something I really need to show you," she added.

"What's up, Munchkin?"

As if on cue, Olawale Adebayo appeared in the doorway with a fresh cup of coffee and a plate of piping hot scones.

"Ollie!" Julia yelped and jumped up from her seat.

She wrapped her arms around the massive Nigerian, who had to evade her flailing arms for fear of spilling the coffee and scones.

It wasn't as though Alan was uncomfortable about the bond between Julia and Ollie, it was more a case of being slightly envious or possibly even jealous about their relationship.

He understood the reasons and while in retrospect he was grateful, it still irked him a little.

During her formative years, he had been entirely consumed with forging an empire and was often preoccupied and distant, missing out on key milestones in her life.

She had consequently grown up in the big man's presence. While most adolescent girls had a group of friends to confide in and hang with, Julia had a Nigerian giant.

Whether working or at rest, Ollie had always been there for her. Whether driving her around, entertaining her or merely just spending time with her, he had always been available to her.

Ollie was a two metre tall, one hundred and fifty kilogram

slab of extremely dark Nigerian beef and referring to him as such was in no way derogatory, as this was how he had introduced himself when he was first interviewed by Alan Swan.

Ollie was more than just Alan's butler, chauffeur, bodyguard and all round dog's body. Over the years, he had become a close friend and confidant. He was totally devoted to the Swans and his service to Alan and his family for the past twelve years was beyond reproach.

He was remunerated exceptionally well as Alan believed that his job function was ultimately more important than those of his numerous business advisers and managers. This was obviously a bitter pill for his advisers and managers to swallow, as they had business degrees and often multiple graduate qualifications, while Ollie was, in their minds, just a muscle-bound oaf.

To the contrary, Alan's perspective was quite simple; Ollie took care of him and his family while his advisers and managers took care of the businesses.

Which function was more important?

Now, who could really fault that logic? Besides, who would dare?

This was, after all, Alan Swan.

As a result, Ollie had amassed a small fortune during his tenure with the Swans. But even with his accumulated wealth, he remained a very humble, quiet and reserved man.

He was in the enviable position where he could retire at any stage and be more than comfortable for the rest of his life, so it was certainly not the money which retained his service.

He had literally become part of the Swan family and since he had no reason or desire to return to Nigeria, why would he leave?

He lived on the property with them, he ate at the same table with them, he was even regularly asked for his input on family and business matters.

Ollie was part of the inner circle and kept in the loop on everything.

Alan believed that Ollie's involvement in all matters was of vital importance, as he was the common denominator in all their lives. When he was not with Alan himself, he accompanied his wife, Claire, on her errands and commitments. Julia required his attention less frequently, as she no longer resided at the mansion. He was within minutes of her, if ever required. Basically, Ollie would be wherever he was needed.

As a consequence, he needed to know where each family member was at all times and this, he seemingly managed to do with consummate ease.

Chapter 8

Dwarfing Julia, Ollie stretched over her and placed the coffee and scones on the table and then returned his attention to her, reciprocating the affection with a huge, but tender, bear-hug.

"Where have you been, Jules? We haven't seen you for days," Ollie asked in his measured baritone voice.

He hadn't totally lost his Nigerian accent, but it had definitely been transformed by the subtle strains of South African English.

"I've been around. I think the last time I was here, you were out with Mom."

Ollie nodded and philosophised, "Maybe out of sight, but never out of mind, Jules."

"So what have you got to show me?" Alan interjected, in an effort to regain some of Julia's attention and direct the discussion to the reason for her visit.

"It's hopefully nothing, Dad, but I think your advice is crucial here."

Julia reached back and rummaged in her bag, which she had hung on the backrest of her chair. She handed the envelope to Alan.

"What's this?"

"Open it," she insisted.

Alan flipped the envelope and extracted the letter, noticing that it was simply addressed to 'Julia Swan'.

"Read it," Julia prompted.

Alan took his time scanning the letter, his facial expressions changing all the while.

Julia and Ollie chatted softly in the background, so as not to distract him. A practical impossibility, since he was totally engrossed in the content of the pages he flipped through.

Finally he turned his attention back to Julia.

"What's this about?" he asked curiously, while trying to figure out what it meant. "Who's this guy?"

Julia shrugged her shoulders. No words were necessary.

"Do you think he's for real?"

"I don't know, Dad. It sounds like it, but then again maybe he's just a total whack-job trying to get some attention. He does, on the other hand, sound extremely intelligent and his command of the English language places him firmly in the well-educated bracket. But being educated and well-spoken doesn't preclude him from being a whack-job. We can all attest to that."

"Okay, so from the beginning, Jules," Alan directed, unconsciously tapping his left index finger on his temple, while focussing all his attention on Julia.

Julia inhaled deeply and regaled them in detail of what had happened.

Ollie looked on curiously and, on noticing this, Alan handed him the letter.

"This might be serious, big guy. Julia might have attracted the attention of some lunatic. There could be trouble brewing here."

Like Alan, Ollie studied the text.

He finally nodded, placing the letter in front of him on the table and steepled his massive fingers together on his chin.

"Sounds like a whack-job to me."

"Maybe, but whack-job or not, will he follow through with

his threats and more importantly, is Julia in danger here?" Alan queried, pursing his lips and nodding his head ever so slightly.

"Well, we can't ignore it. That's for sure. I'll get the team on it immediately," Ollie stated matter-of-factly and excused himself from the table.

Alan turned his attention back to Julia.

"I want you to move back in here until we figure this out."

"Dad, you know that's not going to happen."

"But Ollie and the team can be more effective with you here," Alan pointed out.

"I can't go into hiding every time something like this happens, and besides – if this guy's true to his word – I'm not his target. He just wants me to publish a play by play account of his exploits," Julia countered sternly.

"You can do that all from here, Julia, even though I would advise against getting involved in this at all. There's no reason to put yourself in danger until we know what this guy's up to."

Julia could see the concern in her father's face and knew that what he was saying made perfect sense, but she couldn't and wouldn't change her life-style over a letter, which was in all fairness, most probably just a hoax.

"I just can't, Dad. I have my life and it can't be thrown into turmoil over issues or non-issues like this."

Alan looked off into the distance, as he contemplated an appropriate counter-argument. He knew that he would not change her mind. But he had to try.

When his eyes locked onto hers again, he unfortunately knew that whatever he said would be futile.

But, in a last ditch attempt, he added, "You asked for my advice, Julia, so here it is. I think you should move back in with us where we can protect you more effectively. This will give Ollie and the team time to figure this out without being stretched too thin surveilling you."

He continued, "Ollie has built up an interesting and influential network over the years and will get to the bottom of this sooner than the authorities can. Leave the letter here for him so he can get it analysed, then we can track down this nut case before you or anyone else gets hurt."

"Okay, keep the letter and let Ollie do his thing, but as for me moving back, it's not going to happen. I really do appreciate the offer and concern, Dad, but I can't have my life turned upside down over this. I also need to brief Moses. If he's to allow me to publish the exploits of some anonymous whack-job, he'll need to understand the story behind it."

Alan sighed.

"All right, Julia, let's do it your way, but just understand that I'm not happy about it, so don't expect me to sit idly by and do nothing. You got me involved and I have the resources to protect and keep you out of danger and that's what I'll do," he stated categorically. "Also, please give us a day or so to get a jump start on this before you get Moses involved. He might be obligated to get the authorities involved and we can do without the red tape for now while we investigate."

Julia understood his concern and loved him even more for it.

"Fine! But the guys can't get in my way. I can't be surrounded by bodyguards the whole day like some dignitary."

"Great, you won't even know they're there," he promised, already knowing that it would be easier to apologise than to ask for permission if the team did encroach on her movements.

Julia stood and retrieved her handbag, forcing closure to the conversation.

She had learnt this tactic from her father many years before and now used it expertly against him.

She kissed him again and whispered "I love you" in his ear, did an about turn, and left.

"Love you too," he replied, but she was already out of earshot.

Chapter 9

Dan had been watching his first victim for weeks already and was all too familiar with his day to day routine – which never changed.

When would people realise how vulnerable they made themselves when they adhered to strict routines?

Mix it up, people, he thought to himself. *You're setting yourselves up.*

The thought of what he had to do actually galled him, but what choice did he have and for that matter, what alternative was there to get the authorities to pay attention?

Half the police force was overweight and totally unfit to perform their duties and those who did try their best and were prepared to assist citizens in trouble, could not. Police vehicles were either damaged, without fuel, or totally beyond repair. Police stations looked more like scrapyards than law enforcement premises.

How had it come to this in such a short space of time?

He had additionally heard stories of the public phoning in to report a crime in progress and being astoundingly asked by the officer on duty whether they would like the police to be sent to the crime scene or not.

He shook his head in absolute dismay. Why would someone be calling for help if they didn't want immediate response from the police?

How had things become so bad so quickly?

Dan prickled with frustration, but brushed these thoughts away as he forced himself to re-focus on the task at hand.

He waited, in position until the sun finally crested the hilltops and twilight cloaked the valley. He was crouched out of sight – patient and alert – waiting. The street lights, along with any garden or house lights which were programmed on timers, would soon activate and bathe the semi-darkened area in a soft glow of light. As the darkness of night intensified, the shadows steadily became more and more apparent, ultimately stretching themselves out to fill and obscure all the recessive areas.

The house he was staking out was a beautiful semi-modern simplex, located in an up-market and fairly affluent neighbourhood. The exterior walls and roof were recently painted and the house was generally well maintained. A concrete slab driveway cut its way across a lush and well-manicured lawn along the side of the property, leading up to the doors of a double-garage which adjoined the house.

There were no real flower beds to speak of but a few over-grown oak trees had been strategically positioned around the erf to provide shade in the summer months and now would unwittingly offer excellent cover for Dan when he slipped into the yard.

He glanced at his watch, mesmerised for a brief moment by the second hand which ticked metronomically along.

Any minute now, he thought.

True to form and right on schedule the sleek silver BMW pulled into the driveway. It was not the latest model on the market, but was still in itself a status symbol and rather desirable.

Without even a cursory glance to the left or to the right, Craig Davis thumbed the remote to activate the electric gate. The motor kicked in and the gate opened slowly, sliding steadily along its rusted and worn guiderail.

It was almost too easy to follow the car up the driveway, but Dan remained on high alert. Although under the cover of darkness, it was still the trickiest and most dangerous part of his plan.

If his timing was even slightly out, his movement would be noticed in the rear-view mirrors and his ambush would go up in smoke.

But, his execution was perfect. He ducked into the yard and concealed himself behind the bole of a large oak tree just as the BMW came to a halt in front of the garage doors; its brake lights now illuminating the entire length of the vacant driveway.

As the gate closed behind them, the motorised garage door began its ascent. It was quite noisy as the wooden slats rolled up on themselves, but an all too familiar sound in this class of neighbourhood.

No need for concern from anybody.

The car inched forward once again, coming to rest in its parking bay inside the garage.

In his preparation visits, Dan had noticed that Craig always cut the engine and climbed out of the car before activating the closure of the garage door.

This was the moment.

Dan waited anxiously for the garage door to start its descent and then bolted into the garage, crouching slightly as he ran and slipped though under the descending door.

Craig never knew what hit him.

The crushing blow to the side of his head felled him where he stood.

As he dropped to his knees and then fell forward onto his face, his brief-case and keys spilled from his limp hands.

In a flash, Dan retrieved the keys, unlocked the interleading door and effortlessly lifted Craig's limp body off the floor. Craig weighed about ninety kilograms, but to Dan, this was like just another day at the gym. He hefted the 'dead-weight' over his shoulder, squatted to retrieve the brief-case with his other hand and casually strolled into the house.

Chapter 10

Craig lived alone.

He and his wife had separated many years before. It was a marriage that should never have been. They had both been so ambitious and career driven that their nuptials were realistically doomed from the outset. Unwittingly, however, they had followed through with the romance and the subsequent wedding, paying no heed to how much hard work and effort a marriage required.

Each day, they both left before sunrise for work and arrived home way after sunset; too self-absorbed and exhausted to give each other much attention. Expectations and demands led to contempt and finally, the writing was on the wall. A year later they both agreed to an amicable divorce and ended up in court signing the dreaded separation documents.

Children were never part of the equation. They were both far too engrossed in their own careers to even contemplate consummating their marriage with children. This was ultimately a blessing and the imminent divorce had no complications. A neat little fifty-fifty split of their estate and they were on their way.

Craig had ended up keeping the house in which they'd lived and his now ex-wife had moved out, soon after to be transferred to Pretoria on a promotion.

It was destiny, he always believed.

Memories of good times gone by triggered once in a while, when he walked through the house, but he was not the nostalgic type and paid little heed to them. He had moved on, both physically and emotionally.

He would never have thought that living alone would be the kink in his armour. He had been singled out by Dan as target number one purely because of his reclusive behaviour and precision routines.

He had made himself such an easy target.

Dan knew, from weeks and weeks of surveillance, that Craig was a loner. In all that time, he'd never once witnessed anything close to what could be defined as a congenial encounter. Craig avoided interactions whenever possible.

No-one would show up unannounced or accidentally come to his rescue.

He shook his head, as if clearing his mind of these thoughts, and slowly and methodically busied himself with the necessary preparations.

Craig finally stirred and winced as a razor-sharp pain raced around behind his eyes, making it impossible to focus clearly on anything. He blinked repeatedly. What he could see from his position on the floor seemed so distant. Everything was framed by a hazy aura and seemed to pulse in time with the throb of pain in his head. He squinted and nearly cried out as the ceiling light caught his attention, shining acutely down on him.

Through his clouded vision and muddled thoughts, he finally reasoned that he was severely concussed.

What was happening? he wondered.

He tried to speak, but his mouth was clogged with a gag and he could form no words. Instead, a gruff, garbled sound emanated from his throat.

Dan slowly lifted himself from the recliner and stood over Craig's prone form.

He waited patiently.

Craig looked up and blinked repeatedly again in an attempt to clear the fog which hung like a curtain before his eyes.

Dan waited and watched in anticipation. This was a memory he would savour and always hold dear.

Recognition and realisation slowly filled Craig's eyes.

"Ah, you remember," Dan mouthed – a hint of a smile appearing on his countenance.

Craig squirmed, but totally in vain.

His hands and feet were securely bound with cable-ties and the acrid tasting gag was held in place with some sort of sticky bandage or tape.

Dan looked downwards in amusement as Craig repeatedly tried to work his hands and feet free, only to fail again and again with each attempt.

How long could a person courageously struggle before hopelessness finally settled in and all thoughts of escape were relinquished?

Not very long, it turned out.

Chapter 11

"You tormented me for years, Craig! You and your cronies had a lot of fun at my expense."

Craig tried to reply, but an agonised groan was all he could muster.

"How could you take advantage of someone so much younger and smaller than you? You were a bully – you and your friends. It's all coming back to you now, isn't it? I see it in your eyes. You remember what you did."

Craig moaned.

"Well, times have changed – and so have I – as you can see."

Dan flexed his pronounced pectorals to emphasise the point and glanced over at his bulging biceps, barely contained by the tightly fitting shirt he wore.

"Congratulations!" he added good-naturedly. "You have been singled out as number one. But fear not, the rest of your cowardly cohort await a similar fate and they will all pay dearly for making my life a living hell."

Craig moaned even louder and wriggled feverishly in another attempt to free himself.

Dan sighed audibly as he flashed back to the constant torment, the abuse and ultimately the raucous laughter which inevitably followed. He had been mentally and physically abused for years, enduring such cruelty to the point where he finally begged his parents to move him to another school. He couldn't, or more accurately wouldn't, tell them the reason why, while paying meticulous attention to concealing any cuts and bruises he had suffered under make-up and numerous layers of clothing. He had actually become quite adept at using concealments to mask any lacerations and skin discolorations.

His unsubstantiated request was initially dismissed as a stage he would outgrow. But when his grades starting sliding and skipping school became routine, something had to be done. His parents, now extremely concerned, pestered him for answers, but he had remained tight-lipped – saying anything would just aggravate the situation.

Craig shouted again into the gag, which brought Dan back from his painful reminiscing.

"Shhh, Craig." Dan whispered softly. "Nothing you say or do can stop the inevitable now. You see, destiny is calling and your fate is vitally important in the bigger picture."

Dan finally stood and slowly moved out of Craig's line of sight.

Craig's body stiffened as he felt a noose being slipped over his head and firmly secured around his neck. It wasn't a rope. It felt rubbery. He panicked and thrashed violently, but all in vain. He couldn't dislodge it.

What was going on? his mind screamed.

If only he could just talk, explain, rationalise, even apologise. Maybe they could laugh it all off as school high jinks and maybe he could get out of this. But he couldn't talk, in fact he was now having difficulty just breathing with the noose around his neck.

Dan looked down at the pitiful sight lying before him and suddenly didn't feel disgusted any more. He didn't feel anything any more. He embraced his quest and what he had to do, as a calm numbness descended over him. His mind and body drifted onto auto-pilot.

He calmly lifted Craig's legs and slowly, but firmly, pulled them towards him, inching backwards all the while.

Craig's eyes widened in fear, as he felt the rubbery cord tighten and then constrict around his neck.

His body tensed, while his mind exploded with the sudden realisation that he was being hung... horizontally.

There would be no quick release, as would be the case in a normal hanging. Gravity was not at play here and his neck would not suddenly snap as his free-falling body reached the full extent of the hangman's rope.

This was no rigid length of rope... it was a bungee cord.

Dan gazed intently at Craig's face, which was now a purple-blue hue as his eyes began to bulge. Unadulterated panic was quite evident.

Too soon. Too quick. Minimal retribution.

He released Craig's legs and the bungee cord snapped the man's body backwards into the pillar to which it was anchored. A searing pain erupted in Craig's head at the site of the impact. Warm, sticky blood seeped from the wound in the top of his head and dripped onto the floor. His concussion was now a hundred times worse than it had been and, through the haze, he tried desperately to focus on not throwing up.

Craig coughed through the gag and snorted vigorously through his blocked nose to allay vomiting while concurrently trying to inhale the oxygen his body desperately craved. Throwing up would be fatal, as he was still gagged and that would only lead to one thing... choking and possibly drowning on his own barf. This realisation totally immobilised him and with nostrils flared to the extreme with each intake of oxygen, tears started flowing from his eyes.

"That's it, Craig, you made me cry on many occasions. You relished in my anguish. How does it feel?"

Craig's mind flashed back as he remembered ambushing the boy and tying him to the poplar tree in his parent's back garden. They had stripped the boy naked. He had been ashamed of his nakedness and sobbed and pleaded incessantly for his release and his clothes, but then soon realised that his nakedness was the least of his worries. The four older boys had spent the entire afternoon painfully shooting elastic bands at every part of the little boy's exposed body. They laughed ecstatically, while he cried in agony.

Finally, they let up with the torture and released their prisoner, who grabbed his clothes and ran from them.

Dan could almost follow Craig's thoughts and finally broke the silence. "Well, well, now here's the irony; you lying here now all bound up and at the mercy of a maniac with a rubber band. Kind of poetic, isn't it?"

Dan again lifted Craig's legs and took a few paces backwards. The bungee cord stretched and strained again as Craig's body lifted horizontally into the air.

Milliseconds before his demise, Dan again released him.

The sudden release again catapulted Craig headfirst into the base of the pillar, opening another huge gash in his pate. Blood spattered the base of the pillar and pooled rapidly on the floor tiles.

The thud was alarmingly loud and the result was strangely satisfying to Dan.

Craig came to after thirty minutes.

Concussed and bleeding profusely from the two gashes in his head.

While unconscious, Dan had cut away his clothes.

"Embarrassing, isn't it, Craig? All your bits hanging out.

Well, this is how you will be found! And I will personally make the missing person's call if your absence isn't noticed soon enough. I can't have a spoilt crime scene now, can I?"

Craig mumbled weakly into the gag, as if acquiescing to his fate and with that Dan raised his legs one last time and retreated with purpose. The bungee cord stretched to its limit, crushing down on Craig's throat and cutting off his air-supply.

Dan held him firmly in position.

Craig writhed and gasped in a last-ditch effort to free himself, but soon enough the struggle was over. Mercifully for Craig, his suffering had come to an end.

Dan looked on inquisitively as Craig's life force was snuffed out. And then for good measure released Craig's legs for the last time and watched again as his now lifeless body crashed headlong into the pillar smashing Craig's skull and turning the top of his head into a mushy mess.

It was much later than he had intended.

He still had a lot to do and while being ultra-careful, he hurriedly staged the crime scene.

He then scanned his handiwork.

Perfect, he thought to himself.

Dan then calmly and casually left the house, as though nothing untoward had happened, locking the door securely behind him.

Chapter 12

Julia's mind had been racing for the past few days since she had received the letter. Her body was constantly on high alert. Every stranger she passed looked suspicious. Eye-contact with anyone seemed threatening. She had been struggling to concentrate and even sleeping was nigh on impossible.

Sleep disorders were foreign to her but she soon realised that she had to do something about it. She'd been walking around like a zombie for days now. She resorted to a natural remedy rather than any of the prescribed medications.

She had heard that Melatonin was the way to go, as it wasn't a sleeping pill per se, but rather just switched off the brain's beta wave activities, which were ultimately responsible for thought.

The pills had actually worked a treat. The incessant activity in her mind had finally stopped and she'd managed to get a few hours of shut-eye, albeit filled with the most graphic and lucid dreams she'd ever had.

Quite frightening actually, but at least nothing to do with her current situation.

Nonetheless, she woke early, feeling relatively refreshed for a change.

The room was still dark. The blackout drapes, which were seldom drawn, had on this occasion done their job to perfection and had kept the room gloomy.

She casually reached over and fumbled for her cell phone on the bedside table and with dexterous fingers keyed in her PIN to activate the luminescent screen.

It was still early, very early, but she felt great. The best sleep in what felt like an eternity. Realistically, though, it hadn't been more than a few days since she'd received the disturbing letter.

She lay there, now wide awake, checking her emails and messages. She had done nothing to comply with the requests, or rather demands, made in the letter.

What would happen next? she wondered.

Should she be doing something?

What would happen if she didn't comply?

Would Dan come after her?

How would he enforce his demands?

If he was capable of following through with murder, what would he do to her if she didn't play her part?

Would her family be in danger?

Would she be looking over her shoulder for the rest of her life?

Would she ever lead a normal life again?

Julia mulled these thoughts over, becoming increasingly anxious all the while. She reflexively covered her face with her hands. It was a totally instinctive reaction, probably dating back to the beginning of mankind.

Protect your face when in danger; physical or emotional.

Anyway, whether true or not, it comforted her.

Slowly but surely the anxiety ebbed.

And with that, she decided to comply with Dan's demands.

Whether right or wrong, it certainly couldn't harm her career. She might actually benefit by being at the coal-face of a cutting-edge story, while the drama or tragedy, for that matter, played itself out.

She would start with some research of her own… today.

The morning sun was now just peeping over the horizon when she opened the curtains and even though her eyes were accustomed to the dark, at this time of day, the sun wasn't bright or full enough to assault her eyes with its dagger-like rays.

Within a half hour she was ready to face the day. Abnormal for a woman, but her job didn't entail a uniform, or even make-up. She simply slipped on a pair of jeans and a T-shirt, brushed her mousy-blonde hair and made a turn in the kitchen, where she poured herself a steaming cup of freshly brewed coffee from the percolator. She sipped the steaming liquid, careful not to scald herself, until the caffeine took effect.

"Ahhh, that's the ticket," she murmured.

She gasped in exasperation, as her perfunctory glance came to rest on a white envelope protruding from under her front door.

It was again clearly addressed to her, **Julia Swan**.

She stooped to retrieve it when the intercom buzzer next to the door rasped loudly and nearly stopped her heart. She swore animatedly, trying desperately to compose herself before answering.

"Who is it?" she called out. Maybe a bit louder than usual, but quite understandably under the circumstances.

"It's Phineas at the gate, Ma' Julia... Ollie is here to see you."

"Oh, hi, Phineas. Thanks. Please send him up."

Julia left the letter where it lay, as she wanted Ollie to witness her opening it.

Moments later there was a light knock on the door. "It's Ollie, Jules," the Nigerian announced his arrival.

Julia exhaled deeply through sheer relief and went through the process of sliding back the deadbolt, then unlocking the dual locks on her door.

The huge frame of the amiable Nigerian dominated the space vacated by the opened door.

"Ollie, another one," Julia stammered, indicating the envelope on the floor.

"I know," Ollie responded casually, "the guys caught this little bugger doing the drop with Mr Kilburn outside the gate an hour ago. I came as soon as they called."

"Well, you could have warned me, I nearly had heart failure when I saw it; and frankly, I still haven't even picked it up."

Reflecting then on Ollie's last words, Julia tried to look past the bulk of the man, but his sheer size prevented her from getting a glimpse. The confusion was etched on her face, though.

Noticing this, the huge Nigerian moved his bulk to one side.

A small African boy stood there, shaking fearfully as he was supported on either side by two significantly larger African men.

Julia had seen them before, but didn't know their names. They were obviously part of Ollie's team and had been staking out the apartment building on her father's instruction.

"Themba questioned him in the time it took for me to arrive, but with little success. The boy stutters a lot, which makes communication a bit difficult. He keeps referring to the madala in Currie Street, who gave him R10 to deliver the letter to this address. He seemingly couldn't gain access, so he gave it to Mr Kilburn, who was on his way in after his morning run."

"Madala? What's that?" Julia asked, looking for clarity.

Ollie smirked. "At least I knew that one," he said proudly, not having picked up too much of the local languages during his time in South Africa.

"It means 'old man', but we couldn't get any more specifics than that from the boy."

"And Currie Street… that's just around the corner, Ollie."

"Yes," Ollie concurred. "We already have some guys scouting the neighbourhood. Hopefully they will track down the old man and bring him in to answer some questions."

"Was the old man black or white?" Julia asked.

This had already been established, but for Julia's sake, Themba engaged in another brief exchange of words in Xhosa with the youngster and it was confirmed that it was an old black man; a homeless old black man.

"That's not our guy, Ollie. From his letter, I profiled Dan as more of a well-educated, middle aged, white man. Although, that was my totally unprofessional opinion."

"I agree, Jules, this guy is smarter than we give him credit for. He knew that we'd be staking out your apartment, so he used the classic hand-off strategy, making the trail back to him so long and arduous that following the breadcrumbs would probably keep us busy for weeks or more."

He then added, "After a few hand-offs, it's actually quite amazing that the letter found its way to the correct address at all."

Ollie turned to his two-man team and instructed them to take the boy and continue the search for the old man with the others, hoping that the boy would add value in the identification process.

"What do we do with the boy after that?" Themba asked Ollie.

"He's had the scare of his life, so let him go," Ollie replied, "but give him your cell number. Any future information would be good."

And with that Ollie handed over a crisp R50 note to the boy, whose tearful eyes suddenly showed signs of delight – it must have felt like Christmas.

As the guys left, Ollie turned and followed Julia into her apartment, waiting for her to stoop and timidly retrieve the envelope.

"R10 is food for the day to these street kids, so I wouldn't be surprised if this happens again," Ollie muttered, more to himself than to Julia.

Julia set about brewing more coffee, ignoring Ollie's protests that she should sit while he prepared the coffee.

"You are in my house as a guest, Ollie, now behave like one," Julia admonished him sternly.

They moved to the living room and took up seats opposite each other, separated by the centrally positioned wooden coffee table.

Julia's nerves were still quite frazzled and it took a while for her to regain her composure; the taste of the fresh coffee soon sorted that out.

"What did you find out about the first letter, Ollie?" she finally asked.

"Nothing much really, no finger-prints, no DNA, commonly available paper and envelope and nothing special about the printer used either. Frankly that letter was the definition of ordinary."

"Any other leads from your connections or informants?" she probed.

"Nothing at all! I didn't divulge too many details, for obvious reasons, but still, nobody had heard anything remotely connected to our guy."

Julia glanced down at the coffee table where she had placed the second letter and Ollie's eyes followed hers.

"I suppose I'd better open it," Julia said and stooped forward to retrieve the letter.

Chapter 13

"How careful should we be?" Julia asked, hesitantly reaching for the envelope.

"There's probably no use dusting for finger-prints or anything like that. We can safely assume that this letter was touched by many fingers during the hand-off process and, by the looks of the envelope, odds are its standard stationery anyway, just like the first letter," Ollie responded matter-of-factly.

Nonetheless, he still examined the envelope thoroughly.

"No additional clues. No clues at all. This guy is ultra-careful," he added.

Julia took it from him and used a sharp cutting knife which she had brought from the kitchen to slit the envelope open at the fold.

As if confirming Ollie's prior assessment, the letter she extracted was identical to the first, even down to the detail of the Calibri font and *italic* type-face.

No surprises there then.

Unlike the first letter which comprised of many pages, this one was surprisingly shorter – obviously less detailed – and more to the point.

She looked across at Ollie and frowned. He mimicked her expression as if to encourage her or to say 'Whenever you're ready'. The silence was deafening. The anticipation hung like a thick mist around them, making it difficult to breathe.

They would both end up reading the letter, so she decided

that reading it to herself and then passing it across to Ollie would be futile.

Julia finally inhaled deeply and proceeded to read the letter out loud.

Dear Julia,

I had hoped that our second letter would be of a more professional nature, but unfortunately through your actions, or should I say lack thereof, I am forced to wear the paternal hat and chastise you.

You've been a naughty girl, haven't you?

I implored you not to waste your time or mine in trying to track me down and your first action was to get your father and his bodyguard involved.

I am well aware that you have limitless resources at your disposal, but use them wisely, if you have to.

Do you really think that I am that foolish to leave trace evidence on the letters?

Do you really think that I will present myself, in the flesh, on your door-step?

Do you really think that I am that simple?

Now really, after what I have planned, would I really stumble at the first hurdle?

I, too, have numerous resources at my disposal, and am also well aware that your apartment is under constant surveillance.

A simple case of watching the watchers.

And now, as a result, my method of communication with you is consequently hampered and I will have to employ other ways to keep you informed and apprised of the latest developments.

This is truly most inconvenient.

As I guaranteed you before, you are in no danger, and I stand by my word, unless of course, you continue to snub me.

So, it would be easier for all if you got the guard dogs to back off and let us get on with our lives and the inevitable.

You play a crucially important role in this process.

I don't want unnecessary complications to delay the process. That aside, I have seen nothing in the media as yet.

*I would have appreciated an introductory passage by now, as the first **die** has already been cast.*

This will confuse the public if the reasons for phase one are not satisfactorily introduced. He becomes just another meaningless statistic in a sick society.

A common occurrence, about which the public are probably already numb and emotionless.

Even the best article will just garner a cursory glance.

That's the effect our ailing society now has on the individual. Nothing fazes or shocks us any more. We tolerate, albeit with disgust, the senseless number of murders and rapes, amongst all else.

Julia, I am depending on you to make sense of this mess for the public and, suffice to say, this could really put you on the map as the top-class investigative journalist you've always wanted to be.

Your previous articles will, in contrast, pale in comparison, possibly even just be considered page-fillers at the most, compared to this.

Now, either we leave the history behind us and move forward or you can continue to defy my wishes and suffer the consequences.

The proverbial ball is in your court, but I sincerely hope you choose the former.

Starting the process over with another journalist would be a complete and utter waste of my time.

You now have twenty-four hours to get the introductory article published before the police investigate the missing person's report and find our dearly departed friend, after which it will be too late, and this will make me very unhappy.

Rush, rush, rush now!

Best Regards,

Daniel Nathan Anderson

Chapter 14

Julia looked up from the letter, meeting Ollie's big brown eyes again.

As if reading her thoughts, Ollie said, "Sounds like we need to take this guy seriously, Jules, he's way ahead of the game. He's done his homework on you, your family and even me. He's even been watching our every move... and now you even have a strict deadline."

Julia nodded sagely.

"I know Dad won't go for this, but your team needs to back off a bit and give him the space he's demanded. If he's tracking your surveillance team, any sight of them could push him over the edge and I now believe his threats for non-compliance are as real as they come."

"Jules, you know your father, he will never allow that. If he thinks you're in danger, he'll force you to move back into the mansion, at least until we have a better idea of who this guy is and, more importantly, how dangerous he is." Ollie pursed his lips and frowned.

"The other thing which bugs me now is how he's been able to watch us without being seen. My guys are too well trained to miss something like that."

Julia mulled this over for a second. "He claims to have killed someone already, which, if true, doesn't take him out of the 'whack-job' category, but definitely places him in the 'dangerous' category. But think about it... moving back home would just further hamper his so-called communication channel with me. This might just irk him enough to interpret it as non-compliance and to come after me, or us, for that matter. I still somehow believe him, when he says he won't hurt me. Besides he seems to need me desperately to fulfil his plans."

"Sure, but what about when it's over? You'll have served your purpose and he might want to tie up loose ends."

"We'll have to deal with that when the time comes, but until then, I have to comply to stay safe. Look, I'm not saying back off completely, we can still look for leads to tracking him down and putting a stop to this. Maybe just increase the perimeter of your surveillance team and take the subtle approach until we know more."

"Jules, your father will never go for this and you know it. We have enough men and fire-power to take on a small army if needs be and your father's approach has always been to fight fire with fire. He won't back down, no matter what," Ollie responded curtly.

"I know, but this is completely different from the previous threats and attempts on our safety. No-one is presently in the line of fire. We are not his targets. Realistically, right now, there is no threat against us."

She shook her head vigorously from side to side to emphasise her point.

"Your father needs to be involved in this, Jules. We can't make these decisions without his input and consent," Ollie concluded.

"Okay, so let's thrash this out and think this through from all angles before even going to him," Julia conceded.

Ollie pursed his lips again and nodded slowly.

Julia started counting off scenarios on her fingers.

"One – I do as he demands, he does what he does and we all live happily ever after.

"Two – I do as he demands, he does what he does and then he finally tries to eliminate me to tie up loose ends.

"Three – I don't do as he demands, he still does what he does, but his publicity stunt is now toast, so I am immediately part of the problem and no longer part of the plan.

"Four – I don't do as he demands, he gets upset and now directs his attention to me, as his plan now has no effect without the publicity. I inadvertently save the lives of his victims, but am in constant danger until he finally figures out how to get to me."

They discussed her scenarios at length, searching for scenario five and a way out of this predicament, but they both drew a blank.

The best scenario would obviously be to find him in a hurry and take him out of the equation permanently, but neither of them was naïve enough to believe that to be a possibility.

Julia finally added, "So, big guy, what's your take? I definitely don't like options three and four. Option one would obviously be the best and with time on our side, even option two could be countered or even prevented."

Ollie shrugged. He couldn't find fault with Julia's summation, but he knew Alan too well when it came to being protective of his family. There would be no quarter given or taken. He would shoot up or burn down the entire city to find this guy before he could lay a hand on Julia and Ollie knew he was Alan's weapon of choice.

Chapter 15

Alan's face progressively transformed from a lighter hue of crimson to a dark shade of burgundy as he progressed through the letter.

"The gall of this lunatic," he shouted, "does he have any idea of who he's messing with? I'll rip off his legs and beat him to death with the wet ends! Nobody messes with my family!"

He stood up abruptly, knocking the chair over backwards in his haste, and started pacing the living room.

Julia was deeply touched by his instinctive paternal protection, but after her in-depth discussion with Ollie, she was well prepared to rationalise with her father – even in his current state and frame of mind.

"Dad, he's not after me. His only interest in me is that I cover his exploits," Julia retorted.

"What do you mean, he's not after you? His glaring threats are abundantly clear," Alan fumed.

"His threats only become a reality if I don't comply with his requests," Julia responded calmly, knowing full well that getting into a shouting match with her father under these circumstances would be counter-productive. "If I comply with his demands, the threats will never materialise. He's only strong-arming me with the threats to get me to do what he wants."

She paused, before continuing, to let her rationale sink in.

"As you read, he seems to have studied our family and knows what resources come into play if this goes full-circle. I really doubt that he wants to go down that road if at all he can avoid it."

"Yes, I understand, but he's still demanding that you do something you might not want to do… that's intimidation no matter how you paint it and with the threat of harm, it becomes extortion or even blackmail, Julia. It's precisely the same as coercing you to rob a bank for him by threatening to kill your family. It's totally unacceptable and moreover, criminal. And anyway, why are you defending him?"

Julia had never seen her father like this before. He was beyond fuming and paced the room purposefully, like a caged feline ready to pounce. Ollie and Julia were tying themselves in knots trying to following his movements around the room from their seated positions.

"I'm not defending him, Dad, actually far from it. But let's face facts; we have no leads as to who he is or whether he is serious about his quest or threats. He claims to have murdered someone already, but we have no confirmation of this. He claims to be watching us at all times, but no-one has been noticed by Ollie's team, who are well trained in surveillance and counter-surveillance."

Ollie winced at this last remark, but stayed quiet as Julia continued.

"So far, we have nothing! It's safer for us, especially me, if I just go along with what he wants. This gives us more time to mount a proper investigation and hopefully put a plan in motion to catch him, which then ultimately negates the entire issue."

"Julia, I can't condone this, you are my flesh and blood. I will do everything in my power to protect you."

Julia's voice trembled slightly as she replied, "Thanks, Dad, and I do appreciate the sentiment, but I'm only asking that for now everything gets done from a distance. If I'm in no imminent danger then we can afford to slack off a bit on the surveillance and protection detail. If we give this guy enough rope, he might hopefully get careless and hang himself."

Alan was not convinced or happy, but ultimately offered a concession: "Fine, but either you move back in with us or Ollie moves in with you. He doesn't leave your side when you're out in the open."

Julia shook her head emphatically, expressing her exasperation.

"This won't be acceptable to him, Dad. He wants to be able to communicate freely with me and anything other than the status quo won't fly."

"Julia, how can I defend you if you keep objecting to everything I say?"

"That's just it, you don't have to protect or defend me at this stage, Dad. I'm not his target. He needs me. He wouldn't jeopardise…"

"You can't know that for sure," he interjected. "I'm not happy."

Alan focused his attention on Ollie now. "Ollie, you and I really need a serious chat after this. Besides, I'm starting to think that this whole story is a ruse. Maybe he is someone we know. Someone who does have a gripe with me. Maybe he's trying to outflank us with some elaborate cockamamie story to get us to lower our guard or back off."

He turned back to Julia.

"Maybe you are his actual target as he tries to get back at me. You know that I've ruffled a few feathers over the years, Julia. I just don't like it. Something feels off and normally my instincts are very reliable. How can you trust anything this mad man says in his letters?" Alan continued with his tirade.

Julia responded quickly, "I don't know, I just can't believe that someone would go to such extremes to research a subject, like he did, merely as a red-herring to put us off the scent of his real motive. He could have got the same mileage and effect with far less effort. Until we have more information or evidence, we have to take everything at face value. We have no option at this stage."

Alan's pacing became manic.

He now covered the length of the living room within a couple of strides.

His turns were executed with near-military precision before pacing back again.

Julia and Ollie continued to follow his movements, but now it was as if they were watching a tennis match.

Her heart broke to see him in this state.

"Dad, I'll be fine. We have to believe this. Put whatever play you like in motion, but whatever you decide, it must be done discreetly. We can't afford to spook him. I honestly believe that he'll be too concerned with his master plan anyway to bother with me, as long as I keep his mind at ease and write about his exploits," Julia concluded.

Alan abruptly stopped pacing and raised his index finger as though reprimanding a child. "Okay, Julia," he said, "but don't think I'll just sit back and do nothing. We've dealt with odd-balls like this before and this is just another one who's crept out of the woodwork. I have the resources to protect you and, by God, that's what I'll do."

Ollie had been quiet throughout, astutely captivated by the exchange between father and daughter and now decided it was time to interject.

"Boss, while you have many valid points, I believe Jules is correct with her assumptions that this guy is toying with us. He knows our moves before we make them. In our defence, we didn't see the necessity of approaching this with extreme caution. Our immediate concern was Julia's safety. We can certainly go deeper under cover and drop back to give the illusion that we have complied and retracted our surveillance. We'll always be near, though, of that you can be assured."

It was an indictment to their close and valued relationship that Alan listened intently and acquiesced to Ollie's experience and perspective.

"Fine," Alan snapped, feeling totally aggrieved, as if Julia and Ollie had ganged up on him, "but if something happens to Julia there'll be hell to pay, Ollie."

"Understood," replied the big man.

Chapter 16

The drive home was mundane and uneventful, but inside the car, Julia's mind was racing at a million miles an hour. She was overly alert to every vehicle passing her and kept glancing behind her in the rear-view mirrors to check if she was being followed.

Paranoid, maybe, but rather overly cautious than reckless and careless.

If she was to get an article out by the following morning, she only had the rest of the day to research and write it and there would be no second bites at this cherry.

What if he didn't like what she wrote?

What if the exposé wasn't what he envisaged?

It needed to be well researched and factual for it to have the impact he desired, but then again also slant to the fact that he would be murdering people.

No, she couldn't write that – or could she?

Thoughts bombarded her like machine-gun fire.

The realization of the situation she was in sent a sudden wave of panic through her body.

She took some deep breaths and forced herself to relax.

She also couldn't just upload anything onto the *DispatchLive* website.

Oh shit, she thought. She needed to run this by Moses Mamabolo, her editor, first.

Time was running out and the pressure was mounting.

This had to be done in person, she decided, so instead of

taking the turn to her apartment, Julia headed out to the *Daily Dispatch* building.

She called Moses via her hands-free kit in the car to see if he had time to see her, impressing on him the urgency of the matter and that she'd explain in detail when she arrived. As usual and no matter how busy he was, he always made time for her. He was probably like that with everyone. He was just that kind of person.

Julia hung up, breathed a deep sigh of relief and cautiously drove on.

Moses shifted uneasily in his chair, slightly confused by the call from Julia and how desperate she had sounded. Deep down he knew that Julia had more integrity than to waste his time with anything insignificant.

She had done this to him once before, but to her credit, the article had proved a phenomenal success for the newspaper. She knew what was important and from a business perspective what sold newspapers. Furthermore, she somehow always seemed to find herself in the centre of some newsworthy debacle. Gut feel and experience told him in no uncertain terms that Julia had something worthwhile.

He shook his head and closed his laptop. He needed a leg stretch anyway to get the blood-flow going again. The experts always say that taking a walk every hour or so is a good thing. And while he was at it, a cup of coffee would also be a fine idea.

Although only a freelance journalist, Julia was by far one his best columnists and his favourite to boot, not that he could ever say it out loud.

As he walked around the building his mind wondered, reminiscing about his first meeting with Julia.

It hadn't been an interview, per se, but he had promised Alan Swan, an acquaintance at the time whom he had met at numerous prestigious city events, that he would meet with her.

At the time, Julia had just completed her Bachelor of Arts degree, specialising in journalism and media studies, at Rhodes University in Grahamstown.

With flying colours, it might be added.

Subsequently, she had received job offers from all around the country; many from very successful and renowned publications.

It turned out though, that home truly was where the heart was and she had rejected a few very lucrative recruitment offers to stay in East London and be near her family and friends.

At the time, there were no vacancies at the *Daily Dispatch* and Moses had made that fact abundantly clear. He certainly didn't want to make promises to Alan Swan which he couldn't keep.

Coming from an ultra-wealthy and prominent family, Moses had prepared himself for a meeting with an arrogant and self-righteous brat with an overbearing sense of entitlement.

He still chuckled to this day about how mistaken he was.

During their time together, Julia had completely won him over. Firstly, with her intellect and knowledge, but predominantly with how down to earth she was. She was intelligent without being a know-it-all. She was confident without being condescending. And even though from a mega-wealthy family, she was surprisingly humble.

They had spent an extremely pleasant afternoon together, chatting for hours about journalism, the industry in general and her future prospects. Finally, Moses had stuck his neck out and proposed that she work for him as a freelance journalist – remunerated solely on submissions – and that was where it had all started.

Chapter 17

Moses returned to his desk and now sat slightly hunched over his computer, perusing the content and layout of the following day's newspaper, when Julia was ushered into his office by Martha, his personal assistant.

He casually looked up from his computer screen and on seeing her a genuine smile spread across his face.

"Julia!" he exclaimed amicably in his rough and raspy voice.

He just had this way of engaging which made the recipient feel like the most important person in the world. This was undoubtedly the primary characteristic which had fuelled his meteoric rise through the ranks of the media world.

"Hi, Moses," Julia replied, her smile also evident in her voice.

"We haven't seen much of you for a while?"

"I know," Julia responded, "It's been a bit crazy of late."

"So, to what do I owe this pleasure?" Moses joked in his usual jovial manner.

Julia's tone changed slightly, revealing a hint of the panic she was now feeling. "Moses, I know this is a very late request, but I really need to get an article through in tomorrow's run."

"No way!" Moses retorted, shaking his head to emphasise the point. "I'm just signing off on the content and layout this minute. The templates are nearly complete. It's just too late in the day for changes now."

"I understand, but I'm in a bit of spot here, Moses, and

literally this is a matter of life and death and I don't use that cliché lightly," Julia countered.

"If you have the article with you right now and there's merit to it, I can possibly see where I can fit it in. Even then I'll be putting everyone under enormous pressure to finalise the run," Moses responded.

"I don't have anything here. I'm still working on it," Julia confessed, knowing that in her desperation, a small half-truth had slipped out.

She still had a lot of work to do on it.

"I don't think online will be as effective, but I understand it's very short notice, and it will have to suffice. After you hear my story, I'm absolutely positive that you'll agree that this story could run front page above the fold."

"That's pushing it… so no promises, you hear?" Moses responded. "But let's hear what you've got."

Once she started though, time constraints and other matters of urgency evaporated completely. The astounded look on Moses' face said it all, as he listened intently to the tale she told. And then the questions began. And then he needed to read the letters, which she fortunately had on hand. And then finally, he wanted to read her article.

Julia ashamedly admitted that she had previously misspoken and that the article was actually in its infancy and still needed a lot of research and work before being finalised and ready for publication.

"What do you mean, you haven't written anything yet?" he asked, with a note of concern punctuating the question. "You said you needed this to go online tomorrow?" he added questioningly and raising an eyebrow.

"I know, I know," she admitted, starting now to panic as time ticked steadily away. "I need to get my head around what I'm going to write and how I'm going to phrase things without being too antagonising and judgemental. In reality, I needed your approval before proceeding," Julia countered and then added, "I'll get it done by the early hours of the morning, after which you can read, approve and upload it... if it's good enough. I know I'm asking a lot, Moses, but the timing is critical and I could be in serious trouble if I don't comply."

Moses sat where he was, absolutely dumb-founded. His jovial temperament lost under the circumstances.

But, Julia was in a predicament and he was in a position to assist, so of course he would do whatever he could.

"What about the police, Julia? Have you spoken with them?"

"Not yet, Moses. This issue unfolded rather quickly and I only grasped the reality of this not being a hoax after the second letter was delivered earlier this morning."

"Your article will blindside the authorities if they are not in the loop before I publish it. I can't afford to tarnish our relationship. I've spent too long nurturing the trust between the media and the police."

"I understand," Julia said, "but one way or another, this article must go out tomorrow. I've delayed for too long already and the possible repercussions could be disastrous."

"Okay," Moses finally said. "It is totally mind-blowing and, as you alluded to earlier, it might eventually be a front page, above the fold story, which will definitely increase sales. However, let's approach this one cautiously. I'll arrange for an urgent meeting with the East London station commander, Brigadier Jola, today and at a bare minimum give him a rudimentary outline of the story we're about to run. Maybe the police already know about the murder, but at least we'll put them on the front foot if they are still in the dark. In the interim, I suggest you start writing… you have a long night ahead of you."

"Perfect," Julia agreed, "And thank you, Moses. We'll talk soon."

As Julia stood up to leave the office, Moses caught her eye and casually commented, "I don't know how you always end up knee-deep in these stories, but your work is truly commendable and your articles are really compelling. That's the only reason I'm willing to take this chance on you."

He was absolutely sincere with his compliments.

She appreciated that about him.

"Thanks again, Moses. You won't regret it," Julia responded and exited his office.

Chapter 18

Julia spent the rest of the day scouring the internet for information on the DNA Project and the South African DNA legislation.

There were definitions and general explanations on how DNA is processed and how the results were used in assisting with investigations, eliminating suspects and combating crime in general.

She also found that there were now three Forensic Chemistry Laboratories in South Africa, one in Cape Town, one in Pretoria and one in Johannesburg and none of them scored very well when last audited.

Astoundingly, and according to an article by Wilmot James based on the auditor-general's findings, she also found that the Johannesburg and Pretoria laboratories were not even fully accredited with the South African National Accreditation System (SANAS) which ensures formal recognition that a laboratory is competent to perform its tasks in line with international criteria.

When the audit was conducted, the following additional shortfalls were highlighted:

Low staff morale

Inadequate storage space for samples

High turnover and vacancy rates

No back-up power supply to prevent samples and specimens from spoiling

Poor management, leadership and information systems

Wow, that doesn't bode very well for us, pondered Julia. Hopefully after the findings of that last audit were published, all the issues had been addressed, but she somehow doubted it.

Besides the Biology Unit, which dealt primarily with all DNA found in body fluids, human tissue and hair, there was a Ballistics Unit, a Scientific Analysis Unit, a Question Document Unit, a Chemistry Unit and an Explosives Unit.

Julia was fascinated as she scanned through the functions of each. She, like most others, had been exposed to most of these concepts through the CSI New York and CSI Miami series on television. But it was never prudent to base impressions on television programmes. She was well aware of this. Processes ran smoothly, incriminating evidence was always found and the good guys always prevailed within the space of a few days. The detailed functions of each unit she perused was far more holistic and comprehensive than she had been led to believe.

Further to her research on the Biology Unit, she stumbled across the creation and maintenance of the South African National Forensic DNA Database or NFDD. This database was, in essence, pivotal to the functions of the Biology Unit and was comprised of the following indices:

The Crime Scene Index

The Arrestee Index

The Convicted Offender Index

The Investigative Index

The Elimination Index

The Missing Persons and Unidentified Human Remains Index

Julia was totally riveted. The intricacies and complexities were beyond intriguing. But, while captivated, she was periodically keeping an eye on how quickly time was flying. This was going to be an all-nighter, of that she was sure.

She continued unfazed and found that Dan was spot on the money when it came to the issues of backlogs, delays in processing, as well as the dismal statistics on follow-up investigations once outcomes had been processed.

She also pondered the reason for it taking the country so long to formulate the laws and legislation supporting and pertaining to the use of DNA results in investigations and legal proceedings, but came up fairly empty handed in her research.

Crazy, she thought, *are we really that far behind the more progressive countries in the world?*

No wonder Dan had lost his sense of humour.

'Tick tock, another fifty murders and one hundred and eighty-three rapes reported as each day passes.'

She scanned the notes she had made and then read and re-read Dan's first letter trying to find some flaw in his facts or reasoning, but what she had found on the world-wide-web seemed to confirm everything.

South Africa was definitely not the most transparent of countries and even though there was mention of frequent audits, meetings and reports, very few were uploaded into the public domain.

Could it be that certain data with negative connotations was being suppressed?

Besides, not everything you read on the internet is true, she mused.

But in this case, whatever she could find supported Dan's claims and accusations, and these included the Auditor General's report, political party reviews as well as some of the annual reports compiled by the National Forensic Oversight and Ethics Board (NFOEB).

Julia shuddered at the thought of Dan being a regular man. She had previously thought of him as a madman, a ranting lunatic, a nutcase, a whack-job. But he was as normal as the man next door.

What had happened to push him over the edge?

Surely he hadn't just woken up one day and flipped out. Something had derailed him and if I can just get to bottom of that, I might be able to find out who he is and stop him, Julia thought, *but first I need to show him that he can trust and rely on me.*

And with that she went to work on the introductory article that he had demanded of her.

Chapter 19

Julia awoke to a bright and beautiful day. The weather had been immaculate of late, not that she'd even noticed. Her routine had been turned on its head.

But, even after only a few hours of sleep, this morning she felt revived and quite vibrant. Probably more out of relief than anything else.

She had finally finished her article at around four in the morning. After proof-reading it a dozen times through drooping eye-lids, she had emailed it to Moses and had almost immediately passed out from physical and mental exhaustion.

She now reached for her cell phone and noticed that it was only 06.48. Thumbing quickly to her emails, she disappointingly found no response from Moses as yet. *Of course not,* she thought, *he obviously hadn't sat up the whole night waiting for the article. It was still early and he would read it soon enough* – even though the anticipation of waiting for his feedback was killing her.

The day held no urgency for her, so she just lay in bed for a while, for no other reason than simply because she could. She wouldn't fall asleep again. She knew that for a fact – being far too hyped up as she waited expectantly on the response from Moses. Her bedroom curtains were hardly ever drawn at night, as she loved going to sleep by the light of the moon and positively adored waking up as the first shards of sunlight peaked over the horizon.

It felt so natural to her.

Prying eyes or a potential invasion of her privacy were non-issues, as her apartment was on the second floor with her bedroom overlooking the ocean to the south-east, while the external walkway which serviced each floor was on the opposite side of the building.

Unless you could fly or dangle off the balcony of the apartment above, there was no way of getting a glimpse into her bedroom.

Security and an insane view of the azure ocean were the two main reasons for her badgering her father into letting her move out of the house and rent the apartment in the first place.

She yawned and stretched. It was time to get the day started.

She freshened up, slipped into some very casual house-wear and headed to the kitchen. She was finally able to relax and her thoughts immediately drifted to her girlfriends. She hadn't seen or spoken to any of them for days.

What would they be thinking of her?

She hadn't been this preoccupied in a long while and with a sudden pang of guilt, she made a mental note to call them later that day. She consoled herself with the fact that she wasn't really to blame, not that they would believe that. She knew they would probe until she opened up and regaled them with the entire story from start to finish. The article was coming out later that day anyway, so whether they read it themselves or heard it from her would be immaterial.

Julia was, however, very concerned about their safety. At this delicate stage it might be dangerous being near her, although if Dan knew as much about her as he claimed he did, then it followed that he would already know everything about her three best friends.

As she sipped her coffee, her thoughts again drifted to Dan

and the turmoil he had caused in her life in such a short space of time, as well as the subsequent disagreement and confrontation it had caused between her and her father.

They obviously had a difference of opinion as to how best to handle the situation, but ultimately a consensus of sorts had begrudgingly been reached.

They had, at least, partially agreed on a game-plan. The nagging uncertainty she still had was that this was just the beginning, even though for now, with the completion of the article, a weight had been lifted from her shoulders.

Julia lay back on the sofa for a while and basked in the glow of the weak early morning rays invading the room.

The sun was still relatively low over the eastern horizon, but the yellowish hue complimented the browns, beiges and burnt oranges of the room and reflected warmly off the ivory-coloured walls.

Her earthy colour schemes might have been regarded as fairly bland and boring, but she'd never been one for the girly-girl pinks, lavenders and purples. She had heard and partially attributed that to being a Capricorn, even though she'd never really put much stock in astrology. Coincidence or not though, Capricorn was definitely one of the earth star signs.

It was coincidence; at least in her mind.

Chapter 20

Alan had Ollie on speed-dial and summoned him to his office.

The room was lavish without being overly-ostentatious. He did most of his work from home, so the room needed to be more functional than flashy. His pride and joy was, however, his mahogany desk, which he had painstakingly sourced and imported from Jepara, Indonesia. The art of furniture making in Jepara was legendary and had been passed down from generation to generation. The city boasted some of the most talented woodworkers and furniture makers in the world. The details and accents had been to his specifications and he had paid handsomely for this masterpiece of perfection. The production had been a meticulous process and the importation had resulted in a further delay, but the wait had been ultimately well worthwhile.

The desk obviously held centre-stage in the room and was punctuated by comfortable and functional seating. His leather office recliner stood sentinel behind the desk while two visitors' chairs were evenly positioned in front.

The plush carpet with its thick pile was a Scandinavian rya and was both comfortable on the eyes, as well as the feet, while augmenting the spaciousness of the room by complimenting the light colour paint on the walls. The walls were in turn sporadically accentuated with colourful abstract paintings, creating a warm and peaceful ambiance to the room.

Ollie knocked politely before entering Alan's domain. They

might have been closer than brothers, but Ollie respected Alan immensely and never crossed the line between employer and employee, if such a line even existed between them. Ollie handed Alan a cup of coffee since it was still early and neither of them had eaten breakfast yet. Ollie thought the inevitable discussion would be over breakfast, but seemingly Alan hadn't slept very well and the urgency of the situation warranted immediate attention.

"Morning, Ollie. Come. Sit," Alan said, motioning Ollie in.

"Morning, boss," came Ollie's response.

Alan had never insisted on being called Mr Swan or boss, but it was Ollie's way of showing his respect.

"Any updates, Ollie?"

"Nothing concrete, as yet, but Themba did phone me in the middle of the night with some news. The guys managed to track down the old man from Currie Street. It turns out he's just a homeless old man. He was given R50 by another old man to give the letter to someone else, who then needed to make the delivery. He found the youngster we caught and paid him R10 to deliver the letter. Sounds like the letter and a bit of money regularly changed hands to mask the trail."

"So, no progress then?" Alan summed up.

"The old man did add that a message must be passed along with the letter and money to each person, warning them that if the letter was not ultimately delivered to Julia, they would get a visit from some very nasty men, who would chop off their hands. On the upside, there was also more money to be made if future letters needed to pass through their hands."

"A stick and a carrot," exclaimed Alan. "We're dealing with a very clever and street-wise person here. We won't catch him this way."

"I agree," concurred Ollie. "We'll spend too much time and use too many resources chasing these shadows with little to no chance of tracing the process back to the source. Besides, Julia doesn't want us to interfere with the communication channel at the risk of her being targeted."

"Shit!" Alan exclaimed, banging his fist on his desk. "This guy's got us by the short and curlies and it's starting to piss me off. How do we get ahead of this, Ollie?"

"I have my guys out in the field. They'll find something for us soon enough. I've even spread the word of a reward for information. I hope you don't mind?"

Alan shook his head vigorously and waved off the question. "Not an issue, Ollie, as long as it turns out to be reliable and gets us results."

Just then, Alan's phone rang. The caller-identity displayed Julia's name.

"Hi, love," Alan answered affectionately.

"Hi, Dad – great news – Moses just read my article. He loved it and will upload it in the next few minutes," Julia replied.

Alan could hear the sound of relief in his daughter's voice. It irked him that someone had literally held his daughter to ransom to get this article written, while he felt side-lined and impotent, and could do absolutely nothing about it.

Julia continued, "It took me the entire day and most of the night to write and then fine tune it, but I think it'll work as an introductory piece."

"You must be knackered after those long hours?"

"I am, but I'm more exhilarated than anything else, just knowing that it's done and will go out today as instructed."

"No other contact as yet?" Alan asked, the trepidation evident in his voice.

"No, nothing, but I'm sure he'll be in touch once he's read the article. I just hope he'll be happy with it and that it is what he wanted from me."

"So, you think we now have some time to track this whack-job down before he barges into your life again?"

"Yes, I do."

"Okay then, Julia. We're doing everything we can from our side, so you just make sure you stay safe. Ollie's team will be watching, but don't now go out of your way to make it difficult for them. They're there for your safety."

"I understand, Dad. Now go read the article. It should have been uploaded by now. I'll talk to you later."

"Okay, Julia… love you."

"Love you too… bye!"

And with that, Julia hung up.

"You heard all that, Ollie?" Alan queried with raised eyebrows.

"I sure did." Ollie nodded in a slow and measured manner, even though the phone had not been on speaker.

"We have a bit of time now, so turn over every rock you can find and let's hunt down this vermin and squash him before he aggravates me even more," Alan instructed.

Ollie silently concurred with another nod of his head and left the room.

A man on a mission.

Chapter 21

After the call to her dad, Julia rummaged around the kitchen fixing the makings of a hearty wholesome breakfast. She was famished after her all-nighter and lack of sleep. Coffee alone would not answer the questions her grumbling stomach was asking.

Her buzzing cell phone snapped her rudely from her thoughts.

Even though the pressure was off her for a while, her mind just wouldn't let up. Her thoughts bounced erratically from one subject to the next – all Dan related.

Who was he?

Why was he doing this?

What had happened to make him suddenly snap like this?

How would they stop him?

Could they stop him?

Should they stop him?

Would his tirade have the desired effect?

Would anyone care?

It was all consuming. She had been sucked into someone else's world. A world where she didn't belong or even want to be.

"Hello!" she answered, wedging the handset between her shoulder and ear, to keep her hands free.

"Hi, Jules," replied the familiar voice. "What ya doin'?"

"Caths! How are you, honey? I was just thinking about you girls a little earlier."

Premonition – a very strange thing.

She had planned to phone later and now she suddenly gets a call from the person she was intending to call. She shook her head. It was quite surreal and baffling.

"Just fine, stranger," Cathy responded sardonically. "Where've you been the last few days? Fall off the radar again?"

"You'll never believe me even if I told you, Caths."

"Deadlines again, huh?"

"You can say that again, but a hundred times more intense. I got done with the article in the early hours of the morning after pushing through the whole night. Then I tried to sleep. Too much happening in the old noggin. Just couldn't get to sleep and when I finally did, it wasn't for very long. And now I'm famished, so I'm fixing breakfast. How about we meet later? I need some downtime and some quality girl time with all of you. I'll get hold of the others a bit later and we'll meet for sundowners and maybe an early bite. How does five o'clock suit you?"

"Sounds perfect. Righto me matey!" Cathy answered her, in her best pirate drawl.

Cathy had always been the comedian in their little foursome and her constant wise-cracks kept everyone entertained.

But, even though she was being her normal light-hearted self, she knew something was up with Julia – something big. It wasn't too often that Julia fell off the grid, but when she did, everyone knew that she was onto something important and being the friends they were, they always respected this and backed off, giving her the space, she needed. As always, Julia would resurface in time and life would continue where it had left off. None of them took it personally. They just got on with their lives in her absence, knowing that soon enough, she'd finish her project and re-join the group.

"Give me a little hint then?" Cathy prompted. "It's totally unique and ground breaking… even for me. And that's saying something. It's better if we're all together before I get into the details. Saves me from having to retell the story. Moses has actually just uploaded the piece, so as an entrée you can go check it out. There are going to be too many questions, so it's better if we wait until we're all together. Sorry to keep you in suspense the whole day."

"Okeydokey, I'll just have to soldier on through the day, left in the dark without a torch," Cathy conceded reluctantly. "See you later then, Jules," Cathy added and then hung up.

Julia finished her breakfast, washed the dishes and tidied the kitchen. She wasn't really a neat freak, but the thought of unwashed dishes or an untidy apartment just irked her. The irony was that she had been waited upon hand and foot during her formative years, but now she really enjoyed being independent and doing all the washing, ironing, cleaning and housework herself. A minor aspect her parents couldn't understand.

Her calls to Anne and Samantha were similar in content and nature, with her stone-walling their questions with the promise of full disclosure when they met later. She had already read and re-read her article which Moses had uploaded earlier and had patted herself on the back for a job well done. Both girls were briefed about this appetizer and would surely read the exposé immediately after hanging up.

Julia now had the day to herself, with no plans until five p.m. Although, keeping busy would be key to stop her fixating on Dan and his issues. If she could just subdue her thoughts for a while, she might even be able to sneak in a few hours of sleep, which she desperately needed. That would be bliss.

Chapter 22

The exposé was a sensation from the moment it was uploaded, giving it the requisite credibility and importance it warranted. The tracked hits were astronomical, as the article gained momentum via word of mouth. The fascination by the public was almost tangible. The dropped cookies recorded data which stretched beyond the boundaries of the East London area and even the provincial boundaries of the Eastern Cape. This was going national, there was no doubt about that.

Alan sighed deeply, as he re-read Julia's article.

But he still shook his head emphatically from side-to-side, as he knew the backstory which she had not included.

How had this maniac become a part of their lives?

Life was complicated enough without being sucked into someone else's deranged world or sick sideshow.

The article was good – very good. Julia had done a fantastic job and, although disconcerted, he was extremely proud of her. She had complied with Dan's instructions and had captured all the salient points and even expounded with her own research and analyses.

No wonder the readers were captivated.

Facts and figures – the way of the world in which we now live, he mused.

No time for bullshit.

No time to smell the roses.

Everything succinct and to the point.

Everyone was a CEO in the making.

Know the detail, if asked, but until then only abridged versions or executive overviews were required.

At least it was written in proper English and not that crap shorthand the kids of today used on their phones.

U, R, DAT, DEM, LOL, FOMO! What garbage was that? Kids didn't even have time nowadays to write properly. What the hell was their rush anyway? It's not like they were rushing off to save the world.

Twitter, Facebook, Instagram – whatever!

Why did everyone need validation from Joe public these days, anyway?

Get a life, and stop revelling in the details of other people's false realities.

Alan fumed, just thinking about the time wasted, especially by the youth of today.

He needed to clear his head. He put his iPad down, removed his shoes and walked down the stone stairway to the lush and expansive garden sprawling before him. He was a proponent of earthing, so he spent at least thirty minutes to an hour every day in contact with Mother Earth. The theory was that direct contact with the earth was therapeutic and healing. The ailments afflicting people these days were aggravated – and possibly caused – by them insulating themselves from the earth. Shoes were believed to be the worst invention ever by mankind and telling kids to put their shoes on when going outside was counterintuitive.

It all had to do with the magnetic charges and energy received while in direct contact with the earth. Negative energy out, positive energy in.

He hadn't noticed any significant improvements in his

health, but conversely, he suffered from none of the maladies plaguing the elderly.

His garden service had done an immaculate job. The grass was lush, green and manicured to just the right length. The trees and bushes were pruned and trimmed neatly with no branches extruding at odd angles. The flower beds boasted a variety of flowers. A veritable collage of colours.

He walked casually across the lawn, bunching his toes slightly with each step. A great workout for the plantar fascia. As he walked, his mind drifted to Julia's article once again.

He was no profiler, but a few traits were apparent, even to him. It was evident that Dan desperately didn't want to be thought of as a monster.

This seemed to be very important to him.

He wanted to be regarded as a crusader, forced to act through circumstances. Fighting for a cause because nobody else would. He was imparting to the world that he was actually a good guy – that what he was about to do was not by his own design. He had no bloodlust, but was coerced into doing what he had to do to draw attention to the issues being ignored, and as a result for the betterment of the country.

Someone needed to take a stance and the end would justify the means.

He would be the martyr.

He would take the bullet to correct the injustice.

This was all speculation though, Alan realised. Dan hadn't done anything as yet. He had them all bouncing around chasing their tails and he'd done absolutely nothing besides write a letter or two.

Alan's conjectures continued as he strolled bare-footed

across the lawn.

Was this article just a ruse to raise attention to a cause he believed in or was it really a cautionary shot across the bow? An opening salvo, if you might. And more would follow if nobody paid attention.

Could it all just be a cover, while deep-down he was just a regular everyday psychopath? A serial killer who would go to great lengths to mask his actions, while actually just craving attention.

He was so wrapped up in his thoughts that even without being aware of it, he had returned to his chair on the veranda and was busy retying his shoes.

He shifted uneasily in the chair as his thoughts now drifted to Julia.

This was a very dangerous game for her to be involved in and it was all his fault. He had always pushed Julia to be the best and now look where it had got her. He was proud, but at the same time was mad with himself.

She had been chosen by this nut-case because he had recognised her talent and ability to document his story and broadcast it to the wider community.

Alan scowled – not on his watch – not while he had a breath of life left in his body.

And certainly not where his family was concerned.

Ollie's sudden appearance in the doorway startled him. He was unrealistically quiet for such a big man. Always in stealth mode.

Alan needed a distraction from his thoughts and self-deprecation and hopefully Ollie's appearance would facilitate that.

Ollie looked hot and sweaty and constantly mopped at his

face with a small towel. He had just finished his morning workout. Alan had previously witnessed the man's workout before. He effortlessly handled dumbbells and weights which the average man would battle to even lift off the floor.

His black sweatpants looked more like tights on him, as they stretched over the sheer bulges of his enormous thighs and calves.

The white tank top he wore left nothing to the imagination when it came to his massive forearms and biceps. He was barrel-chested as all power-lifters and strongmen were. He was not a bodybuilder per se – so chiselled abdominals were not a concern – he worked relentlessly on unmitigated bulk.

With his size and talents, he really could have been a pro-wrestler or even a cage fighter, but the allure of popularity and fame were not part of his make-up. He loved, more than anything, being part of the Swan family. With no airs and graces, he was just plain old Ollie and that's the way he wanted it.

"You're up," he casually commented.

"For quite a while now," Alan replied matter-of-factly. "Couldn't wait to see what Julia had written!"

"Can I get you some coffee, boss?" Ollie queried.

"No thanks, Ollie, I'm good for now. Why don't you go freshen up and we'll catch up over breakfast?"

Ollie nodded and left the room.

Chapter 23

Dan sat alone in the coffee-shop, quietly sipping his coffee.

It was a typical mom and pop type coffee shop, which he enjoyed more than the commercialised, impersonal, brand-named establishments. Here you were a customer. There you were just a number.

It was a quaint little shop catering to a maximum of thirty-six people with its six square tables tightly arranged in the seating area and a few booths fixed along the side walls. The tables and chairs were solid wood, and while initially comfortable, would not facilitate long-term occupation. The cushioning on the chairs was just way too compressed and worn for that.

The business of any food outlet was after all reliant on turning tables as quickly as possible. Mom and pop had definitely achieved that goal by not replacing the chairs or their cushions in years – if ever.

The walls were neatly painted and sparsely punctuated with framed 'thought-provoking' quotes. These could possibly be perceived as a bit kitsch by some, but actually played an important psychological role in the dining experience. Patrons would generally be too busy and distracted, digesting these quotes, and wouldn't be inclined to monitor the time taken between placing and receiving their orders. Old school common sense and practices. You couldn't beat the old timers.

That was Dan's opinion on the subject, anyway – whether correct or incorrect.

Two young waitresses, probably university students, hustled around between the patrons, multi-tasking. They took orders, delivered the food, bussed the tables and then operated the till to close out the customer service. Mom or pop – or maybe both – were more than likely in the kitchen preparing the food. In a tiny outlet like this, the turnover couldn't be very much, so they would surely need to be very hands-on in their business to ensure that everything ran smoothly.

The prices charged couldn't leave too much of a profit margin, so staff wages would probably consist of a small basic wage and then supplemented with tips, but the two waitresses seemed cheery enough and content with their work.

Dan's coffee was strong, with just a hint of milk, which he found took away that sharp, acrid taste of genuine black coffee. He had ordered a breakfast of two eggs, two rashers of bacon, half a grilled tomato and two slices of toast. He generally had the appetite of a bull elephant when fully entrenched in his body-building routine, but occasionally enjoyed the slightly meagre offerings of this establishment. Besides, his enthusiasm for training had recently dwindled as his other exploits had demanded more and more of his time and effort.

He thumbed through the media pages on his iPad while he waited for his breakfast and there it was. Julia had finally acceded to his request, then his demand, and then finally his subtle threat.

Dan spent the next few minutes studiously reading her article: their article.

Slowly but surely his eyes narrowed as a smile spread across his face.

She had really done a sterling job.

All the relevant points had been succinctly captured in black and white for all to read, just as he had intended.

He didn't particularly appreciate or agree with her references to him and his crusade, but at this stage she had very little with which to work, so a little latitude would be tolerated.

He had also pre-empted that she would immediately pick up on the DNA acronym of the name he had given, but to refer to him as DNA Dan was actually quite insulting and unforgiving. It didn't sit right with him and seemed to reduce the impact of the intended message significantly. Almost like ascribing a Deputy Dawg reference to a serious article.

The article was out there though, and at this stage, that was all that mattered.

He was in such deep thought that he nearly jumped off his chair when, Sharon, his waitress, suddenly appeared at his side and placed his food order on the table.

"You should wear a bell!" he chastised her.

If she had only known about the dark place he had just visited in his mind – well, how could she?

So, not knowing whether he was joking or not, Sharon just shrugged her shoulders slightly, offered him a forced smile, turned and walked away.

Dan was left alone to tuck into his breakfast and drift off into his own mind once more.

Chapter 24

It was edging closer to five o'clock when Julia left her apartment building.

She felt extremely guilty about not seeing her friends in such a long time, but knew that they'd understand once she brought them into the circle of trust and disclosed the details. Strangely enough, though, there'd been no phone-calls nor messages from any of them during her absence. This could mean a few things. They intuitively knew that she was deeply engrossed in whatever she was busy with, or they were all as busy as she was, or they were upset with her. While believing it was the former reason, it still offered her no reprieve. She was guilty of neglecting her friends and she really felt bad about that. While she promised herself it would never happen again, deep down she knew that this was a promise she would inadvertently, but inevitably, break.

She jumped into her red Suzuki Swift and sped down the beachfront.

Her father had insisted on giving her a new vehicle on her birthday, even though it went against her principles of making it in life on her own. He had insinuated that she was an embarrassment to him and her mother whilst driving around town in her beloved, but thoroughly beat up, 1995 Citi-Golf.

It was a real skorokoro, but she had adored it. It had been her trusty transport throughout her varsity years and until recently, had served her very well.

But her father wouldn't relent this time and she had

eventually conceded, with one stipulation, of course – the choice of car would be hers.

She knew full well that if left to his own devices, her father would have bought her a Porsche or a Ferrari, or the likes.

A part time, freelance, investigative journalist driving a Porsche or Ferrari around East London – come on, not happening! Besides, when investigating a story, how likely would people be to open up to her if she pulled up in some fancy car. It would not work for her.

She had finally decided on the Suzuki, which had cost a pittance compared to what he would have spent on her. But, it was new. It was reliable. It would get her from point A to point B and most importantly it was very economical and on her wages that was extremely pertinent.

Again, she had managed to keep the powerful Alan Swan in check. He must have taught her well.

Bed down the terms and conditions before entering into an agreement, he had always said.

The drive was uneventful, as Buccaneers was literally ten minutes away, if that.

Not that getting anywhere in East London would take anyone very long. It was really too small to be called a city, but in reality, too big to be called a town. It didn't come close to the likes of Cape Town, Johannesburg, Pretoria or Durban.

While the economy ticked steadily over, East London also just seemed to exude a more laid-back atmosphere and nobody ever seemed to be in too much of a hurry to do anything or get anything done. It somehow just worked.

Julia cruised along the beach-front, weaving her way between the slower moving vehicles... those evidently out to enjoy the bracing sea breeze or early evening ocean view. It wasn't long before she arrived at the entrance to Buccaneers from the slip-road into John Bailie Road.

She'd been delayed for a while at the Moore Street intersection behind some slow-moving cars, as traffic was always backing up at this intersection, but the vibe between motorists always seemed to be that of acceptance and tolerance.

The carpark at Buccaneers was filling up nicely when she arrived. It was going to be a busy night for them. She found a parking bay relatively easily and swung effortlessly into it. The joys of having a small vehicle.

Buccaneers was a very popular watering hole in East London with an unparalleled location. It was well positioned, overlooking the beachfront, with the ocean less than one hundred metres away. It was an absolute goldmine, with constant patronage, not only from the local clientele, but also from visitors to East London, who stumbled across it whilst driving along Esplanade Road, admiring the sea view.

It would be difficult, if not impossible, to find a more perfect venue for sundowners. Their food was good and their prices were very reasonable.

It was currently rated as the number one of nine bars in East London and number nine of ninety-one restaurants in East London. These were very well-deserved and prestigious accolades.

Chapter 25

The restaurant was already buzzing. Sundowners and post-work drinks were really popular here. Julia stood still at the door, scanning the room for her friends. It took her a good while before she spotted the girls through the crowded room. She bobbed and weaved between the tables, dodging the waiters and deftly side-stepping the patrons, who stood milling around in groups.

The girls were seated outside at a table, at the far end of the deck. It was a perfect day to be out on the deck, but Julia knew that that wasn't the real reason for their choice of tables.

Cathy and Sam were both smokers, so it was always their choice as to where the group sat and as usual the non-smokers ended up in the smoking area, passively smoking with every breath they took. It was outside, after all, as Cathy and Sam would routinely remind them, resolutely defending their position and rights. But it didn't really matter to any of them, they were all together and that was what mattered.

"Hi, girls," Julia blurted out as she made her way across the crowded deck to her friends, her voice barely audible over the hubbub of the crowd.

"Finally, girl," Cathy shouted back, "When you say five o'clock, you know you need to be here earlier. This place is a madhouse at this time!"

"I know. Just happy you got us a table," Julia responded, taking her spot at the table.

"So, Jules, tell us all about it," Anne hurriedly interjected, hardly even waiting for Julia to squeeze in.

"Yeah," added Sam, "you got us all to read the article and now we need the juicy bits."

Julia gazed at each of her friends in turn, taking in every detail, as if she hadn't seen them for years.

The last few days were a stressful blur and had passed in the blink of an eye. But, how she'd missed these girls.

Cathy was, of course, her best friend. They had been childhood pals and that relationship had just flourished as the years passed. Growing up together had been an absolute blast. Julia had been the rational mind in the duo, while Cathy was always the consummate clown. She had never been overly serious about anything. She laughed and joked her way through life, her magnetic charm and personality, a beacon of light, even to the most downhearted.

She had studied with Julia at Rhodes University in Grahamstown and after graduating cum laude had been recruited by one of the largest accounting firms in East London and was presently doing exceptionally well for herself.

Cathy was a typical "work hard" and "play hard" type of girl and Julia could sense that this was going to be one of those "play hard" times tonight.

She smiled at her friend as she pondered the irony. Accountants were usually sombre individuals with little or no inter-personal skills, and yet here was Cathy, a total anomaly in the world of debits, credits, assets and liabilities.

She must be such a hoot in the boardroom, thought Julia.

Next was Anne, a sexy blonde gym instructor, who plied her trade at the Virgin Active gym in Aquarium Road. Like Buccaneers, it was perfectly located.

The treadmills lined the huge front windows where not even

dripping beads of sweat could obscure the beautiful view of the azure ocean.

Julia and Cathy had met Anne on opening day when they had enrolled at the gym and had been inseparable ever since.

Anne was muscular, lithe and toned. Stunningly beautiful to boot.

With her blonde hair and sculptured body, she was the proverbial Barbie Doll in the group, although the Sports Barbie version.

She was actually quite tom-boyish by nature and mostly dressed in sweats and T-shirts or tank tops when she needed to reveal those unbelievably defined abdominals. Guys ogled her every movement and were drawn to her like moths to a flame, even though she had no interest in a committed relationship or settling down at the moment. Her sister had married young and was now just plodding through life with a deadbeat husband and two small children. She definitely was not ready for that life yet.

Finally, there was Samantha, or Sam, as she preferred to be called. She was the last to join the quartet. She was not originally from East London and had only met the others when she relocated.

She was the drama queen in the group and well-suited at that, since she was after all a high school drama teacher. She lived for the theatre and all told would have loved to find work in one of the major centres, like Johannesburg, Pretoria or Cape Town, which were the current hubs for the theatrical arts in South Africa. Then possibly instead of just teaching drama, she could perform as well. A dream of hers.

Sam was slightly on the plump side, but her striking facial features and magnetic personality made her desirable nonetheless.

She was not at all a health freak like Anne and smoked like a chimney given the opportunity. This was exacerbated by Cathy, who lit up as frequently, and over a few drinks they tended to match each other cigarette for cigarette.

The girls were all young, single, and a tight-knit group of confidants. Their regular gatherings were safe spaces and nothing was discussed outside the group unless expressly permitted.

They shared their innermost secrets and discussed all sorts of unspeakables.

Julia loved them all dearly.

Chapter 26

Cathy followed Julia's eyes as they moved around the group and not being able to bear the suspense any longer, she finally broke the silence.

"So? Spill the beans, Jules!"

Julia surveyed her surroundings and took a sip of the freshly poured wine which Sam offered her. She definitely needed to whet her whistle before sharing the details of her current situation.

After satisfying herself that the noisy environment would obscure the conversation, she sighed deeply and began to regale the group with the events of the past week.

She gave a detailed account of Dan's first letter and the astounding statistics he had quoted, which she had verified in her research. This elicited gasps of disbelief from her captivated audience, augmented by the looks of astonishment on their faces.

But, before the imminent questions interrupted her train of thought, she raised a hand to settle the girls and soldiered on.

They would have to park their questions for now.

She then dealt extensively with her father's and Ollie's involvement, the meeting she'd had with them, the surveillance and protection detail and finally the hand-off strategy and the delivery of Dan's second letter.

Julia could not only pen a good story, she was a consummate narrator.

The crowd, the noise, the outside world, all disappeared as

if the four of them were now locked in their own isolation bubble, held captive by their own concentration, focus and attention.

Cathy drained her glass and raised her hand to summon a waiter. When Fred arrived, she quickly ordered another bottle of wine for the table. There was no way that they would get through this story with empty glasses. The others drank up to keep pace with Cathy.

It took several minutes for the wine to arrive, as the waiters were literally run off their feet bustling hastily between the patrons and the bar, but it gave the girls a chance to head to the toilets. They took turns and went in pairs for fear of losing their table, which would have been catastrophic on a busy night like tonight.

The leg stretch and interruption by the waiter turned out to be a welcomed reprieve and Julia used this opportunity to gather her thoughts and choose the correct words in preparation to continue her story.

"Thank you, Fred," said Sam, raising her voice to be heard above the commotion, as the handsome waiter proceeded to uncork and pour the wine.

Fred smiled charmingly and winked covertly at Sam, instantly bringing a pretty pink hue to her cheeks.

Once he had departed, Cathy looked inquisitively at Sam and asked, "What's with that, now?"

She had noticed the secretive little wink.

"What do you mean?"

Cathy knowingly responded. "Well, the overly polite 'thank you', the wink and the schoolgirl blushing."

"Oh, it's nothing," Sam replied. "Just being polite."

"Come on, that was far more than just being polite, something's going on there, isn't it?"

"Not really, or not yet, should I say," replied Sam, suddenly grinning sheepishly.

"I knew it," replied Cathy, snickering openly. "I thought you could act. You're as easy to read as an open book."

Sam took a few moments to recover and quickly countered, "Bite me!"

All four of the girls burst out laughing.

They took a while to quieten down and settle again.

The distraction had broken the tension and lightened the mood and Julia was actually quite relieved that the attention had been directed away from her for a while. After what she was going through, the levity of it all almost brought back a bit of sanity to her world.

But the reprieve was short lived.

Anne reached out across the table and touched Cathy and Sam on the arms, as if to say *'Are you quite done? I want to hear the end of this story'.*

She then turned to Julia, "Please continue, my friend," she almost beseeched.

Julia took another big glug of her wine and readied herself to continue with the saga.

The rapt attention from the group returned and was almost tangible, while at the same time the surrounding noise from the crowd again became almost unnoticeable. The girls immersed themselves once more in Julia's adventure, as she continued from where she had left off.

Chapter 27

The big man sat quietly in the corner sipping his whiskey. He was thick-set and frankly, over-sized in stature. He was not very tall, maybe average height, but he was wide and tipped the scales at an extremely impressive one hundred and thirty kilograms.

It had taken years of determination, all-consuming effort and extremely hard work, not forgetting the supplements and steroids, to transform his physique into what he admired in the mirror each morning.

He would never be the victim again.

But tonight, ensconced in his large leather jacket, he looked quite normal while seated amongst the crowd. It concealed his bulk very effectively.

He had positioned himself at the foot of a much larger communal table, as there were no single seats available anywhere. As a result, he was inconspicuous as an individual and looked to be part of the larger group. He just hoped that some garrulous halfwit wouldn't take up the seat alongside him. He couldn't be bothered with polite conversation.

From his vantage point, he had surreptitiously been watching the girls for the past hour, furtively glancing their way every so often while he sipped his drink.

They were a captivating group and he was astounded that the guys in the crowd had not hit on them yet. He had, of course, noticed some of them leering in their direction every once in a while, whether biding their time, building up the courage to approach or just appreciating the eye-candy.

He couldn't be sure.

But then again, it was a classic female defence mechanism to gather in groups, so as to intimidate intruders. Strength in numbers and protection of the herd, it would seem.

He couldn't see Julia's face from his vantage point, as her back was towards him. He smiled discreetly to himself, wondering what she'd do if she knew he was there and only a few metres away from her.

She entranced the group with what appeared to be a lengthy and mostly uninterrupted monologue. The quizzical and disbelieving expressions from around the group said it all.

She could only be recounting her recent experiences.

And the girls were riveted.

He obviously couldn't make out what she was saying over the ruckus from the crowd, but he didn't really need to. He knew that the entire narration was all about him.

His smile broadened as he took another deep swig of his drink.

Almost a toast to himself.

He consoled himself that this wasn't his doing. He was merely a tool. A means to an end. Someone had to do something, and that someone was him. Self-appointed, maybe, but appointed nonetheless.

He was the judge, jury and executioner. A catalyst to instigate a resolution – to force change.

He wondered whether she was painting a dark picture of him to the group, maybe describing him as a monster. A monster with an agenda of murdering some random individuals.

What would they do if they knew how close he was to them? Would they scream hysterically and scatter, spilling their drinks in the process?

It would be like telling a ghost story and then suddenly the ghost would appear. They would shit themselves, he thought and chuckled malevolently into his drink.

"Careful, buddy!" he grumbled, as the guy next to him stumbled and by some miracle avoided dousing him in what smelled like rum and coke.

"Shhhorrrryy," came the slurred, quick-fire response, as the youngster pirouetted and brought his drink under control before moving away.

He probably wouldn't even remember it in the morning.

Nothing more came of the altercation, which suited the large man just fine. Getting into some frivolous pushing and shoving match, or at worst a barroom brawl, would draw too much unwanted attention to him. His cover could not be blown so early in the game.

In the past few weeks, he had managed to avoid a couple of exchanges when his antagonists suddenly realised what bulk they would be facing and as a result backed down very quickly.

This was, of course, the sole reason and motivator for pushing himself so hard to develop his body in the first place... even if pharmaceutically assisted.

He was tired of getting the shit kicked out of him.

In his case, the school of hard knocks was not just an adage, it was an actual account of his life.

His mind drifted back to his master plan which was gaining momentum.

He smiled, quietly stood up and miraculously found another unoccupied seat, which must have recently been vacated, as the place was really buzzing now.

From this new position, the girls were situated diagonally across from him. He had a great side-on view of their table and could now discreetly watch them without being overly noticeable.

Although he could see Julia's face from the side, he still couldn't make out what she was saying, but at least he saw more of her now than just her back.

Chapter 28

Another man moved stealthily around the crowded deck area. He didn't have the formidable bulk of Dan, but was extremely lethal in his own lean and sinewy way. His senses tingled as he inched his way along, surveying the crowd with heightened intensity.

"Come on," he muttered to himself, "show yourself. I feel you're here!"

The buzzing, jovial atmosphere engulfed him, as he moved from group to group, taking special care not to spill the drink he sported as an accessory in order to visually fit into the scene – camouflage of sorts.

He paused every so often to greet someone who had made eye-contact with him, but then just as abruptly moved on again.

He'll surely be alone, the sinewy man rationalised, as he casually did a three hundred and sixty degree turn to survey the scene for any loners. Nobody caught his eye and of course, there were no single or double seaters in the area for a solitary person anyway. The smallest table was a four-seater and in this crowd no individual would manage to reserve an entire table for themselves.

Not as easy a target as the man had thought.

In fact, the place had filled substantially and was now packed to the proverbial rafters. Even the smaller groups were no longer very prominent as they seemed to have merged into one large mass. Patrons were sitting together, standing together or moving around – it was just one amorphous mass.

Nobody could stand out in this throng.

Sundowners was a major event at Buccaneers for both young and old, blue-collar and white-collar, not forgetting all the different races constituting the South African rainbow nation.

Twenty-odd years prior, this scene would have been unheard of, with the enforced race segregation of the apartheid era.

But now, it was a vision to behold, as multi-racial groups congregated; chatting, joking and laughing in gay abandon.

There was, at last, a commonality, a singularity of purpose, especially amongst the younger generations. Those who had heard about the struggle, but had not physically been part of it. It was easier for these youngsters to forgive and forget the injustices of the past and consequently easier for them to associate with one another. These more affluent youngsters had commingled from birth and were quite comfortable with one another and the diversities amongst their various cultures.

The animosity, however, still existed with the less prosperous youths, who were very vocal and militant about the inequalities of life. This then often resulted in protest marches, riots, looting and vandalism. Burning down schools and public service buildings were common occurrences and to the rational population made absolutely no sense, as the destruction of these facilities just widened the division between classes, as the country now had to spend more money on rehabilitation or reconstruction instead of investing these funds in housing, health or infra-structure, which would ultimately assist the poor.

One step forward, two steps back.

A large percentage of the older generations unfortunately also still harboured dark feelings from their pasts and as much as they might want to keep those feelings under wraps, in tense or stressful situations, the hateful emotions and words would boil to the surface, subsequently straining the already tenuous race-relation situation.

But seemingly, not at Buccaneers.

As the man scanned the crowd, everyone seemed to be having a blast, irrelevant of whether they were black, white, yellow, pink or green. Good times flowed with a liberal dash of alcohol.

There would always be a bit of pushing and shoving, but this was generally due to a combination of testosterone and alcohol. The crowd mostly policed itself and most scuffles were broken up in record time by a sheer mass of people intervening and separating the aggressors.

He glanced over at the four girls seated at the far end of the deck. They paid no attention to the crowd. Their heads were drawn together, as they leaned in across the table to hear one another without having to raise their voices too much above the music and cacophony of the crowd.

For now, they were still safe, but the man had an ominous feeling that the status quo would be short-lived. They were engaged in deep conversation and totally oblivious to their surroundings. They looked and acted so natural, making surveillance a doddle.

Chapter 29

The sinewy man, better known as Manny, had been a part of Ollie's crew for years now. His instincts were razor sharp, along with his reflexes, through years of experience in this line of work, so it baffled him that he could not get a bead on his target. They had been so sure that Dan would be there, rationalising that for him to stay ahead of the game, he would need to keep a close eye on Julia. But now Manny was starting to doubt that rationale.

Okay, Buccaneers was ridiculously crowded now, so spotting an unknown, suspicious-looking person was close to impossible. But still, it concerned Manny that Dan could remain so elusive.

Maybe this was a long-shot.

Maybe he was home in bed, reading a book or maybe he was staking out his next victim.

Two hours had passed since Manny had been in position, but so far he'd come up empty. This was definitely not an indictment of his prowess or adeptness.

Either Dan wasn't there or he was extraordinarily skilled at operating below the radar. Manny decided that if he was amongst the crowd he must be ordinary and unremarkable in every way, making him undetectable.

Or could it be that he wasn't here at all, Manny wondered.

Suddenly, in unison, the girls rose from their seats – they had decided to call it a night.

Manny caught the sudden movement out of the corner of his

eye and forced himself not to turn in their direction, but rather to survey the onlookers. Now that the girls weren't sedentary, he hoped to catch someone paying extra special attention to the girls. The problem was that many heads turned to check the girls out. Men, being men, made his job tough tonight. The girls were ogled from head to toe by all in close proximity, but Manny's keen eye picked up no maliciously lengthy stares.

Spotting the vacant table, a nearby group of four moved in quickly, as if caught in a vacuum created by the girls leaving, and hurriedly claimed the unoccupied seats, even though the table had not even been cleared yet.

Realistically it wouldn't be cleared any time soon anyway, as the waiters were still running their butts off between the bar and the patrons.

The girls' empty wine bottle and glasses were therefore nonchalantly pushed to the corner of the table by the new occupants and they continued their conversation unabated, but now comfortably seated.

Manny followed the girls, but not noticeably so. He needed to maintain his distance, while simultaneously being close enough to protect them.

Would their worst fears be realised?

Would Dan strike?

Should he have agreed to the backup offered?

Could he protect them all collectively if something went awry?

They were relatively confident that Julia would be safe, as Dan needed her to fulfil his demented plan, but their real concerns were Cathy, Anne and Sam. Their safety was paramount. The significant leverage Dan would have over Julia, if he managed to get to her friends, would be a game changer.

Manny glanced cautiously in the direction of the girls, but had now lost sight of them as they moved inside from the deck. He moved carefully, but quickly, remaining alert to the tight groups of patrons cluttering the path to the exit while concurrently looking for anyone in pursuit. They were well ahead of him and now exited the main door. Julia briefly turned to check behind her for anyone following and then contentedly moved on.

Good girl, thought Manny, *her instincts and training served her well.*

Nobody.

That was a good sign.

He sighed inaudibly and continued after them, pushing through the crowd.

The next time he caught sight of the girls, was when they were walking casually through the car park towards their cars, chatting away, oblivious to their surroundings. Julia had obviously spent the night informing them of the situation, but it obviously hadn't registered with any of them that they might now be potential targets. They strolled on, casual and unaware of any latent dangers.

Suddenly a man moved out of the shadows and shouted in the girls' direction.

"I've been waiting for you," he hollered.

It was the last thing the man recalled, as a powerful bony hand grabbed his wrist, twisted it, then moved swiftly to just below his elbow and finally connected with the pressure point in his neck, felling him swiftly and silently where he had stood.

Manny was that good.

The girls heard the shout and their heads spun around in perfect synchronicity. They scanned the car park curiously, now on high alert, but saw nothing. They looked curiously at one another, almost in disbelief that they'd heard anything at all. But really, what were the chances that they'd all heard something that wasn't there? The conclusion, although not expressed in words, was that the voice obviously was not directed at them.

With nonchalant shrugs and frowns, they gave each other the perfunctory hugs and kisses, climbed into their cars and went their separate ways.

The big man had witnessed the spectacle from the door. He hadn't noticed the bodyguard, but was now extremely relieved that he'd decided to bide his time and not make a move.

Everything could've been ruined in one fell swoop.

Just not acceptable, he chided himself.

He had completely misread the situation. He knew from the start that Julia would be constantly surveilled and protected. He now postulated that all the girls were protected or, at a minimum, under surveillance twenty-four/seven because of him. Such was the reach and influence of Alan Swan.

He turned on his heels, reprimanding himself quietly for this oversight.

He had just dodged a bullet.

Chapter 30

Roger awoke in an unfamiliar and dingy room. He was propped up on a rickety wooden chair. His hands and feet were bound to the chair with cable ties, and his mouth was dry.

Confusion was etched into his face.

What had happened to him?

Why was he here?

Had he been drugged?

Why did he feel so dazed?

His mind raced back to what he could recall. He was at Buccaneers. He was having a good time with a group of his mates. After a few drinks he had finally built up the courage to make his move.

But now, he was bound tightly to a chair and surrounded by six very intimidating looking men. Four of the six wore skin-tight shirts, stretched ominously over bulging muscles – as muscle-shirts were designed to do.

He looked from one to the other, his anxiety building all the while.

Roger then wet himself, as his bladder involuntarily released.

"This is not our man," said the largest man in the group.

"I'm not your man," Roger whimpered, not caring what he was admitting to or not. He just wanted to get out of there alive.

"He just pissed himself," another of the muscle-bound giants mumbled.

"If he's not our man, then this has to be the most classic 'wrong time, wrong place' story in history," said another man.

"Well, he came out of the shadows and shouted to the girls that he had been waiting for them, what was I to think?" said the skinniest man in the group.

Roger started crying.

He had never been so frightened in life.

"P-p-p-p-p-l-e-a-s-e, it's not me you're looking for? I don't even know what I did wrong or why I'm here," he snivelled.

"Quiet!" the largest man instructed.

Roger tried his best, but he was fretting like a child and couldn't control his sobs. Tears and snot ran freely from his facial orifices and dripped off his chin.

"Either this guy is the best actor I've ever seen or we really do have the wrong guy. I mean really, who would piss themselves if they were putting on an act?" asked the sinewy guy again.

Roger strained backwards as Ollie leaned forward and really got in his face – almost nose to nose. The unsteady chair on which he was precariously perched nearly toppled over.

"Okay, so answer me this, why were you hiding in the shadows and why did you shout at the girls? It would be very wise to tell me the truth," Ollie probed and warned in a deep ominous tone.

Roger again shifted his head backwards, this time to evade the spittle that jetted at him along with the questions. Not that any more bodily fluid on his face would make much difference.

Roger's mind raced back to what he could remember.

Instantaneously, the wracking sobs ceased as the realisation suddenly dawned on him. He inhaled deeply, taking his time to suppress the last of his sobs and then began to regale the group with a staccato version of what he could remember – "I was inside Buccaneers with some mates, drinking and having a good time. Then I joined a friend outside to have a smoke. That's when I saw Cathy sitting with her friends at the end of the deck."

He stopped to regain his breath, the words now flowed quickly and freely as he rattled along. "Bad timing, I guess, because as soon as I noticed them, they stood up to leave. I've always had a thing for Cathy. She's the woman of my dreams. The timing has just never been right to have a decent conversation with her, you know?"

Roger was gaining in confidence now, as his story built to a crescendo.

He continued, "So, I left ahead of them and waited outside. I tried to calm my nerves, hoping that I'd still have the courage to talk to her before she left. They walked right by me, but I'd lost my nerve again by then. Only once Cathy was well past me did I regain my confidence and that's when I shouted to her. I don't recall anything after that, except waking up here. That's the truth, I swear."

Roger exhaled deeply, as though he'd just run a marathon, but was relieved and now confident that the truth would set him free.

Ollie looked over at Manny and smiled. "The worst timing ever, my friend," he added matter-of-factly.

He turned to glare once more at Roger, squinting his eyes menacingly and concluded, "Right, my friend. I believe you. This seems to have been a huge misunderstanding and very bad timing on your part. Like we said, wrong place, wrong time. I apologise for the inconvenience. We will escort you back to Buccaneers."

On hearing this, the sinewy man's hand flashed from his pocket, revealing a knife, which gleamed menacingly, even in the darkened room.

Roger flinched and jerked backwards again, nearly fainting in the process. He would have pissed himself again, had his bladder not already been emptied.

"Relax, buddy," Manny reassured him, as he cut the plastic ties around his arms and legs.

Roger was then lifted to his feet and guided to the door by two of the men.

Their firm grips on his upper arms would surely leave marks, but he didn't care, as long as was getting out of this mess alive.

"You'll have to wear this until we get you back," another said and without warning pulled a hood over his head, blacking out his view.

Roger was absolutely helpless and totally in their control as they shuffled him forward and stuffed him unceremoniously into an awaiting vehicle. Space was limited in the back of the vehicle, as two of the behemoths flanked him tightly throughout the journey, not that he had any intention of making a move anyway.

The drive took forever. All the while Roger breathed deeply through the blackout over his head. It was not very porous and severely impeded normal breaths. He wandered just how far they had driven, but soon realised that, with all the turns they were making, they were just taking detours to mask their original location, route and distance.

Finally, after what seemed like an eternity, the vehicle came to a halt and he was brutally bundled out. Once again, the vice-like grips moved him forward until he was brought to a halt. Roger had no idea where he was. It was eerily quiet. He really hoped he was back at Buccaneers, but for all he knew they might be somewhere off the beaten track and he was about to take a bullet to the back of the head. He started to panic again.

Just before he was about to piss himself again, the hands loosened their grip on his arms and the hood was removed. He reflexively inhaled deeply. The fresh air which bombarded his lungs tasted so good. He blinked repeatedly to regain his focus, but all was dark around him. As his eyes slowly acclimatised to the darkness, he could make out a wall in front of him. There was about a metre between him and the wall.

What now, he wondered anxiously?

He waited in anticipation for whatever was about to happen to him next.

All was quiet – definitely some deserted place.

He slowly inhaled and exhaled in an attempt to keep himself clam.

The eerie silence was suddenly shattered, as the man alongside him whispered gruffly in his ear, "Lean forward and place your hands against the wall. If you turn around before we're gone, we will come back and that wouldn't end very well for you."

Roger instantly complied and placed his hands against the wall and faced forward. He definitely had no intention of turning around. That was never going to happen.

"This never happened. And we'll be watching you," the man added, before leaving.

Roger stayed motionless until the sound of the vehicle's engine faded into the distance and then waited a little while longer.

There was no way he was giving them a reason to return.

This was a chapter in his life best forgotten.

Chapter 31

Alan and Ollie sat together on the veranda, enjoying the early morning freshness while hungrily tucking into the healthy breakfast that Mavis, the cook, had prepared for them.

This was their routine.

Most days started like this for them.

In the corporate world, this would have been termed a morning meeting and would have been formal and staid. Alan even detested the thought of that. Everyone tarted up in suits. The boss touting a red power-tie, of course, while barking orders from on high. In what world? That attire was certainly not appropriate for the African heat, but somehow it had been adopted from the cooler European countries where it was more practical and was now accepted as the world-wide norm. Absolute bollocks.

On the contrary, their morning ritual was very informal and essentially a no holds barred discussion. There were no secrets between the two of them, but confidentiality was a given. Their relationship had evolved to that extent.

When there were business issues to discuss, facts were separated from fiction and assimilated into a strategy and decisions were made there and then.

If there were no important points on the 'agenda' the conversation was just that – a conversation.

"So, did we have any luck last night?" Alan asked between mouthfuls.

"Nothing," replied Ollie, "Manny was sure he was onto

someone. We took him to the safe house for questioning."

"And?" Alan prompted impatiently when Ollie paused to take another bite of a wonderfully juicy apple.

After chewing, swallowing and wiping his mouth with his napkin, Ollie continued, "Well, straight off the bat, the guy pissed himself. What a mess. All down the front of his trousers, down his legs and into his shoes. Manny cleaned up the mess." Ollie grinned. "He wasn't happy about that, but it was his take-down and mistake, after all."

"So, nothing useful?"

"No, he was just an admirer. Really the worst timing in the history of rotten timing. This Romeo shouted from the shadows in the car-park to get Cathy's attention and instead he met with one of Manny's pressure point knockouts. When he woke, we had him tied up in the safe house and that's when the water-works started. Poor bugger got the fright of his life."

"Just don't tell Julia," Alan cautioned. "What about at the bar?"

"Definitely not, and nothing from the bar. Either he wasn't there or he's better than we anticipated. Manny did say that it was extremely busy, so while the crowd effectively concealed him, it could have done exactly the same for Dan. If he was there."

"Damn, back to square one then. What about camera coverage?" Alan asked.

"We might have some luck, but according to Manny there were only two cameras on the deck and from his account, very general views. But it is a lead we'll follow up on today. It might take some 'sweet-talking' to get the footage, though." Ollie made the quotation signs with his huge fingers, but Alan had already got the message.

"Do what you have to, Ollie, this won't be the first time."

"No problems, boss."

The sudden ringing of Ollie's cell phone interrupted their conversation.

Ollie checked the caller ID, frowned and turned the phone to show Alan.

'Detective Phiri'

Not to be rude, Ollie excused himself from the table and took a stroll around the garden as he spoke animatedly to his friend, Alfonso Phiri.

Alan watched Ollie intently from the veranda. He was very animated in his discussion with the Captain.

Something was wrong.

Something had happened.

Oh God, don't let it be Julia.

How could it be? They would have phoned me first, not Ollie, he thought.

But whatever it was, it was important and concerning.

He could see it in Ollie's body language and facial expressions.

Seconds felt like minutes.

Minutes felt like hours.

And still Ollie paced the garden.

He listened intently, occasionally speaking into the handset, probably to gain clarity on what had been said. He offered very little. The plan was just that, to be the information centre and only offer titbits here and there, but only if absolutely necessary. That way they could control the situation and find this animal first. Obviously Ollie had warned the police Captain of a possible situation arising, but had been vague enough to avoid too many questions being asked.

Alan had the sudden urge to pace as well. He couldn't stand

the suspense.

Finally, Ollie dropped his hand holding the cell phone. Obviously, the call had ended. He made his way slowly back onto the veranda, his expression betraying his thoughts, which were a million miles away. He edged his way into his chair and unhurriedly raised his head to meet Alan's curious glare. He had heard and seen it all before, but nonetheless, he had a faraway, dazed look in his eyes.

"What, Ollie? What?" he demanded, anxiety and anticipation coursing through him like a raging river.

"They found a body. The crime scene was a disaster zone," Ollie answered and then paused, not for effect, but to get the facts he was just given ordered properly.

"And?" Alan urged.

"Well, the vic's name was Craig Davis. Divorced. No children. Lived alone in the suburbs. He was found two days after his murder. His colleagues eventually noticed his absence and phoned in a missing person's report to the police."

"Are they certain it was murder?" Alan interrupted.

"Absolutely positive," Ollie replied and then added, "Get this – his corpse was found in situ with one end of a bungee cord tied around his neck with the other end secured around a structural pillar in his living room. The blood splatter pattern and the pool of blood suggested significant trauma prior to his death. It's suspected that the killer had repeatedly pulled the man by his legs to stretch the elastic and then released them to allow him to smash head first into the pillar. The police are still unsure whether the cause of death was blunt force trauma or strangulation. Either way, it was a horrible and extremely traumatic way to go. Nobody seems to have ever seen anything like this before."

Alan listened intently to Ollie recount the message and was

mesmerised by his hand movements as he imitated how the murderer had killed his victim.

"And forensics?" Alan finally prompted, tearing his thoughts away from the vivid picture Ollie had painted.

"Well, that's another issue altogether," Ollie answered with raised eye-brows. "They're still busy at the crime scene. Shoe prints everywhere, different shapes and different sizes. Various colours and lengths of hair everywhere. Blood where there shouldn't be blood and even some liquid here and there which reportedly smelled like urine. It looked like a whole platoon went through that crime scene."

"So the scene was staged," Alan said – stating the obvious – while nodding his head.

"They're still dusting for fingerprints, but a buck gets ten, they'll find none… or a ton," Ollie added.

"Bastard! His gripe is with the police and the capability and quality of forensic investigations in South Africa. So what does he do? He swamps the crime lab with a single crime scene. We could wait forever for results."

"They have this scene prioritised when all the evidence collected arrives in Cape Town."

"Offer them the use of my plane, if it will expedite the process."

"Will do. My worry is that we won't even know if his real prints or DNA are amongst the evidence collected. He might just have contaminated the crime scene to throw us off his track – and implicate numerous other innocent people at the same time."

"We'll have to follow up on all leads, Ollie. What choice do we have? My biggest concern is the turnaround time to get the results. How many more murders could he commit before we get the results back from Cape Town?"

"We can't just sit on our hands until then," Ollie added, shaking his head. "We'll have to stick with the surveillance and hope he slips up and reveals himself in the meantime."

"Shit!" Alan cursed and without warning slammed his fists on the table.

The noise brought Mavis running, who had to sidestep Alan as he stormed indoors.

Ollie shrugged at Mavis. He understood Alan's frustrations entirely and swore to himself that above all Julia would be kept safe and that they would track down this maniac. Hopefully sooner than later.

Chapter 32

Julia heard the doorbell… loud and clear this time. She had slept soundly and was already dressed and puttering around the apartment when the raspy noise of the doorbell broke the silence.

She moved cautiously to the door and squinted through the peephole.

It was a very sweaty looking Mr Mathe.

She had only met him a few times, but he was always amiable and open to conversation, but they'd never really had the time to get to know each other. So, it was always more of a greeting in passing that they'd share.

After sparring with all the locks on her door, she finally opened it. The reinforced security gate still securely separated her from her visitor.

"Morning, Mr Mathe," Julia greeted, although her smile didn't quite match the curious expression on her face.

"Good morning, Julia… and please… call me Alfred. All my friends do," he responded dryly.

"What can I do for you, Mr – Alfred?" Julia asked, feeling quite uncomfortable about addressing her elders by their first names.

"Nothing for me, Julia, but I was given this for you," he explained as he handed an envelope to her through the gate.

"Where did you get this, Alfred?"

"I was at the end of my outrun when a lady approached and begged me to deliver it to you. I really didn't want to break my stride as I need to do at least a half hour of exercise each day to achieve my Vitality goal, but she implored me, so I relented… and here we are. I do apologise if it's a bit sweaty, but it wasn't my intention to run home with an envelope in my hand."

"I'm so sorry for that, Alfred, do you perhaps know who this lady was?"

"Never seen her before. She literally just appeared in front of me."

"Oh, it's all right, thank you, I'm sure the letter will explain everything."

"Have a great day then, Julia," Alfred responded and turned to walk away.

"You too, Alfred, and thanks again," Julia shouted after him.

Dan! It could only be Dan, she thought to her herself.

I wonder what he wants now.

This was the second time he'd used one of the tenants to deliver a letter to her. She still hadn't found out who the first person was, but the faint smell of deodorant on the first envelope still lingered in her memory and she would eventually put two and two together, if and when she bumped into that person. She would get a similar explanation to that of Alfred's, of that she was sure, but she still needed to know.

She poured more coffee and headed over to the couch.

As was the norm, her name and surname was emblazoned on the front of the envelope. No frills, just printed in bold black capital letters.

Julia Swan

She unceremoniously ripped open the envelope. No caution needed. She knew exactly who it was from and since she believed she was still safe, there was no need to worry.

Without further ado, Julia started reading.

Dear Julia,

I read your article with immense pride and admiration.

You really outdid yourself and, as with me, I'm positive you captivated the minds and interest of the broader community.

Actually, in passing, I have heard numerous people discussing the article. They seemed fascinated. Probably just ignorant and unaware of what is going on around them or the nightmare they are living in.

The facts and figures speak for themselves, and as your competent research verified, I fabricated nothing when quoting this data.

However, I was immensely disappointed and even upset about the 'DNA Dan' moniker. Whilst clever and catchy, it just detracts from the gravity of the situation and the importance of my mission.

I'm sincerely hoping that it was just a strategy – an attention grabber – to introduce me and my exploits.

I do not mind 'Dan', but let's keep it to that, shall we?

Now, maybe you've already heard or maybe you haven't. My first victim has been discovered. And just in case you might not believe me – his name was Craig Davis. I wouldn't know that yet if I wasn't involved, as no press release has been made. He was tortured and then hung with a bungee cord in a most unique and intriguing way.

You can verify the facts when the details are released, but you might as well take my word for it, as I would never take the credit for someone else's work.

I also ensured that the crime lab would be kept very, very busy for a very, very long time with all the evidence I left at the scene. They've been complaining for years about inadequate staffing levels and an unsuitably small budget, so I'm making sure they have enough bullets to fight those fights going into the future.

Now it's a case of seeing whether they have competent staff and reliable systems.

I sincerely hope they won't just take short-cuts and brush some of the DNA and testing under the carpet. I've heard that this has happened before – purely to achieve targets. Can you imagine; recognition as 'Employee of the Month' for exceeding targets when all you've done is discard tests or falsify results?

If they do that again, they might just miss the clues I've left them.

Lastly, let's also see if our police department will follow-up and investigate the DNA results produced by the lab, as this was also an area recently identified as a short-fall.

Anyway, this wasn't meant to be a lengthy letter.

Please continue with the great work and I'll expect your second edition to follow soon; pending the media release by the police. The public must be made aware of the reasons for a crime which could have been averted.

Julia exhaled. It felt like she'd subconsciously been holding her breath the entire way through the letter. She reached for her coffee, which was now tepid and not as hot as she usually liked it, but she drank it thirstily anyway.

So, he didn't like 'DNA Dan', she pondered.

She had thought it was a stroke of genius herself, as it created the bond between him, or rather the name he'd given her, and the motive behind the murders he was committing. She wondered whether she could still make use of it if she ensured that it didn't lighten the mood of the article. In her mind, it was the perfect moniker to encapsulate the exposé holistically.

She would take Moses' counsel on that one.

"No time to muck around," she muttered to herself.

She needed to share the latest events with her father and Ollie.

If they were lucky, one of Ollie's guys would have been watching Alfred Mathe this morning and they might be able to qualify what had transpired. It sounded like another handoff though, so even if they saw the woman or managed to trace her, it would probably just be another dead-end.

There were as many women as men begging for loose change at every intersection these days, so to get a letter delivered for a R10 or R20 note would be too easy.

Poverty and desperation didn't discriminate between races, gender, culture or creed.

Chapter 33

Neither Alan, nor Ollie, were at the mansion when Julia arrived. It was no problem though. It would give Julia some quality time with her mother while she waited for them.

Claire Swan was not the aloof 'I'm married to a millionaire' type of woman. She carried herself proudly, but without being overly prim and proper. She dressed well and always ensured that her hair and make-up were immaculate when the occasion demanded it. But in her down time, she could rough it with the best of them. After all, she wasn't born into the role. She came from a middle-class family and had a public-school background and was proud of it. She played tennis and golf regularly, and swam in their heated pool nearly every day to stay fit and toned.

She was at that age, when tiny feelings of vulnerability started manifesting themselves. She'd heard too many war stories from her friends about those younger women who preyed on rich and powerful men, armed with nothing more than the allure of their beauty and youthful bodies. It didn't even seem to matter whether they had one or two brain-cells between their ears.

Rich and aging men were highly insecure and evidently vulnerable to this shallow form of seduction.

Alan wasn't like that – she knew that – or rather she hoped that that was the truth. He'd never strayed before or, more accurately, she'd never heard or suspected that he'd strayed before. As far as she was concerned, he was the most faithful man on the planet.

Besides, she had Julia in her arsenal… and she had nuclear potential.

Julia would disown him in a heartbeat, if she found out that he had cheated on her mother, which would totally destroy him. His love for Julia was eclipsed by nothing. Not even his love for her, she often believed.

Julia had been blessed, or maybe cursed with unwavering morals. She believed in loyalty, trust, honesty and integrity above all and would never tolerate anything like that. She would never forgive him. Not in a million years and not for all the money in the world.

If she currently had no interest in his money and the promise of a cushy life, then Claire couldn't even imagine how Julia would feel if she went nuclear.

"Hi, Mom." Julia announced loudly, as she barged into the bedroom.

Claire was totally accustomed to this invasion and didn't even flinch as Julia rounded the corner and found her in her walk-in closet. She was in the process of selecting an outfit for her tennis game later that morning.

"Hi, my love," replied Claire, turning to kiss and embrace her.

The hugs were always firmer and longer than really necessary, but merely served to affirm the degree of love shared between her parents and herself.

"Tennis today," Julia asked, stating the obvious.

She was well aware of her mother's routine.

"Yes. I'm playing with Wendy, Edith and Rosanne," Claire replied proudly.

Edith was, of course, the club captain and number one player in the senior division for the past few years, so it was always an honour to be drawn to play against or alongside her.

"Well, a special occasion calls for a special outfit then," Julia joked, winking slyly to provoke her mother.

Claire lovingly punched her on the shoulder, knowing full well that Julia was having a laugh at her expense.

"You watch yourself, young lady, before you know it you'll also be in the senior division."

Claire had maintained her fitness and youthfulness much better than her counterparts and it actually irked her that she was classed as a senior, but she tried her best not to let on how she felt.

"In many, many years, Mother dear," Julia replied, still ribbing her mother, although at the same time realising that time was indeed flying by.

She was in her twenties already and it seemed like just the other day that she was a young and carefree teenager.

Just then, Alan strode purposefully through the door, having heard the girls' voices from the bedroom.

He looked briefly at the outfits on display. "That one," he pointed out, sensing that the girls were undecided.

Claire smiled lovingly at her husband. He knew her so well. She had already decided on the same outfit, but was humouring Julia by involving her in the selection.

Knowing very well that Alan and Julia needed to talk, Claire turned to Julia, "Well, you two go on then, I'll catch up on the details later. Be safe."

"Will do, Mom. Enjoy your game. See you later then," Julia responded with a brief wave and followed her father out of the room. Claire was left alone in the closet, perusing the garments and wondering whether their choice of outfits would really suit the occasion.

Chapter 34

This time they seated themselves in the gazebo at the bottom of the garden. Strategically positioned facing away from the house.

It was purposely designed that way so the occupants could only view the lush green grass, the huge perennial trees and the colourful flower beds, thereby immersing themselves in nature and the feeling that they were totally removed from civilisation.

When Alan really needed to clear his mind, he would retreat to the gazebo.

It was a beautifully designed tropical hardwood structure, hexagonal in shape, fully roofed in, with solid walls in the rear. A canvas tarpaulin with a transparent window section protected the interior from the elements, but today, owing to the great weather, it was rolled up to create a gaping entrance, which permitted all occupants to simultaneously enjoy the view.

The wood was dark, but the entrance was large enough to allow enough ambient light to enter, which naturally illuminated the gloomy interior. The wooden floor boasted a few treated animal-skin rugs, which fittingly added to the outdoor African ambiance. Typical adventurer or explorer paraphernalia and equipment sparsely adorned the walls. Enough to create a mood without being overly distracting. Four comfortable armchairs were positioned alongside one another creating an arc of seating in the entrance, while a round table with four upright chairs stood in the rear of the gazebo and was available on those very rare occasions when a light meal was served.

On this occasion a low table had been placed in front of the armchairs. Coffee and a selection of biscuits and snacks adorned it.

Mavis was dilly-dallying in the back when they arrived, but was very quickly in attendance to pour them both a steaming hot cup of fresh, aromatic coffee.

"Thanks, Mavis," Julia said, smiling awkwardly. She preferred doing things herself, so felt a little uncomfortable being waited upon.

She had grown up being served by the waitstaff and at the time had loved it, but now she lived in a completely different world.

She was self-sufficient and efficient.

"We'll pour for Ollie when he arrives," Alan stated, effectively dismissing Mavis from her duties in the gazebo. "I wonder where he is this morning?" he added.

Julia preferred not to repeat the story when Ollie arrived, so instead she steered the conversation to small talk so as to pass the time. They sipped their coffee while shooting the breeze about his businesses and all current and proposed projects.

It was a good chat but the anxiety building in her father was visibly noticeable.

He could sense that there were developments and was dying to probe her for an update, but constantly cautioned himself to play it cool and let her get to the story in her own time.

He was intrinsically not the patient type, but with Julia, he would wait an eternity if required.

"Ollie!" Julia finally exclaimed, as the big man rounded the corner. A broad smile adorning her beautiful face.

"Hi, Jules," Ollie replied enthusiastically.

"Where've you been, Ollie?" Alan queried.

The big man's absence had been the cause of his nightmare. Julia had procrastinated pending Ollie's arrival.

Ollie bent over to pour himself a cup of coffee, offering a refill to Alan and Julia in the process. They both declined politely.

Before Alan could tell Ollie to hurry up and sit down so Julia could finally get to her story, Ollie blurted out, "I've been with Detective Phiri. He took us up on your offer of using the plane to get the evidence samples to Cape Town. What a tedious process. He had to put all the protocols in place, vet it for safety and security and then clear it for landing in Cape Town, before it could even take off. We've been hanging around the airport since the crack of dawn this morning."

"So, what turnaround time are we looking at?"

"Well, it seems that with the few details I've shared with him – obviously trying not to divulge too much – he managed to convince the powers-that-be to fast track the testing. I cautioned him that this could be the work of a serial killer and that we needed quick results. He wasn't really sold on that, since one incident, no matter how horrific, could not be classified as the work of a serial killer. I couldn't elaborate more than that, but I think your position and standing did grease the wheels."

"Excellent, a bit of influence comes in handy sometimes," Alan said, trying not to smile too broadly.

Ollie finally looked over at Julia with a questioning frown on his face.

"Apologies for being late and then telling my story first. What did I miss?" he asked, glancing curiously between Julia and Alan.

"No. We were just chatting. I was actually waiting for you, so I wouldn't have to repeat the story," Julia chipped in.

"Well – he's here now – get on with it," Alan interjected.

His patience had finally run out and his anxiety was off the charts.

Chapter 35

Julia once again regaled the men with her tale, but this time with the sequel. She unravelled the story at a slow and steady pace, as though she'd rehearsed it many times over in her head. She obviously hadn't, but by slowly and methodically telling the story, she made sure that she didn't miss a single detail or jump around excessively, confusing the threads or timelines.

The men sat motionless, totally transfixed by what she had to say.

She was confronted by a myriad of facial expressions during her soliloquy.

Intense concentration, raised eyebrows, pursed lips, confusion, concern, anger and finally an intense desire for retribution.

Questions were pensively filed for later.

Neither man was willing to interrupt her until she had concluded the saga and read the letter to them.

Finally, Alan could contain himself no longer.

"This bastard," he fumed, his face now a crimson hue. "He's now demanding another article from you and more publicity. I'm going to rip him apart when I get my hands on him. He's going to regret the day he barged into our lives."

Julia reached over and patted her father on his leg comfortingly.

"It's all right, Dad. He just wants publicity. He hasn't threatened to come after me. He needs me."

"I know, but it's not like you have a choice in the matter and that is the part that irks me."

Alan detested this feeling of helplessness he was experiencing. Nobody had ever had the audacity to cross him to this extent and while it was quite a new experience and emotion for him, he was extremely concerned about his daughter and her involuntary and coerced involvement.

"From the amount of evidence from a single crime scene which was loaded onto the plane this morning, I can't see anything coming back from the lab any time soon," Ollie stated, adding to Alan's frustration.

"So we still have nothing to go on," Alan cursed.

Julia focused on Ollie. "Did you have anyone following Mr Mathe this morning?"

"I'll find out," Ollie replied, "but I doubt it. He runs every morning. Same time. Same route. You could probably set your watch by him. And since we know his routine there was never any reason to follow him, but I'll check anyway."

"It was probably another hand-off again anyway." Julia shrugged, concluding that it would once again be a futile exercise. "I'll also need all the info and detail on the murder that you have. If he's expecting another article, I better know everything about what happened and I can't wait for some half-baked police report either."

She finally stood and took a few steps outside to remove herself from the testosterone-filled atmosphere. The men were left chattering and visibly broiling behind her, as she strolled the grounds, taking a time-out.

She knew it was time to go. Nothing more could be achieved with those two carrying on like mad men threatening to bring the world to its knees.

Sometimes she wondered whether it was worth keeping them in the loop at all, but realistically she knew that she had to. Besides, Ollie's surveillance team looped him in anyway and probably knew more about what was going on than she did herself. They had a complex network of informants, and eyes on far more than she would ever know or care to know about.

The massive trees cast a huge umbrella of shadow over the gazebo and its surrounds. She looked up at the dense, leaf-bedecked branches and shivered ever so slightly as the cool morning breeze pricked through her sweater with its chilly shard-like fingers. Winter was on its way.

She wandered aimlessly for a while taking in the beautiful scenery and then finally decided that it was time to go.

She approached the two men, who were still in the throes of heated debate and planning. They probably hadn't even realised that she'd gone for a walk in the gardens.

"Time to go," she calmly interjected, bringing the discussion to an abrupt halt.

She leaned over casually and kissed and hugged her father.

She then turned to Ollie.

The big man was already on his feet and Julia wrapped her arms around his bole-like neck and gave him a hug.

Without further ado and no backward glance, she left, knowing full well that the two men would stay where they were until they had solved the world's problems – or rather – in this case, hers.

Chapter 36

Peter Roland surreptitiously watched Anne from across the gym, as he grunted and groaned through his upper body routine. His glance shifted regularly to his thick arms as he admired his own biceps, flexing and relaxing under the strain. A narcissistic trait apparent in all body-builders.

His physique was beyond impressive.

Hours and hours of dedication had got him this far and he was by no means done. Big enough was just not part of his vocabulary nor would it ever be.

The only part of his stature he was not very happy about was his height. He would have loved to be on or around two metres tall. His bulk would have been even more proportional and way more intimidating in a taller frame.

Anne was busy with her second class of the day.

This time it was a step aerobics class and the bodies in front of her – mainly ladies – glistened with sweat.

This was one of her advanced classes and Peter could clearly see why.

The participants were past the stage of this workout being torture. They were seasoned, smiling and having fun. This was in all likelihood their fix for the day. Some would head on home after the workout, some would head to the office, while others would gather for refreshments and engage in general chit-chat to while away the vacuum of superfluous time in their lives. But aside from their diverse lives, currently they were singularly committed to this activity and he appreciated that unwavering dedication immensely.

He took a breather to wipe himself down and give his aching muscles some well-earned respite between sets. He stared at the group for slightly longer than intended, totally mesmerised as all the participants moved in unison to the rhythm of the music.

The room was glassed in, but the energetic music still somehow managed to permeate the joints in the glass panels and doors, and drift faintly over to him.

Peter bobbed his head subconsciously to the beat of their music.

He suddenly became aware of Anne looking directly at him over the heads of the class members.

He really hadn't meant to stare and quickly looked away, quite embarrassed that he'd been caught ogling the ladies.

He was a proper gym-rat and the thought of taking part in an aerobics class had never even occurred to him. He pumped iron. That was his thing.

An hour later, he had finished his workout, showered and dressed. His hair was still a little damp, but he figured the cool air outside would resolve that very quickly.

He had his backpack slung over his shoulder and was heading for the exit when Anne suddenly appeared before him.

"Hi," she said, showing no intention of moving out of his way.

"Hello," he stammered, being caught slightly off-guard by her sudden appearance.

"Saw you watching our workout this morning." Gesturing with her head and eyes towards the aerobics room.

"Uh, yes, it was a sight to behold," he answered,

immediately feeling rather silly about his reply. "I really didn't mean to stare," he added, not wanting her to think he was some kind of deranged pervert.

"No worries," Anne replied nonchalantly, "ever thought of joining?" she continued, always looking for new acquisitions for her classes.

"Not really," he replied, his confidence now returning. "I'm not so sure I have the right body or fitness for all that jumping around."

"Don't be like that, everyone needs cardio."

"I'm sure, but still… I'm carrying a bit too much weight for that. Besides I have two left feet and would probably kill myself or someone else doing what you make look so easy."

Anne chuckled. "That group even has me challenging myself, but we have beginner's classes too, you know. Everyone has to start somewhere. Besides, it's the ultimate for burning off any residual or unwanted fat."

"Sounds tempting, but I'm more into packing on the bulk than burning any of it off," he responded, subconsciously flexing his pectorals beneath his tight-fitting shirt.

Anne was perceptive enough to realise that there was no chance of signing him up any time soon.

"Oh well, if you change your mind, you know where I am."

"That I do," he replied, "and I'll be here a good few times over the next couple of weeks, so I'm sure we'll see each other around."

"Good to know," Anne responded, "I'll see you around then."

Even though he wanted to make more out of this chance interaction, he knew better than to push his luck too soon.

A girl like her was probably hit on all the time and resented the constant pick-up lines and come-ons.

"Well, see you next time," he concluded, heeding his instincts. "And maybe we can even do coffee if we can find the time."

He stepped around her, not waiting for an answer and casually left the building.

Anne stood where she was, a tiny bit confounded by the encounter and yet a little intrigued by the man's brazen, confident, yet nonchalant closing remark.

Who was this guy? she wondered and before she even realised what she was doing, she was heading to the reception desk to search through the active client logs.

Chapter 37

After a brief stop at the supermarket to stock up on some essentials, Julia pulled into the parking spot allocated to her apartment. The bags weren't heavy, but were nonetheless still a little awkward to carry.

Luckily she'd learnt a while back to do part-shopping, as and when she needed something in particular. Lugging bags and bags of groceries from her parking bay to the elevator and then down the passage to her apartment was a lesson she only needed to learn once.

"Hold the lift, please," she called out, noticing a youngish man entering the elevator a little ahead of her.

He turned, stuck his head back out through the doors and smiled at her... not a face she recognised.

He jammed his arm between the doors, preventing them from closing until she had climbed in.

"Hi," she greeted amicably.

"Hi," he replied, pressing his floor number into the key-pad.

He was a lanky young man, probably in his early to mid-twenties. Possibly a year or two younger than herself. His dark wavy hair was untidy but yet not unkempt. He fitted the typical student profile perfectly. Probably working a bit here and there while studying through correspondence. Basically living off daddy's money while exploring opportunities to find his own feet and settle down.

"Third floor," she prompted.

"I'm also on three," he said, indicating the lit button on the key-pad.

"Oh, thank you. I haven't seen you around before," she added.

"New to the neighbourhood," he replied curtly, not offering more.

They stood in silence, as the doors closed fully and the elevator began to ascend.

It wasn't a totally uncomfortable silence as most encounters in an elevator tend to be, but Julia decided it was an opportune moment to get to know a new neighbour.

"I'm Julia," she blurted out.

"I know," he responded. "Julia Swan."

"How's that?" Julia questioned, knitting her eyebrows and suddenly becoming a bit wary of the stranger sharing a very confined space with her.

"It's not what you think," he smiled disarmingly.

"How is that, then?"

"Well, I made a delivery to your apartment the other day. The letter had your name and surname on it."

Julia backed away slightly, not that there were many places to go in a tightly confined metal box.

She was visibly shaken, but still managed to catch a vague whiff of a scent which processed some vivid memories in her head.

"The letter," she spluttered, quickly piecing together the puzzle from a few days back.

"Yes, the letter," he repeated and then elaborated, "I rang the doorbell a few times, but figured after a while that nobody was home, so I left it on your doormat. I presume you got it?" he added.

"Um, yes, I got it. Thank you. Thank you very much."

The elevator dinged and the doors began to open slowly, having arrived at their third-floor destination.

"Was the letter from you?" Julia asked, quite frankly not knowing what his answer would be. Maybe Dan had rented an apartment in her building to get as close to her as possible without attracting any attention. She mulled this over in her mind for a micro-second and then discarded it just as quickly, realising how improbable that would be.

"What do you mean?" he rallied, stepping out into the corridor. "Was there no name on the letter?"

"It's a long story," she countered, "but no, it was anonymous."

"Well, it wasn't from me," he replied quickly, not knowing whether he had incriminated himself in something or not.

"So, what's your name then?" Julia probed, as she also stepped out into the passageway.

"It's Justin. Justin Kearney," he volunteered quickly, hoping that this would clear him of the sudden suspicion he could see in her eyes. "Really," he continued, "I was just handed the letter and asked to deliver it to you on my way up. I saw no harm in that, so I agreed."

"Who gave it to you?"

"Some old lady, at the corner café. I thought nothing of it at the time, but now I'm not so sure."

"And all she asked you to do was to deliver it to me? Nothing else?"

"Nothing," he expounded. "Just simply whether I could deliver the letter to you when I went past your apartment. It seemed innocent enough."

The tables had turned and it was him who felt a bit shaken

now.

What have I unknowingly become involved in? he wondered.

They walked side-by-side in silence until Julia reached her door.

"Well, this is me," she said.

"I know," he replied, his shaky voice betraying him and his initial cocky confidence.

How has she managed to rattle me in such a short space of time? he wondered.

"See you around then… Justin."

"Okay," he responded, instinctively knowing that this would not be the last he would hear about this incident.

Chapter 38

After entering her apartment and going through the protocol of securing all the locking mechanisms on her front door, Julia dumped her shopping bags on the kitchen counter and rifled through her handbag for her cell phone.

She keyed in Ollie's speed dial number and within seconds the big Nigerian's voice crackled in her ear.

"What's up, Jules?"

"Ollie, I just found the guy who delivered the first letter. According to him, he stays in the building, right here with me on the third floor."

"Where are you?" he asked, a little panic rising in his voice.

"I'm at home, Ollie, I'm fine."

"Doors locked?" he queried.

"As safe as Fort Knox," she confirmed.

The relief was evident in his voice when he continued. "So, who is this guy?"

"Well, he claims to be Justin Kearney. He's apparently new here. I'm not sure whether that means he's new to East London or whether he's new to the building."

"We'll check that out easily enough," Ollie assured her.

"He also claimed that the letter was given to him by an old lady down at the corner café, who simply asked him to deliver it to me on his way past."

"Sounds innocuous and about as promising as all the other leads we've had."

"At least those pieces have started falling into place," Julia added, always being positive and looking for the silver lining.

She was never blinded by the colours, but always looked at life through rose-tinted glasses.

Ollie smiled to himself, knowing how important it was for Julia to piece the entire puzzle together. Even when she was younger, it was never good enough for the end to justify the means. She had to know and understand how everything fitted together from start to finish. She'd always had such an enquiring mind.

He loved her like a father loved a daughter. She'd grown up in front of him – in his care – and they'd spent countless hours doing whatever her heart desired.

She'd filled the void in his life which he had believed only his own children could have, and since there were no plans for that ever happening, he was truly indebted to her and the Swans.

"You still need to brief me on the details of the murder, Ollie. I need to start formulating my thoughts for the next article and I need more than just the victim's name."

This abruptly jolted Ollie back from the warm memories lurking deep down in the abyss of his mind.

"Jules, from what I can gather, it was beyond gruesome. The police were even saying that they'd never seen anything like this before."

"Really?"

"Craig Davis was found tethered to a structural pillar in his house. One end of a bungee cord was secured to the pillar in his living room while the other end was tied like a noose around his neck. The top of his head was totally caved in. The investigators believe that he was lifted by his legs, retracted like a catapult and released. The elasticated bungee cord would then snap back and pull him headfirst into the pillar. The blood spatter indicated that this was done more than once."

"That's hideous, Ollie," Julia exclaimed.

Ollie nodded in agreement. "The part they are still unsure about is whether Craig was killed by this repetitive bashing against the pillar and therefore the trauma to his head or whether the noose cut off his air supply and therefore strangled him to death. The petechial haemorrhaging is prevalent but not quite answering that riddle just yet."

Julia shook her head from side to side in disbelief.

"The killer then totally contaminated the crime scene, mostly with all types of biologicals. He must have brought with him a few shoes of varying sizes, some blood and urine samples, as well as hundreds of hairs."

"Any updates on the forensics?" she queried.

"Too soon to tell. The police and the lab have a lot to get through before we'll know anything, but the working theory is that since the strands of hair were clearly from different donors, the blood and urine will prove to be the same. He surely wouldn't make it that easy to identify him."

Julia suddenly changed tack.

"Well, please let me know what you find out about Justin and keep Dad in the loop too."

"Will do, Jules."

"Thanks Ollie – and I really do appreciate all you do for us and especially for me."

With that, she concluded the conversation and hung up.

The warmth of those simple, yet heart-felt, words washed over Ollie and his murmured response of, "Thank you, Jules," fell on deaf ears, as she'd already ended the call.

Julia unpacked her groceries and settled in for the rest of the day.

She might be taking a brief time out, but her thoughts and ideas jostled around in her mind vying for pole position in how she was going to continue with her exposé on Dan, the serial killer, without divulging too much 'insider' information.

Chapter 39

It wasn't the norm for her, but she found herself constantly tuning into radio stations every hour on the hour in the hope of catching some breaking news on the murder in the Nahoon area.

Nothing.

What was taking them so long?

Surely inquisitive neighbours were asking questions?

Surely news teams had heard the rumours and were badgering the police for details?

Surely the police needed to get ahead of this?

She wondered whether anyone had joined the dots to her exposé yet.

Too early, she concluded.

When the details were eventually divulged her exposé would suddenly transpose from fiction to non-fiction and the city-folk would go into high alert. But, as with any event, this wouldn't last very long before life returned to normal.

Hour after hour dragged by and then finally, at eight p.m., the news broke.

It was without much detail, but at least the police spokeswoman confirmed that a man had been found dead in the East London area, after being reported absent from his workplace by his colleagues. The usual tag-line of 'no further details were available at this time as the police were still busy with the investigation' was quoted.

But she did allude to unusual circumstances and probable

foul play.

"Finally," Julia mumbled and sighed with relief.

She found this to be an odd and self-serving response to the press release and frankly she didn't like herself much for responding or feeling like this.

She would never have reacted or felt like this in the past knowing that someone had just lost their life.

What had Dan done to her?

She felt like a monster.

Her job was now predicated on animals like Dan and reporting on their vendettas or revenge.

Suddenly what she did for a living became a reality and she hated herself for it. The public infatuation with gore and misfortune and more so the psychopaths who constantly fuelled these fires.

Gone were the days of genuine newsworthy reporting and the gentler, more joyful, news creating a stir and talkability.

Nowadays the economics of news reporting pivoted solely on depravities and the negativities of life. The more insidious the better.

Life was spiralling out of control without anybody even realising it.

It sickened her.

She now understood why her father was so riled up about this. She had thought at the time that he was over-reacting, but now she saw the light and she, of all people, was facilitating this pandemic.

But what could she do about it?

Dan had taken her free-will away and forced her into doing his bidding. What was worse, was that she would end up with a very good pay check when this concluded.

Julia had wound herself up so tightly that she was on the verge of tears.

Never again, she swore to herself.

She needed to pursue better stories going forward – controversial for sure – but definitely not murders or glamorising evil.

This was the last, she was drawing the line.

She jotted down the details of the news report so she could quote the spokeswoman and the date and time of the breaking news.

She then went online and searched for any other scraps of information on the incident. She was positive that some eager-beaver reporter would have been on site the second there was any hint of a story and it wasn't long before she found exactly what she was looking for.

It was a nice, neat and tidy story penned by someone she had never heard of before. It described the quiet suburban setting, as well as the activities of the police investigators and the forensic team.

It was well researched and included interview snippets with neighbours and furthermore went on to name and describe the owner of the property, although the author was very careful to avoid making assumptions that the owner was the victim.

This was some great work, Julia concluded, and frankly had just saved her a lot of time in probing for the details herself.

Craig Davis, she pondered.

He owned the property and, in all likelihood, resided there.

Could he be victim number one?

Dan had assured her that he was.

But could he be trusted?

Could she put her credibility on the line because he said so?

Not happening, she concluded.

She couldn't afford to make those assumptions, but she could dig into his background and prepare herself for the big reveal if it did turn out to be him.

No social media presence, but this was merely a bump in the road. Julia, like most reporters, had figured out many other ways and means of prying into people's private lives and thus her search began.

After an hour, she had accumulated a fair amount of detail on Craig Davis.

She'd summed him up as married, divorced, no children, a financial broker, little to no social affiliations or activities and a solitary existence.

She looked at the words she had noted down and with pursed lips, shook her head ever so slightly.

A very easy target, she thought.

Craig had to be victim number one.

Based on what she'd discovered, Dan's resentment could not be recent and had to stem from further back in his life, so now the real deep dive would need to begin and she'd have to dissect whatever she could find going right back to Craig's childhood.

And so, the search began.

Chapter 40

Julia was so engrossed in her research and follow-up article that when she finally resurfaced, it was two days later. She had disappeared down a rabbit-hole before, but this time had been chronic. She didn't remember eating, sleeping, bathing, changing her outfit or even brushing her teeth. She'd been all-consumed by this story and her life had effectively come to a standstill although the tell-tale date on her cell phone had discreetly progressed by two. Nobody had phoned her or curiously queried her whereabouts.

Great friends and family I have, she thought to herself.

I could have had a heart-attack, a stroke or maybe even have been lying dead in a puddle of blood and nobody would have been any the wiser.

She knew this wasn't the case though.

Ollie's team was bound to be in the vicinity surveilling her around the clock. They were never evident, but she knew they were always there. Her father would have Ollie's head if anything happened to her under his watch, besides, Ollie would find a way of having his own head if anything happened to her. Just the thought of this warmed her heart and brought a glisten to her eyes.

"Hi, Dad," she said, as Alan answered her call within the first few rings.

"Good morning, my love."

"Sorry, I must've fallen off the radar again."

"We gathered so, not hearing from you for a couple of days. Ollie's guys kept reporting in that you hadn't left the apartment, so we figured you were busy."

"Yes, I started investigating Craig Davis. You know, the owner of the house where the murder took place?"

"Craig Davis, you say? I believe Ollie mentioned that name to me. Do you need any help with your research?"

"Actually, yes, the guy has no social media presence and I hit a wall on his current work portfolio and client list."

Alan paused, the cogs in his brain turning slowly, while tuning into Julia's train of thought.

"You think he might have wronged Dan in a business transaction?"

"I didn't believe so at first, but now I think it might be possible. At this stage, I'm just covering all bases and since he's a financial broker, it crossed my mind that Dan might have been a client and maybe took a bath on an ill-advised investment. It's pure speculation for now."

"Maybe speculation, but quite feasible," Alan replied, knowing all too well the challenges and pitfalls of successful investing in the current economic climate.

"It's definitely an angle to investigate, but who has access to client lists and failed investments?"

"Leave that to me," Alan responded emphatically, "I know people who know people."

"Thanks, Dad. In the meantime I've written the next exposé for Dan and I was wondering whether you'd proof-read it for me."

"Sure thing, Jules, bring it over and I'll give you the best critique I possibly can."

Julia could hear the elation in his voice, brought on by

simply being included in her work and life.

"Is Ollie there?" she followed up curiously.

"Not right now. You need something from the big guy?"

"Maybe. This might be a wild goose chase, but I was wondering whether Ollie, through his contacts, could get more information on Craig's early years. Not much history has been digitised or captured online, so hard copies would be the only source of records. Ollie could then look into his classmates for me. There might be a connection or possible lead there."

"Of course," Alan immediately committed. Ollie would walk on water if he asked him to.

"I also wanted to know if he had found out anything about Justin Kearney yet. You know, the guy who delivered the first letter?"

"He hasn't mentioned anything to me, so either he's clean or he's still being investigated."

"Thanks, Dad, you guys make my life so much easier," she added, stating the absolute obvious, but knowing that just including him in her 'adventures', made his day.

"Right," he replied, "then I'll see you later. Why not come over for dinner? Your mother would love that. If you don't have other plans, that is?" he quickly added, not wanting to impose on her too much.

"You know, that sounds like a great idea. Please let Mavis know there'll be one extra for dinner."

"Consider it done."

"Bye, Dad, and thanks again."

"Goodbye, my love," he said, hanging up the call.

Chapter 41

The gym was starting to quieten down now after the usual morning rush.

Business levels typically ebbed and flowed throughout the day, starting with the usual frantic action on opening. Once all those patrons had left to start their work days, there was an hour or two of recovery, and time to wipe down and straighten up all the equipment. After that it was the turn of the housewives and shift workers, who would generally invade the gym during the mid-morning hours, keeping the staff busy once again.

The afternoon was never very productive, with limited patronage, generally by those less committed. This respite was brief though, as capacity was once again reached after the normal working day ended.

Anne was dressed in her usual Lycra leggings, today a black and pink patterned three-quarter fit, revealing just enough of her calves to make the average woman look twice. A slightly over-sized pink t-shirt hung loosely down past her butt. This would generally be discarded when she had a class, which would then reveal her usual crop top or sports bra and the most enviable abdominals any woman could ever dream of having.

Between classes, she did her rounds in the gym, offering assistance and advice on posture and form wherever needed – mainly to the women.

"Well, well, well, if it isn't Peter Roland," she commented to herself after noticing the bulky man working out on his legs in the corner of the communal area.

She ambled casually over in his direction as though she hadn't noticed him.

"Need any help?" she offered when their eyes met, knowing that the offer was frivolous and nothing more than a conversation starter.

Peter cracked a huge smile.

His smile was near perfect and quite dazzling, as he sported an almost perfect set of pearly-white teeth.

"Yes," he replied, pointing to the loaded leg press machine, "please show me the correct form to lift this."

Anne smiled, knowing full-well that he was having a laugh at her expense. It also looked to her as if the machine was at full capacity and nearing its breaking point.

"I did legs earlier this morning and don't want to overdo it today," she retorted, smiling broadly at her spontaneous comeback and ready wit, "but I can watch you and critique your form."

The smile remained plastered on his face as he enjoyed the banter. Anne was stunning and had a really sharp sense of humour.

A spectacular combination of beauty and brains, he thought.

"It's Peter, isn't it?" she queried, already knowing the answer.

His smile broadened. "So, who's a stalker then?" he challenged.

"Not at all," she responded too quickly. "After our last little encounter, I just happened to mention you to a colleague and they volunteered your name." She was amazed at how easily she could lie, retaining a stoic face throughout and giving nothing away.

"Oh, is that so?"

"Yes, that's so."

"Okay then, let's say I believe you," Peter remarked confidently.

"Okay, let's say you do," Anne parroted him.

"How about that coffee then, after I finish my work out?"

Anne glanced down at her watch. She had some time to spare.

"The juice bar, in half an hour," she said, indicating the Kauai juice bar just off the reception area, with her head.

"Great, it's a date," Peter replied, wiping the sweat off his face with a small hand towel.

"No, it's a juice," Anne countered, not wanting anything labelled at this stage.

"Fine, it's a juice," Peter replied sarcastically.

"See you shortly then."

"Right, see you in half an hour then."

Peter grinned inanely at the interaction, as Anne turned and walked away rather less confidently than when she had approached him.

Peter was right on time and looked as fresh as a daisy. A total contrast to the sweaty behemoth she had spoken to earlier.

Anne already had an orange juice in front of her when Peter sat down, placing his backpack carefully on the floor next to his chair.

"So, what did you order for me?" he asked casually, noticing her half-finished drink in front of her.

"Don't know you that well yet." Anne shrugged. "But I was thirsty so I took the liberty of getting a head-start."

The waitress approached the moment Peter raised his hand.

"Hi, Patty," Peter addressed her, not even glancing at her

name badge.

"Hi, Peter," she replied. "Green tea smoothie?" she added knowingly.

"You got it," he answered, "I need to catch up with Anne here."

Patty smiled professionally at Peter and then turned to Anne, boring into her with her eyes.

Anne frowned, sensing a bit of hostility in the air, but not knowing what she had done to deserve the glare.

Patty swivelled on her heels and headed off to place the order.

"What was that all about?" Anne asked quizzically.

"Oh, nothing much," Peter countered indifferently. "We're just friends. We got talking the other day and she turned out to be quite pleasant."

"Seems like she thinks you're a bit more than friends."

"You think? I never picked up on that vibe before."

"Well it was clearly evident. You ever been here with another woman before?"

"No."

"There's your answer then. She's jealous."

They sat in silence for a moment contemplating the encounter until Patty retuned with the green tea smoothie.

"Your drink, sir," Patty remarked while directing her attention at Anne, every word dripping with contempt.

"Thanks, Patty," Peter replied, her tone sliding off him like water off a duck's back.

Patty stormed off leaving Peter sipping his beverage and Anne totally bewildered.

"Green tea smoothie?" she finally remarked.

"Yup, packed with green tea, spinach, grapes and avocado

and just a hint of honey to offer some well-needed sweetness," he replied, "want a taste?"

"No thanks," Anne replied, being caught slightly off-guard by his impudence.

The conversation, while they finished their drinks, was broad and extremely general, until Anne finally looked at her watch.

"Oh shit," she exclaimed, "I have a class in ten minutes. I need to run."

"I've got the bill, don't worry," Peter stated, noticing that Anne was about to un-zip her wrist-purse.

"Thanks Peter," she replied. "I really need to run. We'll have to do this again sometime," she added, as she turned and scrambled away.

"Look forward to it," Peter shouted after her.

He sat where he was for a moment longer contemplating how well their 'date' had gone. While she had still been a little reserved, he felt that he'd more than made up for it and had effectively navigated the quieter, more awkward moments.

Patty interrupted his thoughts when she suddenly appeared beside him with the bill. He downed the dregs of his beverage and casually placed a R100 note in the bill-fold and told her to keep the change.

She smiled broadly at his generosity and even broader when he winked and silently mouthed the words 'Thank you'.

Chapter 42

The autumn day suddenly turned miserable. The weak sun had simply been overrun by a mass of clouds which now covered the sky in a thick, grey blanket. Rain was uncommon in the autumn and winter months, but not unheard of.

The breeze now picked up quite significantly and the sea became choppy with little white crests punctuating the swells.

Julia had desperately needed some fresh air and to escape from the confines of her apartment. Her dinner date with her family the night before had been great and although they'd tried their best to stay off topic, the conversation always seemed to meander back to Dan, the murder, the evidence and mostly his motive. It was quite disconcerting that of late they had so little else to talk about.

She hadn't left too late and had by all accounts had a decent night's sleep but today she'd felt claustrophobic and her thoughts were again rampaging uncontrollably through her head.

The walk from her apartment down to the promenade was refreshing but now as the breeze picked up, she wished that she'd worn something a little warmer. She shivered ever so slightly, but still gazed out over the ocean. She forced herself to pick up on each and every detail, in an effort to clear her mind.

For a while she became fixated on the sea gulls fluttering and swooping above the waves in search of their next meal. Their flight patterns were totally mesmerising.

In the distance a cargo ship edged slowly along the horizon

probably making its way up the coast to Durban to offload its bounty.

A few couples walked hand-in-hand along the water line leaving a trail of footprints imbedded in their wake. It was cute how couples always held hands when they walked on the beach. Somehow the ambiance always seemed to bring out a bit of romance in people's lives.

Julia suddenly felt quite alone.

She'd had her fair share of romances, but presently wasn't seeing anyone and the romantic scenes playing out before her left her feeling isolated and depressed.

Her phone vibrated in her pocket snapping her back to the present.

She'd once again forgotten to reactivate the sound.

She always switched it to silent when she was busy researching or writing, relying solely on the vibration haptic to alert her to any incoming messages or calls.

She looked at the display. It was Ollie.

"Hi, Ollie," she answered cheerfully, placing her self-pity on hold.

"Enjoying the view?" he responded, catching her squarely off-guard with this question.

She looked around, intently scanning her surroundings for the whereabouts of the big guy.

"I'm not there," he added, vividly picturing her looking around to find him. "I just got an update from the guys on where you were and what you were doing."

"Just getting some fresh air and at the same time wallowing in a bit of self-pity."

"Sounds like you could do with some company."

"No, I'm good, thanks. I just really needed to get out of the apartment and focus a bit on myself again."

"You sure, Jules, you sound so depressed? Maybe a distraction is needed? We could go for ice-creams," he offered in his most tempting tone. "Like we used to when you were younger and feeling a bit down. Maybe relive some of the good old times?"

"I'm too old for that now, Ollie... but you know what?" she said, after reconsidering his proposition, "let's do it anyway."

"Great... so where should we go?"

"You surprise me. I'll wait where I am and you come fetch me."

"Done. See you in a few minutes."

As promised, Ollie arrived in a matter of minutes. It made Julia wonder whether he was nearby all along, keeping that ever unobtrusive eye on her.

"So, Wimpy, Windmill Roadhouse or the number one rated Friesland Dairy Bar?" he enquired with a twinkle in his eye.

"Your call," she replied, already knowing where they'd be heading.

The big guy had a thing for the Friesland Dairy Bar and never needed much more than an excuse to pay them a visit.

"Then it's the Friesland Dairy Bar," he answered unsurprisingly and pulled away from the kerb.

The ice-creams were fantastic and for a long while they just sat in silence, licking the cold, creamy, smooth delights.

"Justin Kearney," Ollie finally murmured between licks.

"Yes?" Julia answered questioningly, raising her eye-brows.

"Nothing to him."

"What do you mean, nothing to him?"

"Totally harmless. He's not Dan."

"What did you find out?"

"Well, simple middle class up-bringing. Finished school. Went on to complete his B-Comm Degree through UNISA. Moved to East London. Bounced around between jobs for a while and then finally ended up in his current marketing job and when he started making some decent money, he moved into your apartment building. Like I said… nothing to him." He shrugged.

Julia frowned. "Another waste of time and dead-end lead."

Ollie could see the frustration on her face.

"Don't worry, Jules," he consoled her, "we'll get the break we need. We just need to play the waiting game for now. This guy will slip up sooner or later and we'll be on him in a flash."

"I truly hope you're right, Ollie. This is really starting to wear me down."

"I know. And he'll pay for it when we finally pick up on his trail."

He put a fatherly arm around her shoulders and gave her a reassuring squeeze.

"We've got this."

They spent the rest of the afternoon reminiscing about years gone by. It was immensely therapeutic just sitting, chatting and enjoying each other's company. Ollie made certain that the conversation steered clear of current events and could clearly see the stress start leaving Julia. She finally began to relax. She needed this and he was happy that he could play such a pivotal role in her therapy.

Chapter 43

It was just after eight a.m. when Julia arrived at the *Daily Dispatch* offices. She sat in her car in the parking lot and took a few slow, deep breaths to compose herself. In her right hand she clutched the memory stick. Hours and hours had become days and days of research to support her article residing in this micro-device. She had not risked emailing any of it to Moses this time. The data and detail was becoming more and more sensitive and extreme, and although she was protected by the latest and greatest anti-virus software, she could not vouch for the security of the data once it left her device and wound its way through cyber-space to its destination.

Moses was generally in his office quite early in the morning and she hoped that today was one of those days. She hadn't even made an appointment to see him. She knew that this could be construed as impudent, but she'd decided to take her chances nonetheless. Over and above that, she also hoped that he had no early meetings lined up. She really needed him to squeeze her in.

As luck would have it, he was in his office early, he had no meetings lined up and he was more than happy to indulge her and discuss her article.

She shook her head subconsciously, thinking to herself how wonderful a human being and boss he was.

Julia spent the entire morning with Moses, discussing her follow-up article and which angle would be the best for the news provider.

"It needs to be as objective as possible," Moses insisted.

"I understand," Julia agreed, "but Dan is holding all the cards here and he wants this to be as subjective as possible to illustrate the point he is trying to make."

"We can't glamourise his actions or even be seen to condone what he is doing."

"I know, I've been facing that conundrum for days now. That's why I did all the research and have painted such a broad background in the article. It's not to condone his action, but more to ensure that the public are aware of the crisis we're facing as a country and thereby give context to his actions. We have the DNA Act in place now, but if we can't enforce it or reap results from it, then it's totally ineffective."

"It still boils down to the same issue. While giving context allows a greater measure of understanding, it ultimately condones his actions as necessary."

It wasn't an argument as much as a spirited debate, but Julia had one last ace up her sleeve.

"It really irks me to say this, but we currently have the inside track on this story and much more detail and insight than any of the other news providers. We have to capitalise on that. For his own reasons Dan has confided in me and as long as he is still confident in my reporting, we can't miss out on this opportunity."

"Okay, fine," Moses finally conceded. "But somehow you need to tweak your article to shift the focus more to the murder than the murderer. I know Dan wants the attention…" he raised his hand to prevent her from interrupting "… but we can't have him being portrayed as some kind of saviour on a well-intentioned crusade."

He continued, "Concentrate on the bizarre manner in which Craig Davis was murdered, the staged and contaminated crime scene and then finally include Dan's reasons for doing all of this."

"Done and done," Julia replied, knowing that the story was ninety per cent there already and only minor focus shifts were required.

She knew this would antagonise Dan though and she actually feared the repercussions, but he would just have to understand that she also had constraints and needed a platform to publish his 'activities' and that platform came with its customs, rules and ethics.

"Great, then I'll get this to you first thing tomorrow morning then."

"The sooner the better," Moses added, knowing how big this story was and how important it was for them to stay ahead of the other newscasters.

"I'll send it as soon as I'm done then," Julia agreed and while indicating with a sideways glance and raised eyebrows, added, "you might want to keep the memory stick with the supporting research for future reference or clarity."

"Good work, Julia. Really good work," Moses said, as Julia turned to leave his office.

"Thank you, Moses," she noted and then added, "and thank you for making time for me today. I know it was impromptu and I know you're busy, but I had to take the chance that you could make time to see me."

Moses smiled and dismissed her gratitude and comments with an indifferent wave of his hand.

Chapter 44

Julia's article exploded over the internet.

Moses sat in his chair raptly watching his computer screen. He had never seen the hit counter on *DispatchLive* go bananas like this before and he could hardly contain himself. He so badly wanted to phone Julia to let her know, but he couldn't tear his attention away from the odometer ticking steadily over as each hit on the website was counted.

He had heard that registrations and subscriptions had recently been on the increase, but hadn't as yet put two and two together.

He had now.

Julia's first article had been the appetiser and had created the interest and talkability. Now that the main course was served, the appetite of the public was insatiable.

They had struck gold.

He could barely contain his ebullience.

This also couldn't only be Eastern Cape clientele. The population was too small to generate these numbers. This story had gone national – possibly even international. He would have to analyse the statistics as soon as they were made available. But for now he could only sit in awe, riveted to the monitor before him.

Across town, Julia had been logged in for hours already, waiting in anticipation for the site to be updated.

She had managed to get the revised article through to Moses

at around eleven p.m. the previous night.

It was now just a matter of time, she consoled herself.

She had slept in fits and starts and had risen early after what could only be classified as a totally restless night's sleep.

She was well into her second cup of coffee when the breaking news article was activated. The home page refreshed to include her story and simultaneously a shrill bleep notified her of the update – rather redundant under the circumstances.

Julia read her article, even though she could practically recite it word for word.

It was intimately familiar to her after dedicating so many hours to its revision, editing and proof-reading.

She smiled to herself.

It was good.

Hell, it was brilliant, even if she thought so herself.

Her thoughts suddenly drifted to Moses.

I wonder what he thought of it, she wondered.

He must've liked it, she immediately concluded. *After all he was the one who had approved it and forwarded it on for publication.*

She had heeded his advice and instruction and had turned the story on its head.

The murder, evidence and crime scene were now at the forefront of the article with Dan playing a more secondary – you might say, almost insignificant – role.

As a result it was untouched by Moses. He had made no changes at all.

The words, syntax and grammar were all her own.

Julia's phone started buzzing minutes later.

She fielded calls from her father, her mother and her friends.

The accolades flowed in thick and fast, and containing her

pride was becoming more and more challenging. She'd never needed validation in the past from anyone where her actions or achievements were concerned, but since this had been such an ordeal, the compliments somehow fortified her and endorsed her efforts.

It was wonderful hearing from all the people she loved so dearly.

A sudden premonition flooded over her. It was a vivid sense of how Dan would be feeling after reading her article.

He would be seething.

He claimed that his actions were justified and that he was on this crusade for the greater good, but it was clearly evident from his letters that a large portion of the publicity was to fluff his own ego.

He wanted the story to be about him and how he was making a statement to change the status quo for the benefit of everyone else.

His response would be undeniably vicious and she wondered whether she'd be ready for it or, more importantly, in danger now.

She already felt quite traumatised and the ordeal had only just begun.

Would his verbosity be muted?

Would his words turn into actions?

Would his anger now be directed at her?

Her initial elation abated as rapidly as it had begun.

She'd gone and let him set up house again in her mind and it intimidated and scared her.

She had to find a way of permanently evicting him from her life. He had no right to invade and monopolise her every thought and more so hold her captive like this.

She looked down at her hands – they were shaking.

A slight tremble, but a nervous, fearful tremble nonetheless.

It all became too much for her.

The emotional turmoil comingled with her fatigue and drowsiness were overwhelming.

She lay down on the couch and within seconds was out like a light.

Chapter 45

A loud knock on the door roused Julia from her sleep.

She opened her eyes wearily, blinking repeatedly to regain some focus.

The room was dark, even though she noticed that the curtains were still open. *Where had the day gone?*

Julia looked curiously at her watch – it was six thirty p.m. already.

Had she really slept the whole day away?

She rubbed her eyes with her knuckles and then worked a bit more fervently with her little fingers, at the build-up of crusty debris in the corner of her eyes.

"Hold on!" she shouted, as the incessant knocking continued. "I'm coming."

She worked her way around the room switching on the lounge lamps, forcing the darkness to retreat into the unlit corners of the room.

She peaked through the peep-hole in the door and sighed deeply.

Was she really up for this?

Then it became a battle with the door locks again.

It really was like Fort Knox, but for good reason. And she knew it.

Cathy, Anne and Sam stood sheepishly on the other side of the security gate, all grinning inanely at Julia.

"We've come to celebrate," Cathy erupted.

"What a masterpiece," enthused Sam.

"We've read it a dozen times each," added Anne, without exaggeration, "and each time we have more questions than before."

They all nodded in unison, silently concurring with Anne's sentiments.

"You look tired, babe," Cathy continued, "Looks like we woke you."

"You did," Julia replied, although her lop-sided smile conveyed that there were no hard feelings. "The exhaustion just caught up with me and I fell asleep over there," she added, stretching her stiff neck from side to side and indicating the couch which still boasted the indentation of her body.

She blamed it all on her tiredness.

She didn't want to let on how mentally anguished and emotionally distressed she actually was.

She should never have 'named' him.

It had personified him.

'Fear of a name only increases fear of the thing itself.'

These words, by Hermione Granger in the Harry Potter series, rang true in her mind, but she fought back her emotions in the presence of her friends.

The girls poured the wine while she freshened up in the bathroom. She felt like a bus had driven over her, but the cool water she splashed on her face staved off some of the stubborn fatigue.

"How did you get up here anyway?"

"Come on, Jules," Sam answered matter-of-factly, "Phineas probably knows us better than some of the residents who stay here permanently."

"You could get him into trouble... breaking the rules like

that."

"Oh come on, who's going to tell? Besides, he really enjoyed the idea of us wanting to surprise you," added Cathy.

"Especially when we showed him the wine," said Anne, passing the freshly poured glasses around.

"Anyway, cheers, my friend," Cathy continued. "To a job well done!"

They all raised their glasses and clinked them together to acknowledge the toast.

One thing you couldn't say about Cathy was that she was slow out of the blocks... and persistent.

She immediately pressed Julia for more details on her article.

"Is the state of our forensics as bad as you say?"

"It seems so, from all the research I've done, even though we had and probably still have state of the art facilities."

"So, what's the problem then?"

"Crime scene contamination, lack of training for those collecting the evidence, lack of personnel, under-qualified forensic technicians, insufficient budget, an insurmountable workload, no follow-up on results. Tell me when to stop."

"Ouch," Sam interjected, "so these are the statements Dan is trying to make?"

"It would appear so, even though his methods are totally counter-productive. All he's doing is adding to the workload and compounding the problem."

"Have they managed to get some results from the evidence collected?" questioned Anne.

"As far as I've been told, the analysis of this evidence has been prioritised, but we're all still waiting anxiously for some feedback and results."

They all sat in silence for a while, pondering the situation and its implications.

"Calls for more wine," Sam finally added, shattering the silencing and startling the others.

The smokers exited the apartment to get their fix on the balcony, which was usually the preferred spot for their visits anyway. It was furnished with an outdoor weather-proofed table and four chairs. It was only just spacious enough to accommodate the four of them and a small braai. The South African pastime of having a few drinks and cooking meat on an open fire was commonplace and an area dedicated to this pastime was, for all intents and purposes, essential in every household.

Unfortunately for the smokers, the autumn chill prevented this tonight.

Anne and Julia, meanwhile, refilled the wine glasses and ordered a few pizzas.

Mr Delivery had become an integral service for fast food outlets and many would rather pay for the service than be bothered with ordering and collecting their own food.

It would take thirty minutes, which suited them perfectly.

Cathy and Sam lit their second cigarettes.

These days, when an opportunity to smoke presented itself, you had to make the most of it, and they did just that.

Even though it was a brightly lit night, they couldn't really make out the ocean, but the sound of the waves crashing in the distance was quite mesmerising.

"I can't quite grasp what Jules is going through here," Cathy commented between puffs on her cigarette.

"Me neither," Sam concurred, "and to think, this could just be the beginning."

"Don't you think Dan has made his point already?"

"I would think so, but according to his first letter, there could be a few more scores to settle."

"That's just it, though? Is it now a case of continuing to make a point or just an excuse to settle old scores?"

"I think it's a vendetta under the guise of making a point," Sam concluded. "I can't believe that it started out as such, but now that his point has been made, what other purpose would there be for an ongoing crusade?"

"And he's certainly getting all the mileage possible with Jules providing insights and running commentary."

"Agreed. There'd be no other reason."

"Bloodlust. Media sensationalism. Take your pick. He's had a taste of it all now."

They stubbed out their cigarettes in the flip-top ashtray, which was designed to contain the butts and smells, and went indoors to re-join the others.

On leaving, as was their routine, they would empty and wash the ashtray and bag all the debris for disposal in the trash skip outside the apartment building.

Considerate and well trained you might say.

Chapter 46

Dan once again sat in the mom and pop coffee shop, this time reflecting over the article Julia had written and what his response should be.

"Your usual, sir?" the waitress asked.

"Just coffee for now, thanks, Sharon," he answered without looking up from his iPad.

She was impressed that he had remembered her name without even glancing up at her.

"Coming right up," she responded, suppressing a broad smile.

Within minutes she had returned with his order.

Know your customers and know what they want, he thought to himself.

Personable and friendly didn't hurt either.

Best advice for anyone in a sales position.

The coffee was good. Actually, it was excellent.

The coffee shop was still quiet and he'd purposefully selected a table in the far-right corner of the establishment with the intent of having his back to the wall to ensure his privacy.

Julia's article was intriguing.

Her facts were undeniably accurate, but that's where the article flopped. It would captivate the average Joe, but to him, it was dry and impersonal. He was expecting a bit more. The facts were the facts, but that's where the story ended.

As a reader, he'd want to know more.

Why had she not divulged the detail?

She knew why he'd killed Craig. She even knew how he'd killed Craig. Lastly, and most importantly, she'd known that he'd manipulated the evidence left at the crime scene and the reasons for doing that.

Yet there was nothing in her article about any of that.

She'd merely captured the facts.

Any two-bit reporter could have written this.

A man was found dead, presumed murdered.

This was his address.

The evidence was sent to Cape Town for further analysis.

Game, set, match.

He could feel his face gradually redden with anger as these thoughts slowly worked their way through the synapses of his brain.

"Anything wrong?" Sharon questioned on a routine walk-by.

"No," he snapped. "Everything's just great!"

She flinched at this sudden eruption, not knowing what she'd done since their previous encounter.

Dan knew it wasn't her fault, but he felt slightly better after taking his frustrations out on someone else.

Humans were strange creatures; garnering pleasure out of demeaning each other.

As Sharon skulked away, his thoughts returned to the point in question.

There was so much more to the story, so much meat she'd left on the bone.

Her report was leaps and bounds ahead of the others he'd read, as she'd dwelt quite extensively on crucial aspects like the DNA Act, forensic analysis and the predominant shortfalls currently experienced in the South African environment. But it wasn't enough.

A neatly dressed couple walked in and sat at the table

alongside him. The man wore dark blue formal trousers and a light blue open neck shirt, while the lady donned a very professional grey pantsuit.

It could possibly be a breakfast meeting between two colleagues or even a 'breakfast before work' tryst between spouses or lovers.

No matter which, the man was attentive and polite, as he pulled out the chair for the woman to seat herself.

Who said chivalry was dead?

They politely greeted Dan when he looked up and made eye contact with them, even though the scowl on his face sternly warned them off.

He was in no mood for small talk with strangers and wanted to make that quite clear from the get-go.

Sharon was quick to make a turn to attend to the new arrivals and after taking their drinks order, again offered to get Dan his usual breakfast order.

"Just toast and a refill," he muttered, having totally lost his appetite.

Sharon skulked off to place the orders, leaving the couple to make small talk and Dan to wallow in whatever had just upset him.

He fingered the iPad screen, paging from one article to the next and then it suddenly dawned on him.

He had chastised Julia for using the silly DNA Dan moniker and now she couldn't or didn't know how to refer to him without fear of retribution.

No wonder it's all factual.

How stupid of me?

With this realisation, his anger slowly dissipated and when Sharon dropped off his order, he was all smiles again.

"Thank you, Sharon."

She just shook her head and walked away.

Chapter 47

Julia jumped, as her phone suddenly began to vibrate in her pocket.

She'd been straightening up and cleaning her apartment after the exhaustive gathering the previous night.

She'd been quizzed six ways to Sunday by Cathy, Anne and Sam and had been totally drained by the time they finally left.

"Hello?"

"Hello, Jules," replied the familiar gruff Nigerian voice of Ollie.

"Hi, Ollie, what's up?"

"We finally have some feedback on the forensics, Jules," he answered. "I just got off the phone with Detective Phiri."

"Please tell me we have him," she implored.

"I can't do that, Jules."

She exhaled disappointedly.

"All the shoe-prints were staged. The shoe sizes ranged from a toddler's size two to an adult male's size fourteen, accompanied by many of the variations in between."

"His must be in there somewhere."

"I'm sure it is, but which one?"

"What else?"

"Hair – lots of it. All colours and lengths. You couldn't find a bigger variety if you swept the floor of a barbershop, which is probably what he did."

"Any DNA hits on the hair?"

"They're still busy, but so far not too many positives. Most of the donors are probably not in the system anyway. You're well aware of the state of our databases by now."

"Which leaves us where?" Julia wailed in exasperation.

"The blood and the urine," Ollie replied thoughtfully.

Julia waited for him to continue.

"Well, there definitely weren't as many 'donors' as with the hair samples, so the analysts believe that their best chances in finding a match will come from these bodily fluids."

"But the reliance still rests on whether a match will be found in a limited and unreliable database, right?"

"Exactly," Ollie confirmed. "There's no guarantee that Dan's DNA has ever been captured or, for that matter, retained."

"He must be in there somewhere. He claimed to have left some valuable clues which could be useful in identifying him," Julia prompted.

"He probably did, but forensically speaking, it might not even be possible to tie them back to him."

"Unless we get a sample from him," Julia added, "and how do we do that, if we don't have the faintest idea who he is?"

She started pacing the room in utter frustration.

"This is high priority, Jules, so they're doing the best that they can under the circumstances."

"It's not good enough, Ollie – and I'm not blaming them – even after all the hard work we'll probably circle back to a 'no match found' outcome, as he won't be in the database."

"You're right, Jules, linking all the evidence won't necessarily give us a name. From a DNA perspective, we could know exactly who committed this crime, but never know who he is."

"Damn, this is so frustrating," Julia blurted out loudly.

"Finger-prints would have been the most definitive, as everyone with an ID or driver's licence has them on file, but as expected, the scene was scrubbed clean and didn't give up a single print besides those of Craig Davis," added Ollie.

"So, what do we do now?" questioned Julia.

"Nothing much we can do, except wait for further analyses or for Dan to slip up."

This was not what Julia wanted to hear.

"Ollie, I can't take this much longer. This animal has me caught up in his exploits, broadcasting his wrong-doings to the world and what's worse, is that I'm getting accolades for reporting on these heinous events."

Julia burst into tears and Ollie's heart broke.

He so badly wanted to be there for her. He so badly needed to be there for her.

"I'm sorry, Jules, we're doing everything possible to get this guy. He just stays one step ahead of us all the time."

"I'm sure he'll make contact again," she sniffed. "I really think the last article will have pissed him off properly."

It wasn't often that Julia let her emotions get the better of her, let alone spew profanities, but this was evidently one of those times.

"And hopefully he'll slip up and we'll have something more substantial to go on," Ollie added – and then we'll break every bone in his measly little body – he thought to himself.

By this time Julia had regained her composure and with one final blow of her nose, she said, "Thanks for getting back to me and keeping me in the loop, Ollie. I know you've got my back, but please be extra vigilant now, as I believe I've really annoyed Dan with this last article. He would've wanted the story to be about him, but Moses instructed me to downplay his part and concentrate mostly on the facts. It will rile him, I just know it."

"Don't worry yourself about that, Jules. We have you covered… morning, noon and night."

"Thanks, Ollie," Julia concluded and hung up.

Chapter 48

Julia padded around her apartment like a zombie.

Her good intentions of doing a thorough clean up were now as distant as her thoughts were.

She tried unsuccessfully to distract herself with making breakfast, watching television and even reading a couple of the latest unrelated news articles.

It was all in vain though, as her thoughts kept drifting back to Dan.

The long, hot shower didn't even work. She leaned her head against the far wall letting the powerful jet of water beat down on the back of her neck and willed the stream to massage her stress away, but to no avail. She finally scrubbed mercilessly at her skin with the loofah until she was bright pink all over, but not even an external purging could make her feel better.

He was in her head and that's where he now lived.

Only a handful of cars populated the parking bays when she arrived downstairs. The majority of the tenants were still of a working age and had left hours before to keep the wheels of industry turning.

She hadn't planned to go anywhere in particular. She just needed to get out and drive.

Phineas waved and smiled broadly as she exited the complex, but she was in no mood to socialise with him, or anyone for that matter.

A polite wave in return was all she could muster.

Once she turned onto the open road, she turned her music up high, rolled down her window and allowed the tunes and wind to overwhelm her senses.

A good while later, she realised in dismay that she was on the N6 highway heading to Stutterheim.

How had this happened?

She had no recollection of any part of the journey.

The deafening music along with the wind blowing gales through the opened window and mussing her hair, had totally engulfed and cleansed her.

Looking down at the speedometer, she also noticed that she'd unconsciously and quite recklessly been speeding and quickly slowed the vehicle down to comply with the speed limit.

At this revised speed, she could admire the country-side and scenery through which she was travelling.

It was a lovely part of the country.

The farmlands on either side of the highway were picturesque.

The pastures were a collage of vibrant shades of green after the great summer rainfall the area had received.

Dirt roads and fence-lines sliced between the adjoining fields and created the most breath-taking farmland mosaics.

The occasional farmer's truck or tractor navigated the farm roads casually going about their daily tasks, while seemingly oblivious to the hustle and bustle of the outside world.

Cattle, mostly dairy herds, congregated in some of the meadows, grazing leisurely and chewing their cud without a care in the world.

Julia wished she could be that care-free.

A cow would only care about the basic necessities of life – eating, drinking, sleeping and procreating.

How the human race had complicated the world for themselves.

So much for being the most intelligent species.

The Bluetooth enabled stereo system in her car suddenly interrupted the music with the ringing of an incoming call.

Julia punched the 'answer call' button.

"Going somewhere, Julia?" her father's voice questioned over the speaker-system.

"Dad?" Julia responded surprisingly.

"You didn't think we'd let you slip off the radar, did you?"

Julia had to smile.

She was slightly annoyed that her cell phone had been bugged and tracked, but at the same time was pleasantly relieved to know that her father and Ollie were looking out for her.

"Just out driving," she answered. "Didn't plan to end up here, but it's obviously where the world needed me to be right now."

"Been there," Alan replied, not meaning her exact destination, but more so having needed to just get away from it all and clear his head.

"It's so beautiful out here," she continued, as she gazed out the window at the panoramic view while simultaneously driving and talking.

"That's nature for you. It has a very soothing effect. Why do you think I built the gazebo at the bottom of the garden facing away from the house and civilisation?"

"I know, Dad. No need to go off on your earthing tangent again."

"It's been scientifically proven, Julia," Alan said through the smile he had on his face. "Contact with the earth is vitally important and all we do is insulate ourselves from it the whole time."

Julia sighed audibly and Alan swallowed back his follow-up statement.

"Okay, so where are you going and when will you be back?" he asked.

"I didn't even realise where I was until just now. I'll be turning back any time soon," she replied.

"Okay, I'll let Ollie know not to worry too much."

"Don't tell me I have a tail?" It was more a statement than a question.

"They're about two kilometres behind you according to their last update and don't be upset, you know as well as I do that you need protection now more than ever before."

"I know, Dad. I'm not upset. I even asked Ollie this morning to be more vigilant than usual."

Alan was elated that Julia had finally realised that her safety had been compromised and had subsequently conceded to his initial wishes and plan.

"All that's left is for you to move home for a while then," he pressed on.

"Don't push it now, old man," she responded jokingly.

"Okay, chat soon then and drive safely."

"Bye," she answered and ended the call.

Chapter 49

Russell Dwyer sat alone in his garage tinkering on his latest project. It was his place of refuge. A man cave of sorts, but not like any other man cave.

Instead of a bar and fully stocked fridge, he had an electronics workbench.

Instead of a big screen TV on the one wall, he had drawers and drawers full of electronic components.

Instead of vintage and neon signage adorning the other walls, he had huge tool boards with all his tools hanging in a very orderly manner.

Instead of comfortable recliners with side tables, he had a central height-adjustable fabrication platform for his bigger projects.

It was good for a man to have a hobby – but his hobby had become an obsession.

He had longed for the day when his kids no longer demanded all of his time and attention.

Most parents dread that imminent day when their children become more independent and have their own friends and consequently require less and less attention from Mommy and Daddy.

That time couldn't have come soon enough for Russell.

It wasn't as though he didn't love his children or devote time to them when it was required, but he didn't miss the constant badgering of young children.

'Look at me, Daddy.'

'Is this right, Daddy?'

'What are you doing, Daddy?'

'Can I have this, Daddy?'

'Come play with me, Daddy.'

Those days couldn't have ended soon enough.

He needed his own space and now he had it.

He wasn't anti-social by nature, but could spend hours whiling away his time in his garage – no company required.

Russell and Penny were in their early twenties when they tied the knot. They hadn't rushed their courtship, but once it had run its course and when it had felt right, they had followed through and made the ultimate commitment to one another.

Christopher was born a year later, followed closely by Mary-Anne nineteen months after that.

It was absolute chaos in the house for the first few years and coping with two babies really took its toll on the young couple, but like most families they put on brave faces and soldiered on through it.

It was only now that both children were in their early teens that they both had a bit of time on their hands.

Penny loved her arts and crafts and, as a compromise for Russell taking over the garage, they had refurbished one of the bedrooms in the house to fulfil her requirements.

The room generally looked like a bomb had exploded in it. Paper, cardboard, material and essentially any off-cut of anything, no matter the size or shape, was stacked here, there and everywhere, awaiting future use.

An arts and crafts aficionado never throws anything away.

To an outsider it looked a mess and very disorderly, but to Penny the storage methodology made all the sense in the world.

The floor was tiled for practicality, but old stained sheets were often spread out in a mostly ineffectual attempt to prevent paint and other liquid spillages from blemishing the tiled surface.

Besides the laminated work table positioned against one wall, there were also easels, palettes, paints and brushes ready for use against another wall.

Various works of art – completed or works-in-progress – haphazardly adorned the walls.

The state of this room depicted hours of messy fun.

Mary-Anne, having been exposed to arts and crafts her entire life, had caught the bug many years prior and consequently now spent a lot of time with her mother in – what was now called – 'their room'.

Chris was the odd one out.

He showed no interest in either of his parents' hobbies.

He didn't have a creative or inventive bone in his body – but this hardly fazed him – he was an academic, through and through.

When he was not out with his friends getting up to mischief, as typical boys do, he was in his room, ear-pods in place, devouring text-books, theories, and papers, way more progressive and advanced than expected for a child his age.

Chris had already been recognised as a child-prodigy for his advanced intellect, which really irked his little sister. It was more than simple sibling rivalry or jealousy. She felt she was justifiably annoyed.

At her tender young age, she was already an accomplished artist and had won numerous art exhibitions and had even sold a few paintings, but being creatively brilliant seemingly did not measure up to being intellectually brilliant, which she felt was grossly unfair.

These unusual challenges aside, the Dwyer family was like

many others. A loving couple with two teenage children, living a comfortable life in a four-bedroom house in a middle-class suburb, while occupying their spare time on the pursuits they individually enjoyed.

Life seemed good.

Chapter 50

It was late in the afternoon when Peter and Anne met for another of their non-date, juice bar 'dates'.

Anne had managed to squeeze in a quick thirty-minute break before her late class.

It was that quiet twilight period before the evening masses arrived after toiling away the entire day in their offices or other places of work.

Most of the staff were diligently straightening up and cleaning all the equipment before the imminent evening rush.

She had done her bit a little earlier immediately after her last class. Her domain had been swept and mopped and was currently spotless and prepared for her next session.

It was only a question of time though until the droplets of sweat would again sully her floor and the cycle would repeat.

"So, is it a date this time?" he prompted, as she strolled up to the table looking as breath-taking as ever.

"No, it's still not a date," she countered, trying to hold her composure as his dazzling smile nearly caused her to cave.

They had become more and more comfortable with each other in recent days and the chemistry was evident to all and sundry.

Their 'dates', however, were still confined to the juice bar at the gym, where they remained resolutely in their comfort zones.

"Well, if this is not a date yet, maybe we should take it to the next level," Peter prompted.

"And what next level is that?" Anne queried in an effort to tease the answer out of him.

"How about dinner sometime?" he replied.

Anne looked around, making sure nobody was watching or listening – especially Patty. She had been a real nutcase lately when she'd seen them together. Peter claimed he couldn't see it, but to Anne it was as clear as crystal could get.

Nobody was nearby. In fact, the juice bar was practically deserted at this hour.

The calm before the storm for them as well, Anne thought.

"Okay, let's do it," Anne finally replied, "let's do dinner."

"Great," Peter replied. "Any preferences?"

"You choose, but not tonight, Peter, I have a class soon and I need a 'date-appropriate' outfit," she smiled and fluttered her eye-lashes at him.

He nodded supportively, although knowing that she'd look absolutely gorgeous in anything she decided to wear.

"Well, then it's dinner for one tonight," he said through pursed lips while sighing deeply to enhance the point.

Anne laughed. "Afraid so, what's on the menu then?"

"I'll probably just slum it and hit some burger joint on the way home," he answered indecisively, "or just phone in an order."

She actually felt sorry for him, even though she knew that he was just playing on her emotions.

"Well, when can you squeeze in this dinner date then?" he asked.

"I'll get back to you on that soon. I first need to get a stand-in for my late class and then find something to wear. Not easy when sportswear and casual clothes are all you own," she confessed.

He chuckled at this.

It had never dawned on him that someone like Anne would have clothing, or lack of clothing, issues.

The arrival of Patty, to check on them, disrupted their conversation and the jovial banter.

"Everything all right here?" she asked, almost too cordially.

"Fine, thanks," Peter replied. "We're just finishing up."

"Oh, then let me get the bill for you then."

Peter nodded and watched her as she turned and walked away.

Anne couldn't help but get the feeling that there was more to Peter and Patty than he let on, but they weren't at that stage in their relationship where she could ask such a personal question.

Relationship?

Had she really just classed what they had as a relationship?

Well, that was progress for her.

It was heading for six p.m. when she looked at her watch and the evening patronage was now steadily filtering in. She needed to shake a leg and get herself prepared for the upcoming advanced class, which would have them all, bar none, drenched with sweat.

He nodded knowingly when she looked at her watch. She had to leave.

As was now routine, there were no long goodbyes between them.

Peter paid the bill and they parted company with a generic 'see you, then'.

It was cheesy, but breaking out of a comfort zone was never an easy thing to do.

Chapter 51

Julia pulled into the drive just as the late afternoon sun was setting behind her. It had been a long, but pleasant, day. The drive in the country-side had done her the world of good and she felt refreshed and almost back in charge of her life.

Wind gusting through your hair, loud music and singing at the top of your lungs.

Who would have guessed?

This non-medicinal prescription proved to be the best stress reliever ever. She would definitely be doing that again.

Maybe her dad had a point. Getting in touch with nature was indeed medicine for the soul.

She would possibly try it more often, but she'd never admit it though.

She'd never hear the end of it. Her dad would have a field day rubbing it in.

Phineas was just about to end his shift, but quickly raced out of the guard-hut as she drove in.

She automatically thumbed the remote on her key fob and the electric gate motor kicked in. But before she could proceed, Phineas appeared at her window, urgently motioning her to roll it down with a circular hand motion.

Even though the electric window had replaced the outdated window winder decades before, this circular hand motion was still somehow the universal sign for 'please wind down your vehicle's window'.

This struck Julia as very odd.

What's up with Phineas, she wondered.

"Hi Phineas, what's the matter?" she asked apprehensively, as the window rolled down.

"Mr Delivery for you, Ma' Julia," Phineas responded, holding up a bag of take-out food to the car window.

"I didn't order any food, Phineas," she replied, frowning in confusion.

"It arrived for you fifteen minutes ago," Phineas continued, looking down at the very old and scratched watch he sported on his left wrist.

Julia's gaze followed his to his watch and she immediately made a mental note to buy him something better and a bit more modern for his next birthday.

"But, I didn't order anything," she repeated.

"I kept it warm in the guard-hut for you," Phineas continued unfazed, not picking up on the confusion or consternation in her voice.

As was his nature, he just wanted to please.

Julia considered telling Phineas to keep the food, but then another thought suddenly struck her.

"How much did you have to pay for it?" she asked, reaching for her purse on the passenger seat.

She couldn't allow Phineas to be out of pocket. He was already struggling on his meagre wages.

"Nothing, Ma' Julia. The driver said it was already paid for when I told him you weren't home and that he had to leave it with me."

Julia frowned again in dismay.

Who had ordered food for her and who would have paid for it?

Who would even have known that she wasn't home and hadn't prepared anything for dinner?

Finally the penny dropped and she nodded ever so slightly.

It must be her dad. He knew where she'd been and that she probably wouldn't want to cook anything when she arrived home.

He obviously thought he'd save her the trouble of either cooking or ordering out or possibly even going to bed on an empty stomach.

He cared too much for her for that to happen.

She dipped into her purse and came out with a R50 note, which she handed over to Phineas in return for the bag.

Phineas looked confused, "I didn't pay anything for it, Ma' Julia," he clarified.

"I know, Phineas, it's just my way of saying 'thank you'."

"Thank you, thank you, Ma' Julia," he exclaimed, nearly jumping with joy.

The cost of tonight's meagre rations didn't have to come out of his own wages now.

Julia placed the take-out bag carefully on the passenger seat, shifted the car into gear and proceeded carefully up the drive to her parking bay.

The smell of the food was overwhelming and she salivated expectantly. It would take days for the smell to dissipate and for her car to regain its usual odour, but she didn't care as her stomach grumbled in anticipation.

I wonder what dad thought was fitting for tonight's meal, she wondered, as she juggled her hand bag, house keys and the newly acquired take-out bag en route to her apartment?

Chapter 52

The apartment was dark and she clicked on lights as she made her way to the kitchen, where she unceremoniously dumped her baggage on the counter-top.

She fished around in the take-out bag and discovered that it was a burger and chips from Steers.

Nice, she thought, *good choice dad.*

She really enjoyed the taste of the Steers beef patty and had argued with many and on numerous occasions that it was by far the best patty out of all the fast-food franchises. She obviously received counter-arguments, but that was her opinion and she'd stick by it.

As was standard practice, the burger and chips were packaged separately with the burger in its own cute little box and the chips peeking out of a wax-proof packet.

She snacked on a few chips before progressing to the burger.

It was only when she lifted the burger from the box that she noticed it.

Under the burger was a transparent square of plastic and under the protective plastic square was an envelope, which was neatly and most recognisably addressed to **Julia Swan**.

Her heart sank and her appetite instantly deserted her.

She dropped the burger alongside the box.

A tear formed in her left eye and slowly began to trickle down her cheek.

She tried to blink it away, but more tears rapidly replaced it and now both eyes were tearing up and ultimately the taps really opened.

It took a whole five minutes for her to gain some composure and even then, she was perched precariously on the edge of meltdown.

All of this, and she hadn't even opened the letter yet.

She wiped her eyes and blew her nose on the serviettes, which had accompanied the burger and chips, and then plonked herself down in her favourite living-room chair.

Her mind drifted back to the first three letters she had received. All were opened and read in this chair. She suddenly thought of changing seats, but really, how would that break the cycle?

Dear Julia,

They always began like that – warm and friendly.

But this time she knew better and was expecting the worst, which was the reason for her teetering on the edge of an emotional cliff.

Congratulations!

The media fraternity are in awe of your latest article.

Prize-winning stuff, I might add, with nothing but accolades splashed everywhere.

I knew you were good, but you've taken this to a whole new level.

It was truly impressive and was investigative journalism at its best.

And yet, while you captured the essence of the incident, I somehow can't help but feel a bit disappointed by your efforts.

Here it was.

She just knew what was coming next.

Her hands shook uncontrollably and it took a good few

minutes and colossal effort to regain her self-control before she could continue to read.

Sure, you did your own DNA research, but merely to verify the facts which I had already given you.

Sure, you described the murder scene in meticulous detail, but again, mostly just regurgitating the detail I had already given you.

You beat the other journalists to the punch because I gave you the details – details which nobody else had or could possibly even get.

But somehow the reason for Craig Davis being murdered, received fairly scant commentary and yet I'd given you all the detail you needed for that as well.

Why is that, I wonder?

That question consumed me.

I've been trying my best to understand why this is and how we can progress with our symbiotic relationship if important details are flagrantly omitted.

And then it dawned on me.

It is my fault.

Julia inhaled deeply as though someone had thrown a bucket of ice-cold water in her face.

Had she read correctly?

Yes, there it was, as clear as daylight.

Although hesitant, she also couldn't wait to continue reading now.

He was bound to elaborate.

How can you personalise something without a name?

How can you write about someone when you don't know what to call them or how to address them?

Maybe I was a bit hasty in chastising you about the use of the *'DNA Dan' moniker. I truly believed it would trivialise my character and the story I had to tell. And yet you might have been spot on the money. It would probably work well to tie me to the cause, the incidents and the reasons for the incidents.*

I accept the errors of my ways and for this, I do apologise.

I should have gone with your original instincts.

You are, after all, the expert in that field.

Julia shook her head in surprise.

She had just received an apology from a psychotic, megalomanic, cold-blooded murderer.

Was this some sort of alternate reality?

Could she have misread this?

She re-read the last paragraph.

No, it was there, a clear apology for not agreeing with her naming convention.

I cannot expect a revision of the article you've already written, but then again as we both already knew – we've only just begun.

The adventures ahead of us are untold and with me on my quest and you documenting every step of the way, it will be an epic tale.

Best Regards,

Daniel Nathan Anderson

A pang of fear suddenly gripped Julia, as she placed the letter on the coffee table. The realisation that she would now have no way of avoiding what he wanted written in future, scared her to bits.

How would she convince Moses to give her such latitude without fully confiding in him? He had believed in her from the onset and had taken a chance on her without knowing anything about the back-story. Sure he was basking in the glory of her exposé, which was written under his guidance and supervision, but would he be as tolerant and forgiving if he knew that she was in contact with the murderer and writing these articles at his behest?

The thought paralysed her with fear and she sat frozen to the spot for what seemed like hours.

Chapter 53

Alan didn't take the call from Julia very well and he and Ollie raced over to her apartment.

The streets were already quiet at this time of night and although no unnecessarily dangerous driving was required, Ollie's foot was still a bit heavy on the pedals.

Alan sat quietly in the passenger seat swaying to the movements of the vehicle as Ollie gunned the engine down the straights, skipped stop signs whenever possible and took corners slightly more hurriedly and tighter than usual.

Alan had denied Ollie the detail, but when he had said they needed to get to Julia's apartment in a hurry, the big man needed no further reason or explanation.

Julia was safe, that he knew without a doubt from the updates he regularly received from his surveillance team.

If she wasn't, and he hadn't already been informed of this by his team, someone's life was about to end by his massive hands this very night.

With a squeal of tires, the vehicle finally skidded to a stand-still in front of the security gate, but there was essentially no delay, as Julia had already informed the guard on duty to allow her father and Ollie access the moment they arrived.

Ollie recognised the guard, but had no idea of his name, so merely greeted him with a nod and a forced smile.

The guard in return greeted Ollie and Alan enthusiastically and with reverence, and even saluted them, although improperly, as they proceeded through the gate.

Julia already had the security gate and door open, as the two men came striding along the dimly lit corridor.

Alan immediately saw the distress on his daughter's face and engulfed her in a warm and loving embrace – she desperately needed to be comforted.

Ollie squeezed past them and edged his way inside the apartment. It was second nature and part of his job to secure any area before his boss entered, but since this was Julia's apartment, he had to fight back the instinct to rapidly search the kitchen, living area, bathroom and bedroom. He took up his position in the living room not quite knowing what he should be doing.

Julia was crying rivers of tears on Alan's shoulder now and although both men were beyond uncomfortable, not a word was uttered. Alan rubbed and patted her comfortingly on her back, but otherwise was statuesque in the embrace. He had learnt over the years that sometimes you just had to be there and restrain the urge to speak, offer advice or solve the problem.

After, what seemed like an eternity, Julia finally let up and took a step back.

She had literally cried herself out.

Ollie handed out tissues, which he had found in the living room and while Julia wiped her eyes and blew her nose vigorously, Alan dabbed ineffectively at his wet shoulder.

Alan led the way into the living area. "Let's sit," he prompted.

The two men both noticed the letter on the coffee table, but neither were brazen enough to reach for it. Julia would need to open that particular door.

She plonked herself down in her chair and between sniffs, began to re-count the story.

This came close to qualifying as a déjà vu moment.

They'd been through exactly the same before, but just not in Julia's apartment.

The men sat and listened intently, mentally filing any questions for later, so as not to break her rhythm or train of thought.

They were becoming expert at this by now.

Once they'd heard about her day and how the letter had been delivered, she reached for the actual letter and began to read it to them. She figured it would be better if they both heard it simultaneously, rather than taking turns reading and digesting it. She sobbed and sniffed occasionally, but painstakingly managed to control herself throughout the reading.

Alan found it impossible to sit still. When he needed to understand or assimilate information, he needed to pace. Somehow his brain functioned better when he was moving.

So, while Julia essentially read the letter to Ollie, who stayed in attendance, Alan paced her living room. He moved behind her, striding from one end of her living room to the other.

When she finally finished, she looked up at Ollie and then turned to locate her father behind her.

She daubed her eyes again with the tissue and wiped her slightly runny nose, and then asked the most relevant and apt question ever:

"So what do we do now?"

Chapter 54

Alan moved forward and wrapped his arms around Julia's neck from behind.

A hug from a father – nothing beat that.

Julia sniffed repeatedly but was totally cried out. Instead, she snuggled into her father's forearms which cradled her head. "It'll be okay," he stammered.

They all knew this wouldn't be immediate, but trusted that in the medium to long-term they would remember this – not with fondness – but more out of relief, that they got through this unscathed.

While Alan comforted his daughter, Ollie excused himself and made his way to the balcony to make a few phone calls.

The cool breeze coming off the ocean had picked up significantly, but Ollie was unperturbed by it. He had important work to do and nothing would detract from that.

There were only three Steers franchises in nearby proximity to Julia's apartment block, with a few more a little further away.

Start close and progressively work outward, he thought.

He struck gold on his first call.

Manny had personally been on stake-out duty and had seen the delivery bike arrive and minutes later, leave again. He couldn't remember the entire registration number, but out of habit, he had committed the first few alpha and numerical digits to memory while the motorbike was stationary at the gate.

Ollie barked a few orders into the mouthpiece and could

vividly picture his team getting organised and mobilizing themselves into action.

A steaming cup of coffee was waiting for him on his return to the living room.

It was most welcome after the cold wind had brushed him down with frigid strokes while he was outside on the balcony.

Alan had done the honours, as Julia was still perched in her original position, legs tightly retracted under her. She stared almost catatonically into the distance.

Ollie broke the silence as he sat down. "Good news," he said, "Manny got a partial plate number on the delivery bike. The team will find it in no time."

"Good," Alan replied. "At least we'll know which outlet dispatched it and then we can interview the employees. Someone must know something."

"Agreed," Ollie continued. "One of them must've had a hand in putting the envelope in the burger box and covering it with a plastic square to prevent the juices from the burger spoiling it."

Contrary to what the sombre situation demanded, a faint smile appeared on Julia's lips. "He's way ahead of us." She shook her head and continued, "He gave the instructions and paid someone off again. He's too clever to be personally involved and risk the possibility of being caught on camera."

"We need to follow the leads, Jules," Ollie commiserated genuinely, "even if they lead us nowhere for now. He will slip up sooner or later. His type always do. His arrogance will lead to complacency and that will be his downfall."

Julia nodded, understanding the rationale, but knowing that it was another long-shot.

Ollie's phone rang in his pocket and he quickly reached for it.

"What you got?"

He listened intently for a minute before responding.

"Mmm, well get down there and intercept the rider when he returns."

He listened to the response and finally added.

"I don't care, interview all the staff if that's what it takes.'

There was another brief pause, as he was given further information.

"Okay, if the manager has a problem, let me know. Mr Swan knows the owner, so it'll only take one quick phone-call to sort out any issues."

Alan looked over at Ollie as the conversation progressed, the frown-lines on his face deepening all the while.

"Right, let me know then," Ollie concluded, stabbing the disconnect button on his handset.

Ollie didn't wait for either Alan or Julia to prompt him and got right into it.

"The delivery came from the Esplanade outlet – just down the road. They're waiting for the delivery bike to return from its latest delivery run to the Kennaway Hotel and then the Cozy Nest Guest House, so they can question the rider."

"What was the part about the manager?" queried Alan.

"Well, Manny was anticipating issues from the manager when requesting to interview the staff."

Alan nodded sagely, "Doug Smith owns that franchise. That'll be easy to resolve."

"That's what I said. Any issues and you can just make a quick call to Doug."

Alan pulled out his phone. "In fact, I think I'll do that anyway. Let's get Doug in the loop right away, so the manager is briefed accordingly and doesn't give Manny any unnecessary problems."

Ollie nodded in agreement, as Alan searched through his contact list for Doug's number.

Julia's apartment had suddenly been transformed into a command centre.

The conversation with Doug was brief and to the point.

He was initially a bit defensive, believing that Alan was complaining about a service delivery issue, but once Alan had shared a little more detail with him, he agreed to his staff being questioned, albeit with his manager present.

Doug's curiosity was inevitable, but Alan adeptly sidestepped most of his questions and mostly reiterated that nothing was wrong and that all he required was some information on who prepared the order for delivery.

Alan could picture Doug phoning his manager and explaining the situation, the moment he hung up.

Ollie gave it another ten minutes before contacting Manny and giving him the thumbs-up to call for the manager.

And then they waited.

Chapter 55

It was an agonising wait.

Time always ticked by so slowly when expectant news was pending.

It had ultimately been a long and stressful day and Julia felt utterly drained.

She left the men and disappeared into the sanctuary of her bedroom.

The elated and stress-free emotions from her country-side drive were now a distant memory. A time long forgotten.

The day's events meandered casually through her mind as she lay down and drifted off to sleep.

Alan and Ollie now both paced the living room, every now and then having to side-step one other, as their paths came close to colliding.

Both were deep in thought and wrapped up in their own worlds when Ollie's phone finally rang.

Even though they were expecting the call, the sudden ringing caused the men to jolt with surprise.

"Put it on speaker," Alan commanded.

Ollie complied.

Manny's voice came through loud and clear although with a slight electronic twang and delay. It sounded like he was miles away, while in reality he was just down the street.

"Hey, Ollie?" he questioned, due to the delay in Ollie answering the phone while pressing the speaker button.

"I'm here," Ollie confirmed. "You're on speaker, Manny."

"Okay, so this is what we have so far. We waited for the delivery guy to get back to the shop and started with him. He clearly recalls the delivery made to Julia earlier this evening, but maintained that he just collected the order and drove it over to the address stipulated. He was not allowed in..."

"We know all this," Alan interjected, "he dropped it off with Phineas, who then gave it to Julia."

"Yes, sir," Manny stammered and then continued.

"We then called for the manager, as instructed, who could not assist with any questions asked. He called the dispatcher to his office and she had a similar story to that of the delivery guy. She just received the order, wrote down the address and dispatched it."

Alan was getting impatient now.

He loved the old adage of 'Tell me the time, don't build me a watch,' and Manny was building him a damn watch.

He forced himself to take a deep breath and relax, even though he would have usually demanded an executive summary.

Manny pressed on. "So, we got the manager to call in the food prep staff one by one. They'd made so many identical burgers during the course of their shift that none could remember anything in particular about a specific burger destined for Miss Julia."

This time Ollie jumped in. "It was a pretty standard burger, the difference was in how it was packaged."

"I was getting to that, boss," Manny added excitedly. "It was only when we spoke to the supervisor that we managed to get the detail we were looking for. She told us about the handover she'd received from the day-shift supervisor before he knocked off and went home. He'd given her the letter and the plastic square and had instructed her what to do with them and when and where to deliver the order. She complied with the instructions and as it turns out, that was her total involvement."

"Did you get the name of the other supervisor?" Alan asked.

"More than that, sir, we got his address as well."

"Well, get over there. We need the full story tonight still."

"Thuso is on his way already," Manny confirmed. "He'll phone in once he has more details."

"Good work, Manny, you've done well," Alan acknowledged.

He'd been in business long enough to know how much a pat on the back meant to an employee. Recognition was a primal desire. It didn't even need to be material or financial. Just watch any child. 'Look at me. Look how far I can kick the ball.' Affirmation and recognition was ingrained in everyone, no matter their race, religion, culture, age, ability or upbringing. It was one of the great levellers in life.

Once Ollie hung up, both men entered their holding patterns once again and continued to orbit the living room. The silence was deafening as they paced the area. Both were engrossed in their own thoughts, wondering where this information would lead them.

Finally the call from Thuso came through to Ollie and he once again activated the handset's speaker.

"What'd you get, Thuso?" Ollie asked when answering the call.

"Not much, boss!"

"Did you find the supervisor?" Ollie prompted.

"Yes, we found him at this house, but there's not much to his story. He received a call from a customer before his shift ended. The customer wanted to surprise his girlfriend with a letter. The supervisor offered to put the letter in the bag with her order, but the customer was worried that she would just remove the food and not see the letter. The customer then asked if it was possible to put the letter under the burger, so that when his girlfriend took out her burger she would notice it. The supervisor initially objected as it would get ruined under the burger. The customer then suggested that he place a transparent square of plastic between the letter and the burger, which would then protect it. The supervisor agreed that this would work and ensured the customer that it would get done."

"Sounds plausible," Ollie responded. "But this doesn't answer the question of where the letter and plastic came from."

"That's the interesting part," Thuso replied. "When he asked the customer the same question, all he was told was that the letter would be delivered to him along with the plastic square, the order, his girlfriend's name and address and the time it needed to be delivered."

"So, when and how was the letter delivered?" Alan interjected.

"Hello, big boss," Thuso greeted Alan enthusiastically, not often having the opportunity to speak to him directly. "A few minutes after the customer hung up, a waitress brought an envelope into the back office. It was addressed to 'The Supervisor'."

"And of course, since it was still too early, he had to hand over the customer's request to the oncoming supervisor?"

"Yes, sir, that's all he can remember."

"Thanks, Thuso," Ollie added before hanging up.

Julia arrived just in time to hear the end of the conversation.

"Dead end?" she asked quizzically.

"Not quite," Alan answered. "We have a better

221

understanding of what happened, but more importantly we have three more leads to explore. Firstly, who was the waitress who took the letter to the supervisor? Secondly, how did that waitress get the letter? Thirdly, if hand-delivered, who gave the letter to the waitress? But it's a bit late now to follow those leads, so we'll find answers first thing in the morning."

Chapter 56

Julia woke early after another dismal night's rest. She slept in fits and starts, her mind churning relentlessly with a constant turmoil of thoughts.

She needed to clear her conscience and bring Moses into the picture. Her only concern was that he would feel obligated to inform the police and potentially bring the house of cards tumbling down around them.

Alan and Ollie had been vehemently opposed to her disclosing the entire story to Moses. If the police got involved, they might be ordered off the case for obstructing a police investigation. They would have to turn over the letters and all other information they had accumulated so far, which would ultimately jeopardise their own investigation and could impact on Julia's safety.

While Julia understood all this and had promised to be cautious, she emphasised that the next article would need to be far more personal in nature and without consent from Moses, it would be a non-starter. She had to come clean now. Later would be a problem no matter how she looked at it.

Her meeting was scheduled for ten a.m. and she couldn't wish any harder for it to be that time already. Moses had managed to squeeze her into his schedule at the last minute simply because she was his star writer at the moment, and also because she had said it was urgent. He was at that stage where he believed, if she said it was urgent, then it was urgent.

She had certainly delivered for him after their last meeting and at least on this occasion she'd made an appointment to see him, which was in stark contrast to just ambushing him again.

He had been praised by all levels of the organisation for her work on the last article. The publicity for the media house had been immense and although he had not readily accepted the accolades for himself, everyone knew that he had acquired and nurtured the talent reporting into him.

Julia pulled into a visitor's parking bay at the *Daily Dispatch* building fifteen minutes before her appointment. She looked in the review mirror and touched up her make-up which was generally applied minimally, but was a bit more outlandish today. A poor night's sleep had left its dark marks under her eyes and she'd felt self-conscious enough to attempt to mask the imperfections with make-up.

She was dressed in a pretty red mid-length chiffon dress, pleated to emphasise her curves and rounded off with a beautiful pair of low-healed Lady Violette red shoes. Her intention hadn't been to look too formal, but she knew that jeans and a t-shirt would not be appropriate.

The ensemble was spectacular and heads turned as she walked by. Men predictably gawked, mostly in admiration, possibly sprinkled with a dash of lust, but when women leered as they did today, it was mostly out of jealousy. Julia hated being objectified, whether by men or women and for that reason, mostly dressed down whenever possible. But this occasion had demanded a more professional appearance.

Moses was waiting for her and even he couldn't resist a double-take at her appearance when she arrived at his office. He caught himself before it became awkward and promptly welcomed her with, "Well, well, is it Lady in Red or Little Red Riding Hood?"

Julia broke into a huge grin. "I tried not to overdo it, but from the looks I've been getting, I think I failed dismally."

"You look beautiful," Moses confirmed in his most professional and fatherly tone. "Don't take notice of anyone else."

"Thank you," she replied, gaining more confidence in preparation for what she had to discuss.

Moses continued, "The hype around your last article hasn't stopped. What a great job you did. Is my position in jeopardy?" he grinned, as he closed off with the last sentence.

Julia brushed the accolades aside. "That's actually why I'm here to see you."

"Okay…" Moses cautiously replied, drawing out the word and leaving it hanging, as he quizzically waited for her to continue. "You need a raise? You've had a better job offer? You're leaving us?"

He was quite flustered by the time he'd finished. He took a deep breath to calm himself.

"Nothing like that," Julia answered and then added, "but there is something I need to disclose."

Moses was nearly beside himself by now. "What is it?" he questioned, his mind racing in all directions, as he tried to pre-empt what he was about to be told.

"Coffee anyone?" came a voice from the door. It was Martha, Moses' personal assistant.

"Not now!" Moses uncharacteristically exploded, but immediately realised how out of line he was and apologised sincerely. "Sorry, Martha, Julia was just about to share some important news with me."

He rapidly composed himself and turned back to Julia, "Julia, would you like some coffee?"

"I'd love some, thank you, Martha," Julia politely responded.

"Be back in a jiffy," Martha smiled and left the room.

Chapter 57

Moses waited for the sexagenarian to exit his office and then promptly turned back to Julia in anticipation.

"Well?"

"Well, it's quite a delicate issue and I need you to be as open-minded as possible about what I have to tell you."

"Okay, I'll try my best."

"What would you say if I told you I had a source who was feeding me all the information and details about DNA Dan?"

There was a deliberate pregnant pause, as Julia waited for Moses to assimilate what she was saying.

"Most journalists have sources," Moses finally added, not understanding why such a common practice was suddenly a big issue to Julia.

"No, it's not that," she replied, noticing the confusion on Moses' face.

She opened her mouth to clarify, but the words caught in her throat as Martha entered the room holding a tray containing a pot of coffee, a jug of milk, two mugs, two teaspoons and a small bowl with an assortment of tubular sachets of white and brown sugar and sweeteners. She usually just carried in two mugs of pre-prepared coffee, as she knew very well how they took their coffee. But today was seemingly not one of those days.

Noticing the surprise and confusion on their faces, she nonchalantly looked over at Julia and addressed her, "You look so beautiful and official today, I decided a more formal approach would suit what is obviously a special occasion."

The elderly lady smiled graciously as Julia replied, "Thank you, Martha, but there's no special occasion. I just wanted to look good today."

"Well, you certainly present very well," Martha added and placed the tray on the desk between Moses and Julia.

"Should I do the honours?" she asked, looking over at her boss.

"No thank you, Martha, we'll take it from here."

And with that she once again departed.

Although his curiosity had built to a crescendo, Moses had let the formalities pass undisturbed, but now he was getting anxious waiting for the big reveal.

Julia stretched over and poured the coffee after which they each added their own accoutrements and began the stirring process.

It wasn't until after her first sip that she resumed her story.

"So, to continue, I've had plenty of sources in the past, but this source is rather unique."

"How so?" Moses queried.

"Well, I've been getting letters delivered to me," she continued, "containing all the information and details I've included in my articles."

Moses raised his eyebrows.

"So, what you're saying, is that we're just publishing someone else's letters and this is not your work?"

"No, no, it's definitely my work. I've had to do days and days of research and investigation and then ultimately stitch everything together to finalise the articles."

"I'm not with you then, Julia. What's so concerning about this that you needed to schedule a meeting with me?"

Julia had tried to be subtle and obscure but now realised that she'd need to employ a more direct approach.

"The letters are from him," she finally said, almost whispering the words.

Moses strained to hear what she'd said and then when the penny dropped, he asked, "What do you mean 'him'?"

"Him," she replied. "They're from Dan himself."

"What?" Moses erupted, his professional demeanour deserting him in an instant. "The murderer has been communicating with you?"

Julia looked down at the floor like a scolded child.

"Yes," she said, almost inaudibly. "For some reason, he chose to confide in me. He has been coercing me to do his bidding by threatening to harm my family, my friends or myself."

Moses took a little longer this time to compose himself.

He shook his head, "No wonder you were first to flight this story. And then after the murder, you also had far more information and details than our rivals, who were literally camped out at the crime scene. I had a feeling that something was awry, but I was never quite able to put my finger on it."

A hushed silence descended over them.

"So why come forward with it now?" Moses asked, finally breaking the silence.

"The last letter…" she answered, pausing slightly. "The demands he made in the last letter made it impossible for me to keep it a secret any longer."

"How so?" Moses asked, as the questions began to multiply at an alarming rate in his mind.

"He demanded that he, himself, his views and his cause get more publicity in future reports. Bearing in mind that you'd instructed me to stick to the facts and avoid the individual in the last article, I saw no alternative."

"What do you mean, he demanded?"

"Let's just say that, to date, his threats have been more intimated than direct. But we all now know of his capabilities and violent tendencies."

"How do you even know the letters are from him?"

"Nobody could have known all the details he divulged to me, even my dad agrees with me on that one."

Alan Swan – Moses had forgotten about the illustrious Alan Swan.

"What does your dad think?" he probed.

"Well, he didn't even want me talking to you about this. He and his team of investigators are entrenched in finding this maniac."

"What about the police?"

"We all know how slow and inept they can be. Dad would rather handle this himself and at the right time hand it over to them."

"But that could be seen as withholding evidence or pertinent information in an ongoing investigation."

"We know, Moses, which is why I'm appealing to your extreme discretion," she responded in her most imploring voice. "If this gets out, I could be in danger, my friends and family could be in danger, even you could be in danger," she added, driving the point home. And besides that, his contact with me might stop and then there goes our coverage and story."

She relentlessly chiselled away at him with all the justification she could think of to create some emotional conflict within him, between his professional aspirations and his sense of duty to report the situation to the authorities.

It hadn't hurt to belabour the fact that she could be in

imminent danger as well.

He couldn't fault her rationale, but it still plagued him that this should be a case for the authorities. He was an honest and upstanding man who knew the difference between right and wrong, good and bad, and what she was asking of him was wrong on so many levels. But for the right reasons, he concluded.

"Okay," he finally answered, "since your father and his team are actively pursuing the case and will then hand it over to the police, we'll let it play out a little while longer before I'm obliged to inform the authorities."

"Thank you, Moses." Julia exhaled deeply, truly relieved at this outcome.

"Just one more thing," she added.

Moses shrugged and gave her a look that she could only interpret as 'is there more?'

She continued unabated. "Well, the next article will have to be different. It needs to be more personal and not so much about the facts. But I'll make sure not to glamourise him or his actions too much."

"Fine," Moses conceded, shaking his head with disdain, as though he'd been check-mated by a real pro. "But we'll continue this discussion when your next article is ready. I can't just give you carte blanche to write what you want."

"I understand. Thank you, Moses," Julia replied, hurriedly standing up and leaving his office before he had a chance to reflect too much and come up with any plausible reason to change his mind.

Chapter 58

The weekend had crept up on everyone like a ghost in the night. The week was a mere memory. Whatever hadn't been done by now would have to wait for Monday. While the commercial and economic sectors closed their doors, literally and figuratively, on a busy week, the leisure industry was just gearing up to take over for the next few days and then the cycle would begin again. The wheels of industry. Wash, rinse, repeat.

Dan stood in the lengthening twilight shadows waiting for the onset of total darkness. He keenly observed the activities in the house across the street. Behind him was an old three-bedroom house, probably mid-seventies by the look of it. It was shoddy and rundown. General upkeep and maintenance were definitely not a priority to the owner and this was probably the reason for it currently being unoccupied. This suited Dan perfectly.

He could concentrate on his objective without concerning himself about who could be observing him.

As darkness engulfed the neighbourhood, windows intermittently began to illuminate, as residents flipped light switches to keep the darkness at bay.

The house across the street remained in semi-darkness, as was the norm for this time of the evening.

In accordance with their routine, the family would now be clustered in the lounge or adjacent dining room, chatting about the day, the week or anything and everything which required discussion. Family time was after all very important, even for those who desperately yearned for the sanctity of their own sanctuaries.

It would be at least another hour before they'd disperse and he could get to work.

He ran through his plan once again in his head.

It was far from perfect and yet it could just be.

Interruptions were uncommon, but on occasion were always an inevitability.

He hoped that tonight was not one of those nights. He had no qualms with the family and frankly didn't wish any of them any harm.

But if he was backed into a corner and had no alternatives, the chips would fall where they might.

He truly hoped that this would not be the case, but for the sake of due diligence, he'd prepared for all contingencies.

As total darkness gradually overpowered the twilight, Dan's eyes slowly adjusted to the absence of light and his vision became more and more acute. He squinted ever so slightly to adjust his focus as his eyes probed the darker areas of the garden. Nothing moved. Not even a breath of wind disturbed the leaf-laden branches of the trees which lined the street.

It was the perfect night. The perfect night to execute part two of his plan.

He smiled ever so slightly at his own wit – execute part two of his plan – very clever indeed.

A bedroom window suddenly lit up causing him to flinch a little with surprise. He'd been waiting for it, but was still startled when it finally lit up. The curtains were already drawn so he couldn't make out who it was, but a buck gets ten, it was Chris. It was his room after all and, besides that, he always seemed to leave the gathering first. Teenage behaviour was so predictable.

It took another twenty minutes – probably just time enough to wash, dry and pack away the dinner dishes – before the roll-up garage door was framed by a thin bright outline of light. After another few minutes the light in the arts and crafts room came on.

Dan cautiously scanned the street for any activity.

Still nothing moved.

He crept stealthily across the tarmac and came to a sudden stop just outside the gate.

He heard a screen door slam shut and then a voice ring out in the stillness.

It was an elderly man's voice.

"Come on Fudgey, do your business. It's nearly time for bed."

It came from two doors down, but still nearly gave Dan a heart attack.

The beam of a flashlight darting to and fro through the air now caught Dan's attention.

What was the old chap up to now, he wondered?

He'd rather use a flashlight than use electricity and switch on the porch light for the poor mutt. *Old people,* he mused. They work their entire lives to have a steady pension to retire on comfortably and then they become overly frugal and consequently forget to live. The old chap probably thought he'd be around for another sixty years and still needed to scrimp and save for the future.

Dan shook his head in disbelief and waited for the dog to do its business and for the old-timer to retreat back into his house.

The recently oiled gate opened soundlessly under his gentle, but persuasive, touch. He pulled it closed again, but left it unlatched, in case a quick escape was called for.

It was now or never, he thought to himself, as he hefted his bag of goodies over his shoulder and edged his way up the drive.

Chapter 59

He could vaguely hear Russell tinkering away on something inside. After all, the roller door was not very thick and even thinner at the joints. He listened intently for any voices. Russell needed to be alone for this to work.

Besides the clinking and scuffling noises coming from behind the door, it was dead quiet.

He readied himself and then rapped quietly but persistently on the door.

Russell's voice broke the silence. "Is that you, Chris?"

No answer.

Dan continued with the slow and steady knock.

"Forgot your keys again?" Russell mumbled. "Didn't even know you were going out."

Dan smiled. This would be easier than he thought.

The roller door suddenly came to life and before Russell could utter a single word, Dan dipped down low and reappeared on the other side, Taser in hand.

Russell's body jerked spastically as the voltage immediately subdued him.

Dan dared not catch the falling body for fear of shocking himself and just looked on in awe as Russell lost total control of his muscles and dropped to the floor.

In the quiet surroundings every sound was vastly amplified.

Dan stood motionless for a few seconds, straining to hear any noises which would indicate that somebody had heard the commotion.

Nothing.

Perfect.

Dan slowly rolled down the door and prepared himself for the night's activities.

The first point on the agenda was securing the inter-leading door to the house.

After all the planning, any interruptions would be most inconvenient.

Unfortunately, the key was in the lock on the opposite side of the door. Dan moved to plan B and quickly grabbed a workbench chair and wedged it under the door handle. It wasn't the perfect solution, but it would suffice.

Dan looked around, scoping out the detail of the garage.

He nodded approvingly.

Nice job, Russell, he thought to himself.

It was comfortable, as well as functional.

He had no idea what Russell had been working on, but numerous tools lay scattered around the workbench cluttering up what would usually be a pristine work area.

Russell broke the silence with an almost imperceptible – and probably involuntary – groan.

Can't have that, Dan thought, deciding that a sharp kick to the head would be more effective than another tasering. Russell's eyes rolled back in his head as his body slumped into unconsciousness.

Dan continued exploring the garage as silently as a cat-burglar.

He soon found what he was looking for and wouldn't have to improvise.

In the far corner stood a handmade wooden structure.

It had a really robust frame, crudely but creatively crafted with solid creosote poles. It was bolted securely to the wall. Eight-millimetre boards spanned the void between the poles, masterfully fashioning it into a utilitarian shelving unit. Russell's heavy-duty tools and equipment adorned the shelves.

Perfect.

Dan spent a few minutes moving these items and creating a bit of work-space for himself.

It was taking too long.

His plan was unravelling.

He had anticipated a relatively quick in and out, not having to worry continuously about being interrupted. As a consequence, his anxiety levels were through the roof and he could feel the sweat streaming down his torso under the heavy-duty bodysuit he wore. It was fairly cool, even inside the garage, but with his adrenaline flowing, Dan's body was generating excessive heat.

He wasn't particularly concerned about a few drops of sweat here or there, as he had a few bottles of trace evidence prepared to mask such an eventuality. He was armed with concoctions of sweat, blood and urine to contaminate the scene once he had completed his work.

But he was concerned about the time.

He needed to get a move on.

Footsteps suddenly crunched audibly on some gravel in the front yard, with a twig snapping loudly under the pressure of a human body.

Dan froze.

His body went into high alert and his mind raced at a million miles an hour.

He had never even contemplated an intrusion from the

garage door side.

Time for improvisation, he thought to himself.

Silently he tip-toed into position alongside the door, now brandishing a dowel, about the size and shape of an average broom-stick which he had found en route.

If the door started opening, he would be ready to swing.

But it never came to that.

"Hey, Dad, just going to the shop with Tim and Rob quickly. Be back in about an hour," shouted Chris from the driveway.

Dan didn't know whether to answer or not.

Would Chris come back and check on his father if he didn't answer?

In his confusion he just grunted loudly – hopefully audible, possibly not.

And then he remembered the gate.

He'd pulled it closed, but had left it unlatched.

Would that raise alarm bells?

Dan winced as he tried to put himself in the shoes of a teen.

Could something so tiny derail his plans?

He waited and waited for what felt like an eternity, but true to form, the oddity hadn't even raised the slightest suspicion in the mind of the teenager.

How inattentive and naïve, Dan pondered and resumed his preparations.

Chapter 60

Russell blinked a few times to clear his blurry eyes. His face ached and his muscles groaned as he tried to move. He grimaced in pain.

His mind was still muddled and his current situation had not registered with him yet. The form standing before him slowly became clearer, but it was all too surreal to fully comprehend.

"You awake?" Dan whispered.

Russell's eyes widened, as he realised his hands and feet were secured and he couldn't move.

"Not a great predicament you're in," Dan taunted, pursing his lips and shaking his head slightly from one side to another.

Russell suddenly realised the danger he was in and tried to scream, but the gag stuffed in his mouth prevented any sound from escaping his lips. He groaned throatily, but that would never be enough noise to attract any attention.

Dan gazed into Russell's eyes, waiting in anticipation for some sort of recognition, but all he saw was fear – desperation and fear – and not only for himself.

Dan saw the concern and added, "Don't worry, Russell. Your family is safe. Chris went out with some friends. Penny and Mary-Anne are both in the craft room and safe for now… unless they interrupt us, of course."

He paused and grinned, letting the words sink in and the fear build to a crescendo.

Russell was going out of his mind.

There couldn't be anything worse than being a husband or father in a totally helpless situation. Possibly one of man's greatest fears of all time. Put their families at risk and the biggest, wealthiest and most powerful men in the world could be reduced to putty and would comply with anything.

Snapping out of his thoughts, he continued, "Since you obviously don't remember or don't want to remember, I'll remind you. There was once a little boy who was terrorised by a group of four friends or should I say a gang of four thugs? And that little boy is no longer that little any more."

Russell's eyes widened as he suddenly recognised the behemoth before him.

"That's right," Dan added, "and it's now payback time."

Russell tried to say something but no words were forthcoming.

Dan shook his head, "Too late for apologies, I'm afraid. You did what you did and you all went on with your lives as though nothing had ever happened."

Russell again tried to form a few words through the gag, but all he could elicit was a groan.

"Remember the time you tied that little boy to a tree? Where was it again? Oh yes, in Cameron Long's back garden. Wasn't that a day to remember? The bonds were so tight, they cut into the little boy's wrists as he squirmed relentlessly – in such a vain attempt – to escape."

Russell screamed though the gag.

"I know, I know. Very similar to the predicament you now find yourself in. Now, what was it you did then? And if memory serves me correctly, it was your idea, wasn't it?"

Russell was beside himself. Tears streamed down his face and snot bubbles started forming in his nose.

"Right. You decided it would be very funny if you all peed in a cup and forced the little boy to drink it. He cried, just like you're crying now, and snot ran freely down his face too." Dan nodded and then shook his head at the sight of the helpless man tied to the shelving upright before him.

"Well, we're all set up for a re-enactment," Dan said, indicating the apparatus next to Russell's head with his eyes.

Russell tried to turn his head to look, but discovered right away that any head movements were limited. His head had been secured and stabilised with a belt, tightly fastened around the top of his cranium and the pole.

"I'll show you," Dan offered, casually leaning over Russell's shoulder and unhooking the IV bag of urine attached to a transparent plastic intubation pipe.

The panicked look in Russell's eyes was beyond anything Dan could ever have imagined. That expression would live on in his memory for eternity.

"Now, now, just relax Russell, and take your medicine like a man," Dan said calmly, now enjoying the tormenting far too much.

Russell's eyes betrayed his intentions and Dan could see that he was just playing possum until the gag was removed.

How stupid do you think I am, he wondered?

A tiny smirk spread across his face.

He cocked his right arm and a powerful roundhouse connected with the side of Russell's head, whose lights went out for the second time that evening. The impact was hard enough to shift his head slightly inside its restraint but not too excessive to lay him out for too long.

Dan went to work quickly by removing the gag and roughly forcing the intubation tube down his throat. It would be as good as a gag in preventing him from screaming for help when he awoke.

Dan couldn't wait much longer and viciously slapped Russell across his face to rouse him from his unconscious state and then waited anxiously until he was again fully compos mentis.

Russell couldn't believe what was happening to him and shook vigorously at his bonds until his head, wrists and ankles were raw.

Dan waited patiently for him to relax and then looked on in amazement as he strained vigorously to suck whatever air he could get through the intubation tube and his snot-filled nose. After his unsuccessful efforts to free himself, he needed to gasp, to inhale great lungful's of air, but the tube was like a straw and all he got for his struggle was more and more light-headed.

"No more fighting now," Dan commented casually. "It's time."

He slowly opened the tap and watched in fascination as the orange liquid inched its way down the tube from the IV bag and into Russell's mouth and from there, down into his lungs.

As soon as the choking began, Dan closed the tap.

He couldn't end it too soon – it was pay-back, after all.

Russell coughed, spluttered and choked to clear his lungs of the liquid, but the pipe firmly blocked his airway. He thrashed around once more, jerking his head frantically to and fro while working to dislodge the tube with his tongue, but it wouldn't budge and the blockage allowed nothing to come up.

"You made that little boy drink your piss. How does it feel?"

Dan grinned savagely as Russell battled on.

His sweaty face slowly changed colour, from a bright red to a purplish-blue.

Dan gazed deeply into Russell's eyes and sneered, "Look at me, you bastard. I bet you never thought I'd be the last person you ever saw before your miserable life ended. And now you probably regret what you did. Well, too late for that."

Dan chuckled silently.

As much as he wanted to prolong and enjoy this, he realised that time was of the essence. He couldn't take too long to finish Russell off. The risk of discovery was just too great.

And with that he opened the tap wide and watched the horrific spectacle of Russell Dwyer thrashing around as he drowned in urine.

Chapter 61

It was late, very late, but when Ollie's sleepy eyes eventually focused on the caller ID, he was wide awake and ready for action.

'Detective Phiri' was emblazoned across his cell phone screen.

"DC Phiri?" he answered expectantly, although with a slight bit of trepidation in his voice.

Detective Captain Phiri could hear the sleepiness in his voice.

"Apologies for waking you, Ollie," he said, genuinely remorseful, "but I think you'll be interested in this."

Ollie was all ears.

"What is it?" he asked inquisitively.

"Well, a call came in around eight p.m. from a very distraught lady. She claimed that her husband had been murdered and we needed to get our butts there immediately…"

"Go on…" Ollie prompted when DC Phiri hesitated.

"Dispatch sent out the alert and once the first patrol car had checked out the scene, I was called in."

He paused again for effect, which actually irked Ollie, but how could he rush this man's story?

"You're never going to believe this," he continued. "The scene was nearly identical to that of Craig Davis."

"What?" Ollie replied in a slightly elevated tone, which revealed his surprise. "He was horizontally hung as well?"

"No, no, no," the detective responded. "His death was far

more gruesome, if that's even possible. I mean the scene was staged like that of Craig Davis'. Hair all over the place – a variety of colours and lengths. Blood droplets here and there, which we assume are from different donors again. And finally puddles of liquid, which I'll bet are urine samples – again, most probably from various sources."

Without much hesitation, he continued, "We believe it's the same guy, getting his kicks out of overloading the forensics lab."

Ollie listened carefully and soon realised just how important it was to have DC Phiri on the payroll. He wasn't corrupt, or anything like that. Nothing illegal was ever asked of him. Mostly it was just a heads up here and there. After all, information was king and to get the inside track on whatever they needed, was always a boon.

Before DC Phiri could continue, Ollie interrupted him, "What did you mean that the murder was even more gruesome than that of Craig Davis?"

"You won't believe this – and neither did I. It's actually the first time in my career that I've seen something like this."

"No way! Another first?" Ollie remarked, very surprised by this.

"DC Phiri continued unabated, "He was drowned."

"Oh, that is awful, but what's so gruesome about that?" Ollie asked, now very confused.

"He was tightly secured against a pole. His hands, feet and head were tied, so no movement was possible. He had a tube shoved down his throat and above him hung a bag of urine. Picture an IV drip setup. The liquid was then pumped into his lungs until he drowned."

"No way!" Ollie repeated, even more surprised than previously. He broke out in goose bumps and cold sweats at the thought. Drowning was his worst fear, but this took drowning to a whole new level and he shuddered violently at the thought.

He repeated what DC Phiri had said, just to make sure he had heard correctly, "A tube was connected to a bag of urine. The tube was then rammed down the man's throat. The urine then flowed down the tube to fill the man's lungs ultimately causing him to drown?"

"Correct," DC Phiri responded, shaking his head emphatically, even though Ollie couldn't see him. "The coroner had to reconfirm the cause of death twice before I would believe him. Never in my life!"

DC Phiri had painted a picture far too graphic for Ollie to comprehend and he shook his head as if that would erase the image.

"We'll also need to use the plane again," DC Phiri continued. "There's another ton of evidence to get to the lab in Cape Town. No rush though. It'll probably take the team a few days to bag and tag it all again."

"And we'll probably hit a wall again with the results," Ollie commented. "Identifiable DNA but nothing in the database to compare it to."

He continued, "And it's probably exactly the same hair, blood and urine, as this punk spread about at the first scene."

"Probably," DC Phiri confirmed, "but we can't take short-cuts and make assumptions now, can we?"

"I suppose not. That's exactly what he's counting on to prove his point."

"Which reminds me," DC Phiri chimed in, "I read Julia's articles with great interest. She seems to know an awful lot more about this murderer and his motives than is common knowledge."

Ollie shrugged, not that DC Phiri could see him on the other end of the call.

"I know what I've told you, Ollie, and I know what general details have been released to the media, but Julia's articles have had that little bit extra. Anything I should know?"

Ollie hesitated, then finally answered, "Not that I know of. She's a great reporter and probably has some informant feeding her the juicy bits."

"Uh huh?" DC Phiri replied, unconvinced, but hesitant to pursue the subject.

Plausible deniability, Ollie thought to himself.

If the DC knew anything, he would be obligated to follow up, which would hamper their investigation and be very bad for them all.

He smiled to himself, knowing that DC Phiri would never follow through on this line of questioning. He would always have his suspicions, but to knowingly bite the hand that feeds wouldn't be too clever and he knew the detective to be a very shrewd man.

"Well, please keep *us* in the loop, DC," Ollie requested, emphasizing the 'us', as if DC Phiri wasn't aware that Alan Swan was the one paying the bills and pulling the strings. "Oh, and the plane is yours whenever you need it," Ollie added. "And a rush is probably needed before this animal strikes again."

Ollie bid the detective a good evening and lay back in his bed, absorbing the new information and knowing that falling asleep again would not be possible.

Chapter 62

After only a few minutes Ollie gave up all ideas of sleep.

He was tired, but his mind was swimming with all the information he'd just received. He washed his face, brushed his teeth and dressed. Jeans were his favourite, worn with a cotton long sleeve shirt with a few buttons at the neck, which were essential just for show. The typical Sam Hanna look that LL Cool J pulled off so well in CSI Los Angeles. It made muscular bodies look even more sizable without being overly ostentatious. He hated the latest fashion of ultra-short sleeves or wife beater vests, except of course for gym use.

In his opinion, if you had to wear those shirts in public, you were just vain and narcissistic. An attention seeking arsehole. Everyone could see you worked out and had a good body. Why rub it in their faces?

Ollie lived in a self-contained flatlet on the Swan property, even though he mostly ate and socialised with the family in the main house. It was not lavish, but he was comfortable. He was not a materialistic person and quite content with his meagre creature comforts.

He stuck the kettle on and waited patiently for the water to boil. He then took the cup of coffee and stood on his tiny patio drinking it while admiring the beautiful setting. It was faintly illuminated in the darkness by a nearly full moon. His familiarity with the grounds assisted more with the visualisation than his sight did, but nonetheless, it was an immaculate, kempt garden.

He lived in paradise and while he didn't own paradise, he was eternally grateful that he had met Alan Swan when he had, and furthermore had made enough of an impression on him, to at least become part of his world.

It was still early. In fact, it was only three o'clock. It was far too early and the information was not nearly urgent enough to rouse Alan from his slumber.

He decided to check out the scene for himself.

The streetlights shone brightly in the darkness, casting puddles of light every hundred metres or so, as he drove along the deserted roads. He was forced to activate the wipers, as the mist hung low and periodically built up enough on the windscreen to obscure his view of the road. It was quite an eerie and desolate night to be out driving.

DC Phiri had mentioned the address to him and he knew he was in the right neighbourhood when he turned the corner and was confronted by a fleet of police and civilian vehicles.

The house on the corner was receiving an inordinate amount of attention.

The area was haphazardly cordoned off with police tape and huge floodlights stood sentinel in the garden drenching the house, and in particular the garage, in bright light. The garage and driveway reminded Ollie of a beehive, as a swarm of SAPS employees bustled around busily.

Ollie pulled his car over a little way away and took a leisurely stroll up the street. He joined a group of on-lookers and reporters and tried to blend in as best as he could. Even with his contacts, he wouldn't be allowed near the crime scene. It was fresh and active.

"What happened?" he asked an elderly lady who stood clutching a shawl around her shoulders.

"We're not quite sure," she replied without shifting her gaze from the scene. "We overheard some cops talking and heard the name 'Russell' mentioned."

"Russell?" Ollie prompted.

"Yes, Russell Dwyer," she confirmed, "Marty, over there, claims to know the Dwyers and confirmed that they live in this house." She pointed to a middle-aged man standing on the edge of the group to indicate who she was referring to.

"So what actually happened?" Ollie continued, probing the little old lady for more information.

"It could be a murder or maybe even a suicide," another man standing nearby answered.

He was toting a camera, so Ollie made the assumption that he was a reporter, although no reporter lanyard or accreditation was evident around his neck.

Ollie looked over at him curiously.

"They carried somebody out earlier in a body-bag, so we know someone must have died," he continued, "but there's been no statement or mention of who or how. We believe it must have been Russell, as Marty confirmed, because we saw his wife and two children being escorted from the house earlier. They were so distraught."

Ollie lowered his head in deference to the sad news. "Very tragic," he muttered. "Sounds like you've been here for a while already?"

"Since the beginning," the reporter proudly exclaimed. "My police scanner is always on. You know how much the media pays for newsworthy photos?"

"No, actually, I don't," replied Ollie, "but it must be a lot to get you out of bed at this time of night."

"Yup, you can say that again."

"So you heard the first call come in then?" Ollie asked.

"Code 504 was called in and although that just means 'sudden death', when it was followed up shortly with code 507 which means 'admit body to mortuary', I rushed over."

"Been doing this for a while then?" Ollie grinned at the man.

"In this country with its high crime rate, most times deaths and murders aren't very newsworthy, but once in a while you get a real gem and I'm in the business of sniffing out those gems."

"Sounds fascinating."

"It is," the reporter continued and added, "so, what's your angle?"

"Nothing – nothing at all. I couldn't sleep, so was out driving around for a while. I literally turned the corner and came face to face with flashing police lights and danger tape. I thought it was a police blockade at first, but the activity didn't fit. Curiosity got the better of me and the next thing I knew, I'd parked my car and was standing here with you getting schooled on media photos and police codes," Ollie lied.

The reporter accepted the legitimacy of his answer and smiled broadly, as if to say 'been there, done that, buddy'.

Chapter 63

Ollie had seen and heard what he had come for and didn't want to overstay his welcome or make his presence too obvious.

His size and stature had already commanded a bit too much attention, as a few sideways glances had earlier confirmed.

The crowd had mostly dispersed and only the ardent reporters were still assembled when he decided that it was time to get going. They were too far away to see anything clearly anyway.

It was nearing six o'clock already.

He yawned and left the scene.

Traffic was building and the roads were getting busier as he made his way back to the mansion. For most, the work day generally only started at eight or even nine o'clock, but for some it seemed there was a seven o'clock start of which he was unaware. He wondered which industry began its workday that early.

He took a detour along the beachfront, as he still had a bit more time to waste.

The sun had just cleared the horizon and yet there was already a humdrum of activity in the ocean.

Ollie was impressed to see this much activity at this early hour. He was usually in the gym around this time, but each to their own, he guessed.

Surfers, donning full wetsuits to protect themselves from the chilly morning temperatures, were already paddling out and riding the waves back in. A kayak or surf-ski, Ollie could never figure out the difference, was making its way along the shore line beyond the breakers. Fun and fitness or fitness and fun? The motivation differed from person to person.

Seven o'clock finally arrived.

Julia would still be fast asleep, but he felt obliged to get her and her father around a table to give them the news.

He pulled over into one of the beachfront parking bays and with a picture-perfect view unfolding before him, he dialled Julia's number.

Her phone rang in his ear for what seemed like an eternity before her weary voice answered.

"Ollie?" she crackled.

He could hear that he'd woken her. "Sorry to wake you, Jules…"

"It's seven o'clock, Ollie," she interjected, as though he wouldn't or didn't know this already.

"I'm sorry, Jules. This couldn't wait."

"What couldn't wait?" she responded, now wide awake and fully alert.

"I'll tell you everything. How soon can you get to the mansion?"

Julia could hear the urgency in Ollie's voice. "Give me time to shower and dress and I'll be on my way."

"Okay, Jules, see you shortly."

Ollie then phoned Alan.

He was already awake.

"You're up bright and early, big guy."

"Morning, boss," Ollie answered respectfully, "unfortunately yes, the bad guys never sleep."

"Bad news, I take it?"

"Yes, but not business related."

Alan frowned. "What do you mean, not business related?"

"We believe that Dan has struck again."

"How'd you know?"

"DC Phiri called me in the early hours of the morning."

"How could he be so sure that it was Dan?"

"The crime scene was staged exactly as before."

"Son of a bitch!" Alan cursed into his cell phone.

Ollie had to move his handset away from his ear.

"Sorry, Ollie, that wasn't called for," Alan apologised.

"No problem, boss," Ollie replied, swapping his phone to his right ear, to give his deafened left ear a chance to recover.

"Well – go on then," Alan prompted.

"I'm on my way back home now and Jules will meet us there too."

Alan cursed again under his breath. He hated having to wait for anything, but as was becoming commonplace, when it concerned Dan, he was made to wait. He understood the practicality of relaying the story once and then taking questions, but it still frustrated him.

"Fine," he mumbled. "When will Julia be over?"

"She was just taking a shower, dressing and then would be on her way."

"I'll get Mavis to start with the breakfast."

"Okay, boss, see you shortly."

Ollie made a few more brief calls, issuing curt instructions to his team, and then begrudgingly relinquished his parking bay with the perfect view of the ocean. He'd been watching the aquatic activities while making the calls and had found the experience immensely cathartic and therapeutic.

In retrospect, he could have sat there the entire day if he hadn't had matters to attend to. He subsequently vowed to do it more often, although instinctively he knew that it would be far less frequent than he wished.

Chapter 64

It was barely eight o'clock and the mien of the garden outside the dining room was cloaked in a veil of mist or possibly even a low hanging cloud. A typical morning in a seaside town until the sun eventually managed to break through. The mansion was nestled in a shallow valley, which compounded the effect. The dew point and subsequent condensation wouldn't last long though and would disappear the moment the sun cleared the surrounding higher ground and baked the valley.

Alan, Julia and Ollie once again sat around the breakfast table.

Déjà vu, it would seem. This was becoming a habit and not one that any of them enjoyed.

They were all starving, but no-one touched the food Mavis had prepared, even though the tantalising aroma permeated the air. Coffee was a priority at this time of the morning, but that was all for now. They were gathered for a briefing after all – their grumbling stomachs would have to wait.

With the pleasantries and apologies, for the early disturbance, out of the way, Ollie took centre stage. He regaled them with the events of the night. The call he had received in the wee hours of the morning. The chat with DC Phiri. His trip out to the crime scene. His discussions with those gathered at the crime scene and more especially his conversation with the reporter.

He didn't miss a beat.

He'd had plenty of time waiting until dawn to nail down his recital and he didn't disappoint.

Alan and Julia listened attentively but, as before, there were no interruptions until the tale was told.

Ollie finally took a deep breath, sat back and waited.

"Are we sure it's him?" Alan asked.

"DC Phiri says he's positive and he wouldn't say that if there was any doubt."

"Why's he so sure?" Julia chipped in.

"Well, same evidence strewn around. Obviously, this still has to be verified by the crime lab, but DC Phiri was at both crime scenes and drew an immediate parallel."

Alan nodded in agreement. "He's had many years of experience and has always been rock solid in his judgements and in helping us out, when needed."

Ollie concurred with a few slow but steady nods of his head, but thought better of it than to tell Alan of DC Phiri's suspicions about their involvement at this stage.

"So, what's the connection between the first and second victim?"

"We don't know yet, Jules, but it's one of the leads the police will investigate."

"We'll get our team on it as well," Alan stated matter-of-factly, looking intently at Ollie.

Ollie had already briefed his team and some of the analysts were already hard at work scouring the internet, social media pages and any other platforms to which they could possibly gain access.

"Absolutely, boss, our team has already started digging. I'm waiting for feedback, as we speak."

"You said both victims were pretty much the same age, so

there must be some history there," Julia piped up.

"I believe so too. The team is working that angle as well. Once we have a connection between the victims, the pieces will start falling into place."

"And the evidence?" Alan questioned.

"The forensics team will again be busy for a few days scrubbing the scene and then they'll need the plane again."

"Of course," Alan said. "Goes without saying. We're here to help and to get to the bottom of this as soon as possible."

The room fell into stunned silence, as all three of them regressed into their own thoughts.

They took this opportunity to pick at the spread of food laid out before them. It was more of a Continental breakfast than a Full English breakfast, so only the croissants and muffins had cooled. Mavis was quick to reheat them and replenish the coffee when she heard the sounds of cutlery on crockery coming from the dining room.

"Thank you, Mavis," Julia said.

"Pleasure, Miss Julia," she replied and smiled genuinely, before leaving the room. She'd been working for the Swans for many years now and instinctively knew when her presence was required and when she should vacate the room.

"She's great, isn't she?" Julia quipped, deviating dramatically from the topic.

She was well paid for her services, so Alan regarded her as just another employee, but he shrugged and nodded just the same. She definitely wasn't ill-treated, but she wasn't part of the family, as could be said of Ollie. As long as she performed her tasks as required and expected, she would remain in their employ and that's as much as Alan thought of that.

Chapter 65

Ollie's phone vibrated on the table.

All three of them immediately looked curiously down at it and tried unsuccessfully to read the caller ID.

He always put it on 'silent' when they were in a meeting. He knew from prior experience that his phone was bound to ring at the most inconvenient of times. He was constantly juggling numerous balls for Alan and there was always feedback or a query which required his attention.

He excused himself from the table and walked out onto the veranda to take the call.

It was now a beautiful day outside even though a slight breeze chased a few dead leaves playfully around Ollie's legs.

He paced the length of the veranda while talking animatedly to the caller, while Alan and Julia looked on inquisitively. He re-entered the dining room, hiding his concerns behind a granite mask.

"That was Thuso," he commented almost casually.

Alan looked over at Julia, who looked expectantly at Ollie.

"What, Ollie?" she cried out.

"Not such great news, I'm afraid," he responded. "Thuso has a letter – addressed to you."

"Oh come on," she said, exasperation clinging to every word.

"He was staking out your apartment. A beggar approached him, firstly asking for money, and when he was brushed off, he pulled the folded letter from one of his pockets and handed it to Thuso."

"A beggar?" Alan questioned in a raised voice.

"That's what he said," replied Ollie.

"Another hand-off," Julia added, shaking her head in disbelief.

"Unfortunately yes, Jules. They questioned the beggar and followed his directions but couldn't find the old man who'd given him the letter to deliver."

"Let me guess," Alan chipped in, "the old man got the letter from someone else?"

"Well, we don't know that for sure, but that is the assumption."

"This bastard is driving me insane," Alan commented harshly. "And he's always one step ahead of us. He knows we're watching Julia's apartment. He knows your team members. He knows where they're posted. He knows everything."

Ollie shrugged, but was not defeated. "I'll swap them all out. They'll go deeper under-cover than ever before. He won't get the better of me," Ollie concluded.

"So where's the letter?" asked Julia, trying to stay as calm as possible.

"Thuso gave the letter to Manny, who's on his way over."

"That's four hands it's been through… that we know of," Alan stated.

"As with the others, I doubt there'd be any trace evidence on it anyway. This man isn't going to be caught out with something as simple as that. Forensic evidence is his favourite subject anyway," Ollie answered, concluding Alan's thoughts.

"Well, no surprises there then," Alan added.

Minutes later, Manny appeared sheepishly in the doorway.

None of them had heard the doorbell.

Mavis must have let him in.

Manny looked over at Alan and Julia first and nodded, "Morning sir – ma'am."

Alan nodded in response.

Julia looked up and smiled wanly. "Morning, Manny, how are you today?"

Manny smiled back warmly, "Very well, thank you, Miss Julia."

For years he had watched protectively over Julia and although their relationship could never be classed as friendship, they had forged a genuinely amicable bond over the years.

He could sense the tension in the room and was not very eager to hang around any longer than necessary.

He turned to Ollie and nodded respectfully to his direct boss and presented the letter with a slight genuflect and bow of the head. It was a sign of respect in his culture when greeting, presenting or receiving anything.

"Thank you, Manny."

Ollie and Manny had shared many adventures together over the years and Manny had, on more than one occasion, saved the day and Ollie for that matter. With his unique combination of offensive and defensive skills, he was a formidable adversary.

Ollie was more the bone-crushing giant, while Manny was the sinewy and deft combatant. But in any relationship, there had to be an alpha, and Ollie undoubtedly held that position.

Manny really didn't want to overstay his welcome and with a slight twitch of his head he signalled the door. Ollie nodded subtly, totally understanding the gesture and hence granting permission for Manny to leave.

"We'll talk later," Ollie added, as Manny turned on his heels and departed.

Alan and Julia looked at Ollie expectantly, as he twirled the envelopment between his fingers.

"Should I read it?" he offered courteously.

Julia shook her head. "No, it's addressed to me, I'll do the honours."

Alan wasn't so sure about this, as Julia was in a rather fragile state and he wondered whether she'd be able to get through it before another meltdown began. "Are you sure?" he asked out of concern.

She emphatically ripped the envelope open, as if to put Alan's concerns to rest.

Chapter 66

The torn envelope gave up its contents easily, as Julia widened the tear and tugged at the letter.

Standard white paper again.

Simple typeface and font.

Exactly the same as all the others.

No surprises there.

Dan had been busy, she thought.

A murder last night and already a hand-delivered letter this early in the morning. She wondered whether he had written it before or after the murder.

She cleared her throat and began from the top.

Dear Julia,

As you already know, I was quite a busy-body last night.

Well, that answered her question.

The letter was definitely written after the fact.

Julia suddenly frowned and looked over at Ollie, questioningly. "How could he know that I already knew about the murder, when he wrote this letter?"

Ollie shrugged. "Dumb luck, assumption or deduction."

"There's no dumb luck with this guy," Alan commented. "He wouldn't even rely on assumption. He's far too methodical for that."

"Okay, deduction then," added Julia. "But how?"

Alan thought for a moment, then threw out a whammy, "Observation. He, or someone he trusts, has been watching one of you."

Julia and Ollie both shook their heads vigorously, emphatically denying the possibility.

"We're trained to pick up on things like that," Ollie replied. "He wouldn't tail me and my team is watching Julia day and night.

"Okay then, what's left? Could he be listening in? Could he somehow have cloned or tapped our phones?"

"Unlikely," replied Ollie, "we run regular scans and do regular sweeps for bugs. We have some of the best IT minds on the payroll and we run a very tight ship."

Alan knew this and nodded in agreement. He should've known better than to question Ollie on the security protocols they'd devised and implemented over the years.

"Carry on, Julia, we'll give it some more thought and circle back to it when you're done," Alan conceded.

Julia raised the letter and began again.

Dear Julia,

As you already know, I was quite a busy-body last night.

It wasn't something I relished doing, although I must admit, it was absolutely fascinating and obviously vitally important to give impetus to my agenda.

The police should now be joining the dots. Having seen the similarities between the two crime scenes, the only conclusion would be that a serial killer is roaming the city.

Maybe now they'll pay attention to the issues and deficiencies I have highlighted through your articles.

His name was Russell Dwyer, as Olawale has more than likely already briefed you. Now, while on the surface he came across as a really nice guy – a loving husband and doting father – he was latently as evil as evil could be. He deserved everything that came to him and even more if I'd had the time.

He undeniably brought this upon himself.

I was merely the instrument of justice.

I, again, left a few goodies for the forensics team at the scene.

Still not making it easy for you, I know, but you need to appreciate my position.

I'm not, after all, in this to get caught.

I'm trying to make a point and spur on some accountability and responsibility.

A point, which I hope will be remedied in the really near future.

I have noticed some progress though.

I see the police have seconded the Swan Lear Jet for priority transportation of the evidence to Cape Town.

That is definitely a step in the right direction, even though it probably has no bearing whatsoever on whether the evidence is actually being processed expeditiously or not.

Why would it?

These are just mundane murders of low priority individuals in an unimportant part of the country. Maybe the second murder might raise a few eyebrows, but I'll bet that only the third or fourth will ultimately pique some genuine interest and reaction. Murders in this country are a dime a dozen and we have all become immune to the shock and horror of a human life being taken.

Bodies are piling up around the country, but if the cornerstones of the investigation process are not in place, is there even a chance of the villains being apprehended and justice being served?

I think not.

But once again I digress.

This was just meant to be a courtesy call to ensure that you knew that Russell was one of mine.

I expect more than just the facts this time, Julia.

A bit of that poetic license and creativity needs to shine through and turn a good article into a great article. We can't afford to lose the reader-base, we have already so adeptly established, with some half-baked reporting on just another murder in our valley.

I trust that we now have an understanding.

Best Regards,

Daniel Nathan Anderson

With trembling hands, Julia gently placed the letter on the table in front of her. She tried her utmost to maintain her resolute composure, but the steely glint in her eyes imminently yielded to the glistening of tears, which she tried ineffectively to blink away. She reached for the tissue Ollie offered her and dabbed roughly at the corners of her eyes, as if defying her natural instinct to burst into tears.

Chapter 67

Alan turned to Ollie. "He knew you were there, big guy. He mentioned you by name. First time he's done that. In fact, first time he's used one of your team to deliver the letter to us."

Ollie squinted slightly, stared off into space and regressed into his memories.

Alan had seen him do this before and wasn't surprised when no answers were immediately forthcoming. He waited patiently and used the opportunity to butter a scone and lather it with strawberry jam and cream. The scone had cooled significantly, but every bite was still sublimely delicious.

Julia shifted her gaze between the two of them in utter dismay. She was about to break the silence when Alan raised his hand cautioning her to hold back.

Ollie finally re-surfaced after a few more minutes.

He didn't have a photographic or eidetic memory, but he had honed his observation skills to such a degree over the years that he could replay entire events and barely miss a detail.

He nodded his head as if satisfied. "There were quite a few onlookers at the crime scene, but most of them were from the neighbourhood. Nobody looked suspicious or out of place." He took a deep breath and with a steady pace continued, "Police were milling around going about their business, but not nearly enough of them for an imposter to mingle in amongst them and be overlooked. The only red-flag, if any, was the reporter I spoke to."

"Could it be him then?" Julia queried.

Ollie shook his head. "Average height. Obese. Red-faced. Sweating, even with a cool breeze blowing. This guy couldn't sneak up on anyone unnoticed, even if they were already dead."

"Follow up on him, anyway," Alan instructed. "We might just be overlooking something very obvious. No unanswered questions. We'll also need to re-write the entire playbook. This guy knows far too much about us and how we do things. He's basically toying with us. Probably getting more kicks out of foiling us than from the murders."

Ollie nodded in agreement and stretched forward to grab a bite, as his stomach grumbled audibly.

Alan then turned his attention to Julia.

"Will you manage to get through this, Julia?"

She nodded in affirmation.

"You know you're welcome to move back in?" he reiterated. "If anything, it would make me feel a whole lot better," he added.

"Dad, you know I can't. It's really getting to me but if I do as he says, I'm in no danger."

Alan didn't force the issue. "How did your meeting with Moses go?" The segue caught her by surprise, but she welcomed the redirection, as she hadn't had the time or opportunity to update her father yet.

"As you can imagine, he wasn't very amenable at first and I had to let a bit more slip than I initially wanted to, but he eventually relented. I know it'll put him under the microscope, but knowing what he knows now, he was ultimately willing to put himself in that position."

Alan nodded his head almost imperceptibly as he listened to Julia. "So what does that actually mean?"

Julia was expecting the follow-up question. "Well, I now

have the latitude to expound a bit more on the man and his dogmas, as opposed to sticking rigidly to the facts alone."

Alan looked over at Ollie, who frowned back at him, tilting his head slightly to the side. They weren't stupid men, but Julia's last statement had sailed straight over the heads.

"You can do 'what'?" Alan stammered.

Julia smiled openly. She loved them both to bits, but they certainly didn't have doctorates in language or journalism.

Alan smiled affably. "You're messing with us, aren't you?"

"A little," she admitted. "Basically, I can write more about Dan and his back-story than just regurgitate the facts around each murder case. It's a fine line though and Moses clearly warned me about not glamourising Dan and his crusade."

"That is a fine line," Ollie concurred. "DC Phiri already has suspicions that we know more about this case than what we're letting on."

"And now you'll be confirming that in print," Alan added, finishing Ollie's train of thought.

"There's no way around that," Julia replied. "I can't do one without the other."

Alan's face contorted with concern.

"We can't get caught in the middle of this. It could be misconstrued as obstruction of justice. We need to get ahead of this and quickly."

"What's your suggestion, boss?"

"Ollie, you need to meet with DC Phiri. He doesn't need to know all the details. In fact, nothing about the letters because that's material evidence we have been withholding. Maybe just let him know that his instincts were correct and that the murderer has been in contact with Julia and has been feeding her with the details for her exposés."

Ollie nodded, but not very confidently. "He's no fool. He's bound to follow up with the obvious question of how the murderer's been contacting her. I know I would."

"I would too," Alan answered, cursing softly under his breath. "You need to somehow put his mind at ease that we're investigating that part and we'll bring him up to speed as soon as we have something tangible. I know he's on our payroll, but he's also a principled man, so while he might not break any rules for us, he might just bend them slightly for the greater good."

It was not going to be easy.

Julia had a sudden thought and raised her finger to make the point. "Maybe Dan knows that you talk to DC Phiri often and that more than pleasantries are exchanged."

Ollie shifted uneasily in his chair. "Maybe you're right, Jules. Maybe the police Captain's phone has been hacked and he's been listening into our conversations all along. It makes sense. I'll check it out."

Julia nodded, but began to feel restless. She looked at her watch and then did a double take. How had the time flown by so quickly?

The breakfast gathering had stretched well into the mid-morning hours.

They had all been so consumed with the discussion that they hadn't even noticed the time. They suddenly realised that they all had business to attend to and almost stood in unison. Farewells were brief as they exited.

Alan's words followed Julia out of the room – "Be careful, my love."

Chapter 68

The night had finally arrived.

Anne was anxious, but at the same time rather excited.

It was her first date in a long time.

She had been meeting with Peter regularly at the gym and they'd grown very comfortable in each other's company.

So why the anxiety now, she wondered?

They had decided on the Grill Room for their first 'date'.

It was categorised as a traditional steakhouse combined with bespoke upmarket dining and occupied the ground floor of the Premier Hotel Regent. They had both chuckled at the description, thinking that bespoke referred to really fancy five-star dishes and how that wouldn't suit either of them.

They burnt off far too many calories each day to splurge on tiny portions, no matter how tasty they would be.

It was only later and with a little embarrassment that Anne found out that bespoke simply meant 'custom-made'.

Out of pure convenience, they had agreed to meet at the restaurant at six o'clock instead of driving together. After all, they were travelling from opposite sides of the city.

There was ample parking when Anne arrived and she whizzed into the first vacant spot she found. Peter was already there waiting patiently on the sidewalk for her. She tried her best to be as ladylike as possible when she climbed out of her vehicle. Trainers, tights and sweat-shirts were more her style, but tonight she'd sacrificed comfort for glamour.

Peter gasped as he approached her.

"You look beautiful," he gushed, looking her up and down in admiration.

She hadn't gone overboard shopping, but had found an OBR red-striped bodycon dress which hugged her curvaceous and defined body perfectly. She had completed the ensemble with a pair of elegant black Chelsea boots. Something a little more bulky had been preferable, as trying to balance on heels the entire night seemed too much like hard work to her.

Anne blushed ever so slightly and returned the compliment. "Thank you. You clean up very nicely yourself, Mr Roland."

Peter wore a pair of black trousers, wing-tipped shoes, a dark open-necked shirt and an unbuttoned blazer. It was more than adequate for the occasion, unless the dress code had suddenly changed to formal.

The restaurant had opened its doors at five o'clock and was already quite a hive of activity. Peter ushered Anne through the door ahead of him, by placing his hand on the small of her back. The titillation of the tingle which suddenly coursed through her body took her somewhat by surprise. She hadn't quite expected that reaction to his touch.

"Peter Roland. Six o'clock. Table for two," he announced to the maître d'.

The maître d' scanned the reservation list and ticked the arrivals box. He smiled professionally and said, "Welcome to the Grill Room, please follow me this way."

He deftly lifted two menus and a wine list from his station and strode purposefully across the room where he seated them at a quaint little table alongside the bay window, overlooking the ocean.

"Dinner with a view," he commented cheerfully. He

presented them with the menus and the wine list and directed their attention to a waiter, who had miraculously appeared alongside him.

"This is Ralph, he will be serving you tonight. Please enjoy your evening with us."

And with that, he was gone.

Ralph re-introduced himself, just in case they hadn't heard his name the first time and after a brief orientation of the restaurant, offered to give them a few minutes to decide on their drinks and starters.

The couple took the opportunity to look around and take in the detail and ambiance of their surroundings.

The restaurant was far more lavish than they'd expected.

Audibly, a Jazz and Bossa Nova collaboration created a relaxed but upbeat mood. It was pitched at the perfect volume. It masked all auxiliary noises, but was not too loud to disrupt their conversation or force them to raise their voices.

Visually, dark wooden cladding covered the lower expanses of the walls, while alternately dark and light striped beige wallpaper covered the upper reaches. Polished wooden tables of varying sizes and configurations adorned the area, already set and awaiting their designated occupants. The plush leather seats, while simple in design, were extremely comfortable. It would be a difficult proposition to stand up and leave when the time came. The windows offered a stunning view of the ocean outside even though the setting sun and the onset of darkness would soon negate that feature. But the focal piece was undoubtedly the dark mahogany wine rack partition. The rhombus-shaped voids were filled to varying capacities with red-wine bottles, all intentionally resting horizontally. Possibly grouped by distillery or maybe even by blend. Irrelevant though, it was a masterful design and a vision to behold.

If Peter was asked for his opinion, the only constructive criticism he would have had was that the walls looked too overcrowded with classic and antiquated pictures and photographs. But then again, who would ask him? He was definitely no interior decorator.

The evening wore on pleasantly and while Anne enjoyed the Mozambican Chicken, Peter indulged in a massive seven-hundred-and-fifty-gram T-bone steak.

Neither were big drinkers, so they decided to share a bottle of Beyerskloof Pinotage which they quaffed the entire evening.

From the wine to the food to the company, absolutely everything was just perfect and before they knew it their night was coming to an end.

Peter chivalrously paid the bill, although Anne was adamant that she wanted to contribute. All to no avail, though, as he took the billfold and gently pushed her hand away.

A walk along the beachfront would have been an awesome end to a perfect evening, but it was getting late and they both had early starts the next morning.

Instead, they slowly walked to Anne's car continuing to enjoy each other's company.

When a natural break in the conversation finally presented itself, Peter leaned in and gave her a lingering kiss on the cheek. Just enough to leave her wanting more.

Anne was baffled that such an amazing evening would end with such a simple goodbye, but in retrospect was partly grateful and relieved that nothing more was expected. They were taking it very slow, which was abundantly clear.

Chapter 69

"So, what's happening tonight, my friend?"

Julia was so happy to hear Cathy's voice that she nearly burst into tears. She'd spent the previous day trapped in her own misery again. Between sulking, sobbing, sleeping and a tiny bit of planning, the balance of the day had flown by. The walls were closing in on her and she was getting a serious case of cabin fever even in her own apartment. She needed to get out. The universe had heard her and had responded in kind.

"Perfect timing, Caths. I need to get out. I'm driving myself insane."

"Ex – cellent," joked Cathy. "Should we assemble the troops for later or should we just sneak out now? Oh wait, I can't sneak out right now, I have a meeting scheduled, which will probably d-r-a-a-a-g-g out the whole day."

She was such a hoot. She had a real knack of making Julia forget her worries and very soon the proverbial frown would be turned upside down.

"Same place, same time then?" Julia answered. "I'll call Anne, you call Sam."

"Done and done," replied Cathy. "See you later then. Oh, one more thing – we need an update, girl."

"I wouldn't even know where to start. There have been so many developments. It's even got me all flustered."

Cathy smiled broadly on the other end of the call. "The beginning, Jules, always start at the beginning. Or in this case, where you left off the last time."

"Okay. See you later, my friend." She punctuated her goodbyes with an air-kiss and hung up.

Buccaneers was buzzing again when the four girls arrived. This place never ceased to amaze. No matter what day of the week or time of day it was.

It was barely evening. More accurately, it was late afternoon. The lunch trade was already being replaced by the sun-downer trade, which would in turn be replaced by the dinner trade.

The wind was gradually picking up and it was becoming fairly nippy outside.

At a glance, the girls noticed that the tarpaulin sheets with their plastic transparent windows, had been lowered to enclose the outside deck and protect the patrons from the elements. It was tempting, but after a quick vote they opted for inside seating. Warmth and comfort trumped a sea-view anytime. The smokers would just have to survive.

The four girls spread themselves selfishly around a six-seater table which they found in a back corner. Handbags served as spacers and created the illusion that the table was at full capacity. It was a girl's night out and they really didn't want to share seating with strangers.

No sooner had they made themselves comfortable, than Fred suddenly appeared with their usual order.

The bottle of wine was already opened – ready and waiting.

He smiled broadly. "I saw you come in and thought I'd save you some time." His gaze never left Sam's and yet he spoke to the entire group.

"I thought I'd have something different tonight for a change," piped up Cathy.

This comment instantly tore Fred's gaze away from Sam's,

as he realised he'd made a huge and probably costly blunder. It would come out of his wages or tips, after all.

Cathy couldn't contain herself and burst out laughing.

"Just kidding, lover-boy. You did well. Thank you."

She smiled at Sam, who was not amused.

"What?" Cathy asked curiously. "I was only joking and I did say 'thank you'."

Not wanting to be caught in the middle of this, Fred swiftly turned on his heels and rushed off.

"Did I spoil the moment?" Cathy asked Sam, rolling her eyes mockingly.

Sam fumed.

"All right, you two," Anne interjected before the situation escalated. "We don't often get together any more, so we can't waste time with any of this bickering."

Cathy and Sam knew she was right.

"Sorry, my friend, maybe I was a bit insensitive."

"Yes, you were. We're only just getting things started and I don't need you scaring him off."

Cathy leaned over and gave her smoking partner a big hug. "No harm intended," she whispered in her ear, "and I'm rooting for you. He's quite a catch."

"I know, right," Sam whispered back.

All was instantly forgiven.

With the histrionics out of the way, the girls clinked their glasses in a toast to eternal friendship.

"So, what's been happenin'?" Cathy quipped. Her remark was aimed more at Julia, but Anne decided that this was her cue to take centre-stage. It was safer to just come clean. If this lot discovered her so-called relationship before she'd told them, she'd never hear the end of it.

It wasn't as if she'd never been in a relationship before, but somehow this time felt different to her. Her exploits rolled like honey off her tongue and all the girls picked up on the change in her tone and could clearly sense the intensity.

"Oh, wow," Cathy remarked in dismay. "Soon I'll be the last turkey in the shop. We all know Julia can get anyone she wants, any time she wants, and with you two getting serious, I better get my act together. Couples evening will be awful if I'm the only single."

"Oh, come on now," Julia countered. "We've all been in relationships. It's never messed with our dynamic before. Just because Anne and Sam have fishes on the hooks doesn't mean that the rest of us have to panic. Good for them, I say. It's been a while since any of us had commitments anyway."

"I suppose," Cathy grumbled and shrugged, although not totally convinced. "Now your turn, Jules."

Chapter 70

Déjà vu – again – thought Julia.

Her friends' eyes bored into her expectantly and a sudden rush of self-consciousness flooded over her. Nothing a mouthful of wine couldn't remedy.

She swirled the wine in her mouth, savoured the taste and finally swallowed it down. Now where had she ended off and where should she begin?

Oh yes. Her last article and all the accolades.

The visit from her friends and the celebratory drinks in her apartment.

A lot had happened since then. She knew it and they looked on – anticipating it.

Finally, she began – as advised by Cathy – at the beginning.

Or more accurately, at the beginning of the sequel.

She described her drive in the country-side to clear her head, the delivery of the letter in the burger box and the subsequent apology from Dan about the DNA Dan moniker and his demands on her future articles.

The girls gasped. Totally engrossed in the story.

A flash of sheet lightning suddenly lit up Buccaneers creating some ominous visual effects for Julia's story. The girls all jumped. It was followed a few seconds later by the vague rumble of thunder.

A part of the storm had blown in on the breeze, but based on the far-off thunder, it was really still way off in the distance.

The unexpected staccato of raindrops on the roof refuted any truth in that and progressed into sheets which were blasted across the façade of the building by the gusting wind. The tarpaulin on the deck now flapped loudly under the onslaught of the wind and rain.

Julia waited patiently to continue, as the roar of the downpour drowned out the possibility of her being heard.

Darkness unexpectedly engulfed the restaurant, as the storm knocked out the power. It was pitch black for a few moments until the generator kicked in, but true to form a few girls squealed, while the guys just sat motionless and waited for the moment to pass. Why girls felt the need to squeal whenever the lights failed would always be a mystery.

Not all the lights were connected to the 'gennie', but the dull glow was sufficient to illuminate the surroundings, and for business to continue.

The girls sipped their drinks and ushered Julia on with their eyes. The rain had let up to a degree and the cacophony of the raindrops beating down on the building had faded significantly.

Sam caught Fred's roving eyes and confirmed their safety with a few succinct nods. She then went on to raise her index finger to make a circular motion in the air, which in a restaurant environment was for some reason the universal signal for 'another round for the group, please'.

While they waited for another bottle of wine, Julia continued.

She detailed the meeting with Moses and his eventual acquiescence as to how she needed to compose her next articles.

Then came the murder, the phone-call to Ollie and his visit to the crime scene.

She described the crime scene, as best she could from Ollie's meticulous account and finally moved on to the modus operandi and the litter of evidence contaminating the crime scene.

The fascinated and horrified looks on the girls' faces told a story all on their own.

Fred unwittingly broke the tension when he unceremoniously appeared between Julia and Cathy with another bottle of wine.

He placed fresh glasses in front of the girls, removed the used ones and took his time to unscrew the cap, all the while looking over at Sam.

Cathy had to bite her tongue before she caused another uproar by saying something snarky, like 'get a room, why don't you'.

Fred topped up the glasses and left the bottle with its meagre remnants on the table.

"Anything to eat tonight, ladies?" he asked.

"Not right now," the girls answered tersely, desperately wanting some privacy so Julia could conclude her story.

"Give me a shout if you change your minds," Fred answered, spinning on his heels and heading off to wait on another table.

Julia scanned the room for any unwarranted attention and then without faltering continued where she'd left off.

"The last letter confirmed that Dan was responsible for the latest murder, as it contained names and details which were, as yet, unreleased by the police."

She selectively omitted all details about her mental anguish and near-meltdown.

"And that's where we are right now," she concluded. "The floor is now open for questions."

There was complete silence.

The girls were still digesting all the information they'd just been given.

Finally, Anne broke the silence. "Horizontal hanging and now intubated drowning. Either this guy is the most creative killer on the planet or there's some meaning to the methods he's using to kill his victims."

"He does keep harping on about them deserving what they got, but I just can't seem to put the pieces together," Julia responded.

"Yeah, maybe I'm just reading into things here too. If they'd done the same to him, he'd already be dead. No chance he's a ghost, is there?" Anne grinned, in an attempt to make light of the tension they all felt.

"Doubt it," Julia replied, "but it does make for an interesting hypothesis."

Cathy and Sam nodded in agreement.

"I now have to write an article, not only describing the incident, but also glamourising him or at a minimum, his quest – but without coming across as glamourising. Definitely not looking forward to that."

Heads nodded in unison around the table. They really felt for her and the predicament she was in.

"Shout, if you think of any other angles. I could use all the help possible on this one."

After finishing their drinks and wrapping up with a bit of generalized chit-chat, the girls decided to call it quits and head on home.

Julia wasn't looking forward to the confines of her apartment or being alone while her thoughts rampaged around in her head.

Sleeping pills again, she finally decided.

Chapter 71

The sun hadn't even made its daily appearance when the activity in her head woke her.

She was still groggy from the sleeping pills, but her mind was in hyper-drive. Getting back to sleep would be impossible.

It was something Anne had said. It seemed to race around her mind without making any progress, like a hamster on a treadmill.

'Was he a ghost?'

No way. That couldn't have been it.

Although it certainly would answer some of the conundrums of not being able to identify or stop Dan.

Nah – crazy thought. Julia discarded it.

So what was it that was playing on her mind?

What had Anne said?

'Some meaning to the methods he's using to kill his victims.'

She mulled this over for a while.

There could be something to this.

What was it that was trying to bubble to the surface?

The more she thought about it the more perplexed she became.

"Get up, get dressed and get the day started. It'll come to you when you're not fixating on it," she mumbled to herself.

She had research to do and an article to write anyway.

Many cups of coffee and many hours later, Julia emerged from the rabbit-hole down which she'd descended earlier that day.

Her eyes were burning and her head was pounding, as an incessant headache had built to a crescendo in her temples.

But there it was – the draft article – staring ominously back at her.

She routinely became overly engrossed in what she was doing and generally lost all track of time. The apartment could probably have burnt down around her without her being aware of it. Totally absorbed in her alternate reality.

All too often, she'd only have vague recollections of actually writing these articles.

Yet 'magically', her exposé was there, etched on the screen before her.

She smiled for the first time in a long time, as she scanned through the final paragraph.

Later she would review it thoroughly, as she knew all too well that the first draft was never the final draft.

Her eyes were bloodshot, her head pounded, she felt physically drained and frankly quite faint from not eating the entire day.

Her hands also showed their disapproval by trembling uncontrollably as she lifted her mug to her mouth and nearly spilled the dregs of her umpteenth cup of coffee all over herself.

Coffee alone could only sustain you for so long.

She needed to eat and a substantial meal at that. Fast foods would not suffice this time. A home-cooked meal would be the answer and although she never liked to impose on her parents, especially at the last minute, she would swallow her pride today as her stomach grumbled unhappily.

Besides – she convinced herself – they relished the time she spent with them.

The perfunctory call to her mother was short and sweet, although met with some genuine concern about her wellbeing. A mother somehow always just knew. Julia desperately needed to shower and freshen up. She had to look semi-human before dinner to allay her mother's concerns or she'd have to sit through another lecture on how she wasn't caring for herself.

She was in no mood for a lengthy chat right now and even though she felt bad about abruptly ending the call, she couldn't wait to jump into a nice, hot shower. "I really need to go now, Mom. I'll see you in a bit."

Claire had no option but to bid her daughter farewell. "I'll let Mavis know you're joining us for dinner. See you soon. Love you, Julia."

The bathroom was at best a few square metres in size and the powerful jets of hot water which pounded down on her took no time at all to steam up the confined space.

She briskly soaped herself down until she felt squeaky clean and then just stood under the downpour, allowing the concentrated spray to massage the pain and stiffness from her weary neck and shoulder muscles.

She was usually very conscientious about her water usage, but today was definitely not going to be one of those days, as she let the water power her troubles into submission.

A fine mist confronted her as she exited the shower stall, while droplets of condensation had collected to form tiny rivulets which snaked their way down the walls.

After towelling herself off, she repeatedly wiped down the foggy mirror to get a glimpse of what the labours of the day had done to her.

The shower had been so refreshing and while she felt better, she still looked haggard and dishevelled.

Her face was gaunt and freakishly grey in colour. No sign of her usual lustre or attractiveness. This was taking its toll on her.

Make-up would be an absolute necessity for tonight, she thought to herself.

Her mother would pop her clogs if she saw her like this.

Chapter 72

The aroma was the first to greet her as she walked through the front door.

She had learnt all her cooking skills from Mavis. She'd never been the best culinary student. She'd diligently made copious amounts of notes and copied reams of recipes, but she was still fairly inadequate in the kitchen and quite ashamed of her limitations. It reeked of privilege and although she felt blessed to have had these benefits in her life, she loathed the inimitable feeling of guilt which accompanied it.

She would never starve, but she'd also never be able to put on a worthy spread, the likes of which they were about to indulge in.

Practice and repetition were key and at this stage of her life neither was happening. She'd probably need to get her act together when marriage and family entered the fray.

The dining room was a sight for sore eyes and Julia's stomach grumbled again in acquiescence. The lighting had been dimmed so the soft glow could enhance the intimacy. An ornately patterned, cream-coloured table-cloth covered the table and four place-settings were neatly positioned and poised for the imminent feast.

Alan and Claire had agreed very early in their relationship that even if they saw very little of each other during the course of the day, dinner-time around the dinner table was sacrosanct. Exceptions to the rule were only tolerated under extreme circumstances. It was a time-honoured tradition and was so much more than just making an effort to eat together. It was a time to break bread as well as communicate. They would catch up on the activities in each other's lives, discuss business and even debate the merits of future plans.

Julia fondly recalled these gatherings from her childhood.

The conversations and discussions had mostly revolved around her at the time and in retrospect had served to nurture and shape her journey into adulthood.

It had been a safe space and no subjects were off limits, although occasionally quite awkward.

"Hello, Julia," Claire whispered from behind her.

Julia squealed and jumped in response, as she was ripped from her reminiscing back into the present.

"Hi, Mom. You startled me."

"I could see that you were a million miles away – that's why I whispered."

"Just thinking of the old days and all the times we sat around this table."

"Oh? Well, the table's not going anywhere and we could easily include you and make new memories," Claire joked, prodding Julia with her insinuations of moving back into the mansion again.

"Ha." Julia faked a laugh, not for a second contemplating giving up her independence, even for this luxurious lifestyle.

She reached out and warmly embraced her mother, drawing strength and confidence from this woman who she so deeply admired.

A little too long though, which raised Claire's suspicions.

She eventually backed up a little. "Let's get a good look at you, young lady.

You've lost too much weight. Your face is gaunt. Your eyes are bloodshot. You have bags under your eyes. Your attempt to cover it up with concealer doesn't fool me either."

"Mom! I didn't come over to get the third degree."

"I know, Julia, but I have to say it as it is. This case you're working on is really pushing you to the limits. No-one your age should be subjected to something like this."

"I know, Mom, but what can I do? There's no way out. I was chosen by him and I have to see it through. Dad and Ollie are trying, by all means, to put an end to it, but as you know, there are more dead ends than leads."

Claire moved in again and hugged her daughter again.

Julia melted into her embrace, as though Claire was mystically absorbing her stress and tension from her.

A mother knows when to comfort and just how to do it.

Mavis interrupted them by announcing out loud that their dinner was served.

The ladies turned from the doorway to face the table just as Alan and Ollie entered the room from the study.

"Julia, I didn't even know you had arrived," Alan commented enthusiastically and strode over to embrace her.

"Hi, Jules," Ollie echoed from across the room, smiling broadly as was customary for him.

Claire moved to the table and said, "Come on, let's eat. Julia needs to put some meat on her bones." She sat down and waited for the others to join.

Mavis moved in, removed the lids from the serving dishes and placed serving spoons in each.

"Roast lamb, rice, spinach, butternut, baby peas, roast potatoes and gravy," she stated, pointing to each in turn.

The way these dishes were prepared was far from the norm and no doubt would have had extremely fanciful names and descriptions had they been on a restaurant menu.

Julia inhaled deeply. She was starving and the tantalising aroma was wreaking havoc on her neglected stomach.

Chapter 73

It was late enough in the evening to witness the mass exodus from the gym, but not too late to detract from a good workout. He would be slightly pressed for time before the gym closed, but he would at least get through most of his usual routine.

The area became progressively less congested and Dan could now move around freely between the various apparatus he needed for his session.

The evening was cool and his skin bristled slightly as he stripped down to his workout gear.

He had neglected the gym for too long.

He felt lethargic.

His large frame creaked as he started off with a few stretches and some light weight repetitions to get his blood circulating properly, but once he was into the swing of things, he started piling on the weights to push himself.

It was like riding a bike and it wasn't too long before he cycled into a steady rhythm and the sweat started streaming off his body.

He looked up periodically and admired his glistening body in the wall-mounted mirrors. He was always amazed – even dumbfounded – at how much he had bulked up. The metamorphosis was truly daunting.

It was at times like these when his mind would wander back to his childhood.

He disliked this retrospection, but it had taught him so much.

He had been a scrawny, whiny little runt back then. He would have detested that little runt himself, had it not been himself. But, would he have been who he was today, had it not have been for the enlightenment gained from being who he had been back then? It was doubtful. He had taken the knocks, learnt from them and evolved into the specimen that stared back at him from the mirrors.

Nothing, however, could condone what those bastards had done to that scrawny, whiny little runt, in the name of fun. That was his motivation. His reason for living. He would push himself beyond his limits if only to facilitate the revenge he so desperately desired and deserved.

He swore to that.

He really did look good though.

Facing the mirror, he slowly turned from side to side, checking for flaws in the finished product, but ultimately just admiring, from all possible angles, what his hard work had achieved.

But he had been lazy of late.

Maybe 'preoccupied' would be a more apt description.

He had nonetheless neglected his routine and the burn in his muscles sadistically reminded him of that.

He scanned the gym between sets, but couldn't see Anne anywhere.

The 'fishbowl', as he affectionately referred to the glass-enclosed room where she conducted her classes, was empty. He had caught sight of the last class for the evening as they were leaving, but that class had been hosted by another instructor. If memory served him correctly, her name was Lyn – possibly short for Lynne or Lynette – but that's what her name badge reflected anyway.

289

Maybe Anne had the day off, or was possibly even ill.

Dan was disappointed.

She brought a certain vibrancy to the gym which no other instructor could mimic. The way she walked around and interacted with all the patrons was so refreshing. It was evident that she loved her job and that mingling in this environment came naturally to her.

No pretences or faking it.

She would be an easy target to get to Julia, if he was goaded into taking some form of action. Julia had complied thus far with his demands, but she was a feisty one and might just snub him at some stage. If that happened, she would require some encouragement to comply and that was where Anne would feature. It would be extremely difficult, if not impossible to get to Julia, herself, since she was so heavily protected, but he was a regular face at the gym and as such was already a part of Anne's world. His presence here attracted no attention and therefore no suspicion.

Yes, Anne would definitely be the card to play if any inducement was required.

Dan nodded to himself in the mirror, as if he'd just made a major breakthrough, and then glanced up at the wall-mounted clock.

Time was not on his side and he was forced to forego his last few sets.

He grabbed his towel, wiped himself down and, with kit bag in hand, headed for the change-rooms.

Chapter 74

The company and conversation was from the top drawer, but the food undoubtedly stole the show. Everything was absolutely delicious.

Julia sang Mavis' praises until she had finished clearing the table and had left the room with the dirty dishes.

Dessert would soon be served, but Julia doubted whether she had the capacity for another morsel to pass her lips. She had absolutely stuffed herself. After a second helping, the picking had started. She was with family after all and they were a family who turned dinners into occasions.

She'd been a bit on edge about the direction the conversation would take, but was ultimately relieved and extremely grateful that it meandered through a myriad of topics besides the obvious.

Her mother's doing, she finally concluded.

The men had somehow been warned to refrain from any discussions about the elephant in the room.

Fruit salad, custard and ice-cream rounded off the meal perfectly.

It was such a simple dessert, but an all-time family favourite from when she was a young girl. She forced it down, although being past the stage of overindulgence.

"I'm stuffed," Julia admitted openly. "That dessert just pushed me right over the edge."

"Glad you enjoyed it," Claire responded. "We must do this more often. We miss you and from the looks of it, you need a good meal once in a while."

"Mom!" Julia retorted. "I'm doing fine – I just haven't had the time or the inclination to cook anything substantial lately."

"Exactly my point, Julia. Mavis is cooking for us anyway and preparing food for one extra hardly seems like a contentious point."

"At the moment, I'm so full, that a discussion about food or future meal plans is really not on."

"Well, give it some thought anyway. I'd like to see my daughter more often and if it takes a home-cooked meal to achieve that, then so be it," Claire stated emphatically, ending the discussion.

This was way out of their league and the men sat quietly in their seats, not daring to interrupt or add to the exchange. They almost felt sorry for Julia. It was as if they'd just been chastised by their own respective mothers.

The lounge area was cooler and a lot brighter than the dining room, but the recliners were far more comfortable than the upright chairs they had occupied – especially for those of them with full bellies.

It was customary for the family to adjourn to the lounge for post dinner drinks, which comprised, more often than not, of just coffee. They weren't the least bit pretentious and the ritual had nothing to do with wealth or status, as it was for some. It was just more comfortable to relax in the leather recliners and sip on their beverages while digesting their meals and it had consequently become a routine for them.

The conversation was again steered tactfully towards the abstract and controversial with Alan adding a bit of business news into the mix.

The distraction, for all of them, was well overdue and too

soon the evening was at an end.

It wasn't that late when Julia drove home and yet in the late autumn months, the darkness was absolute. The intermittent street lamps offered some light, but in the absence of street lamps in certain areas, she relied solely on her car headlights to offer some illumination.

What a lovely evening, she marvelled.

Her parents really were the best she could have ever wished for.

Her apartment was in total darkness when her key hit the lock. She had forgotten to leave a few lights burning when she had left earlier in the day.

She glanced nervously around, as she fumbled clumsily in the dimly lit passageway to unlock the door and security gate, but finally managed to gain access. The room exploded into brightness when she fingered the light switch, causing her to squint reflexively. She looked around, but all was exactly as she'd left it.

The evening had been a breath of fresh air and had restored her faith in humanity. She would definitely be doing that again.

Regularly.

Not that she'd openly tell her mother that.

She'd be held to it until the end of time – and beyond.

But right now, she needed to review her article and email it through to Moses for an early morning release.

She'd sleep better once this was done.

Chapter 75

Her ringing phone roused her from a surprisingly restful few hours of sleep.

She wasn't chipper when she answered it, as she hadn't been asleep for that long, but she somehow felt incredibly rested.

Maybe good company and a great meal were exactly what she'd needed to feel more human again. This just re-enforced her mother's perspective and open invitation.

"Hello," she murmured into the handset after thumbing the answer button.

"Hi, Jules," Ollie said. "Didn't wake you, did I?"

"Hi, Ollie, yes, you actually did. I was up late reviewing my article."

"Apologies, Jules, but I thought you'd want to know…"

"Know what?" she interjected curiously.

"We have a lead at last," Ollie replied. "Our research team has been digging relentlessly into our two victims. It took a while because they started with the present and worked their way back in history."

Ollie didn't mean to pause for effect, but it certainly came across that way.

"And—?" Julia prompted.

"It sounds like the two lost contact many years ago, but as luck would have it, they grew up together. They went to the same school."

"That's great, Ollie, at least we finally have a connection."

"Agreed," the big man concurred. "But that's just the beginning. We now have to tie them together and figure out what they did to deserve the wrath of Dan."

"Okay. Send me what you have and I'll start digging from this side," Julia offered.

"It's not that easy, Jules. This is pre-internet. It's old school investigation all the way. The team is busy with school magazines, year books and newspaper clippings. You can imagine how painful it is, going through old newspapers on microfiche. No search engines. Post-internet doesn't even help a bit. Neither of these guys had social media profiles either. We found a few photos on friends' and family's profiles, but none of them together and anyway, far too recent to add value."

"What detail to the connection can the families add?" Julia queried.

"It's more like family and estranged wife, but DC Phiri is busy with the legwork from his side. My guess would be that they don't even know each other. From what we've found, these guys lost contact years before getting married or starting families."

"They might have mentioned childhood friends at some stage though," Julia said. "Even if it was just in passing. It's a long shot, I know, but maybe the spouses would remember a name being mentioned."

"Yes, that's the angle DC Phiri is pursuing," Ollie replied, "but as you quite rightly said – it's a very long shot."

"Any news from the evidence lab?" Julia segued.

Ollie suddenly became bleak at the mention of the crime scene evidence.

He shook his head. "Nothing concrete. The lab has a priority on this evidence, but there's just so much and only so many hours in each day. A few DNA and trichology matches have been found though. These have been passed down to DC Phiri and his team for a follow-up. It's now a case of questioning and eliminating suspects and hopefully, by the process of elimination, figure out the real identity of Dan. To date, we've had limited feedback on the urine found at both crime scenes, especially since it was the murder weapon in the second murder. This lack of feedback is causing untold anxiety and not only to us."

"Well, let me know if I can help with anything, Ollie. My diary is now open for a while."

"I will do. Thanks, Jules."

Julia hung up and logged into her laptop.

She had brought it to the bedroom with her the previous night, expecting her article to be published by the time she awoke, which she'd also thought would be much later in the day.

How wrong was she about that?

There was an email from Moses when she logged in.

She put off reading it.

She first wanted to check if her article had been published.

There it was, making headlines on *DispatchLIVE*.

She navigated back to the email from Moses and double-clicked to open it.

He still seemed concerned about the focal point being Dan and not the murder and crime scene, but had conceded to giving her the benefit of the doubt and relying on public opinion to adjudicate on the success or failure of the exposé.

Chapter 76

Dan was fortunate to find a seat in his favourite mom and pop coffee shop. It was unusually busy for this time of the morning. Business attire outnumbered casual attire by at least six to one.

Could be a company breakfast.

Book out a venue and treat your staff.

Maybe.

He thought about it briefly and then discarded the idea just as quickly.

None of his business really.

He reluctantly moved down the aisle and sat at the only available table – right in the walkway. This was not where he wanted to be.

He usually sat in one of the booths with his back to the wall. That way he had a full view of the entire room and some privacy with what he was perusing on his tablet. He would have to move the moment one of the booths emptied out.

He'd have to wait. Fortunately, he had all the time in the world today.

Sharon was busily serving, refilling and clearing when she noticed him walk in and sit down.

"Good morning, sir," she greeted him. "Coffee for starters?"

"Um, yes thank you, Sharon."

"That table will soon be vacant," she said, indicating one of the booths.

She had noticed him looking around. "They're just paying

the bill and will be leaving shortly. Give me a moment to clear it and wipe it down then I'll move you over."

Dan smiled cordially at her.

Very observant, he thought.

True to her word, the couple in the middle booth soon stood up to leave. She was there in a flash and once the table was cleared and cleaned, she indicated to him with an outstretched open-palmed hand.

Dan nodded in assent and within minutes had been relocated to a far more comfortable and suitable spot.

Sharon disappeared, as he settled in, and almost immediately reappeared, this time bearing his coffee and a small jug of milk.

"Will you be joining us for breakfast this morning?" she asked courteously.

"I believe I will be. I'll order with my second cup," Dan replied.

Sharon nodded and moved along.

Dan added the milk and a sweetener, stirred the coffee and took a gulp. It was hot, but oh so good.

His iPad linked automatically to the house Wi-Fi and within seconds he was browsing the internet. He tapped on a pre-saved shortcut and was soon deeply engrossed in Julia's latest article about him.

The world could have ended and he would have been none the wiser – the exposé was that captivating.

Good job, he thought to himself. *Very good job.*

She had managed to capture the essence of him and his crusade, as well as the empathy it was required to conjure up from her audience, without detracting or losing focus of the heinous murder.

He caught himself nodding his head in approval and

appreciation.

Now we're getting somewhere.

He reached for his coffee only to find that he had already drained the mug.

Sharon was busy behind the counter and he had to wave to get her attention. She nodded and raised two fingers.

He nodded, *two minutes you have.*

Sure enough, she was soon at his side ready to take his order.

"Coffee, two eggs, two rashers of bacon, half a grilled tomato and two slices of toast?" she offered, before he could say a word.

Dan nodded.

She had remembered his order from his previous visits.

"Perfect," he replied, very impressed with her efficiency.

Her tip just got bigger. Today he would surely be doling out a hefty gratuity for her good service.

"It'll take about ten minutes," she informed him. "Would you like the coffee while you wait?"

"That would be great," he responded, even though he actually preferred to have his coffee with his meal. Next time he would need to order before he finished his first cup.

Dan decided to read the article once more while he waited for his food.

The view-counter would be climbing off the charts with this piece. His crusade would inadvertently boost the economy. Newspaper sales and online subscriptions would sky-rocket.

He smiled wryly at this thought.

Whoever was in the kitchen was just as efficient as Sharon.

Within eight minutes, mom or pop had turned out a breakfast worth waiting for. No wonder this place was becoming increasingly popular.

Professionalism, quality and speed of service – a winning combination every time. Just for the hell of it, and between mouthfuls, Dan navigated to the Trip Advisor homepage and proceeded to type in a brilliant review for mom and pop.

He had never personally met either of them, but had on occasion seen the elderly couple moseying around in the background. Many larger or even franchised establishments could learn a lot from this tiny little coffee shop.

He chastised himself for not writing reviews more often.

The culture of only 'putting pen to paper' to complain was something he himself, amongst many others, was guilty of. Taking the time to commend good service was just as important, if not more so. Positive reinforcement would always prevail.

Dan washed down the remnants of his meal with the tepid remains of his coffee and requested the bill.

Sharon was as quick with the bill as she had been throughout and was ecstatic when she discovered a R50 tip on such a small bill.

Dan smiled as he exited the coffee shop.

He had a letter to write.

Chapter 77

Cameron Long had never been the brightest spark in the classroom.

His mechanical and electrical knowledge and aptitude were unsurpassed though. He'd been a petrol-head his entire life, tinkering on motor vehicles whenever opportunities presented themselves.

He was a short, burly man; barrel-chested with a large, rotund belly. His thick arms and muscular stature were all natural and had been crafted over the years by many hours of manual labour and toting heavy equipment.

Oil and grease stains tattooed his skin and were a permanent feature under his nails. No amount of solvent in the world could remove all the ingrained gunge.

He'd actually given up trying – clean dirt was as good as no dirt.

He'd worked for many of the top dealership brands during his career – servicing, solving electrical issues and even doing a bit of panel-beating along the way.

He had been on top of his game and a sought-after resource.

That all came to a grinding halt when computerised systems became more widespread in the vehicle industry.

Not only was each vehicle now governed by a computer, even the diagnostics for servicing and problem solving were performed by a computer. They plugged the car into a diagnostic computer and 'hey presto!' any monkey with a wrench could now sort out your vehicle.

Proper mechanics were a thing of the past.

Cameron hated computers.

He didn't understand them and had no inclination to work with them.

He had a finely-tuned ear and a set of trusty tools and yet somehow, he was made redundant by a robot and a printout.

So, he did what any self-respecting person would do.

He withdrew himself from the corporate world and sunk his life-savings into his own backyard business.

There would always be somebody in need of some good, old-fashioned, mechanical prowess and ingenuity. And he wasn't wrong. There were more die hard, old school, petrol-heads like him than he ever would have imagined.

His expertise was regularly required to soup up performance on a muscle car, to rehabilitate a fixer-upper or even fully restore an oldie.

His yard was full and he was busier than ever before.

The day was ending for Cameron.

It was only four o'clock in the afternoon, but the next job he had would literally take hours to complete, so he decided to call it a day for now and get into it first thing the following morning.

With no time-card to punch and no boss looking over his shoulder, he could come and go as he pleased.

Why he hadn't done this years ago, he would never understand.

The West Bank was predominantly an industrial area and property was very reasonably priced when he was in the market a few years back. The downside was that the area was a bit run-down now and the crime-rate was on the increase.

There were too many easy targets for opportunistic house-breaking and theft.

Once in a while he'd hear about a rape or murder in the neighbourhood, but fortunately those were fairly uncommon.

He wasn't overly concerned about any of this anyway, as his house was directly above his workshop and his property was totally enclosed by palisade fencing and razor-sharp barbed wire.

He doubted that any gentrification would take place in this area during his life-time, but he was hopeful that future generations would be able to experience East London as it had been during his childhood.

Cameron had never married.

He'd dated a few girls back in the day, but had soon discovered that his grease-stained hands and grimy nails were not very appealing to the fairer sex.

And he was not about to give up his passion for motor vehicles for any girl.

So, any thoughts of marriage or family ended before they began.

Following that epiphany, life became a whole lot simpler.

He didn't need the company and when he did, it was a phone-call away and at a very decent price. Even prostitutes needed to make a living and he was frequently afforded preferential rates for being such a regular.

Cameron closed up his workshop, double-checked that the main gate was securely locked and that the yard was impenetrable, and then made his way upstairs to his house.

It was a single bedroom unit, with a small lounge, kitchen and bathroom. He had no need for anything more lavish. It was his little piece of paradise.

The furniture was old and threadbare, the carpets were ratty and the walls were devoid of any decorations.

To say he wasn't materialistic would have been an understatement.

He spent his money on what mattered to him – old cars, spares and the tools and equipment to ply his trade.

His first stop as he entered the house was always the washing machine.

He stripped down to nothing, loaded the washer and set it on the thirty-minute cycle to deep clean his filthy work clothes.

Still buck naked, he then spent a little time at the wash-basin scrubbing his hands with a degreasing agent in a futile attempt to remove the latest layer of grime and then headed to the shower.

He had no television and definitely no computer, so he spent the rest of his down time drinking beer and reading car magazines, especially those specialising in antiques and the older models.

Since his childhood, he had accumulated quite a collection of these magazines, which he had read repeatedly. There was always some schematic or article pertinent to his current project.

Life could not get better.

Chapter 78

The squeal of tires and the loud crash which followed brought the Esplanade to a complete stand-still. The usual flow of traffic along the beach-front was now backed up to block the entire road.

Julia heard the commotion from inside her apartment and hurried to the balcony to get a better view of the spectacle. She always had binoculars on hand, as sightings of dolphins were not uncommon. She grabbed them in passing.

From her vantage point, it looked like at least four vehicles were involved. The first two cars had seemingly clipped each other as their front ends were quite crumpled. It was clear from the skid-marks that a black Citi Golf had been attempting to overtake a slower vehicle and had encroached on the opposite lane, colliding with a blue Toyota Corolla. The other two cars, whose following distances were questionable, had then rear-ended the Golf and the Corolla respectively.

The drivers and passengers slowly disembarked and while some were staggering around slightly dazed, others were already seated on the sidewalk, nursing various injuries. One was screaming at another and it looked very much as if the confrontation would soon come to blows. A few of the bystanders swiftly got involved and a bit of pushing and shoving ensued until the whoop of a police car siren broke up the melee.

Julia watched for a while until the ambulances arrived and the police had the scene under control. It didn't look too serious. All those involved looked a bit shaken up, but the most grievous of injuries was probably only whiplash. Those casualties would be taken away for perfunctory check-ups and in all likelihood would be released within the hour sporting neck-braces.

Thankfully, she didn't notice blood anywhere.

Julia finally lost interest in the spectacle when the police started rerouting vehicles to get the traffic flowing once again and the tow-trucks started arriving on the scene.

That was a different start to the day, she marvelled.

After the excitement of the morning, she busied herself with scanning through her emails.

The one which caught her eye immediately was from Moses. He was crowing about her article and how popular it had proved to be. It was topping the 'Trending Now' list and the hit counter was continuing its upward trajectory.

She had done it again.

A knock on her door startled her. She wasn't expecting any visitors. Besides, how would anyone get into the complex without the security guard alerting her? She eye-balled the peep-hole in her door curiously.

It was Mrs Venske from a few doors down.

"Just a minute," Julia shouted through the door and began to fumble with all the keys and locks, which protected her from the world outside.

"Hi, Mrs Venske, nice to see you again," Julia said, as she finally managed to bypass the last of the deadbolts and open the door.

"Hello, my dear," Mrs Venske greeted her in return. "And please, it's Dorothy."

"What can I do for you Mrs Ve – Dorothy?" Julia queried.

"Did you hear the accident this morning?"

"Yes, as a matter of fact, I did. After hearing the collision, I rushed to my balcony and watched everything from there."

"I was there," Dorothy stated categorically, raising her

eyebrows and widening her eyes. "I saw the accident from start to finish. These young ones in their flashy cars. No respect for the rules of the road any more."

Julia was a bit confused now. She wondered where this conversation was going. Maybe Mrs Venske, or rather Dorothy, just needed someone to talk to about what she'd witnessed.

"I was taking my morning stroll along the Espalanade and it happened right next to me," she calmly continued.

"That must have been terrifying," Julia empathised.

"It was. That sudden squeal of tires and then the loud bang. It had us all jumping in surprise. I'm just happy that nobody was seriously injured."

"Would you like to come in, Dorothy? Maybe sit and have a cup of tea with me to settle your nerves?" Julia offered.

"Oh, no thank you, my dear. There's nothing wrong with my nerves. Sure, it was a shocking experience, but that's not the reason I popped over."

"Then how may I help you?" Julia asked again.

"While I was watching, a young man in the crowd approached me and handed me this book." In her left hand she casually held a book, which she passed over to Julia. "He asked me if I knew you and if I wouldn't mind giving you this book when I next saw you."

Julia reached out and took the book.

It was 'An Introduction to Crime Scene Investigation by Aric Dutelle'.

"It has a letter in it," Dorothy added. "It was sealed with your name on it, so I didn't open it," she confessed rather defensively.

"Thank you," was all Julia could muster and after a moment added, "What did the man look like? The one who gave you the book."

Dorothy thought about it for a few seconds. She suddenly blurted out, "Young man, maybe mid-twenties, tanned complexion, wearing blue jeans, a Nike T-shirt and black boots. His face was dimpled, like a golf ball – probably acne scars. His adolescent years were most likely hell for him."

"Wow, that's rather specific," Julia replied, stunned by Dorothy's description.

She'd expected a vague response from the elderly lady.

"I worked in the banks my entire life. We did many courses back in those days. In the event of a robbery, descriptions were vital. It was drummed into us all the time that we needed to pay attention to the details. It's habitual now – I can't help myself. I just pay extra special attention to everything."

Julia was impressed. "You sure you don't have time for a cup of tea or maybe even some coffee?"

"No thank you, my dear, I need to be on my way."

"Well, thank you for this, Mrs Ve – Dorothy," Julia corrected herself once again, while indicating the book she'd been given.

Dorothy Venske smiled meekly and casually walked away in the direction of her apartment.

As she watched the little old lady, a sudden thought crossed her mind.

Had Dan engineered an accident just to get this book and letter to her?

Couldn't be, she concluded.

Surely it was just a fortunate coincidence, but in retrospect she wouldn't put it past him?

She gazed sceptically at the book in her hand and then flipped it open to reveal the letter.

There was her name again, typed neatly in bold, block letters in the centre of the cover, glaring back at her ...**JULIA SWAN**...

Chapter 79

It was more reflexive than out of surprise, but when she saw her name, she couldn't stop herself. "Ah, crap, here we go again!" she voiced out loud.

She'd been expecting some form of contact sooner or later, but this was even sooner than sooner. She'd only just penned the article and it had only just been published yesterday.

He'd obviously been expecting it.

He had her like a puppet on a string.

He could be setting up alerts to notify himself of updates relating to this topic of interest, but it was more likely that he knew her every move.

He had dictated the terms after all.

She wondered what he'd think of it this time.

The thought and trepidation made her hands tremble ever so slightly, even though she knew the critique was imminent. This was the game he'd played from the beginning – why would he deviate now?

Besides the slight tremble, she was strangely calm this time round.

Had she overcome the fear she'd previously experienced, she wondered.

She actually felt quite numb – not quite indifferent – more a feeling of acceptance or possibly even resignation.

The words to Pink Floyd's song 'Comfortably Numb' flooded her mind.

Memories of her youth. A bygone era when her parents had played this track, amongst others, quite repetitively.

She contemplated phoning her dad and Ollie, but then decided it wouldn't make any difference whether she read the letter now or sat and waited for them to arrive.

Mentally, she was in a different place. She'd progressed from that tenuous and fragile state of mind she was in the last time.

It was the dinner date with her parents. It had somehow rebooted her perspective on life. She'd been reminded of the importance of family and the unconditional love and support they had for her. She'd evolved and flourished. Raised from the brink of depression.

She looked the envelope over.

No distinguishing marks or features.

Just her name.

As usual.

She proceeded without caution.

The envelope gave up its contents without a fight as she slit it open with a kitchen knife.

The letter, similarly, had no distinguishing features or characteristics.

It looked like the same paper, same ink and same font.

She snuggled into the couch and prepared herself mentally for what she was about to read.

Dear Julia,

Bravo! Bravo!

I read your latest article with pride and admiration.

It took us a while to get there, but we're finally on the same page.

Thank you for listening to me and taking me seriously.

I've always believed in a harmonious existence. Much better than threats and sanctions, don't you think?

Russell Dwyer was a bottom-feeder of the worst ilk.

He portrayed himself as father and husband of the year, but he was nothing more than a cretin. He deserved to die and one day you and our audience will hopefully understand this. We cannot have people like that roaming around and evading justice. It is quite disrespectful to law-abiding citizens, like ourselves, as we spend our lives watching our Ps and Qs and just wanting a safe and secure environment to live out our lives peacefully.

Anyway, enough about that piece of garbage.

I, again, left the police some vital evidence at the scene.

Sifting through it might be a bit tedious and laborious, but if they allocate and utilise their resources efficiently, they might just get lucky.

My DNA is there – I can assure you of that.

The ball is in their court though and if they are as determined to stop me, as they should be, then they will have to put in the work.

I also know that once a parallel is drawn between my first two quests and the local police start seeing them as the work of a serial killer, then the likelihood of the Murder and Robbery Squad being called in becomes inevitable.

After your latest article, I would be amazed if national interest and resources are not already in play, but then again, my crusade is for precisely that purpose – awareness, response and resolution from the police and upper echelons of government.

They cannot keep burying their heads in the sand and thinking that the country is running smoothly. Crime is rife and they have the tools at their disposal to stamp it out.

This does, however, make my work a little more challenging, even though the original plan was to escalate the timeline once the detail was revealed and connections were made.

And that time is now.

So, be on the lookout, you will soon have a little more work to do.

Best Regards,

Daniel Nathan Anderson (DNA Dan)

Julia felt – well – almost relieved that Dan had been happy with her exposé. She'd again held her breath for what felt like an eternity whilst she read the letter and now gasped like a fish out of water. The anxiety of waiting to be chastised again had been quite daunting.

But, he'd been happy.

She was relieved because Dan was happy.

What was happening here?

The world had turned on its head.

Unbelievable, she thought. *He'd put her through the wringer and now she was concerned about his feelings and praise for her. Wasn't that the epitome of the Stockholm Syndrome? Forging a psychological bond with a captor during captivity.*

In her case, the man who held her mentally hostage and manipulated her like a puppet.

This was too complex for her to handle.

Dan was about to step up his game. She had a good feeling about this. In his haste, he might slip up and they'd have a chance of apprehending him. She hoped she was right.

But, she needed to bring in the reinforcements.

Her dad and Ollie needed to know about this and the team needed to be on high alert.

Chapter 80

Ollie left soon after he and Alan had read the letter.

The discussion and debate had been brief and the big guy really needed to launch a full-on defensive manoeuvre now.

It was show-time.

Julia and Alan stood, in rapt discussion, in the driveway and looked on as he drove off. He hadn't, as yet, decided on the order of events for the day, but he knew he had a lot to do.

His first call from the car phone was to Manny.

Within the first ring, the call was answered. "Hey, boss," came the jovial response.

"Manny. Burns Street. Everyone. One hour!"

"Yes, boss."

His second call was to DC Phiri.

He wasn't as quick as Manny with answering the call.

He also wasn't as jovial as Manny. In fact, he sounded tired, demoralised and depressed.

"Ollie?"

"Hello, DC Phiri."

He was on the payroll, but besides being their inside man, Ollie still had a huge amount of respect and deference for the aging police inspector.

He'd used his influence on too many occasions to bail Ollie and his team out of a few tight spots. Most of the specifics Ollie couldn't even remember.

Besides, you never kick a dog to teach it. You use finesse

and rewards. Loyalty is always earned, and reinforced with love, affection and recognition.

"Just looking for an update, DC," Ollie prompted courteously.

The feedback was brief and interspersed with conjecture and speculation.

Ollie sifted through the fact and fiction as DC Phiri updated him.

He then updated the inspector on the latest letter.

Secrets were a thing of the past and although Ollie still held a few cards close to his chest, he did relinquish what had been deemed necessary. The last thing they needed was the Murder and Robbery Squads involvement and more so, discovering that they had withheld pertinent information from the police.

DC Phiri listened attentively.

"So according to you, or more accurately – the letter – another murder is imminent?"

"That's what we believe. The timeline has been escalated."

"Do you have any idea where he will strike next? The connection between the victims is still speculative."

"We're not entirely sure, but have managed to link them together in their primary school years."

"That's more than we have at the moment. Send me the details and I'll get our investigators working on that angle," DC Phiri directed.

Ollie's third call, whilst driving, was to Phumzile Maloto.

DC Phiri had introduced him to Phumzile after the first DNA samples were airlifted.

She was supervising the case from an evidence perspective in the forensics laboratory in Cape Town

Although they'd never physically met, they'd made such an

314

impression on one another when introduced that they felt far better acquainted than they actually were.

Phumzile was a typical scientist.

All facts.

No fiction.

Say it like it is.

Ollie liked that about her.

She wouldn't embroider on their progress or findings.

Therefore, he didn't have to sift through any details she gave.

Their conversation was also brief.

There were no major breaks in the case, even though there were quite a few more matches found in the system than before. Ollie couldn't help thinking that Dan had somehow planned this. Finding matches actually slowed down the investigation, as the results of each match needed to be verified and checked out thoroughly to eliminate or implicate an individual. This took up valuable time for lab personnel as well as for the investigators on the ground.

"Most of the matches were traced to dead people though," Phumzile elaborated pragmatically.

Ollie frowned at this response. "Dead people?"

"Yes, dead people. We traced them via the Department of Home Affair's Death Records."

"He has access to a morgue," Ollie said out loud.

"Who has?" Phumzile queried.

"The suspect," Ollie responded. "He must have access to a morgue or at least have raided one to get his samples. Is there any way of finding out if all these people ended up in the same morgue? Do the death certificates have this detail?"

"Absolutely," she replied, "They even have the details of the pathologist and the mortician."

"Phumz, you're a super star. How soon can you send those details to DC Phiri and myself? Both our teams can follow up on identifying the morgue or morgues. Finally, we might catch a break."

"You sound so invested in this," Phumzile said. "Is there more to this than I know?"

"Very much so, but I really can't get into that detail right now. We needed a break and hopefully this is it. I need to run now. Thanks very much for the help, Phumz."

Phumzile smiled to herself as she hung up on the call.

Ollie had been driving around for close to an hour when he finished his call with Phumzile. He'd been so engrossed in the conversation that he'd been navigating on auto-pilot and only now realised where he was.

He was on the far side of the city and only had a few minutes to make the rendezvous point on time.

He would never make it.

He phoned Manny again.

"We're all here, boss."

"Good, I'll be there in about fifteen minutes. Start doing some homework on all the morgues in the city."

"Morgues?" Manny queried. "Morgues... like for dead people."

"Yes, Manny... morgues. We need addresses, locations, GPS coordinates – whatever you can find."

"Okay, boss, we'll get right on it."

Ollie could hear the apprehension in his voice and he smiled briefly to himself.

Fear of the dead was a natural, although irrational, phenomenon, but the black African had cornered the market on this superstition.

Ollie could only imagine what was happening back at the safe house.

Manny would be trying his best to put on a brave face, while conveying the task requirements to the team and probably getting the same responses from them.

For now, it was only names and addresses.

Ollie wondered how they would take to an infiltration plan, if it came to that, and burst out laughing.

He rounded the final corner in just over ten minutes and brought the car to a squealing halt outside the safe house in Burns Street.

The area was one of the oldest in the city and the houses lining the street reflected their age in size, architecture and upkeep.

All were dilapidated, but while the exterior of the safe house presented itself as such, the interior had been modernised and was state of the art.

Chapter 81

Ollie gazed into the front door's 'peep-hole' with his right eye and the door swung open on well-oiled hinges.

To any outsider, the door looked quite unimpressive. To those in the know, it was close to impenetrable. It was lined with reinforced steel with a retina scanner imbedded in the 'peep-hole'. If you weren't in the database, there was no way you'd be entering – at least not through the front door anyway.

The anteroom Ollie entered was equally unimpressive and very sparsely furnished. A few drab floral paintings adorned the walls and added a smidgeon of life to the room. The room had been reduced in size during construction and the back wall had been fitted with one-way mirrors and another steel-lined door with imbedded retina scanner. It had effectively been constructed as a man-trap.

It was unlikely that anyone would get through the first door, but if they did, they'd be stuck in this anteroom like rats in a trap and could be picked off one at a time from loopholes evenly spaced and positioned in the wall below the bullet-proof mirrors.

Ollie wasted no time accessing the second door and entered the large meeting room beyond. It was kitted out with a large boardroom table and comfortable leather swivel chairs.

Team leaders were gathered around the table staring ominously at the large monitor centrally positioned on the wall above the foot of the table.

Numerous smaller monitors adorned the walls on each side,

but all attention was directed at the primary screen.

The analysts around the table typed furiously on their laptops and intermittently projected information, mostly to the primary screen, but occasionally to the secondary screens.

The door kickers all but stood to attention when Ollie entered the room.

The respect for him and the position he held was that great.

The number crunchers continued with their work, unconcerned with rank or military protocols.

Ollie wasn't bothered.

He looked up at the monitor curiously.

"Fourteen in the lower metropole area and probably some smaller operations in between or on the outskirts which we haven't pin-pointed yet."

"Thank you, Manny," Ollie replied and nodded in appreciation. "This could be the break we've been waiting for."

He took up the seat at the head of the table which had been left vacant for him. He had a clear view of all the monitors in the room as well as the group in attendance. He looked sternly around the table at the faces which stared anxiously back at him. Ten of them in total. Nine excluding himself. Six being operators and three being analysts. They'd all worked closely together before which gave Ollie a great sense of comfort. They were the trusted elite and a great team.

Ollie opened the bottled water in front of him and took a huge glug before beginning the briefing on the latest developments in the case.

The latest letter was discussed in detail, followed by the relationship between the first two victims.

"If Dan is about to escalate his killing spree, then we can safely assume there will be at least another one or possibly two more victims," Jeff offered. He was one of the analysts. A typical freckled red-head. Smart as a whip.

"Agreed," replied Ollie. "Maybe three more at a stretch. He must realise that the longer he continues with the publicity stunt, the more interest he will generate and the greater the chances will be of him getting caught. So…"

"We need to dig deeper into the background of Craig and Russell," Jeff interjected. "If we're lucky, we'll find they were all part of a group and then we might be able to identify the next couple of victims before anything happens to them."

"Exactly," Ollie huffed, not overly enthused at being interrupted.

His briefings were never one-sided and he expected a spirited debate with ideas being thrown about, but he did not take kindly to being interrupted.

Jeff looked down at his laptop like a scolded child, avoiding eye contact with the big man.

The briefing finally moved onto the subject of the morgues.

They'd all been morbidly curious when asked to research the morgues in the East London area.

Ollie rehashed his discussion with Phumzile and in particular her discovering that a lot of the specimens in the evidence collected had come from people who were now dead. The speculation being that Dan had stolen the blood, urine, skin and hair samples from a morgue or even a few morgues.

It made so much sense.

Where else would he get evidence like this to taint the crime scenes?

"Maybe a hospital?" Manny replied.

"It's possible," Ollie conceded. "It just seemed strange to us that all the DNA matches were to dead people."

"Maybe they were in the terminal ward of a hospital?" Manny theorised.

Ollie contemplated this for a few seconds. "It's definitely something to consider. But amongst all this speculation, we need to start somewhere."

He looked at the analysts first, "Firstly we need a deep dive done on possible friends or colleagues of Craig and Russell and you'll probably have to go old school again. All connections are worth noting."

He then looked at the operators and added, "Split your teams up and let's get an understanding of the morgues. I want to know everything – locations, points of entry, ease of access, staff names, their addresses and contact details, as well as their movements and routines while at work."

He continued, "Who knows, maybe we get lucky and Dan is an employee or even an owner. DC Phiri will be working a similar angle on this, but will concentrate mainly on any reports of burglaries or break-ins at the morgues. He doesn't have the resources to do the grind work."

Without warning, Ollie stood up, catching everyone by surprise.

"Let's get moving, guys. The next murder could be as soon as tomorrow or God forbid, even tonight."

Chapter 82

Peter Roland opened his tired eyes and blinked repeatedly to adjust his focus.

Anne lay facing him, a marginal expanse of her toned shoulder peeking out above the duvet. Her rhythmic breathing was slow and steady, typical of an athlete in peak form. She was still fast asleep.

He couldn't believe his luck.

Had this really happened?

He smiled and gazed at her sleeping peacefully.

Angelic, he thought.

His mind drifted back to the previous evening.

There'd been no expectations.

She'd prepared dinner for them. Nothing even remotely elaborate. A quick pasta Alfredo, which she'd thrown together in minutes. She liked fettuccine and wasn't really a fan of penne pasta. He'd discovered that later when they were chatting.

That's what he loved about her. She was so simple and unassuming. She had this air about her – 'Take me as I am or leave me be'. She was super evolved and seemingly above any trivialities. She lived in the now and took the world head-on, doing what she enjoyed doing. And all of that on top of being absolutely stunning.

He'd really hit the jackpot this time.

Suddenly he started to panic.

Had he performed adequately?

It had been a while.

He dreaded the thought of having been disappointing, or for that matter, just okay.

After the first bottle of wine, they'd opened another.

Had they finished the second – he couldn't remember?

He vaguely recalled them finally losing their inhibitions. Clothes flew in all directions as their pent-up carnal desires overcame them.

That was all he could remember.

When he finally returned to the present, Anne was staring straight back at him.

She had a broad grin on her face.

"Welcome back," she said.

"Uh, sorry," he apologised, practically confirming that she'd caught him trying to remember what had happened. "Seems like my mind went walkabout."

She laughed out loud. "Now I wonder where that mind went walkabout? Trying to piece last night together, were you? Well, me too," she admitted.

She was so casual about it. It sort of took him by surprise.

"Good food, good wine, good company and a bedroom nearby. It was bound to happen," she continued nonchalantly.

Peter smiled, but only to hide his consternation. "I'm glad you can take it so lightly. I can't remember too much about anything."

"You need details to add to your database of conquests?" Anne said joking.

Peter blushed slightly. "Of course not, it's just... it was our first time and it should have been a very memorable moment."

"You're such a romantic, Mr Roland," she replied and winked seductively at him.

Without warning, her hand moved slowly but purposefully under the duvet – her fingers caressing his muscular body. She started on his thick arms. Her touch was as light as a feather. As she moved to his defined chest and abdomen, she intensified the pressure, enjoying the groans which escaped his lips. His eyes were closed, as he basked under her sublime touch.

He was as hard as a rock when she reached between his legs and throbbed in anticipation as she held him firmly in her hand.

She effortlessly straddled him and positioned herself for ease of entry.

He moaned loudly as she slid lower onto him and engulfed his entire shaft.

The moment wasn't lost on her either, as she shuddered slightly and gasped audibly.

Their movements were limited to minute grinding gyrations in an effort to prolong the experience until he could contain himself no longer. He reached behind her, gripped her perfect buttocks in both hands and with a few animalistic thrusts, he emptied himself into her. His grunting and heavy breathing was all but drowned out by her own guttural groan, as she climaxed with him.

They lay in silence, limbs intertwined and breathing heavily.

Two perfectly honed and toned specimens exquisitely connected in the aftermath of exhilarating intercourse.

"Will you remember that, now?" Anne asked quizzically, looking over at Peter.

He turned his head to face her and grinned. "That will be ingrained in my mind for the rest of my life."

"Aw, don't get too romantic on me now," she replied, chuckling comically.

He realised at that moment how much he adored this woman.

Fortunately, he knew better than to tarnish the moment with talk of such things.

"That was absolutely mind-blowing," he commented, adopting her light-hearted approach to everything.

"Well, then there might be some more of that for you soon enough if you play your cards right."

"I can't wait," he replied, now gazing up at the ceiling and thinking how lucky he was.

Chapter 83

Dan strolled casually along the deserted street now flanked with rundown, ramshackle buildings. It was heart-breaking to see what had become of this previously prosperous neighbourhood. He thought back to his childhood and remembered the area fondly. It had been neat, clean and tidy with quaint little houses lining each street. It was now nothing more than a pitiful slum, sullied with litter and in dire need of urban renewal.

Another blunder by the current government – an inability to maintain or re-invest in aging product and infrastructure. Preventative maintenance was a foreign concept to them and while everyone had their grubby little fingers in every pot, they all pleaded poverty and claimed there were no finances to fix or replace anything.

Disgraceful.

Dan's anger grew with each step he took.

Time was fleeting and Cameron would soon be closing up for the night.

Once those gates were closed, he seriously doubted whether he would be able to convince the man to reopen them, even with the story that he'd concocted.

Living and working in this neighbourhood, Cameron would be on high alert for anything out of the ordinary.

Dan increased his pace.

He had parked his vehicle a few blocks from his destination to prevent being identified, but now he started to wonder whether it would still be there when he returned. It could well be another flaw in his plan.

He rounded the last corner.

The scenery didn't change.

The trees lining the street were bare and piles of discarded leaves lay interspersed with cardboard, papers, tins and South Africa's national flower – the plastic bag.

The sidewalks were municipal property and no resident in this neighbourhood would ever even consider raking up the detritus. Besides, even if bagged, who would collect the rubbish? Dan doubted whether any municipal trash collection route even passed this way. It looked more like a neglected dump site than a residential area.

Dan skirted the litter, as if it were a mine-field, and hastily made his way down the road to his destination.

He stopped outside Cameron's gate, which was closed, but not locked.

He was in time.

He rattled on the gate and called out to alert the owner of his presence. This was not an area where you just entered someone's property or walked up to the front door and casually knocked.

A pudgy, sweaty face appeared over the hood of an old car in the workshop.

"Can I help you?"

"I hope so," Dan replied. "You know anything about a BMW E30 325iS?"

"Ah… the Gusheshe?" Cameron replied, as he made his way over to the gate, a broad smile now covering his face. "I know all there is to know about that car. It is legendary. It was first released into the market in 1989 with a 2.5-litre straight-6 engine. Peak power of 130 kW and a close-ratio 5-speed gearbox."

Cameron's recital really gained momentum as he reached out and unlatched the gate.

"You got the standard sedan or the Evo 1... its 2.7-litre successor?

"Neither, I'm afraid," replied Dan.

Cameron's face dropped, along with his enthusiasm.

"I got my hands on the Evo 2!"

"You're kidding me," Cameron spluttered, as the spark instantly returned to his eyes. "That's 155 KWs of power. The 6-cylinder engine is still regarded by most to be the best-sounding free-revving BMW engine of all time."

He was now just showing off his astuteness and Dan continued to string him along.

"I've always been partial to the Salmon Silver Poly," Cameron added.

Dan quickly realised that Cameron was testing him and without hesitation replied, "Well, sorry to disappoint, mate – mine is the Cirrus Blue Poly."

"That would probably be my second choice," Cameron responded casually, now truly believing that Dan was a fellow enthusiast of fine automobiles. "Come on in, let's grab a cold one and have a chat about what you need."

"Thanks, don't mind if I do," Dan replied. "I heard you were the man to talk to."

Cameron ushered Dan into the property and locked the gate behind him.

Dan was pleased to hear the tinkle of the chain being wrapped around the gate frame and the click of the lock.

"Can't be too careful in this neighbourhood," Cameron said, as he noticed Dan looking down at the chain and lock.

"I hear you. I noticed that it's a bit more rundown than when

I was last in this area."

Cameron nodded in agreement but didn't feel he had to comment.

It was a typical workshop environment.

They passed a few old cars, on which Cameron was working, and simultaneously dodged numerous parts which littered the floor. The workshop looked to be in total disarray and extremely grimy – grease and oil stains everywhere. But not a tool in sight, besides of course those which Cameron had been using when he'd been interrupted.

Dan nodded to himself.

Impressive.

A man who looked after his tools. Maybe he had changed. Unfortunately, too late for that though.

There was an old, faded plastic table and three matching chairs at the back of the workshop. They looked extremely weathered and brittle. Dan wondered whether they'd hold his weight.

At Cameron's direction, he removed his backpack and placed it carefully on the table before easing himself into one of the plastic chairs. It creaked and wobbled too much for his liking.

"It'll probably be better if I stand," Dan said.

Cameron shrugged, turned and moseyed off to a fridge, which was neatly snuggled in next to his work-bench.

With his back towards Dan, he never saw it coming and with a few quick steps Dan was on him, jamming the Taser into his back.

With a few vicious jolts Cameron dropped unceremoniously to his knees and then toppled over like a felled tree.

Chapter 84

Dan knew he lived alone.

Dan knew his closing process.

Dan knew he wouldn't be interrupted.

Cameron was a bulky man, but Dan hefted him quite easily up the stairs to his living quarters and, with the gate locked and the workshop door closed, he had the entire night ahead of him.

Dan emptied the contents of his backpack onto the kitchen table and laid the contents out neatly.

He contemplated leaving Cameron's underpants on, but then decided that it would be far more intimidating if he stripped him naked.

He needed Cameron in an upright position for what he had planned and luckily for him the small kitchen had a breakfast nook with a chair and counter top affixed to the only pillar in the house. The pillar was about as wide Cameron's shoulders. It wouldn't be comfortable for Cameron, but that would be the least of his worries.

Dan temporarily placed a chair in front of the pillar and lifted the unconscious man onto it. He then secured the man's hands firmly around the pillar at his back. Finally, and with a lot of effort, he managed to manoeuvre the man into the correct position. He wrapped duct-tape around his head and the pillar and then around his upper torso and the pillar to stabilize him.

Dan removed the chair and although Cameron's body sagged slightly, he was held firmly in position by his bonds.

Once his legs were finally taped to the pillar and a gag secured in his mouth, Dan took a well-deserved break and sat back on the chair staring at the unconscious man.

"Number three," he muttered, as Cameron finally opened his eyes and blinked away the fogginess.

Cameron was dazed and confused, but Dan waited patiently for him to come to his senses.

"Number three," he repeated, but still he saw no comprehension in Cameron's eyes. "If you'd stayed in contact with your so-called friends, you'd know what happened to them, what this is all about and what is about to happen to you. You don't even read the newspaper or watch the news, do you? You have no idea of what is going on. What a poor excuse of a human being."

Cameron spoke into the gag, but the words were garbled and inaudible.

"Let's get to work then, shall we?"

Cameron's eyes widened as he saw the scalpel in Dan's raised hand.

"You don't remember me, do you?"

Cameron now panicked and tried to jerk free, but the duct tape held him steady.

Dan stood back and laughed loudly.

"Many years ago, a little boy was tied up against a tree like this. Do you remember that?"

Cameron tried again to shake his head, but only his jowls wobbled ever so slightly.

"That's right... you do remember, don't you? It was your idea after all. You and your buddies tormented that little boy in many ways throughout the years, but on this particular day it was you who decided on the method of torture. You wondered how much pain and damage paper-cuts could inflict on that little boy."

Cameron was beside himself, as the memories came flooding back to him, but he couldn't move a muscle.

"Well, I've done a bit of research and it turns out that the Chinese invented this form of torture called Ling Chi. It's roughly translated as the slow process, the lingering death, or even death by a thousand cuts – maybe you've heard of it?"

Cameron gurgled into the gag again.

"Unfortunately, we don't have the time needed for a thousand cuts, but maybe if we try really hard, we could make it to a hundred."

Cameron thrashed frantically, but to no avail.

Dan started with Cameron's face and a few small cuts down each cheek. The scalpel was razor sharp and initially cut so cleanly that only a few crimson lines showed behind the blade as he sliced through the facial tissue. It was only after a few seconds that the blood began to flow in earnest.

The pain was excruciating but all Cameron could do was to bite down hard and wince.

"That's it, Cameron. Fight it. There's no use resisting. Isn't that what you said to that little boy when he tried unsuccessfully to escape your clutches?"

Dan raised his hand to Cameron's line of sight and spread his fingers.

"You see… the lines of scars are still faintly visible," Dan sneered.

Dan administered a few more small cuts to Cameron's arms and torso, staying well clear of the duct-tape.

Cameron's eyes teared with pain and at the same time blazed with hatred.

"We're only up to ten. Only ninety to go. Can you go the

distance?"

Dan dragged the blade along the top of the man's scalp and then swiftly went to work on the inside of his bare legs.

The cuts weren't deep, which was the exact point.

But the pain was beyond anything Cameron had ever felt.

His eyes now remained closed, partly from the anguish and partly to prevent the blood, which was streaming down his forehead, from getting into his eyes.

He endured as much as he could and then finally stars exploded behind his eyes and his body went limp, as he blacked out from the pain.

Chapter 85

Dan took a breather when he saw Cameron finally yield to the pain and pass out. He wasn't about to let this animal miss out on one second of what was coming his way. He issued a huge roundhouse slap to Cameron's left cheek, but his body had totally . shut down for now.

Dan could only sit back and wait it out.

An hour went by before Cameron stirred.

The pain immediately set in and he started crying and moaning; sobbing through the gag. The dream he thought he was having had suddenly become reality.

"Crying won't help you!" Dan shouted at him, repeating what had been screamed in the little boy's ear many years prior. "You can dish it out, but you can't take it, can you?"

Dan pushed the scalpel into Cameron's left bicep. Once. Twice. Three times.

Cameron screamed soundlessly into the gag. The agony was immobilising.

Blood and sweat comingled on his forehead and the crimson liquid streamed down his face; a curtain of gunk blinding him.

"Pathetic. You make me sick," Dan uttered in contempt. "We're not even half way through and you're screaming like a little girl."

Dan could see in the man's eyes that he was about to pass out again.

"Oh no… not again," he commanded and threw cold water

in his face.

Cameron gasped and reflexively inhaled through his nose, as his buccal airway was clogged with the gag.

"Now for a little retribution," Dan said calmly and disappeared behind Cameron.

Cameron tried to move his head to see where Dan had gone, but the duct-tape held him firmly. Suddenly a blazing pain engulfed his hands. It felt like his fingers had been set ablaze. He screamed incessantly into the gag, until he could barely catch his breath.

"Hurts like a bitch, doesn't it?" Dan said, returning to Cameron's field of vision. "Now, how do you think that little boy felt when you sliced him between his fingers?"

"Sooooorrrrrryyyyyy!" Cameron screamed into the gag.

It was muffled, but Dan could vaguely make out the word 'sorry' through the wadded material in his mouth.

"You're sorry? Now you're sorry?" Dan emphasised. "Well, isn't it just a little late for that? You should have thought it through a little better at the time. All small boys eventually grow into big men and sometimes into really big men."

He flexed his pecs a few times and then waved a massive bicep in front of Cameron's face to make his point.

"No, my friend… it's far too late for apologies. You've had years to think about your actions and dredge up an apology. Now, you pay for those actions."

Dan dragged the blade once more across the man's chest with little effect.

He'd heard that after significant trauma the body could adapt and switch off certain pain receptors. Seemingly this was true. He would just have to move on to more sensitive areas.

"I suggest you stay as still as possible now," he whispered

into Cameron's ear, as he took the man's penis in his hand and drew the blade lengthways down the shaft.

There were definitely more nerve endings there and the agonising screams moved down the octaves from frenetic, to guttural, finally settling on heart-wrenching.

Almost.

Not quite though.

Cameron's throat was red raw by the time he finally passed out again from the pain.

Dan smiled and shook his head in disdain.

He had all the time in the world, but beyond slicing away sections of the man's flesh, the process was becoming rather tedious.

Besides that, if Cameron kept passing out, this would take all night.

The Chinese must have been extremely patient, he mused.

He tried splashing cold water in Cameron's face again, but nothing was working any more. He was truly out for the count.

Dan felt for a pulse.

It was weak and slow – but it was there.

He decided to wait it out again and then put an end to it.

Another hour passed and only after another few slaps did Cameron rouse slightly.

"Welcome back," he said.

Cameron moaned in despair.

"Welcome to the beginning of the end. This will be somewhat painless compared to what you've endured, but it's time for you to pay the ultimate price."

Cameron tried to say something, but his voice was so hoarse after all the screaming and obviously still distorted by the gag.

Dan ignored him and pressed on.

"Too late for anything now," and with those final words, he sliced Cameron's femoral arteries in both legs.

Dan looked eagerly into the dying man's eyes.

It wasn't long before his face paled and his life trickled down his legs on the back of the warm blood oozing from the fatal lacerations.

Dan was fascinated, taking mental snapshots of the fray to preserve it in his memory for eternity and then for good measure, stabbed the scalpel into Cameron's chest and left it there.

He took his time to prep the scene as before and then left under the cover of darkness.

He knew he would have to report this or it would remain undiscovered and undisturbed for days, if not weeks. Nobody would miss this low-life any time soon and he definitely didn't have that sort of time.

Chapter 86

Julia woke early, plagued by a nagging feeling that all was not right in the world.

She could just sense that something unpleasant had happened during the night while she had slept.

She couldn't shake the feeling.

It was quite eerie.

She pulled back the curtain and gazed out the window.

The day looked grey and morbid. Possibly another ominous portent.

The clouds filled the skies, but were very wispy and drifted up high. At the same time, the sun was still low, only just beginning its daily journey to cross from the eastern to the western horizon. It was weak and probably would remain so as the date edged ever closer to that of the winter solstice.

Only a few brave souls strolled the beachfront this early.

The breeze, of late, was now more than just a mild chill and jerseys, or even jackets, were becoming a necessity. A few of the pedestrians even wore beanies to keep their heads warm against the bracing breeze and unrelenting chill factor.

She admired them from her vantage point and wished that she had the inclination to brave the elements in the quest for fresh air and exercise.

The sea looked choppy and frigid. White horses ran rampant on the crests of the waves. There weren't too many smaller fishing vessels bobbing on the rough swells, but she could vaguely distinguish a few ships floating steadily along the distant horizon.

Cargo ships passed daily on their trajectories between Durban and Cape Town, occasionally docking in East London or even Port Elizabeth to load or off-load their freight from distant lands.

It must be a really hard life, she thought.

Months and months on the open waters to deliver valuable cargo, only to return to their origins and do it all over again. While it was almost taken for granted, the world economy and trade in general would surely be in turmoil without this service.

She wondered what the deck hands did to pass their time.

Surely it wasn't as simple as sleeping or playing cards for hours upon hours, days upon days and months upon months.

She shook off the thought, as her phone buzzed on the bedside table.

"Hey girl," the familiar voice said as she answered the call.

"Hey Caths," Julia replied.

"You're up early."

"I could say the same for you. It's Saturday morning you know."

"I do know. I just had a terrible night, tossing and turning, until I finally just gave up. So happy you answered. I would've hung up after a few rings if you hadn't. I really didn't want to bug you."

"Don't be silly. I'm here for you. What's happening, Caths? Something going on I don't know about?" Julia asked with growing concern.

Cathy was generally the 'happy go lucky' type and this was totally out of character for her. Julia's concern grew by the second.

The absolute worst was going through her mind.

What had her friend gotten herself into?

The one consolation was that whatever it was, she knew they could work through it. Cathy had always been there for her and she wouldn't disappoint her friend in her time of need, no matter what.

"I think I'm pregnant," Cathy blurted out and started to cry uncontrollably.

Julia inhaled sharply in surprise. "What do you mean you think you're pregnant? I didn't even know you were seeing anyone."

"I know," Cathy sobbed. "It was more of a one-night stand, which then became a two-night and then a three-night stand. That's why I think it's affecting me like this. It was never meant to be anything serious. I also feel like such a fraud. To you... to Anne... to Sam. It's karma's way of punishing me for making fun of Sam and Fred's relationship. Me and my big mouth." She continued between intermittent sobs and sniffs.

"Don't be so melodramatic, Caths."

As soon as she said it, she knew she was out of line. Cathy needed her support right now, not a lecture or her judgemental opinion.

"I'm sorry, Caths, that's not what I meant. I just don't think karma would single you out over some light-hearted ribbing. We were there and it was harmless. I think you'd need to do a whole lot worse than that for karma to pay any attention to you."

"You think?" Cathy sniffed.

"Of course," Julia consoled, "besides, a baby is not the end of the world. It would be lucky to have you as its mother. Besides, three aunties like us to spoil and babysit the little sprog... you couldn't ask for better."

"Thanks, Jules," she replied, a slow smile finally spreading across her face, "you always know just what to say."

"Now, who's the lucky father-to-be?" Julia prompted.

"You don't know him. He's a work colleague. We've been working on a project together and obviously got a bit too familiar and close to each other. It was never meant to be anything serious," she repeated.

"So, how far along are you?"

"It couldn't be more than three months, if even that."

"Well… there's no use in panicking or stressing yourself out over it. What will be, will be. You've always had that perspective on life anyway and besides, you have our support no matter how this plays out."

"I know. Thanks, Jules. Just, um… let's not tell the girls just yet. I am stressing out, but maybe it is too early and just a false alarm. I'll let them know when I've tested and am hundred per cent sure."

"Your wish is my command," Julia joked. "But let's get hold of them anyway and do something tonight."

"Sounds like a great distraction," replied Cathy.

They both sent hugs and kisses down the line and then hung up.

Chapter 87

Ollie was deep in thought.

He had read through the preliminary reports on all the mortuaries and nothing at all jumped out at him as a lead to follow up on.

Just normal people going about the day-to-day business of dressing up and interring dead people. Oh, and dealing with grieving families, which was not a perk of the job. The deep dive had produced nothing. The owners were mostly upstanding citizens abiding by the protocols of their chosen trade, while the employees, although quite evidently a macabre bunch, were likewise mostly above-board. It might not be their chosen profession, but it was a job and that's pretty much all that mattered when the unemployment rate was hovering around 30%.

His phone rang, startling him from his thoughts.

"Hello, Phumz," he said, tipped off by his caller ID.

"Hi, Ollie, how are you this fine day?"

"Mostly fine," he muttered, "hitting wall after wall on this investigation though."

"Oh, I'm sorry to hear that… maybe I have a little something to brighten up your day," she added.

He couldn't hide the delight in his voice. "Anything, absolutely anything would be great. We're getting nowhere in a hurry."

"Well, if you've spoken to Captain Phiri lately, you would know that our leads have also led nowhere. DNA matches, partial or otherwise have also been inconclusive. Like you, we were all losing hope this side too. So much evidence to pour through and nothing concrete from a DNA perspective. Anyway, one of my lab technicians decided to go off on a bit of a tangent. She decided to run some routine blood and urine tests on the samples we had. The idea was to identify other traits or characteristics of the sample donors, as opposed to their exact identifications. A bit of lateral thinking."

She paused, as she often did, which Ollie found quite annoying.

He waited with baited breath for what seemed like forever.

Only once he prompted her with, "And…?" did she continue.

"Well, she identified the likes of diabetes, Alzheimer's disease, anaemia and even leukaemia in the sample. But the strangest discovery was that of a high concentration of HGH."

"HGH?" Ollie repeated, sounding a bit confused.

"Human Growth Hormone," Phumzile elaborated.

"Oh right," Ollie responded, "and by high concentration you mean…?"

"The dose was not being taken just as a supplement. These quantities were ingested to really boost the growth of muscles."

"A body-builder… or power-lifter," Ollie commented.

"On the money," Phumzile answered. "Now it's not possible to say whether this detail has anything to do with your man or not, but eliminating body-builders or power-lifters would be a much easier task than eliminating people who suffer from diabetes, Alzheimer's, anaemia and leukaemia. The inflicted are a dime a dozen."

"Phumz, I owe you big time… again," Ollie said.

Without a moment's hesitation, she replied, "If these aren't empty promises, it seems like you'll have your work cut out for you when you eventually visit me in Cape Town?"

"I know," replied Ollie, not even trying to disguise the broad grin on his face.

Ollie wondered whether the information he had just been given had much merit.

They could be off on another wild goose chase.

He decided to scour the internet for more information and what he found made his blood turn to ice.

He read – '*When asking does HGH show up in a blood test, it is understandable that unless a person knew precisely when to target drawing out the sample in correlation with a timed secretion, there would be no way to get an accurate reading. This is because once GH is secreted, it leaves the bloodstream as soon as it reaches its intended receptor cells.*'

Did this mean what he thought it meant?

Nobody knocking on death's door would be injecting high doses of HGH just before dying.

The blood containing the HGH would have been from a living person and harvested soon after the HGH dose was administered.

He sat back and pictured the scene in his mind.

A body-builder administering the HGH subcutaneous injection by pinching the belly skin and inserting the needle. Then, deciding that while his shirt was off, he would find a vein and extract a blood sample. Finally, he would mix his blood in with his collection of blood stored in a refrigerated vial, beaker or blood bag.

That must be it, he thought to himself.

Had Dan made a fatal error?

Was this the oversight they'd been waiting for?

Chapter 88

Ollie's phone buzzed again.

This time it was DC Phiri.

"Morning, Inspector," Ollie answered, again being tipped off by his caller ID.

"Morning, Ollie," DC Phiri responded and without any further pleasantries got right into the reason for his call.

"We received a tip-off this morning from an anonymous caller. The address was that of a car mechanic in the West Bank. A restorer of antique cars, it turns out."

Ollie scrambled for a pen and paper while DC Phiri rambled on.

"The man's name was Cameron Long. Ring any bells?"

Ollie shook his head. "No, not a name we've come across."

"The crime scene was identical to the others with blood, urine, hairs, some shoe-prints and even faeces this time, contaminating the scene."

Ollie was almost too hesitant to ask about the *modus operandi*.

Sensing this, DC Phiri continued. "The vic was found, naked, gagged and bound to a pillar in his kitchen. It looked as though a vicious cat had attacked and scratched the hell out of him. His head, face, chest, abdomen and legs had been slashed with a razor-sharp scalpel – even the length of his penis had been lacerated."

Ollie involuntarily winced at hearing this.

DC Phiri pressed on. "It was clear that the perp was in no hurry. He knew that he wouldn't be interrupted and had all night to torture this poor fellow. The medical examiner was adamant that no person could have maintained consciousness throughout this torture process and believes that he must have passed out numerous times."

Ollie was about to interject, but DC Phiri continued persistently.

"The death knell was when the killer finally sliced the victim's femoral arteries and let him bleed out. He then buried the scalpel in the man's chest."

DC Phiri paused for a few seconds before continuing.

"It was without a doubt the work of our serial killer," he said. "The crime scene was again sullied with an excess of DNA and other evidence. The inclusion of faeces was new and unexpected, but will undoubtedly be from different donors as with the other DNA evidence. The forensic team is currently busy with the bagging and tagging, as we speak."

"The plane is ready whenever you need it," Ollie said, finally getting a word in edgewise.

"Thank you, Ollie. Please extend our sincere appreciation to Alan."

"Not a problem," Ollie replied. "On another note, have you spoken to Phumzile lately?"

"Not recently, why?"

"Well, I was chatting to her this morning and I think she's stumbled across something we need to follow up on."

"Oh, and what is that?" DC Phiri asked curiously.

"She told me that one of her lab techs had inadvertently found large traces of HGH in the blood samples."

"What is HGH?" DC Phiri queried.

"It's Human Growth Hormone. You can buy it off the shelf as a supplement, but she maintains that the quantities found in our blood samples would only be present if someone was trying to do some serious bulking up and injecting it into themselves."

"Okay, that is interesting," DC Phiri nodded.

"I also did some research and it turns out that all traces of HGH leave the blood stream soon after it attaches itself to the muscle receptors, which then leads me to believe that the blood sample was taken very soon after the HGH was injected," Ollie cited. "It really proves nothing though, as its most likely just a sample taken from another oblivious donor and added to the blood cocktail…"

"But maybe it's not," DC Phiri interrupted, "and either we could find our suspect or at a bare minimum narrow down the search pool."

"Exactly!" Ollie exclaimed excitedly. "We need to find out if the same batch of blood was also used at this scene. Can you access some of the blood from the crime scene and get it tested urgently?"

"Can I?" DC Phiri responded sarcastically. "It's my crime scene. The forensic team will do whatever I tell them to do. I'll get right on it."

He hung up without as much as a 'good-bye'.

A man on a mission, Ollie thought.

This was really exciting news and without a second thought, he punched in Alan's speed-dial number.

The conversation was abridged and to the point – summarising his discussion with Phumzile and DC Phiri.

Alan remained silent throughout, as the big man recited his conversations and emphasised their findings and conclusions.

"That's really interesting," Alan remarked, once Ollie had

concluded his synopsis. "When will DC Phiri have some results for us?"

"That's not something I can answer just yet," admitted Ollie. "We only just discussed the issue minutes ago and he hung up to get right on it. I'm hoping within the course of the day, but – it being a Saturday – I'm not too hopeful."

"Well, it could be something, so keep me informed, big guy," he said and hung up.

Ollie's mind was in over-drive with the new information.

He needed to brief the team – urgently – and find out how this Cameron Long fitted into the picture.

Chapter 89

It was a big night for the foursome. The quartet was about to become a sextet.

Both Anne and Sam had initially declined the invitation, as they'd already made other plans, but on the insistence of Julia and Cathy, they'd succumbed on condition that their new partners could be included.

The girls had all met Fred and since he worked at Buccaneers, they decided on The Cow Shed, along Beach Road, instead. It wasn't too far out of the way and was a great alternative for a few drinks and a good meal.

Julia and Cathy arrived early. They were unusually nervous. They'd often been served by Fred at Buccaneers, but had never socialised with him.

To cap that, they knew nothing about Anne's beau, Peter. She had managed to keep their relationship top secret until only a few days back.

"Was this a mistake?" Cathy asked, looking at Julia for comfort and support.

Julia shrugged. "I'm not sure, my friend. This could either turn out great or totally implode."

"Not very reassuring, Jules," remarked Cathy with pursed lips and a shake of her head.

They walked into the restaurant together and requested a table for six people. The waiter ushered them over to the far corner. He pushed two tables together and rearranged a few chairs, creating a large enough eating area for the six of them.

It was still early and the restaurant was fairly quiet with only a few patrons keeping the waitstaff busy.

The interior was very rustic.

The walls were adorned with white-washed wood panelling, almost grey in colour. The wooden tables were darkly stained and had that sheen which comes from frequent use and regular cleaning. Cathy was reminded of church pews and the way they gleamed from all the butts rubbing against them over the years.

The chairs, other than the cushioned bunk benches, were a combination of both wood and metal and were mostly a lighter shade of blue. The light fittings hanging over each table were similarly a hodgepodge of styles, some archaic metal domes, while others were more modern glass casings.

The girls took their seats and waited in suspense for the rest of their party.

It wasn't five minutes before Sam and Fred arrived and sauntered over to the table, hand in hand.

Julia and Cathy both stood to welcome them and suddenly felt very under-dressed.

Sam had dollied herself up like she was off to the prom, while Fred wore a fairly formal pair of brown trousers, a beige collared shirt and a blazer to match.

They were obviously out to impress each other, but had forgotten to send the memo to Julia and Cathy, who now felt really out of place.

Cathy broke the tension, as usual. "Welcome. Come. Sit," she said, indicating the array of chairs with an outstretched arm.

"Thanks, Caths," Sam replied. "No introductions necessary. You all know Fred and he certainly knows both of you."

"Yes, of course," Julia chimed in. "So, what plans did we

manage to mess up for you tonight?"

"Oh, nothing much," Fred contributed, "we were toying with the idea of a pizza and a movie." He looked over at Sam and smiled broadly.

Madly in love, Julia thought to herself, *how lucky?*

"Should we order some drinks in the meantime?" Cathy piped up, but as she looked over she noticed Anne and Peter entering the restaurant.

"Big boy," she remarked out loud. All eyes followed her stare to see what she was talking about.

"Yikes," Julia commented, "he's nearly as wide as he is tall."

Fred suddenly felt very insecure being a really average male.

"Hi, everyone," Anne said jovially, as they approached the table. "This is Peter. Peter this is Jules, Cathy, Sam and Fred."

Peter looked at each person in turn, nodding and smiling almost robotically.

"Hello everyone, nice to finally meet you all," he responded.

It was always a conundrum whether to shake hands with women or not, so he decided not to risk it, and included Fred in the process. He hoped Fred wouldn't take offence. He really needed an ally tonight amongst this bevy of beauties.

"Enough of the formalities, please sit. I'm tired of craning my neck to look up at you," Cathy said, attracting chuckles from the group.

"You warned me about this one's sense of humour," Peter replied, looking over at Anne.

Julia immediately recognised the look they shared.

Madly in love, too, she thought to herself.

The night was a delightful success.

Drinks, conversation and a good meal rounded off the perfect evening.

Cathy feigned nausea and drank soda water the entire night, which normally would have raised some eyebrows, but it seemed that Sam and Anne were far too distracted by the new men in their lives to ask too many questions or probe for answers.

Fred and Peter proved to be highly intelligent, witty and quite garrulous even though outnumbered by four strong-willed and very opinionated women.

And even though there was quite a significant age difference between the guys, Julia noticed that between themselves they also seemed to hit it off.

When the night ended and they went their separate ways, Julia could only wonder whether their little girls' club was about to take a major turn.

And hopefully a turn for the best.

Chapter 90

The mom and pop coffee shop was very quiet.

Dan liked getting there early on a Sunday morning before the church-goers arrived. They were always hungry after paying their weekly homage and praying for the next week to be better than the last.

Dan smiled at the thought.

Adrenaline was still coursing through his body after Friday night's escapade and there was an ostensible spring in his step as he entered the coffee shop and headed over to his usual table.

Sharon was nowhere to be seen.

Dan saw the other waitress's familiar face, but had no idea what her name was. He couldn't remember ever being served by her.

Would she be as friendly as Sharon?

Would she be as quick and efficient as Sharon?

Would she get his order right?

Would she…?

The waitress suddenly appeared alongside his table and interrupted his thought process.

"Morning, sir… your coffee," she said, smiling broadly and off-loaded her tray's contents onto the table.

"Uh, thank you," he murmured. The boil of his internal rage eased to a simmer.

He looked down at her chest and then quickly made eye-contact with her again before she got the wrong impression.

"Mary. Thank you, Mary." He repeated her name, to ensure that she knew he had only looked down at her chest to view her name-tag.

"It's a pleasure, sir. Will you be having your usual breakfast with us this morning?" she asked, stunning him into silence.

Dan was impressed beyond words and just stared at Mary for what was possibly a few seconds too long before saying anything.

"Yes, thank you. I certainly will be eating this morning," Dan said, eventually breaking the silence.

"Should I bring it for you now, or would you like to have your coffee first?"

Dan nodded. "I'll give you a shout when I'm ready to order."

Dan was blown away by this interaction, but then realised that he was being overly presumptuous.

Maybe she wouldn't know what his usual order was?

Maybe she would still get his order wrong?

He reigned in his thoughts. Accolades would only be deserved if she proved to be as good as she made out to be.

But so far, he was impressed.

He poured his coffee and snuggled back into his chair, his iPad switched on and at the ready.

He browsed the *DispatchLIVE* website, but nothing new had been posted there – about him, anyway.

Nothing new!

He knew it was a little over a day later, but he wondered whether Julia needed another nudge again.

He mulled this over for a few moments and then surfed through to the *Daily Dispatch* Facebook page. He enjoyed this portal the most, as it was far more interactive. He scrolled down to *his* story. In the bottom right corner he noticed that there were fifteen thousand three hundred and seventeen 'comments' and eight thousand four hundred and twenty-nine 'shares'.

Out of interest, he scrolled to other news postings. A couple of hundred 'comments' and a handful of 'shares' if they were lucky.

He smiled to himself. He had definitely grabbed the attention of the public.

Those 'shares' had probably gone viral on Twitter and WhatsApp as well, as those were truly the 'sharing' or 'forwarding' platforms.

He wasn't really in tune with any of these other social media platforms, so his concentration was mostly on the internet and Facebook pages. They encompassed the localised media footprint and his initial intention was to make an impact there. The national and international glamourisation and exposure was cream on the top for now.

He spent the next few minutes scrolling down and reading the 'comments'.

Most of the public still didn't get it – 'Serial killer on the rampage in the East London area'.

Unintelligent, oblivious cretins!

However… there were a growing number, who mostly didn't appreciate what he was doing, but understood and acknowledged the reasons for why he was doing what he was doing.

These were the broader-minded individuals he was appealing to. Those who saw the bigger picture and were sympathetic to his views and interested in changing the status quo.

Mary stopped alongside the table on her way past.

"Ready for breakfast?' she enquired.

"Great. The same as usual, please," Dan replied, putting her to the test.

"Coming right up," she said, performing a perfect about turn and disappearing into the kitchen.

Within five minutes she had returned.

"Two eggs, two rashers of bacon, half a grilled tomato and two slices of toast, just as you like it. And a fresh cup of coffee. Enjoy your breakfast, sir."

"Excellent, Mary. I assumed that in Sharon's absence the service would be found wanting. My assumption was incorrect, I might add. Thank you very much and well done."

She grinned widely and left him to enjoy his meal.

Always over-tip for great service, he reminded himself.

Chapter 91

Ollie followed the same protocols to enter the Burns Street safe house as before. The process was as practiced as brushing his teeth.

It was Sunday morning and he hadn't slept very well. His thoughts, ideas and postulations had plagued him throughout the night. At one stage, he found himself wandering the grounds wearing only his sleeping shorts. When he got back to his flatlet, he was freezing.

He was so engrossed in his own thoughts that he couldn't even remember going outside. He spent the next half hour just trying to warm up again.

This HGH analysis was bothering him.

It was highly fortuitous that the lab tech had done additional tests on the blood samples, but making sense of it was proving to be rather taxing. It could be nothing, but his instincts told him differently.

Maybe the team would have an idea on how best to investigate this.

"Morning," he said as he walked into the boardroom.

"Morning, boss," chorused the team around the table with the operators springing to attention, while the analysts remained seated.

Most of them were extremely large men, but none could measure up to Ollie in terms of sheer mass and power.

Ollie could and would destroy any of them any time in hand

to hand combat.

They practiced often enough to stay sharp and hone their skills.

Manny, on the other hand, was lean and lithe and a completely different proposition.

Ollie wouldn't even dream of taking Manny on in unarmed combat.

Manny was a one-man wrecking crew with his speed and martial arts expertise. Size literally meant nothing if you couldn't lay a finger on your opponent. Ollie had learnt this many times and the hard way from Manny while training.

And while pressure points and submission holds were excellent techniques to subdue an opponent, Ollie remained the 'overwhelm and pulverise your adversary' type.

Manny had rightfully earned his position as Ollie's second in charge.

Ollie looked down at the analysts and grinned.

It was strange to see the three of them with their laptops pushed to one side while paging through hard copies of anything.

He was so accustomed to the sound of fingers fleeting across keyboards, and projections being occasionally pushed through to the wall-mounted screens, that this sight was very unfamiliar.

Instead they now had reams of documents piled in front of them. They had, what they had sourced, along with all the information DC Phiri's resources had discovered. The information on the three victims had subsequently been divvied up and was being thoroughly scoured for any correlations.

"Anything yet?" Ollie queried, looking over at the three of them.

Heads shook all round. "Nothing so far, but if anything, the records don't seem to indicate any contact in their adult lives.

We're working solely on the premise that if they knew each other, it could only have been while they were at primary school."

"All right, carry on then," Ollie retorted.

He looked over at the door kickers. "HGH? Is this a lead or not and if so, how do we proceed?"

They looked at each other blankly.

The silence was uncomfortable.

Manny felt obligated to step up. Luckily he had something to say and possibly being the scrawniest person in the group helped.

He also held the unenviable rank of second in charge, so he felt obliged to contribute.

"Well, HGH is a human growth hormone, like a supplement – for body building, right?"

He looked around at the monoliths in his orbit, expecting some sort of affirmation, but none was forthcoming.

He continued to spell it out.

"So… gyms, right? We need to focus in on the gyms."

"Gyms," Ollie echoed excitedly. "Also, it's quite expensive, which will narrow our search down even more. I would think the blood sample came from a proper gym-rat and one with money."

Manny smiled. Not something he could say, since his boss fell into the category and he wouldn't dare say anything to offend him.

But coming from Ollie, it was acceptable.

"I would think the two Virgin Active branches – Beacon Bay and Quigney – are the places to start. You guys wouldn't look out of place in a gym, so get your sweats and trainers on, work out a rotation, and go lift some weights."

"Manny," Ollie continued, "you and your team can pick up the trail outside when a target leaves the gym."

Manny nodded, although feeling a bit slighted. Gyms were designed for cardio as well, not that the muscle in the room would ever acknowledge that.

"Let's get going then, guys, and let's hope we have more success than with the morgues."

They all nodded, thankful that the morgues were now out of the picture.

Chapter 92

Julia's phoned beeped as an incoming message interrupted her catnap.

She'd been watching some documentary on Pharaohs, pyramids and tombs on the History channel and had dozed off on the couch. How better to spend a Sunday afternoon?

She didn't recognise the number and it obviously wasn't saved as a contact or the caller ID would have appeared.

More spam, she thought.

The number of telesales calls and text messages were blossoming of late.

Who was it this time?

Vehicle tracking?

Insurance?

Cell phone or Wi-Fi service providers?

Debt consolidation?

The list was actually endless and becoming increasingly irritating.

She came close to ignoring it, but at the last second curiosity got the better of her. She opened WhatsApp and the first two words nearly caused her to drop the phone.

'Dear Julia' occupied the first two lines of the message.

She resisted the urge to open the message and quickly scribbled down the number on her shopping list, which was conveniently adhered to the refrigerator with a magnet.

The call she made to her father was answered within the first few rings.

"Hi, Dad, quickly write down this number…"

"Hi, Jules… what?" he interrupted, his cheerfulness abruptly replaced by concern.

"Write down this number quickly. It's him. We need to track it right now."

Sensing the urgency in her voice, he took down the number without further interruptions.

"He just sent me a message," Julia clarified. "I haven't even read it yet, so he might still be connected waiting to see that I've read it."

"Okay, give me a few minutes to set this up. I'll call you back when the tracking has begun."

"Thanks, Dad," she replied and hung up.

The next five minutes took an eternity.

She gazed at the WhatsApp screen as she waited.

All that was visible under the number were the two most frightening words she had read lately – 'Dear Julia'.

She was aching to open the message, but at the same time, she was petrified.

No more letters. He had swapped to messaging. She wondered why.

She all but jumped off her seat when the phone rang in her hands.

It was her father – finally.

The number was being tracked.

She promised to forward the message to him and Ollie once she'd read it.

Hopefully by then the number would have been traced and the guys would be en route to the location.

She thumbed the message to open it.

Dear Julia,

I trust you are well.

I must thank you again for a sterling job done on the last exposé. I have been reading the comments and although Joe public believes that change happens all by itself, there are some more realistic individuals out there who are not as ignorant.

But that is a rant for another day.

I believe I am limited to the number of characters I can use, so must dispense with the pleasantries and get to the point.

I hope, by now, you know all about number three.

To date, the most despicable of them all.

Ling Chi was me being excessively kind to this animal.

Cameron Long deserved his comeuppance and my retribution was long overdue. He actually tried to apologise throughout the evening.

Quite laughable.

I cannot believe he would think that I'd say 'Okay, all is forgiven, I'll leave now and you can go back to your despicable life.'

As you would notice, I've given a few sensitive details again, to assure you that it was indeed me and my work.

I would hope that you have started on the next exposé, but if not, then this message is quite apt in its purpose.

To answer the obvious question, the timeline is increasing exponentially and there is currently no time for the elaborate planning of delivering a letter to you, hence the message.

Furthermore, it would be a futile exercise trying to trace this number, as I have by now either flushed the SIM down the toilet, crushed it or thrown the burner phone in the ocean.

Get busy now.

Best Regards,

Daniel Nathan Anderson (DNA Dan)

Julia reread the message.

It disclosed nothing, yet at the same time disclosed a lot.

She was a bit shaken, but on the whole, was fine. The mere thought of communicating with a serial killer really frazzled her nerves.

She tapped on the message and used the 'forward' option to send it off to her father and Ollie.

In all honesty, she had only heard brief snippets about the murder.

She'd believed that her part had come to an end. Clearly it hadn't.

So much for my Sunday afternoon, she thought.

Chapter 93

Ollie read the message and then read it again.

He seethed.

The audacity of this man made his blood boil.

He had made a quick detour, after leaving the safe house, to check out the Virgin Active gyms in both Quigney and Beacon Bay.

The Swans had a fully kitted out gym at the mansion, so before today he'd never even set foot in one of the commercial gyms.

He was given the guided tour, as a potential new acquisition and was actually quite impressed with the facilities they had to offer.

Anne was not working when he investigated the Quigney branch on the beach front. He made absolutely sure of that before entering or his cover would have been blown.

The guys would now take the lead and flag any probables and possibles for Manny's team to follow and investigate further.

The day had flown by and he proceeded into the main house to meet with Alan on the latest developments. He weaved his way along the footpath on his way from his flatlet to the main house.

Ollie didn't know them by name, but he loved all the greenery. The different shades of green created a beautiful mosaic which really appealed to him.

In summer, the shade the big evergreens offered was gloriously refreshing. In winter, however, they tended to block out the sunlight and covered the grounds in a near permanent blanket of shadow.

He was dressed fairly warmly on this late autumn's day and was fairly well protected against the decreasing temperature.

Alan was sitting on the veranda when he arrived. A glass, of what Ollie assumed was cognac, rested in his upturned hand.

He was also dressed warmly to stave off the chill, even though a fire was already crackling in the hearth. The area was still quite cold, but once the logs had burned down more to create embers, the secluded corner of the veranda generally became a lot warmer.

"Evening, boss," Ollie chirped. "Nice evening for a fire."

Alan looked up at the big man and Ollie could see the stress and concern on the man's face.

"Hello, Ollie. A fire is little comfort to a man in dark times," Alan replied philosophically, feeling helpless about not being able to protect his baby girl adequately.

Ollie poured himself a drink and refreshed Alan's and then sat down heavily in his usual armchair.

"I know," Ollie empathised. "We're chasing every lead we can find. We haven't totally given up on the morgue angle yet, but I've moved most of the guys onto the gyms. This HGH lead – there's something to it. All my instincts are telling me that this is the break we've been waiting for. This is where Dan slipped up – I just know it. There is such a small window before the HGH becomes undetectable and he took his own blood sample within that timeframe. He probably figured that since he still had the syringe in his hand after injecting himself with the HGH that he would simply just withdraw some of his blood at the same time and mix it into his blood sample cocktail."

Alan nodded. "I hope you're right, buddy. I just don't know

how we proceed. We can't very well detain and test every bodybuilder's blood for HGH."

"I agree, but we can tag the suspects, surveil them, do background checks on them and at least eliminate those who don't fit the profile."

"You say this as though we have time on our side. If our understanding is correct, he only has one more victim and he's pushed forward his timeline. None of this bodes well for us."

"I know," Ollie agreed. "It's a long shot, but it's a lead and we need to investigate it. As we know most of the evidence already processed was from dead people and it's just too improbable that Dan stumbled across a dead bodybuilder or one on the verge of dying who had just injected himself with HGH. The chances are just too remote."

Alan was not convinced. "I hope you're right, buddy. We're hedging our bets on this."

Ollie's phone rang in his pocket.

Ollie looked over at Alan, almost seeking consent to answer it.

Alan nodded.

Ollie stood and dug around in his trouser pocket to retrieve the cell phone.

"Manny?" he answered questioningly.

"Hi, boss. Some new information just in."

"What is it?" Ollie prompted in an attempt to speed up the message delivery as Alan looked on expectantly.

"Anne... Anne is dating a bodybuilder. Thuso was tailing Julia and the group on Friday night and Anne arrived at the Cow Shed with a bodybuilder."

"Really? Please don't tell me that Dan's managed to infiltrate the group right under our noses."

"We didn't know at the time that we should be on the lookout for a bodybuilder. The post op brief just mentioned, Julia, Cathy, Sam and her boyfriend, and Anne and her boyfriend. There weren't even any names for the boyfriends. We're digging for details right now."

"Get someone onto Anne immediately," Ollie instructed. "Dan could be using her to get close to Julia. She could be in serious danger as we speak."

"We're on it already, boss," Manny replied. "They're not even together at the moment."

Ollie sighed out of relief. He knew he had a competent team and, as usual, they'd acted quickly on the new information.

"Thanks Manny, let me know what you find."

Ollie looked over at Alan, who had heard the entire conversation, and did not look impressed.

"Nothing happened, boss. It's just another lead we need to follow. The guys didn't know anything about the HGH angle at the time."

"But something could have happened," Alan said firmly, "and we'd have been none the wiser."

"I know, "Ollie confessed. "I'm as concerned as you are, but as much as we've pleaded with Julia to limit her activities, we can't wrap her in cotton wool."

Alan nodded. He knew Ollie was right.

Julia was far too stubborn and strong-willed and would not play by their rules even though it put her in danger.

"Well just don't let Julia know anything yet," Alan instructed.

"We'll do our homework first and then close in on this guy if he's any threat," Ollie confirmed.

Dinner would soon be served, and Claire would join them, so the matter was officially closed... for now.

Chapter 94

Another restless night passed and Julia awoke feeling like she'd pulled an all-nighter, as she had often done in varsity.

Far simpler days, she reminisced. *No other distractions or worries except passing her exams. Now, all she had were worries, oh and of course, a serial killer pulling her strings.*

She caught herself secretly hoping that Dan would just hurry up and kill his last victim thereby releasing her from his control. She quickly chastised herself for having these dark and evil thoughts. This was not her. This was the stress talking.

Her morning coffee didn't even help.

She felt drugged and lethargic, but knew that procrastination was the thief of time.

Ollie was awake when she called him. He was always awake when she called. *Did he ever sleep?* she wondered.

Even though her stupor prevailed, her journalistic prowess took control and she probed him for the next half hour on the details of the latest murder.

It was difficult for her to hear, and her hand was cramping after jotting down the details, but she needed the facts for the article she was required to write.

Ollie could hear that she was not herself, but understood the predicament she was in and patiently walked her through the events as described by DC Phiri.

She came close to accepting the offer of joining him for breakfast, but realised that she had a mountain to climb and needed to get on with it.

After the call, she sat back in her chair and read through the notes she'd taken.

This was horrific, she thought.

The poor man must have been in agony for hours upon hours.

She'd already researched Ling Chi, but the gruesomeness hadn't hit home until Ollie had described the mutilation of Cameron Long's body in detail.

She suddenly wondered if Dan's timeline was based on the release of her article.

Would he wait until her next exposé was published before committing the fourth murder?

It was an interesting thought.

Was that the reason for his urgent contact?

Would he feel robbed if she wrote nothing?

Would he direct his retribution at her or her friends?

She decided that she couldn't risk it. She needed to knuckle down and deliver another masterpiece.

But how could she glamourise his actions after hearing about the heinous crime he had committed?

Julia's mind drifted back to what Anne had said:

"Horizontal hanging and now intubated drowning. Either this guy is the most creative killer on the planet or there's some meaning to the methods he's using to kill his victims."

She now added Ling Chi to his list of methods.

Modus operandi intimated a distinct method or pattern indicating the work of a single criminal in more than one crime, so was not a very good descriptor in Dan's case.

"He does keep harping on about them deserving what they got, but I just can't seem to put the pieces together," she had said,

reflecting once more on their conversation.

"Yeah, maybe I'm just reading into things here. If they'd done the same to him, he'd already be dead."

There must be some meaning to his methods, she ruminated.

Nobody would kill random people using such random methods.

He knew these people.

An idea sparked in her dark and drowsy mind and she quickly reached for her phone and scrolled to the WhatsApp from Dan.

She scanned the message until she came across the passage she was looking for.

Why hadn't she seen it before?

"Cameron Long deserved his comeuppance and my retribution was long overdue. He actually tried to apologise throughout the evening.

"Quite laughable."

Retribution, she thought.

Apologise, she wondered.

Dan had finally overplayed his hand.

Cameron was no random victim.

Dan wanted retribution and would not accept apologies.

The gears and cogs in Julia's mind clicked away trying to make sense of this.

Cameron was a recluse. He was a loner. At no time – past or present – could he have wronged the public. Dan was acting in self-interest. The only possible explanation was that he and Dan had crossed paths at some stage in their lives. Dan still felt aggrieved and was now using this crusade to get revenge.

Could it mean that he was also well acquainted with Craig Davis and Russell Dwyer as well and they were not just soft targets or random victims?

Could it mean that they all knew each other?

They were all the same ages, give or take a few months.

She was onto something. She could feel it. She was so close to solving the back story. A few tweaks here and there and she'd have it tied up with a nice, neat bow.

While she was thinking clearly, or, for that matter, not so clearly, she decided to call her father and bounce her epiphany off him.

Chapter 95

Alan faked intrigue.

He couldn't fault Julia's rationale or reasoning.

He had always assumed that there must be some sort of connection between the victims, and unknown to Julia, the analysts were already working that angle. Purely random killings were very uncommon.

Somehow, somewhere, there was always a connection between a murderer and his victim, or victims in this case.

His mind immediately drifted to 'Strangers on a train' by Alfred Hitchcock. He shook off the idea. Total fiction. Besides, there would be another murderer out there and not just one man claiming responsibility for three murders.

To ratify this, the murderer had already given them the history, the statistics and the reasons for his actions. There was no mystery about that.

There were still some missing pieces to the puzzle though.

Who was victim number four?

Was it only four victims or could there be more?

How did Dan know the victims?

What had they done to deserve the punishment he was dispensing?

They were simply running out of time and needed the answers to these questions sooner, rather than later.

Once the fourth victim was eliminated, the trail could run cold. Unless there were more people of course, or unless he now had a taste for what he was doing and believed he was unstoppable?

We need to ID the fourth person, he thought to himself.

Once we have that figured out, we could walk Dan right into a trap.

Alan phoned Jeff.

The pale-skinned, freckle-faced, red-head answered the call immediately.

"Mr Swan?" he answered, questioningly.

"Jeff… how are you guys doing on that research?"

"Uh… we haven't really made much progress, but we're reading everything we can get our hands on."

"That's not very good news," Alan stated bluntly. "You've managed to find nothing in those piles of documents?"

"Nothing, so far, I'm afraid. Manual reading is time-consuming and tedious, so we're scanning all the documents and then using algorithms to analyse the data."

Propeller-heads, Alan thought, *even reading is now beyond them.*

They would rather design a program to read for them. Where was the world going?

But, had it not been for this team, he would certainly not be as successful in his business ventures as he was, so he did begrudgingly admire them.

"Thanks, Jeff. Keep at it and keep me in the loop."

"Ollie," Alan greeted, as the big man answered his second call.

"Yes, boss," Ollie replied.

"Julia ran some ideas past me this morning, which got me thinking."

"Yes, boss. She called me too."

"Your thoughts on them?" Alan questioned, feeling a little deflated that Julia had deemed it necessary to call Ollie as well. Their relationship often caused him pangs of jealousy. He abruptly brushed the emotions away.

Ollie paused briefly before articulating his response. "I agree with her. We've always believed there was a connection between the victims. Now that we have the third victim, the coincidence of similar ages is no longer a coincidence. We have them being the same ages and attending the same school. But class photos only show Craig and Russell together. Cameron was in the same grade, but in a different class. The assumption we're working on is that Dan was also at the same school, but it is impossible to even guess whether he was in the same class, a different class or for that matter, a completely different grade altogether."

Ollie took a deep breath to recompose himself after the lengthy monologue.

He continued. "Craig was divorced, Russell was happily married and Cameron had never married. No correlation there. No similarities in their careers or pastimes either. Frankly, all we have is, same age, same school and same town."

An idea suddenly sparked in Alan's mind.

"Ollie, have we managed to go through any of the victims' personal belongings?"

"No, boss. DC Phiri still has jurisdiction over the crime scenes. The houses and contents have been sealed until the investigation is concluded."

"Listen, Jeff and his team are hitting a wall. They have every document and photo in the public domain and are coming up empty. We need personal documents. Scrapbooks, snippets or photos from their past. And a buck gets ten, Russell Dwyer will be the one. He was a family man with an artsy fartsy wife and daughter. They'd have spent hours creating a scrapbook of his lifetime memories."

"I'll get on it right away, boss."

Alan patted himself on the back over this current lightbulb moment, but had to reign himself in, as all it was at this stage was a good idea.

He also decided not to raise Julia's expectations just yet and rather keep her in the dark for now. Withholding information from her made him feel quite devious, but he'd find a way to live with it.

Chapter 96

'Peter Roland' – dead ends at every turn.

Philip, an analyst, and one Jeff's subordinates, pondered this conundrum.

He'd completed uploading his stack of documents on Craig Davis and, while he waited for the others, had been tasked to check out Anne's new beau, Peter Roland.

He had a plausible internet history and presence, but Philip's internal radar was bleeping uncontrollably. He'd done these investigations many times before and something was off.

An inquisitive check by someone like Anne would have revealed nothing out of the ordinary.

Peter had a plausible upbringing in Johannesburg. Achieved satisfactory grades in school. Attained a tertiary education from the University of Witwatersrand specializing in business management.

After a few years in various disciplines, he had gained enough experience and had proved his competence in a management position.

According to his biography, he was recently appointed to the position of Managing Director of the East London branch of an international cargo and freight company which operated from its offices located down at the harbour.

This reeked of a manufactured backstory to mask a true identity.

There was just enough information and detail to divert

cursory suspicion.

Philip kept digging.

"Peter Roland is a fake," he announced after another hour had elapsed.

"What's that?" Jeff queried, startled by Philip's sudden outburst.

"Peter Roland is a fake," Philip repeated.

Jeff and Kagiso gathered around his work station and strained to read over his shoulder.

That was impractical.

"Put it up on the screen," Jeff instructed, backing off again to the comfort of his own chair.

Philip powered up the primary screen and hit a few buttons on his keyboard.

The darkened screen sprang to life.

Philip toggled between various research pages while he elaborated on his findings. Jeff and Kagiso nodded in unison, as Philip expounded on Peter Roland, his life to date and then finally his reasons for believing he was a fake.

"His ID number is that of a child born in Johannesburg in 1989 and who died of leukaemia in 1995."

Jeff whistled softly as he grasped the gravity of what Philip had discovered.

Philip continued undeterred. "He has a few bank accounts and a credit card in his name, but only a few sporadic transactions ever go through these accounts. His salary and any meaningful living expenses never appear. I could accept that his living expenses are part of his package and paid for by the company or with a company credit card, but that would not explain why his remuneration never gets deposited into his personal account."

Jeff and Kagiso looked at one another with raised eye-brows.

"Bloody hell! We better let Mr Swan or Ollie know about this asap," Jeff declared and reached for his cell phone.

Within the hour, both Alan and Ollie arrived at the safe house and seated themselves in the boardroom. Alan very rarely frequented the safe house, but on such infrequent occasions he took the seat at the head of the table, which Ollie had no objection to. He was the boss after all and the entire property belonged to him. He could sit wherever it pleased him.

"Right," Alan said. "Let's see what you've got. You sounded awfully worked up, Jeff."

"Yes, Mr Swan. It's what Philip discovered while doing a deep dive on Peter Roland."

Alan directed his attention to Philip. "Well, let's have it, Philip. The floor is yours."

Philip stuttered and stammered throughout his opening, having never addressed Alan personally before, but after a while gained confidence and delivered his discovery at a steady and even pace.

Alan and Ollie gave Philip their full attention. They listened with amazement, not saying a word for fear of interrupting the man and causing him to lose his rhythm again.

They had both worked closely with this team before and felt at ease speaking openly and frankly in their presence. They had never violated the boundaries of confidentiality before.

Alan looked questioningly at Ollie.

"Looks like we have our man," he said confidently. "Bodybuilder. Smoke and mirrors bio. Consorting with Anne to get close to Julia…"

Ollie nodded in agreement. "Seems like the puzzle pieces are falling into place."

"Well, what are we waiting for then?" Alan demanded. "Go get this son of a bitch before we have another casualty on our hands."

"Motive," Ollie responded cautiously. He didn't make a habit of contradicting Alan, but it was his job to raise caution.

"What do you mean 'motive'?" Alan fumed. "Were you not listening to the same thing I was?"

"Yes, boss, I heard every word, but we need to be cautious here. Being a bodybuilder and having a questionable background and biography does not prove that he is Dan. As far as we know, he was born and raised in Johannesburg with no ties to East London. How would that explain the personal vendettas?"

"But, as has been established, his background and bio might just be a smokescreen to cover up his childhood in East London and his association with the victims."

"Yes, boss, but until we're absolutely sure, I reckon we put a surveillance team on him. That way, we have time to investigate him further and be a step ahead of him if he does turn out to be Dan. If we bring him in now, we risk blowing any case we might have against him."

"Fine," Alan huffed, realising that he was again being a bit impetuous and that Ollie was just doing his job and being the voice of reason. "But it's on you if this goes sideways and if he even comes close to Julia, you better have a SWAT team available to prevent anything happening."

"I'll be there in person," Ollie replied respectfully.

The analysts weren't accustomed to these heated altercations and frankly didn't know where to look.

Ollie immediately dialled Manny.

"Where's Peter Roland?"

"At home, in bed," answered Manny, who had ears to the ground everywhere at the moment.

"Stay on him. I need to know his every move."

"Roger that," Manny replied and hung up.

Chapter 97

Once the show and tell concluded, Ollie got into his car, and with tires squealing, departed the safe house. The analysts were left aghast.

Unknown to them, Alan and Ollie disagreed on many occasions. Sometimes Ollie would concede. Sometimes Alan would concede. In their hectic lives, holding grudges was a complete waste of time and effort. They somehow brought the best out in each other. It was a crazy, but effective, symbiotic relationship.

Ollie pressed down heavily on the accelerator. He needed to be at the Dwyer house in a few minutes and breaking the speed limit would not deter him. One of DC Phiri's constables would be there to unlock the property and monitor their activities.

DC Phiri had consented to Ollie's search, but had made it abundantly clear that nothing could leave the property without his express permission.

The constable would be there to enforce these protocols.

Ollie would have agreed to anything.

He was just happy that DC Phiri would not be there himself.

Nothing got past him very easily.

Ollie rounded the last corner, veered into the driveway, and skidded to a halt behind the unmarked police vehicle.

As he arrived, four of his guys exited the grey sedan, which was neatly parallel parked alongside the curb in front of the house. Every extra pair of eyes was vital as they searched for the unknown.

They had been briefed on the search prior to his arrival. Scrapbooks, photo albums, old newspaper snippets – anything which could assist them to identify primary school friends.

Constable Radebe unlocked the front door, but only after sizing up the group and reiterating DC Phiri's conditions.

Ollie acknowledged the instructions with an acceding nod of his head and pushed past the constable to enter the house.

"Lungi, you and Themba... the lounge and dining room. Daniel, you and Mpho... the bedrooms. Call me if you find anything."

Constable Radebe looked on anxiously, realising suddenly that he couldn't be in all places at the same time to monitor proceedings.

The group split up and started rummaging through drawers and in sideboards and cupboards. It was a hurried search, but they were as careful as possible not to trash the place. The family would at some stage need to return to the house and to find it in disarray would be extremely disrespectful.

Ollie headed upstairs to the craft room which he'd heard so much about. It had recently been occupied as unfinished projects lay strewn across the workbench and floor. The girls had most likely been busy in this very room while Russell was being tortured and murdered downstairs in his garage.

Would that memory ever leave them?

Would they ever utilise this room again?

A buck gets ten, they'd sell the property and move out as soon as possible, Ollie guessed.

Every nook and cranny would bring back memories of a husband or a father, and inhabiting this house would be intolerable.

Ollie shook his head to dispel the thoughts. He had work to do.

He scanned the shelves first. Scraps of material, paper and cardboard were piled high. He rifled through the stacks. Nothing but scraps.

The cupboards were next.

He started on the left and began to work his way around the room.

Scissors, Stanley knives, rulers, pens, pencils, paint brushes, paints of all colours and shades, thumb tacks, clamps, Sellotape, stickers, glitter.

Cupboard after cupboard. They could have stocked a stationary shop.

Before he could finish, he was summoned to the lounge downstairs by Lungi and Themba. They had created a large stack of paraphernalia on the dining room table.

Constable Radebe looked on intently as he rummaged through the pile of documents, framed photos of the family and some other odds and sods that the guys had deemed important. They all looked too recent.

Ollie shook his head. "Keep looking," he instructed.

On his way back to the craft room, he popped his head into the bedrooms.

"Anything of interest?" he asked Daniel and Mpho.

"Not in the kid's rooms, boss. We're heading for the master bedroom now."

"Check right in the back of the drawers and cupboards. We're looking for some really old documents. Probably stashed and forgotten about for years."

"Yes, boss," chorused the duo.

Ollie returned to the craft room to continue his search where he'd left off.

He finally struck gold in the second last drawer of a lowboy dresser. Large, bulging scrapbooks filled the drawer.

Good thinking, boss, he thought to himself.

He quickly typed a text message to Lungi downstairs – 'Keep Radebe busy.'

His heart raced as he pulled the entire drawer from the dresser and hurriedly paged through the scrapbooks. The spines were mostly distended and nearing breaking point, as the pages boasted ornate designs and decorations which included feathers, dried leaves, ribbons, cardboard and other bulky materials. The female pairing had been in their element creating these works of art. The odd photo was stuck to a page here and there and decoratively framed with loving care, but again, these photos were too recent to be of interest.

Just as Ollie's excitement and optimism dwindled, he came across the last book in the pile. It wasn't a scrapbook. It was different. While scrapbooks generally had landscape pages, the book he now held opened in portrait and contained faded plastic sleeves instead of paper pages.

It was an old photo album.

The days of the old Kodak camera and manually developed photos.

He flipped through the sleeves. These photos were old.

The majority were of a very young Penny. Definitely childhood photos.

Ollie kept paging. As he turned the pages, Penny grew up and matured into a very attractive young woman.

Russell was a lucky man, Ollie thought, as he found a few snaps of the young couple, most likely taken during their courtship.

Ollie was again rapidly losing hope.

He was nearing the end of the album with nothing to show for his efforts.

The last six photos were his redemption. Three sealed under the plastic cover on the recto page and the other three back to back on the verso page.

Looking at the young boy, he thought, *these must be of a young Russell.*

And there were other boys in the photos.

Jackpot!

DC Phiri was no fool though, so he couldn't just remove the photos. The empty slots would betray him. He had to find a way of getting these photos past Constable Radebe without raising suspicion.

The Stanley knife suddenly sprang to mind. If he could remove the entire sleeve from the album and leave no trace, he could hopefully avert any suspicion.

"Let's go, boys," Ollie finally called out loudly.

Between the teams, they had accumulated a small pile of decoy books and papers, which did not include the photo album or scrapbooks which Ollie had carefully replaced in the dresser drawer.

In the dining room, Constable Radebe meticulously documented the evidence for DC Phiri. He then ushered the group out of the house and locked the door behind them.

He would never know about the sleeve of photos Ollie had stuffed down the front of his trousers.

Chapter 98

Ollie led the way with the sedan following closely behind him. They had extremely valuable cargo, or so they believed.

The roads were quiet, but it wasn't in their best interest to break the speed limit on the return journey.

Ollie's phone rang and his Bluetooth sent the call through to the speaker phone. It was DC Phiri.

"Find what you needed?"

"Not really. We've taken a few documents and clippings, but I'm not hopeful," Ollie lied. "Constable Radebe detailed the inventory. It should be with you shortly. Thanks anyway."

"I was honestly hoping that you'd find something. The garage was a bust when we looked, but we hadn't got to the house yet. Usual old story... manpower, time and money. Resources are limited and I needed to deploy my team as prudently as possible."

DC Phiri was genuinely upset that they'd turned up nothing and Ollie felt genuinely remorseful that he had to deceive him.

"I'll let you know if we find anything in what we did take," Ollie committed.

"Thank you, Ollie," DC Phiri replied. "I'm being pushed for results and so far I have absolutely nothing."

"I actually thought the investigation had been handed over to the Murder and Robbery Squad already?"

"It has been, but I was ordered to stay on and work in collaboration with them. This case is becoming increasingly curious and high profile due to the abundance of evidence, but lack of leads."

"I feel for you," Ollie commiserated. "I'll be in touch."

He ended the call feeling awful about lying to the aged Captain.

The safe house looked cold and desolate when they arrived.

The outside lights, which were on a timer, had just activated as the sun set and dusk rolled in.

Lungi unceremoniously dumped the box on the boardroom table, but pushed it to one side, knowing that it contained nothing of importance. Meanwhile, Ollie slid the sleeve of photos across the table to Jeff.

"Maybe this will get us the break we need," Ollie commented.

Jeff gingerly picked up the sleeve and took a cursory glance at the photos.

"Where did these come from?" he asked curiously.

"Russell Dwyer's house and us finding them never leaves this room… understood?"

Jeff, Kagiso and Philip nodded in understanding.

They had sworn an oath of confidentiality to get this job. And besides, nobody would betray the likes of Mr Swan, Ollie, and his team of mercenaries. These were not members of the church choir.

"Do your magic and find out who these boys are," Ollie instructed.

Jeff looked closely at the photo Ollie indicated. It was old and had faded quite significantly over the years, but he could still easily make out the four random boys standing side by side. At best guess they were probably around eleven or twelve years old at the time. He flipped the sleeve over and scanned the three photos on the verso page. The same boys appeared in some of these photos, but only the one showed them all together.

Jeff gingerly pried the photo from the plastic sleeve so as not to damage it or the fragile plastic, which had ensconced it for decades.

He examined the photo and then looked over at Ollie.

"Magic complete," he said, as he flipped the photo and read the names on the back – "Russell, Cameron, Craig and Dave!"

Ollie scowled.

The group huddled together to get a personal look at the four names.

"So who's Dave then?" Ollie enquired.

"He's the next victim," Jeff shot back quickly before realising how antagonising and patronising he sounded.

"Well done, Sherlock, we need a bit more to go on than that," growled Ollie and then continued, "A surname, an address, an ID number, contact details… everything."

Jeff looked over Philip and Kagiso.

"Back to the school records and yearbooks for a surname. The rest will be easy," he instructed.

They jumped to it.

Ollie was already dialling Alan and exited the boardroom for a bit more privacy.

"Ollie?" Alan answered questioningly.

"Boss, we have him. We have the fourth target."

"You have him at the safe house?" Alan queried.

"Uh, no. We've ID'd him. Well, actually we haven't quite ID'd him yet either," Ollie stammered.

He'd gotten a bit ahead of himself.

"Take a breath, big guy. Nice and slowly now."

Ollie inhaled deeply, feeling quite silly about his blunder. He should have thought the story through a bit better before making the call, but in his excitement he'd rushed into it.

"Well, we found a photo of the four boys at Russell Dwyer's house. Your hunch paid off. The names of the boys are pencilled on the back of the photo. First names only, though."

Alan listened intently. He had questions, but was patient enough to wait.

"Dave is the fourth boy and we believe the next target. The problem is, we don't know who Dave is. Jeff and the guys are reviewing the school books and class photos to find Dave's full name. Once we have a surname, the computer work can start for more detail."

"Excellent work, Ollie," Alan praised the big man. "How long before we have the detail?"

"The guys have just started the search, so no idea yet."

"Right, keep me posted, as we'll have decisions to make when we've ID'd him. Oh, and where is Peter Roland right now?"

Luckily Manny had texted him a little while earlier with the information.

"The latest update was that he hadn't left his house the entire day. He must have decided to work from home."

"Keep a close eye on him. We can't have him slipping through our fingers when we're so close to identifying target number four. And as before no mention of this to Julia."

"Yes boss," Ollie replied and ended the call.

Chapter 99

Julia had been poring over her article for too long now. She needed to get it submitted for fear of reprisal from Dan. The problem was… she had nothing new. Another killing. Another method of torture and murder. Same modus operandi of leaving a cocktail of evidence scattered around.

But nothing new in terms of the reasons behind the murder.

She had belaboured that point in her previous exposé and nothing had changed. Dan was still a monster on a quest for vengeance, albeit disguised as a crusade of disgust and awareness of the crime statistics and related problems which faced the country.

She'd be laughed off as another desperate reporter who tried to squeeze the last drop out of yesterday's news.

Maybe it was time to switch things up a bit? she thought.

Maybe it was time for the acquiescence to end and for her to be a bit more antagonistic?

Maybe her non-compliance would rile him up enough to force a mistake and give them a chance to end this madness?

It would definitely add a new dimension to the story.

She was sure she could pull it off, but was she willing to take the chance?

The flip-side was that he could come after her or, even worse, her friends.

She needed some sage advice on how to proceed.

Her father was in his study on a call when she arrived at the mansion. She had no idea what he was currently involved in, but out of respect, she waited outside his study for him to finish.

He had indicated with two fingers that he'd be another couple of minutes when she had poked her head around the door.

She took the opportunity to pop into the kitchen and greet Mavis.

"Miss Julia," Mavis cried out in surprise. "How nice to see you."

"Hi, Mavis, lovely to see you. How are you keeping?"

"Fine, thank you, Miss Julia. Just thankful every day for what your family has given me. Too many people have no work."

"I know, Mavis, it's really tough times."

"I like what Mr Alan does," Mavis said, although probably not entirely sure of his business acumen.

"What is that, Mavis?"

"He makes businesses and gives people work. People want to work, Miss Julia. Some are lazy, but most people want to work and earn money to support their families."

"I'm sure they do... it gives people a sense of self-worth."

This remark probably flew right over Mavis' head and Julia was actually quite relieved when her father called out from the study.

"Well, nice talking to you again, Mavis," Julia said while indicating that she should go see her father.

"Goodbye, Miss Julia."

"Nice surprise," Alan said, as he stood to hug and kiss his daughter. "How are you?"

"I've been better, Dad. Although, the latest article I'm writing is totally hollow. The facts around Dan's last murder are unique, but other than that, it's a non-starter. In my previous articles I've expounded as much as possible on the reasons for his crusade. I can't keep flogging the same horse. The readers will see right through this and my credibility as a journalist is at stake."

"So don't write anything then," Alan replied.

He couldn't give Julia the details, but he was secretly confident that they'd identified Peter Roland as Dan and he wouldn't be able to do a thing without them knowing about it long in advance. They were also narrowing in on the identity and location of Dave. The pincer formation was being prepped for deployment.

"I had another idea, but it'll probably result in the same reprisal from Dan. I want to write an article which, while understanding his perspective, disparages his methods and vilifies him."

Alan laughed. "You want to poke the bear?"

Julia nodded. "But I have my reservations. What if he does decide to come after me, my friends or even you and Mom?"

Alan nodded astutely. "We have that side covered. You do what you need to do. By the way, what does Moses think?"

"I still need to run it past him, but I want to have two drafts when I talk to him. He needs to read and understand why I need to 'poke the bear'."

Julia was being so courageous about this. Alan had to smile.

The article had been germinating in her mind as she spoke to her father, so it was no surprise when she declined the invitation to stay on for dinner and instead rushed home to compose the second version.

She wanted this article approved and uploaded the following morning, so the pressure was on to get it finalised and rushed through to Moses.

She really needed him to see things from her perspective and allow the affrontation.

He had supported her until now and as a result had benefited immensely, even if only in reputation and self-esteem.

The hours rolled by as her fingers flew frenetically over the keyboard. Her thoughts and pent up emotions raced to her fingertips in search of permanent release.

This was the real Julia.

Putting into words what needed to be said. Not regurgitating some prescribed or twisted version of reality. It was such a rush.

She was elated with the final product.

Now she just needed Moses to approve it and get it posted first thing the following morning.

Chapter 100

"David Winter," Jeff barked elatedly into the phone. "Same grade as the others but in the same class as Cameron Long."

"After-school buddies," Ollie heard Philip add in the background.

"Great work," Ollie replied. "I presume you wouldn't have called me if you only had a name."

This was posed more as a statement than as a question.

"Yup, we have everything, from his ID number, to his home and work addresses, and even his bank account details."

He continued, "Bad divorce. Lost the kids and the house to his ex-wife. He must've had a real cracker of a lawyer."

Jeff added the coup de grace very sarcastically.

"What about the boys in the other photos?" Ollie queried.

Jeff knew exactly where he was going with this. "All the same as in the group photo. There were only four of them."

Ollie breathed a sigh of relief.

He could concentrate on one person only and didn't have to split the team up.

"Thanks, Jeff. We might just have saved a guy's life here. Please text me the details, especially his home address and the GPS co-ordinates."

"Sure thing, Ollie. Should I phone Mr Swan?"

"No. I'm here with him," Ollie replied and ended the call.

A few seconds later his phone beeped.

He immediately opened the message. It was the details he'd

requested from Jeff.

"Lotus Avenue, Bonza Bay," he mouthed.

Not a bad area for someone who'd lost everything to his ex-wife.

Seems like David recovered well after his ordeal with divorce.

He forwarded the text to Manny, who would co-ordinate with the rest of the team and then called him.

"Yes, boss?" Manny answered.

"You get the message?"

"Yes, boss."

"It's the details of the next target."

"Yes, boss."

"I want the house and David Winter under twenty-four-hour surveillance, starting immediately. And we can't afford to be seen. If Dan suspects a trap, it's over, and we lose the only chance we've got."

"Understood, boss."

"Where's Peter Roland?" Ollie demanded.

"Still at his house. No movement since yesterday," Manny clarified.

"I need regular updates on him and David Winter. I have a feeling that tonight is the night their paths will collide."

"We're on it," Manny replied, as Ollie clicked off.

Everything was covered for now.

Ollie strolled down the pathway to the main house.

Alan was already in the dining room sipping on a cappuccino.

He looked up as Ollie entered the room. "Good morning, my friend," he said jovially.

"Good morning, boss," Ollie replied, wondering what had

made it such a good morning.

"It's getting too cold for breakfast on the veranda, so indoors will have to suffice until winter ends."

Ollie nodded. "Speaking about winter, the guys finally ID'd Dan's fourth target. His name is David Winter. He stays in the Bonza Bay area."

Alan smiled irreverently. "Then tonight is the night."

Ollie recoiled in surprise. "That's what I just told Manny. The timeline fits."

"Not only that, big guy," Alan said. "That could still be an assumption. I believe he'll attack tonight, but for another reason."

Ollie frowned and listened attentively.

"Julia came to see me yesterday. Her article, which should be out this morning, will be unlike any of the others. She decided to launch a scathing attack on Dan for his vigilantism. So, while reporting on the facts of the murder, she's decided not to glamourise him and his crusade but rather vilify him and denigrate his actions. She's decided to defy him and poke the bear."

"Do you think that's wise, boss? He promised to come after her if she crossed him."

"Have you got her back, or not?"

"Yes, of course. I just think that she might be looking for unnecessary trouble."

"Well, I fully agree with her. Let's rile this bastard up. He'll read the article on its release and will hopefully be so incensed and distracted that he will make some sort of mistake."

Ollie realised he'd lost this battle before it even started and now needed to plan defence.

"Okay, boss, but once this article is published, Jules needs to stay indoors. Either at her house or, even more preferably, here.

If Dan's attention is suddenly diverted to Jules instead of David Winter, we can't have her out and about in public."

"Agreed," Alan concurred. "I'll phone her and lay down the law. After all, this was her idea anyway."

He paused to assess an idea which had just sprung to mind. "Although, I think Dan's the kind of person who will first see his original plan through to the end and then plan on how to take revenge on Julia. But we cannot let it get to that though. If he targets David Winter tonight, then you make sure he disappears."

Ollie didn't need any further instruction on what was required.

"Understood, boss."

Chapter 101

Dan had just read Julia's article on *DispatchLIVE* and was absolutely fuming.

"That bitch!" he shouted.

How dare she judge me?

He had the interest of the people and the country at heart.

She was just like the rest of them.

He felt like he'd been played.

He thought that by now they'd built a solid rapport and had a common understanding of what the problems were and how best to draw the attention of the public to them.

She'd humoured his demands and strung him along, but now when he was so close to completing his mission, she'd betrayed him.

He paced the room – hatred burning inside him – simulating various scenarios and outcomes. He was extremely analytical that way. Nothing was left to chance.

No matter what the final decision was, she would pay.

She would suffer and then pay dearly with her life.

He would not be tormented and subjected to any form of abuse ever again.

It was too early to 'visit' Dave Winter, but what he needed right now was to get out and clear his head.

A few kilometres away, Ollie's phoned beeped.

It was a message from Manny.

'Peter Roland is on the move!'

'Stay on him,' Ollie texted back.

Ollie wondered whether the day was starting earlier than he had anticipated.

He already donned his black trousers and boots, and was ready for the night which lay ahead, but now he had second thoughts about maybe wearing his green camouflage instead, which was better suited for daytime.

After a period of brief indecision, he threw his green camo kit into a tog bag, tossed it over his shoulder and headed for his vehicle.

He would change outfits if and when required.

Lungi was in the Quigney Virgin Active gym when Peter Roland arrived.

He was going through the motions of a light workout while he surveilled the gym for potential bodybuilding suspects for the team outside to follow and investigate. He furtively wore a microphone with two earpieces which were neatly disguised as an iPod with two AirPods. He blended in with little effort. People loved working out to their own playlists.

"Peter Roland has entered the gym," he whispered surreptitiously into the mic.

"Roger that," a tinny reply erupted through the AirPods.

Lungi knew that they were already following Peter Roland anyway, so his revelation was a little redundant, but he didn't want anyone to think that he was asleep on the job.

He watched as Peter went through an entire stretching routine to loosen all the muscles he was about to torment.

He wasn't as tall as Lungi, but he had packed on the bulk. Lungi couldn't resist comparing himself to Peter. He would guess that their biceps, triceps and shoulders were very comparable. Peter's thighs and calves were marginally leaner, but Lungi found himself admiring the definition.

Peter's pectorals and latissimus dorsi muscles pressed tightly against the vest he wore and Lungi couldn't help but think that Peter's pecs and lats were slightly bigger than his.

He couldn't see Peter's abdominals, but wondered whether he concentrated much on ab workouts. Most of the power lifters didn't mind undefined abs.

All in all though, they probably measured up nicely against each other. He appreciated the effort anyone put in to improve themselves.

Ollie drove the streets of East London very cautiously. He could ill afford being pulled over with the arsenal he had in his double cab. He had spent a small fortune customising drawers and a false floor inside the canopy. With the tailgate down, the drawers could easily be ejected from the rear with a simple push of a button, giving him access to all his equipment which was nestled into snug, moulded and cushioned compartments.

He ran through his personnel allocations in his head.

He had pulled the plug on the morgues, as no new intel was forthcoming.

The gyms were still being monitored.

The parking lots outside the gyms were covered.

Peter Roland was being tailed and his location and activities were frequently communicated.

Julia, Cathy, Anne and Sam all had two-man teams allocated to each of them.

Dave Winter had the deadly duo – Manny and Mpho – allocated to him. He had left his house earlier this morning and was now at the lumber yard where he worked.

At his request, Alan and Claire would be staying at home today, to free-up more of his team.

He, himself, was mobile and could traverse between the teams wherever needed. He was currently on his way to Bonza Bay to recon Dave Winter's house and neighbourhood. He still believed that tonight was the night.

Had he missed anything?

Three of them should suffice for the night's projected activities, but he wondered whether he should pull Lungi and Daniel from the gyms earlier than usual to join the Dave Winter team.

Sometimes unforeseen things did happen and five bodies would always be better than three.

He made the call.

Chapter 102

The day rolled by slowly.

Mostly uneventful, except for the report that Peter Roland had finished his gym workout, had showered, donned a fresh outfit and had proceeded to the Virgin Active gym in Beacon Bay.

Ollie found this very strange and intriguing.

Why would he finish training at one gym and then head to another?

Daniel, who was on location at this gym, reported it in immediately.

Daniel also confirmed that he had a brief-case with him this time and no training gear. Peter then spent an inordinate amount of time walking the facility, checking the equipment and chatting to staff and patrons alike, before finally making himself comfortable in the juice bar. He then literally turned the juice bar into his office for the next few hours.

Very strange, Ollie thought, but it wasn't uncommon these days to work remotely. All that was necessary was a table top and a reliable Wi-Fi connection.

Virgin Active obviously fitted the bill.

Why had he cased the facility and why had he not just stayed where he was at the gym in Quigney if he had work to do?

These thoughts ran amok through his mind.

He gave the instruction that Daniel should stay with Peter Roland and tail him when he left the gym. Four of them could easily cope at the house? And Daniel would be right behind him, to box him in, if he somehow managed to get past them and escape their trap.

Moments later Ollie received the message that Dave Winter had left the lumber yard and was on his way home.

Manny and Mpho were hot on his heels.

Once they were all in position then it was just a case of waiting it out until Peter Roland decided to make his move on Dave Winter.

Contrary to what Ollie had pictured in his mind, Dave's house was not one of the palatial properties with a great view of the river and beach below. It was a small two-bedroom rickety cottage at the end of the road, surrounded by overgrown shrubbery and unkempt grass; bushes and trees on three sides.

Its surroundings were perfect to give him and his team the requisite cover.

He took up his position and hunkered down to wait patiently for the action to begin.

It was only six o'clock when Dave swung his rusted Mazda into the driveway and exited his vehicle. The daylight hours were getting shorter and shorter as autumn made way for winter. Dave blinked his eyes to acclimate them to the impending darkness and then proceeded indoors. Lights came on as he moved through the house, as if tracking his movements from one room to the next.

Manny and Mpho hurriedly parked two blocks away, in a spot which they'd identified earlier when doing their recon of the area.

They kitted up quickly and tested microphone comms with Ollie.

They were good to go.

The pathway through the scrub was well worn and they made their way effortlessly along its course behind the houses to the end of the road. It fortuitously passed less than a hundred metres behind Dave's house, where they broke off and skulked through the undergrowth to take up their respective positions.

Ollie was set up across the road where he could scan for any oncoming activity from the road as well as leading up to the front of the house.

Mpho, who was breathing heavily after the brisk run through the bush, took up his position behind the house with a good two-hundred-and-seventy-degree field of vision, covering mostly the back and left side of the house.

Manny smiled at his out of breath, muscle-bound colleague and scampered off to the far corner of the house. He also had a two-hundred-and-seventy-degree line of sight, which covered the road to his right and all the way up to Mpho on his left.

The only blind-spot, at this stage, was the right side of the house which bordered the neighbour's property. The wall they shared was constructed of solid precast concrete poles and slabs. It was obviously erected by his neighbour as the side facing Dave's property was rough and bland with no design elements, unlike the side facing inwards towards his neighbour.

It was not a great access point, but for peace of mind, it would be covered by Lungi, who was already en route.

Chapter 103

Complete darkness was now setting in, with the moon being the only source of light in the darkened cul-de-sac.

The last two lights along the road had fused but, as with most other municipal services, replacement of two light bulbs was never going to happen.

The issue had been reported by Dave on numerous occasions, who had now resigned himself to the fact that he would just have to live without them.

Lungi arrived and, after following the same footpath as the others had taken, he now took up his position on the far right side, behind the house. They had now effectively covered all four sides of the house and were kitted out with night vision goggles and enough weaponry to intimidate a third world country. But for now all was quiet and peaceful.

Ollie was becoming restless. He wasn't often involved in stake-outs any more.

He finally started doubting himself.

Maybe he'd been mistaken and this wasn't going to happen tonight.

Through his night vision goggles, he could quite clearly make out the heat signature of Manny, even though he was tucked down in the undergrowth.

Mpho was further away and from this distance might have just been a tree or stump which was slightly warmer than its surroundings.

He scanned right, along the length of Lotus Avenue, and his heart started racing.

A heat signature was edging towards him.

It was small and insignificant and possibly just a dog or cat roaming the neighbourhood. As he continued to focus in on the heat signature, it started looming larger and larger. It finally became quite clear and took on the shape and form of a biped. It was definitely a human being.

Ollie whispered into his mic, "Person approaching from the east along Lotus Avenue."

"Roger that, boss. I see him too," Manny whispered in response.

They all held their positions. Any noise now would raise the alarm.

As the form passed the concrete dividing wall, it abruptly stopped and scanned slowly from left to right and then ducked into the driveway and disappeared behind Dave's beat up Mazda.

Ollie was intrigued as to how this would play out.

Dave was still awake, as was evidenced by all the lights shining brightly in the house. The flashes and glimmer of a TV could also be seen through the lounge curtains.

Would he wait for Dave to retire for the night and then pick the lock to enter?

History didn't support that MO.

Ollie was still mulling this over when the heat signature made its way stealthily from behind the car to the front door.

It was going to happen.

Right now.

A loud knock on the door broke the silence.

"Who is it?" roared Dave from within, obviously annoyed at being disturbed.

"It's Ralph... from next door," the man shouted back.

"What now, Ralph? I've only just got home."

"You need to see this, Dave."

"Okay, I'm coming."

Ollie was taken aback.

Was this really Dave's neighbour, Ralph?

Why would he have come from so far up the street?

Something didn't add up.

"Stay alert, guys," he whispered into his mic.

The sound of Dave removing the security latch on the front door and unlocking it was quite audible, even to Ollie and Manny, who maintained their positions.

Dave was not happy when he opened the door.

"What do you want? It's late, Ralph. Ral...?"

The electric visuals of the Taser blinded Ollie and Manny, who were still observing the scene through their night vision goggles, but the shocking sounds were unmistakable.

'Shit!" Ollie muttered as he ripped off the goggles and rubbed at his eyes.

"Was that a Taser?" he whispered

"Definitely," replied Manny, as he rubbed at his own eyes and blinked away the stars.

The sound of the front door closing and being locked again brought them back from their dazed stupors.

Ollie had no time for finesse. He knew that Peter Roland would be preoccupied with positioning and securing Dave for whatever sick adventure he had planned for tonight. He exploded from his position across the road, hurdled the low hedge, trampled through the gardens and hit the front door shoulder on with his full weight behind him.

The door was solid, but he was a monster of a man and the

door frame and locking mechanisms could not withstand the sudden impact.

CRACK!

The door flew open upon contact and although his impetus nearly caused him to fall, he somehow managed to retain his footing and was quick to regain his balance.

Peter Roland was off to his right dragging Dave into the lounge and immediately turned to look in Ollie's direction.

Hold on, Ollie thought. *That's not Peter Roland.*

Ollie shook his head in disbelief and yelled, "Dan!"

It erupted like a war-cry, as he charged across the ante-room to over-power his quarry.

Dan looked up in sheer surprise as this monolith exploded through the front door and came rampaging towards him.

Dan was extremely broad in the shoulders, but still did not match up to the size and probably neither the strength of the madman bearing down on him.

"I'm not done yet!" yelled Dan.

In an instant, the Taser materialised in his hand moments before Ollie's full weight crashed into him. The sparks flew for a split second and Ollie's body jerked slightly, as they slid together across the tiled floor. Fortunately for Ollie, it was only a glancing shock and, although partially stunned, he managed to regain his footing fairly quickly.

Dan was already up and brandished the Taser menacingly. Unadulterated hatred filled his eyes as he retracted his arm to thrust the Taser into Ollie's midriff.

Out of nowhere, Manny entered the fray and with limited angles and options he poked his fingers in Dan's eye.

Dan recoiled reflexively, which gave Ollie a second or two to compose himself.

He then delivered a sharp left jab to Dan's face, obliterating his nose in the process and followed it up with a massive roundhouse right to the side of his head.

Dan dropped to his knees, pitched forward, and remained motionless.

Ollie looked over at Manny, and Manny nodded.

That look was all the 'thanks' he needed. He had done his job.

"Let's get this sack of shit out of here," Ollie instructed, as Mpho and Lungi rushed through the door. They looked almost disappointed at having missed out on the action.

"Put him in his chair," Ollie said, pointing to the unconscious Dave. "Then let's tidy this place up and get out of here. Besides a broken door frame, Dave never needs to know what happened here and we'll never talk about it again."

They all nodded in agreement.

Mission accomplished.

Epilogue

Winter had finally passed, and it had been an unusually cold winter for East London. The days were getting warmer now and with the onset of spring the flowers were blooming and the birds were chirping joyfully in the trees.

Alan and Ollie sat in the gazebo sipping whiskey.

It was late afternoon, and the men had formally decided to call it a day.

The past few months had been intense and stressful for all of them.

Julia's article had been another resounding success. She and Moses had been showered with accolades by the public in general, as well as the journalistic community, who appreciated and acknowledged her stance and candour in telling it like it was with no fear of reprisal.

She had basked in the limelight for a week or two. Then anxiety and depression had set in. The fear of reprisal had become a reality and she began to live in constant fear of Dan getting to her and exacting his sick style of revenge on her.

At the insistence of her parents, she had finally acceded to their offer and had temporarily moved back into the mansion. She would not give up her apartment, as even in her current state, she knew that this arrangement would only be temporary.

Alan, Claire and Ollie had each spent many hours with her, in futile attempts to reassure her that nothing or nobody would ever get to her.

Alan and Ollie were the only two who really knew this for certain, but neither would ever admit to it

She just needed time.

Dan's crusade and the police investigation had suddenly gone suspiciously cold.

Both Alan and Ollie had been repeatedly interviewed by DC Phiri and the Murder and Robbery Squad.

Both men had stuck resolutely to their stories.

They had confessed to running a parallel investigation, including the stakeouts of the morgues and the gyms, but had finally relinquished their investigation as futile with minimal hope of any breakthroughs.

The documents which were removed from the Dwyer house were returned, except of course for the photos, as nobody knew anything about them anyway.

DC Phiri, however, still sensed that something was awry, but he simply had nothing further to go on. Even the evidence analysed by Phumzile and her team had turned up nothing of real value.

He desperately wanted justice for the victims, but with no leads there was simply nothing to investigate.

The investigations had ultimately been allocated to the growing pile of cold cases, which haunted DC Phiri constantly.

Peter Roland had been unaware that he'd ever been implicated as a suspect in a murder investigation. Now that he had found Anne and their relationship was getting really serious, he was the first to admit that he had unquestionably lived a double life. He had indeed created an alter-ego for himself, with a credible backstory. But not for any sinister reasons. Essentially, so that he could do his job more effectively. It turned out that he was a Managing Director – but not of some cargo and freight company. He was MD of Virgin Active, South Africa. He had been moving around the country assessing all the branches as an undercover boss. It had worked very effectively for him, until he had finally fallen for the allure of Anne.

Dave Winter never did report the incident. He had cursed profusely on discovering his broken front door, but since nothing had been stolen…

Besides the conversations and interactions, they'd had with Julia – Cathy, Sam and Anne were oblivious to them ever being in any danger, and that would be the way it would stay.

A few months down the line and Julia was seemingly on the road to recovery, which was great news for everyone. She was a rock, but even a rock sometimes needed support.

She would always wonder what happened to Dan. She secretly hoped that her article had played a significant role in him finally seeing the light and calling off his crusade.

She would never know for sure though

Alan looked over at Ollie.

"Will he ever be found?"

"Not in a million years," replied Ollie stoically.

That was the only detail Alan would ever want.

They clinked glasses.

"Karma is a bitch!" Alan added.

They both took hearty glugs of their whiskey and gazed contentedly off into the distance.

The End